KNOW IT BY HEART

a novel by

Karl Luntta

CURBSTONE PRESS

FIRST EDITION, 2003

Printed in Canada on acid-free paper by
Transcontinental / Best Book Manufacturing

Cover design & illustration: Les Kanturek

This book was published with the support of the Connecticut Commission on the Arts and donations from many individuals. We are very grateful for this support.

Library of Congress Cataloging-in-Publication Data

Luntta, Karl, 1955-
Know it by heart / by Karl Luntta.— 1st U.S. ed.
p. cm.
ISBN 1-880684-95-0 (alk. paper)
1. East Hartford (Conn.)—Fiction. 2. African American women—Fiction. 3. Racially mixed people—Fiction. 4. Interracial marriage—Fiction. 5. Race relations—Fiction. 6. Friendship—Fiction. 7. Teenagers—Fiction. 8. Racism—Fiction. I. Title.
PS3612.U58 K58 2003

2002151446

published by
CURBSTONE PRESS 321 Jackson Street Willimantic, CT 06226
phone: 860-423-5110 e-mail: info@curbstone.org
http://www.curbstone.org

For my family

I'm indebted to my agent, John Silbersack, for his reliable counsel and support, and occasional leaps of faith. And to my brother Mark Luntta, who kept asking about it, as did my parents Anna and Hans Luntta, and to my good friend and ally Steve Dwyer. Marc Swan and Kathy Read, thanks for taking the time and for your thoughtful, candid comments. Thanks also to John Coyne, a faithful supporter of writers, on the edge or otherwise.

I'd like to offer my gratitude to Curbstone's founders and publishers Alexander Taylor and Judith Ayer Doyle for their personal and professional insights, and to the Curbstone staff and associates for their hard work.

And of course, it almost goes without saying, a man isn't much without them that love him—thank you Phyllis, Kaarlo, Jack, and Nikki.

CHAPTER 1

That whole business about God being in charge of the universe and everything in it? I don't buy it. I mean, I'm sure God in His infinite wisdom *believes* He's in control of His eternal plan, and that's fine with me because, after all, He is God and having faith in things is definitely up His alley. But all the same, He ought to admit it's at least remotely possible that He's made some world-class mistakes. Just think about the Nazis and Jews and so on. Are we supposed to believe God let all that happen because He's omniscient and had this inside information that it was actually a *good* thing for millions of babies and mothers to be herded into gas chambers? What happened to the omnipotent part, the part where a half-concerned God would've cut off Hitler at the jackboots before the war ever started? And don't even talk about pestilence and poverty and slavery and disease, or the fact that God took paradise away from us just because a guy ate an apple. I think we need a little perspective here. God may have a winning message, and He's probably terrific at keeping heaven clean and safe and heavenly, but here on earth He's let a lot of good come to a bad end. For no reason that I can see. Either that, or justice just isn't His strong point.

My name is Dub Teed, and if you're expecting some irritating story about how I got the nickname, you can go ahead and relax because, for the life of me, I don't know. Nor, and this is incredible, does anyone in my family. Susan swears it came about because it was a sound I used to make when she and my mother gave me baths as a baby, apparently the only imitation I could make of their "rub-a-dub-dub" noises while I sat like a naked idiot in the tub. But the thought of Susan helping to bathe me, baby or no baby, is not a thought I'm particularly fond of, so the less said about that the better. And my mother says she remembers none of that business anyway, so I've got to think that Susan made up the whole thing just to make me cringe every once in a while, which she probably thinks is her privilege as an older sister. So be it, it probably is. Pop seems to think the name came about when he taught me how to spell my real name, which is Walter, which is his name as well. He figures that in the early days I couldn't get by the first letter, which I apparently pronounced "Dub-oo" or whatever, and there you have it. Anyway, since we share the same name otherwise, we figure the nickname has some practical value around the house.

My mother's name, by the way, is Doreen, and that's what we're supposed to call her. She insists on it, don't ask, it's her big thing in life. She gets a huge thrill out of her kids calling her Doreen, as if she's our big sister or kooky aunt, or even worse, a friend. Personally, I find it embarrassing, and so does Susan, who has made it her life's work to call Doreen anything *but* Doreen. She goes as far as to call her "Mother" or variations on the theme. She's even called her "Mère" in this fairly decent French accent, and that, believe me, irks Doreen to no end, which of course is never a hard thing to do. Pop doesn't really approve of it, he just sort of lets it go. He avoids it actually, as he avoids most of her idiosyncrasies. But thank God he doesn't want us to call him "Wally."

Doreen's family is the wealthy Constantines from over the river, that's the Connecticut River, who, if the truth be told, made their money in bootleg liquor during the '20s. It was a small family operation, but I gather they did fairly well with it because later on they started a few legal businesses like real estate offices and car dealerships. If you've ever driven through Hartford on the highway, you'll have seen one of Grandpa's billboards: "Constantine's Cadillac—Piles of Smiles, Mile After Mile." I think he makes up the ads himself.

Grandpa is Greek, if you couldn't tell by the name, and came over to the States when he was just a kid. His house is grand, sort of like that castle in the Walt Disney movies, and he lives in West Hartford with "all them kikes and lawyers," as he says. He, for one, sided with his daughter during the whole Ricky Dubois business, and I think if he ever had an ounce of fun or whimsy in him he must have lost it sometime during his bootlegging days.

His wife died when I was too young to remember. I have seen photos, but all they show is the smiling, round face of a white-haired woman who looks all comfortable and benign, although I get the impression that she shared Grandpa's attitudes, which only makes sense because they were married for years and years. The rumor is she helped supply the recipes for their bathtub hooch. It's even said that she helped him in the early days on his delivery runs, and kept a loaded pistol in her purse to fend off the gangs that were always trying to steal their booze and money. Since Grandpa doesn't talk much about those days, I'll never really know what Grandma was like, except for this legacy he left with me one Easter: "She could smell a nigger coming round the corner."

Doreen and Pop met at college while Pop was in on the GI Bill, and hit it off pretty well early on. After they got married she dropped out of school, which may be one of the sources of her frustration if you ask me. She's always said that she had wanted to be a teacher, and when I think about that now, I wonder what kind of a teacher she'd have been. My guess is the kind who would have made mincemeat out of me.

Grandpa and Pop don't get along—at all. The rumor is that Grandpa opposed the marriage because Pop had already got a job as a newspaper reporter when he asked Doreen to marry him, and Grandpa has this severe dislike for reporters or the police and everyone else who said anything about him back in his gin-running days, probably because, and this is always the thing with Doreen as well, it was true. Personally, I think the real issue is that Grandpa knows he made all of his start-up money as a thug, and since Pop is a stand-up sort of guy, you can understand how they'd feel uneasy around each other.

Pop is still a newspaper man. In fact, nowadays he's sort of a well-known columnist. Not that he'd say that sort of thing himself, he doesn't really make much of it. His column is syndicated in a pile of newspapers, although he writes for our local paper, *The Hartford Courant*. He writes a great column, though I have to admit to not completely understanding it all the time. It's usually about things happening in our increasingly complex and turbulent lives, like Sputniks or the problems with Hula Hoops or something. Last month he called Richard Nixon "another Joe McCarthy, with a worse complexion," which was apparently a big old hoot because I heard him laughing in his study while he wrote it and I couldn't resist popping in to see what he was doing. He wasn't bothered by me busting in like that, because Pop, like me, appreciates a basic principle of life: there isn't a person alive who can walk by a laugh coming from behind a closed door.

They had Susan first and two years later they had me, and I was supposed to be some kind of joy or something because I was a boy and rounded out the perfect family and the American dream sequence, and that was pretty much the case until Ricky Dubois came to the neighborhood and I learned that it's a hell of a lot easier to dream it than live it.

CHAPTER 2

By late June of 1961, the hot weather was well under way. I still like to think of it in terms of a passage from one of Pop's novels. I know it by heart, and it goes like this:

"It was that time of summer when small communities begin to languish, when the sweet heat of wet streets gives way to dreams of gentle breezes, and summer moves from its initial exuberance to a paced, sluggish existence—a victim of its own lust for consumption and joy. This is when the citizens of small towns respond with a nod and a wink and a good nap, and accept it as they would a doomed love. They know summer will inevitably become the shy paramour, hedging, trying to find the door."

Despite the fact that the novel it came from was as popular as Castro at the White House, at least that's what Pop says, I have always liked the passage. I can almost smell the wet streets. And I think it accurately describes the way our summer was unfolding on the day Ricky Dubois moved into the neighborhood.

I had already been appropriately lazy since school let out, although I did help Pop paint the fence and picnic table, a yearly ritual where we get together and talk about my maturation process. I like those times, and I like the smell of paint. And I like the way Pop gets loose and tries to talk about his own maturation process, which, if you ask me, is suspect in a man who has paint on the tip of his nose.

"What do you say, Dub," Pop had said, "how's life treating you?"

"Good, Pop. Why do you ask?" Which is what I always said. It was more or less expected.

"Because it's a fatherly thing to ask. And I'm an interested father."

"Things are fine, Pop."

"No concerns, problems? Complaints?"

"Nope."

He'd dipped his brush, but didn't look my way. "Let's see.... Well, is it time we had the talk yet? The birds and bees business? You'll be in eighth grade, I seem to think it should be on the schedule for about now." He'd cleared his throat.

This, of course, was not our normal routine. But I'd had a good idea of what he was getting at. I mean, who doesn't? You hear things—school buses are overlooked as institutions of higher education, if you ask me—you put two and two together, and you look up the good words in the old Funk and Wagnalls in your father's study. Then you decide that if you've got any questions about it you can always go to the old man and ask. Like, when you're about thirty-five.

"I think I got it, Pop."

The lines on his face smoothed out. "Good. I mean, any questions?"

"Actually, I've been thinking. A kid gets to puberty, right? Then you have to start shaving. But you get pimples, too, so you have to shave but you've got all these pimples on your chin and everywhere else, getting in the way. So, how do you do that? You know, without turning your face into a bloody mess." It was a genuine question. I mean, I *had* been thinking about it.

"Carefully, if I remember," he'd said. "I'll show you. But I don't see any pimples on you."

"I'm expecting them any minute."

He'd laughed. "Sometimes you're just like your mother, Dub. All worry and wisecracks."

"Except she doesn't have to shave."

"Neither do you, not for a while, anyway. So, ready for Kelly's?"

Then we got down to planning out our summer. We always end up joking about this or that, and he sometimes gets to laughing so hard he cries. I mean, I crack him up even more than he cracks himself up, and he's got this great big laugh, like a wounded horse, the kind of laugh where you'd be sort of cringing sitting next to him at a Jerry Lewis movie or something. But I love him for that laugh, at the very least for that.

First we'd discuss our yearly family camping trip to the Berkshires, where I was sure I would watch, fascinated as ever, as my mother refused for the entire week to use the outhouse toilets of Kelly's Kampground in Stockbridge, Massachusetts. "As Jesus is my witness," she'd say, "I will sit on an electric fence before I sit on one of those godless toilets." You should be aware that my mother, for whom Jesus is the prime witness of her life, hates camping.

It's not that she's fragile. My mother can be rugged as an old man's toenail when she wants to be, but she apparently cannot stomach cooking over fires and fending off mosquitoes as much as Susan and I cannot get enough of it. Pop would take us fishing and swimming at Kelly's Pond, and Doreen would nap in the tent or take the car to town with a few of the other outhouse-vigilant wives for cocktails in the air-conditioned lounge of Kelly's Hotel. And there, since the hotel restrooms apparently had religion, Doreen would find her salvation.

After our annual camping trip came my favorite time of the summer, the week long encampment of the C.D. Lorenzo Traveling Family Circus and Carnival, Rides & Games & Prizes, Come One Come All, starring Simba, Pride of the African Jungle. It was a small circus as these things go, but I loved it for its fanfare and noise, for the dripping fat cakes, corn dogs, teenagers with cigarettes, shooting galleries, all of it. But most of all I was pulled to the elephant, Simba. He was bigger than any animal I'd ever seen, and walked with a slow-motion gait, like a king. I always wondered what was going on inside that head of his, behind those watery, almost sad eyes. A whole lot, is my guess.

Then, after the circus came and left, and this was a yearly

thing as well, Pop would take Doreen on their own private vacation somewhere where she could get a decent meal and a shower, and they would come back all rosy and happy and, predictably, all over each other. Doreen would smile afterwards, and things would go well in the house. For a few weeks, anyway.

That mostly depended on Doreen. Pop has always explained away her erratic behavior, meaning her drinking and her temper, by telling us she's just sort of high-strung. And whenever Pop says it, that she's high-strung, I know he's embarrassed because he's got this awful, pained expression on his face and he looks down at his feet as if they're about to talk back to him. And he tugs at that earlobe of his. It's like a gauge, I swear it, the way he tugs at his ear when he's thinking hard about Doreen or trying to hide the fact that he's confused or flustered or whatever. Sometimes he looks like he's about to yank it right off his head.

But he loves her, that I can tell. I can tell by the way he steals a look at her when he thinks no one is looking. It's not a happy, ain't-it-grand-to-be-in-love sort of stare, but a melancholy, hound-dog look, as if he were sitting with an old friend in a hospital room. The thing is, my father is loyal. He'd do anything for her, even now, even after the Ricky Dubois business. And I have to admit that I admire him for that, despite what she did, despite who she is.

About a week after Pop and I painted the picnic table, I found myself next door, glaring at Doug Hammer over a chess board.

"Looks like cheating to me," I said. "Or close to it."

"Not true," Doug said. "I'm an honorable guy."

"Hate to say it, Doug," Susan said, "but Dub is right."

"I'm telling the truth," Doug said.

"Fine," I said, "then it's reliable information."

"Dub," he said, "that's no way to show that you trust a friend."

"Friends are one thing, trust is another."

"What? Are you saying you can't trust me?"

He looked, for a moment, genuinely hurt. "No," I said. "I'm just saying that in this instance, you might be mistaken."

"Look, you *can* move a pawn sideways," Doug said, " long as it's in your first three moves. It's in the rules."

Which clearly meant it was not in the rules, because Doug Hammer said it was in the rules.

"You can't," I said. "There is no rule."

"My father said so," he said, and huffed.

"Okay, fine, do as you damn well please," I said, and let it drop, because that's a thing about Doug. Whenever he brings his father into it, it's time to let it drop.

Doug lives next door to us, and that makes him a friend by default I guess, although he is a true friend and I do have to say this about him: he may lie, and he may cheat sometimes, but Doug Hammer can be counted on in a fix. At least, if it suits him to be counted on in a fix, which is almost all the time. Susan, the amateur psychologist, figures that Doug's loyalty comes from some intense need to be liked, him being an only child and all—that and the fact that he's a fat kid. Me, I see him as another guy who is maybe spoiled by his mother and who is actually sort of demented when you get right down to it. Doug will hunch down and get into the thick of a fight like a kamikaze on a mission if he's got a stake in it. Which, as I said, he almost always does.

Doug's father is another large guy, with blond hair and a tan and a puffy face who always looks like he just got off a boat—in fact, that's pretty much the case because he's got a job as a musician on a cruise ship. Mr. Hammer is divorced from Doug's mom, and that makes him a sort of celebrity around here—I mean, I don't know any other kids whose parents are divorced—when he drops into town every once in a while to pick up Doug for a weekend or a short vacation. Mr. Hammer's hair is wild, it's ocean hair, and he always pulls up in a big rented Cadillac before he goes into the house to grab Doug and take him for a weekend somewhere.

On the other hand, Mrs. Hammer is a short, thin, delicate woman who loves Dougy to death. Doug, of course, loves her to death, and I can't say it's always a pretty sight. I mean, they get along so *famously*—it almost makes you physically ill sometimes. She's always cooing over him, asking if he's had enough to eat and so on, usually after we've just eaten about the thickest peanut butter and banana sandwiches this side of a bathtub sponge. Dougy, clearly, could not live without her.

"Checkmate," Doug said.

"Well," I said. "It's only because you moved the pawns sideways."

Doug paid no attention. "Did it in eight moves, Dubby boy. What do you think of that?"

"Not a whole hell of a lot."

"Well, think again. Lose today, lose tomorrow."

Susan said, "My turn."

"Good, a challenge," Doug said.

The kitchen door opened and Mrs. Hammer peered out. "Doug," she called, "it's time."

"Shit-burgers," Doug muttered. "Pin cushion time."

Meaning Dougy had to take his insulin shot. In the beginning, when the Hammers moved into the neighborhood, I was in awe of Doug's ability to take it every day. Personally, I can actually feel the pain whenever I think of my yearly booster shots for tetanus and God knows what else, but Doug, though he hates the routine, is all in all pretty nonchalant about the whole thing. He complains but he says it softly, in a resigned way. Susan thinks part of Doug's kamikaze attitude toward sports and fighting and whatever is overcompensation for his diabetes, which she thinks he thinks makes other people think he's weak. I don't know, he's never really mentioned it specifically, although I have got to think that plunging a hypodermic needle into your leg every day of your life has got to prepare you for other, much larger pains.

Doug went into the house, and Susan and I set up the chess board for the next game. We were at the picnic table in the Hammer backyard, under a low crabapple tree at the top of a small hill. The hill ended at a slim creek that flowed through our backyard and through Doug's backyard, and we used the hill for some fine sledding during the winter.

I looked at the huge weeping willow tree in our yard at the bottom of the hill. It shifted quietly with the wind, more so than the pines and white birches and other trees. It was the largest tree on the lot, but Pop says weeping willows are the weakest trees of all. During the hurricane of 1954, he said the tree almost snapped in half. I like to climb it, to get inside it. It's as if I'm on the inside of a waterfall. At night, when my window is open, I can hear it rustle in the breeze, like soft wind chimes.

"Better stay away from Mom today," Susan said.

"What happened?"

"She threw a fit," Susan said.

"At who?"

"You didn't hear it?"

"No," I said. How it was possible to miss something like a person throwing a fit in your own house, I'm not sure. Sometimes you just get used to things like that.

"It was classic," she said. "It was about the Fourth."

"What about it? We're going to Grandpa's, aren't we?" This was one of the few times of the year I liked going to the old man's place. He always has firecrackers, even though they're purely illegal, though that never stopped him before in any of his other efforts. He once let me light a firecracker called the Death Bang, and I don't believe my ears have ever been the same.

"Pop said he had to work. Mom said he was just begging out of the whole thing. Pop said that newspapers come out every day, and that means everyday someone's got to write them, and he had to be at work on the Fourth. So she had a fit."

"But," I said, "we're still going, aren't we?"

"Who knows?" she said. Susan explained to me how it had grown to a milk-tossing fray or something. "She called him Mr. Misplaced Work Ethic," she said. "We had to clean it up."

Well, of course. We always have to clean it up. Don't talk to me about Doreen's anger, about the slaps, about the name-calling. The thing I hate most is cleaning up after my mother tosses things. She has tossed plates of food, radios that were still plugged in, glasses of wine, her cat, which has since died of natural causes, me at various times, a lamp, records, apparently some milk here and there, and forks, knives, spatulas, and other common household items. And we're always mopping up after it all, this includes Pop, like drooling patients in some mental ward. It defies explanation, it really does.

"So, how did it end?" I said.

"She started crying, stomped off, we cleaned it up. What's to say?"

It seemed like just another day, so I shrugged my shoulders. But Susan sighed. It wore on her, and had for some time. Doreen wore on all of us, but Susan was the girl in the family, and whatever Doreen did seemed to affect her more. Or maybe it's that Susan is older than me, and she understood more, even saw more. Whatever it was, Susan was just plain tired. She acted too much like an old woman.

"Do you think it's always like this?" she said. "Do all married women scream and throw things?"

"I doubt it, is my guess."

"I'd kill myself first," she said. "I mean it. Dub, if you ever see me with a glass of wine at breakfast, you have my permission to kill me."

"Okay," I said. "How?"

"Poison. Maybe car exhaust. Nothing messy."

"Push you off a cliff?"

"No, too embarrassing. I keep reading about people who jump off cliffs and don't end up dying. They just get crippled for life, and they're more miserable than ever. I'd be sitting in a wheelchair, paralyzed from the neck down, and someone would ask me what happened and I'd have to say that I was hit by a train or a herd of buffalo or something. My life would be a lie, and I couldn't even kill myself to save my life."

"At least you wouldn't be drinking wine anymore. You'd be paralyzed from the neck down."

"What, paraplegics don't eat or drink?"

Just then Doug came out of the house, all blustery and full of insulin.

"Enough chess," he said, "let's get out of here."

"Why?" Susan said. "We've got the chess board set up."

"Bike trip!" he said.

Susan said no thanks, it was too hot and she was not about to get involved with a couple of guys riding bikes around town getting into who knows what. She begged off, leaving us to our bikes, and went into the house, looking forlorn in a way, but determined to be the voice of reason. At that moment, I found myself wishing there were more girls in the neighborhood for her to be with.

"Where to?" I said.

"Let's go down to Hwan's shop."

Doug grabbed his bike and took the lead. He always takes the lead so he can stop and look at every damn thing, dead squirrels, whatever, along the road. He gets a kick out of putting his hand out to stop traffic behind him—that'd be me—as if he's driving a huge rig or something.

We moved quickly through town. East Hartford is built on the outskirts of Hartford, just a couple of miles outside of downtown, across the Connecticut River. It was hot, and the rotting smell from the river became stronger as we headed to Main Street.

Our bikes were well-oiled and we flew along the gooey pavement, listening to the sounds of radio stations blasting by in convertible cars. Most everyone was going to or coming from a shift at Pratt and Whitney Aircraft, the huge airplane engine manufacturing plant that supports about half the families in the town.

We passed row after row of houses that looked like our own. They were small, toy houses, most of them built after the war. Each took up little space, and the yards were just large enough for a game of tag. The tiny Capes were dull and sometimes dirty, and I knew just about every kid who lived in every house.

Sliding down Silver Lane, the best part of the ride because it was a smooth decline that added just enough speed to allow us pedal air, Doug, predictably, jerked his arms straight up. I skidded to a stop behind him. In front of us was the Silver Lane Shopping Plaza, where most of the town bought groceries at Grand Union and trinkets at Woolworth's.

Doug, despite the easy pedaling, was breathless. He pointed to the vacant lot behind Woolworth's. "Two months," he said.

"You stopped to point at the circus lot?" I said.

"I swear I'm going to see the freaks this year, Dub."

"Like hell. Your mother would crown you and turn you into the Headless Boy."

"No, really," he said, wistfully. "The Cyclops Man, Hitler's Brain-in-a-Bottle, The Two-Headed Cow, I mean it."

"You know you can't get into the freak show. They only allow adults in there."

"They'll let us in. I mean, the circus will. It's just our folks that don't. C.D. Lorenzo would let you pay a quarter to see his mother hump a gorilla."

"That's pleasant," I said. "Bet you a buck you don't get in."

"Where are you going to get a buck?"

"I have it right here. Where's yours?"

"I'll have it by then. It's a deal. The Goat with Five Legs, Dub. It's our destiny."

He crossed the street and we cycled over to the empty lot, a wide, dusty expanse of paper, broken bottles, and oil patches. This was the legacy of the C.D. Lorenzo Traveling Family Circus and Carnival's last visit, the summer before.

I knew exactly where the Big Top would stand, and where the rides, games, animal pens, and performers' trailers would be set up. I closed my eyes for a second and imagined the smells and sounds.

When I opened my eyes I turned and saw a group of boys and their bikes, parked up against the back wall of the giant Woolworth's. They squatted on their knees and were pitching coins against the brick building.

"Look," I said.

"What?" Doug said.

"It's Big Farley."

"Really," Doug said.

At that moment, Big Farley glanced in our direction and drew himself off the ground. He said something to the group.

"Hey!" Big said. Big was built like a Coke machine, with a jiggling gut hanging over his jeans that would, I'd always imagined, develop into a champion beer belly in the next few years. His face was, as always, flushed and sweaty.

"Hey!" Big shouted again. He was quite clever about these things. "School's out, no teachers' asses around here for you to kiss!"

Which about summed up Big's feelings about the education process, by implication. I mean, I did pretty well in school, and Doug did okay, too, but Big, well, let's just say he jumped into schoolwork with about as much enthusiasm as a cat jumps into its bath. Not that he was altogether stupid, actually, it's just that his mind was suited for mayhem, not math.

"Let's go," I said.

"Let's stay a minute," Doug said.

"Why?"

"Oh, I don't know." He had a gleam—*that* gleam—in his eye.

"Hey faggots," Big yelled. "Waiting for the circus?"

"Nope," Doug shouted.

"What?" Big shouted, giggling. The boys had all stood up, adjusting their jeans and tee-shirts. There were six of them.

"We don't need the circus!" Doug said.

"Yeah? Why?!"

"Because the chimps are already here!"

"Oh, good," I said.

Big Farley's face turned sideways for an instant. One of the boys whispered in his ear. His face went dark and he hitched up his trousers.

"What did you say, shithead?" he said.

"Get on your bike," Doug said, and we both mounted instantly.

"I said it's too bad about your mother," Doug called out.

Big was lost. "What?"

"That she keeps trying to have kids, but she always gets butt-ugly monkeys!"

"Wonderful," I said.

"Go!" Doug said, and we pedaled off toward Main Street, an easy cut around the side of the building. As we rounded the building into the parking lot, I caught a glimpse of the Big Farley gang, bumping into each other, jumping on their bikes, ready for the chase.

"Thanks," I said to Doug, ahead of me.

"My pleasure!"

"We're dead, you know."

"Pedal," he said, but quietly.

We did just that, hot air burning our lungs, as we pushed those pedals with our lives. The Farley crowd was behind, but not close enough to hear us.

"Where to?"

"Hwan's!" Doug said, which seemed a desperate move, because that's where we were headed in the first place. I mean, shouldn't you go and hide somewhere when your life is threatened by big, nasty people with freshly minted grudges?

"What are we going to do, buy bubble gum?"

"Yes."

"Good, Doug, real good. Let's chew it up while they smash our faces."

"Trust me."

We pedaled like hell and my legs began to fail. We had about a half-mile to go before Mr. Hwan's grocery store would appear, and all I could imagine was that the people driving by were thinking, "How nice, a group of boys out on a ride. Those two in front sure are red in the face, but, well, *it is* a hot day."

We rounded Silver Lane onto Main Street, past Napoleon's Peek-a-Boo Dance Club, and Mr. Hwan's store came into view. The Farley gang puffed angrily behind, yet hadn't, miraculously, gained on us.

"Bikes into the store!" Doug said.

"You're nuts," I said.

"Do it."

We screeched to a halt, and threw our bikes past the front door, walking with them as if it were an everyday occurrence for us to carry our bikes into small convenience stores.

Mr. Hwan, dozing behind the counter, stood up like someone had walked into the place with an aardvark. His flowered Hawaiian shirt seemed bright against his face, which all of a sudden got clouded. "Whaa? Whaa?" he said.

"Afternoon, Mr. Hwan," I said.

"Got any peaches today?" Doug said, gagging.

Big Farley and his gang pulled up with a start, brakes locked and faces pink. They gathered at the door. Mr. Hwan said, "What now?"

The gang swaggered in as if they were about to do some

minor shopping, glaring at Doug and me, breathing heavily and distractedly picking up Mars Bars and potato chips.

Mr. Hwan, who came over from Korea during the war and was no slouch in matters of evading corrupt people in positions of power, seemed to size up the gathering fairly quickly. He sighed and rolled his eyes. He snapped his attention to Big and said something in Korean, which, by its inflection, I took to mean, "American boy-dogs will cause my first stroke."

"Henry Farley," he said, though it sounded like 'Henny Falley,' "good to see you." His mouth worked itself into a pleasant sort of smile, and he rubbed his hands together. "What can do for you today?"

Big stared at Mr. Hwan in disbelief. This was not Mr. Hwan's normal attitude toward the Big Farley gang. "Nice sodas in the cooler," Mr. Hwan said.

"I, uh, I was looking for...comic books," Big said, looking smug as if he'd just passed a test. Doug and I, and our bikes, were over by the comic book section.

Mr. Hwan darted a sharp glance at us, and gestured with his eyes. We moved away.

"Ahh, a good choice, Henry. Good to read books, good for the mind." He squinted at Big. "Yes, good for any kind mind. Come, I show you."

Mr. Hwan put his arm around Big's shoulder, and gently led him to the comic books. The rest of the gang breathed heavily and stared in wonder.

"By the way, Henry, you been you home lately?"

"No," Big said, warily. "Why?"

"Oh, nothing. You fatha just call me ten minute ago, looking for you. Such a coincident you walk into my shop just now. Very fortunate. Look, today we have new Archie and—" he squinted at Big, "Jughead."

"Uh, what did my father want?" Big said. His wide eyes reminded us all that his father, who was Officer Henry Farley

Sr. of the East Hartford Police Department, was not a man to be kept waiting.

"Oh, he say to go home soon, as fast as can."

"Why?"

"Something about you house on fire."

"What?" Big went ashen.

"You house on fire, I think he want you to help move furniture."

"My house?" Big began to shake.

"But you have plenty time to buy comic book."

"My house!"

"New Batman this month," Mr. Hwan said.

"Jesus Christ!" Big said, and he bolted out the door. His cronies scrambled behind, all wide-eyed in anticipation of fire engines and commotion. It was to be, for them, a field day, the hell with Big Farley's house.

They pedaled off, leaving us in a wake of shouts and gibberish.

Mr. Hwan turned to us and the sparkle was out of his eyes. "Next time I see him I tell him it was crank call," he said.

"Wow," Doug said.

"What you do to him?" Mr. Hwan said sharply.

Doug and I exchanged looks. "I guess I called him a name," Doug said.

Mr. Hwan clasped his arms behind his back, and waited.

"You know, like a name or something," Doug said.

Mr. Hwan rocked on his heels. "Yes?"

"A chimp," Doug said.

Mr. Hwan's eyebrows rose. "Chimp?" He shook his head. "Some more, I think."

Doug looked at his toes. "Maybe I said something else. Monkey, maybe it was. Butt-ugly monkey."

"Oh? Very bad thing you say. No good."

"I didn't mean it that way."

"Nobody mean it that way," Mr. Hwan said. "But everybody say it that way."

"He called us names first," I said.

"Yes, yes, am sure he did. But you invite it, I think."

"No, we didn't, we were just hanging around," Doug said.

"No man innocent. No man victim. Every man bring his own trouble. Now, you go before Henry think about possibility of fatha calling from burning house."

Mr. Hwan pointed to the door. "And never bring bike in here again."

"Thanks, Mr. Hwan," Doug said.

"No thank. You go."

And we took off. I imagined the scene at Big's house, the gang bursting in, eager for mayhem. Big's three or four—I was never sure how many—younger brothers and sisters would laugh, and his mother would probably shake her head and blink. Actually, that's all I could imagine of her. I'd only seen her at church, half the size of her husband, her hair pulled back in a bun, shoulders hunched, eyes cast down and blinking about a million times a minute, like she'd just stepped out from a cave into the sun. She was quite the blinker. And she never looked anyone straight in the eye, and I mean anyone, let alone talked to them. I have never heard her speak a word, even to her husband. It was as if she was afraid to talk, or had nothing left to say.

And if Officer Farley, known to most of us as Officer Bigger Farley, was home, there would be hell to pay. Not that Big deserved it, at least this time. It's just that there was always hell to pay at Big's house, we all knew that. Outside of Big and his mom, Officer Bigger was the only person I knew who *never* smiled, at least in a nice way, even at Christmas Eve Mass, and certainly never when we saw him cruising by in his patrol car. When Big came to school with bruises on his arms, on his neck, even a black eye once in a while, all I could think of was Officer Bigger's dark face. For a moment I actually felt sorry for Big, even though he's the type of kid whose behavior crossed the border between mean and dangerous long ago, who once *swallowed* a baby garter snake in front of a schoolyard full of numbed children, and who'd be a great candidate for becoming a celebrated mass murderer. But not that sorry. I mean, family psychology is probably enlightening and all that, but when you find yourself at the meaty end of Big Farley's fist, Dr. Spock can take a flying leap at a rolling doughnut for all I care.

When we arrived home, Susan greeted us on the lawn of our house. She was agitated, and spoke quickly.

"Dub, you remember the old Glasser place?"

"The one for sale?"

"It was sold last month," Doug said.

"Yeah, well, the new people are moving in," Susan said.

"They've got trucks and vans and everything down there."

The house, which was at the end of the block, was of little consequence to me. The Glassers, an older couple with no children, had moved to Florida at the beginning of the summer. No loss, no gain. I hadn't paid an iota of attention to the whole thing, and I couldn't see what Susan was so excited about.

"They're Negroes," she whispered.

CHAPTER 3

I hadn't given much thought to Negroes.

It's not that I avoided Negroes, exactly. It's just that there weren't any, not even one, at school, or at church, or at any of the places I hung out. I mean, I never had even *talked* to a Negro, really.

And now we had Negroes moving in down the block. I certainly hadn't expected it—it sort of hit me like a snowball on a summer day. I wondered if I would like them, or if I was supposed to like them. Or if they would like me.

But the thing is, if you don't know any Negroes, how could you know any of that?

The truth of the matter is, as I said, I never really gave any of the other races much thought. Other than Mr. Hwan, who is Korean and a refugee from the war and all, I never knew a person of another race. And, believe me, I hardly know Mr. Hwan, and that's not my choice.

I did know some things about Negroes. They were in history books of course, having been slaves at one time, which, in my opinion, is almost impossible to imagine.

And I knew about singers like Sam Cooke, Chuck Berry, and Harry Belafonte. The Five Satins and this new group called The Supremes were all over the radio. You could always see Negroes on television. Louis Armstrong, Nat King Cole, and Rochester were on all the time. And, of course, Negroes were in the news.

Ever since the late '50s, during the time of the bus boycotts in Montgomery, in Alabama, and the desegregation of the high schools in Arkansas, when President Eisenhower had to send troops to keep the peace, the big news had been about race relations. I knew names like the Reverend Dr.

Martin Luther King and the Southern Christian Leadership Conference, and the N-double A-C-P, the National Association for the Advancement of Colored People. The Civil Rights Act, which Pop told me was passed in 1957, was apparently a big step for Negroes who were trying to get equal this and equal that.

And by the summer of '61, the papers were full of reports about demonstrations and what they called "sit-ins" for civil rights. It had started, the sit-ins at least, the year before when a Woolworth's lunch counter in North Carolina refused to serve four Negro college students. They, in turn, refused to move from the counter, which raised all kinds of hell in Greensboro. That set off a series of sit-ins and strikes around the country, and the situation began to get testy. Soon, blacks and whites, who called themselves "Freedom Riders," got on buses and drove around the south, joining in the demonstrations whenever they could. Of course the Freedom Riders were heckled and attacked along the way, even by, if you can believe it, the police. It was getting to be a huge mess, and the strikes, the demonstrations, and the Negroes, you can be sure they scared a lot of people, even in our neck of the woods.

I didn't know quite what to make of the sit-ins. When Pop first brought them up at dinner one night earlier in the summer, he'd said they were at least a good start. Doreen said a start of what? Pop said a start in recognizing that everyone has the right to be in any public place and eat or urinate next to someone else, regardless of color. Doreen said we don't talk about urinating at the table no matter who's doing it. Pop said that urinating was not the point, the point was everyone had the right to be somewhere with other people and reap the same benefits from the Bill of Rights.

Doreen stayed silent, but after a moment Pop said,

"You know Doreen, lots of good and decent people, even famous people, weren't white."

Doreen rolled her eyes."I feel a cliché coming on Walter.

You aren't going to tell me about Jesus Christ again, are you?"

Pop said—and you really had to cringe because he said it like a kid baiting his mother—he said, "Yes, as a matter of fact, I was going to mention Jesus Christ. And, for that matter, the apostles. Even some of the early popes probably weren't exactly white."

Now, there are three people you never attempt to reconfigure in my mother's book, and they are Jesus Christ, any past or future pope, and her father, not necessarily in that order. Forget the truth. It's just something you don't do.

And even though what Pop said, about Jesus probably not being precisely lily white, was something people talked about all the time, I didn't have much time to think about it myself because Doreen got into an instant snit, a fury really, and after a couple of minutes of shouting about heresy and high-and-mighty liberal Democrat journalists, buttered carrots started to fly and we were once again mopping it up like a chain gang. Doreen went up to her room sobbing and wondering what was becoming of her world. While we were mopping up, Susan, under her breath, said, "Bad move Pop," and Pop said, "I know, I knew it before I said it and I'm sorry." And I'm sure he was truly sorry because he kept shaking his head and after we finished cleaning up, he went upstairs to find Doreen and I guess they made up or something.

Anyway, other than that, other than Negroes on the radio or television, and other than Negroes in faraway places like down south or in Africa, I did have two minor experiences that stick in my mind. I wasn't going to mention them because the first one occurred even before I was born, and the other happened so quickly it never seemed to have made any difference up until just now. It's funny, but I didn't think about it when Ricky and her family moved in, and I hadn't thought about it during all the troubles later. But I thought about it just now.

To hear Pop talk about the first one, it was something

that really confused him, and that is saying a lot when you get to thinking about his days in the Army and as a reporter and everything.

It was in the year before I was born, when Susan was still a baby. We had neighbors on the block named the Churmans. Mr. Churman was an executive over at Pratt, and Mrs. Churman was just a tight bundle of nerves who looked like she always was about to have a migraine, as Pop remembers her.

The telling incident came one summer, when Mrs. Churman had ordered some living room furniture from over at Sears, which was a completely normal, suburban thing to do. On the day it arrived, the delivery truck pulled up and the driver and his helper got out to offload the chairs and sofas and things. Pop was writing in his study and he happened to notice the truck pull up. The driver and his helper were Negroes.

After the furniture came off the truck, with Mrs. Churman standing in the driveway the whole time, Mr. Churman signed some papers, gave the guys a tip, and they went away. This was all very ordinary, everyday living.

But the next day another Sears truck came by and picked up every stick of furniture that had been delivered. The drivers, this time, were white, and Mrs. Churman didn't come out of the house.

The way Pop tells the story, he figures that Mrs. Churman was sort of a loon. He reckoned that she was not just a racist, but that she had this obsession with germs, which is why she sent back furniture that had been handled by Negroes. Years later, when I heard this story for the first time, I asked him why someone would think a Negro is germy and he said, "It's not really about germs, Dub, it's about ignorance."

"Okay," I said, and hadn't a clue what he was talking about.

"And racism," he said, "is all about not understanding people. White people don't understand Negroes, so they call them names to keep them at a distance. It's an ignorant thing to do, but unfortunately, I think it's a human thing to do.

"Which leads me to give you a fatherly directive," he said, and put his hand on my shoulder. "I don't ever want to hear you calling someone a name because of their race or religion or anything. You will learn enough about hate and pain in life without distributing it yourself. Whatever you may feel about someone—take Doug, for instance, he's overweight but you'd never say that to his face—there is no need to be verbal about your thoughts. Understand?"

"Sure," I said.

"What I mean is, if you ever use the word 'nigger' you will have to answer to me."

"Grandpa uses it."

"Grandpa is of a different generation. He was an immigrant himself, and he made his living in a rough section of Hartford. I'm not making excuses, but you are not Grandpa."

I asked him what Mr. Churman had thought about his wife going mad and all, and Pop said this, carefully: "You do what you have to do."

The other incident with Negroes happened in Hartford. I am not proud of it, because the moment I admit to it I have to take blame for some sort of racism, and it's actually a larger bit than I want to admit to. But in the end, and now, I think all white people are guilty of the same sort of thing, to an extent.

Hartford is about a twenty-minute ride from East Hartford by bus. The city has its "ends," as people call them. They're really neighborhoods, but big ones. Hartford's South End is where the Italians live, and it has Italian street signs, Italian newspapers, and some of the best bakeries around. West Hartford is where my grandfather lives among, as he says, "them kikes and lawyers." What he really means is the rich people, who he apparently thinks are mostly Jewish. The east side of Hartford, just over the Connecticut River, is really a town by itself, our town. East Hartford, the factory village.

The North End of Hartford is where the Negroes and Puerto Ricans live. It's known to be a part of town that's gloomy and dangerous to drive through late at night, no matter what race you are. It's a rough place, and getting rougher. The streets are lined with spilled garbage, the people are poor, and there doesn't seem to be much for them to do. I've walked places in my life, but to walk through the North End would take a whole lot of strength I still don't believe I have, even after the Ricky business. I just don't have it, and it's one of the things I think about almost every single day of my life. To tell the truth, I couldn't say now if I'll ever have that kind of strength.

Anyway, Doreen and I took the bus to downtown Hartford one late summer day a few years ago, to buy new clothes for school. It was a blistering day, and the round of clothes-buying at the G. Fox and Sage-Allen department stores was excruciating. I hate trying on clothes. I hate shopping with my mother. The city was full of fumes and oil smells, and the taxis were loud and busy.

After we'd bought the clothes, we stopped at an ice cream parlor and Doreen bought me a cone. On our way to the bus, we passed a drugstore, me in the thick of pistachio ice cream, and Doreen said she had to run inside and pick up some tissue paper. She told me to wait outside for a moment, because of the cone and all, and she'd be right out.

So there I was, looking fairly dopey standing outside of a drugstore with my face in a pistachio cone, when three Negro boys walked up. I knew they were from the North End. I knew trouble was with them.

The oldest was about fourteen, and his T-shirt was ripped in a symmetrical way that made me think he'd done it himself. He did the talking.

"Got a quarter?" he said.

"No," I said.

"But you do got a dollar."

"No," I said.

He glanced around. "Empty your pockets," he said.

"My mother is in the store," I said.

"Yeah?" he said, and lunged at my shirt collar with his right hand. The cone toppled and spilled to the ground. His free hand plunged into my pants pocket and one of his compatriots went into the other. They came up with a stick of Juicy Fruit.

"Shit," he said. And he spit a huge, dripping, hawker in my face, shoved me, and they all ran away.

All I had in my hand was the napkin from the cone, and I immediately brought it to my face, gouging my cheeks and lips to get the spit off. My mother walked out of the store moments later.

"Lord, Walter," she said, "if you think I'm going to buy you another cone just to have you drop it, you will have to think twice, Mr. Buster Brown. And stop your whining."

And that's about what I thought of Negroes up until the point the Dubois family moved to our neighborhood.

Susan said she'd seen the mother standing on the driveway, gesturing to movers to carry this here and that there, and running into the house every few minutes directing pieces of furniture to the right places. There was a young girl on the porch, who Susan guessed was about our age. She said she hadn't yet seen a father around.

There were a couple people around, neighbors, standing in their yards and watching the proceedings, whispering to each other. Susan said the girl had just stood there, gazing out at the neighbors with a sort of blank look on her face.

I did ride down by the house the next day, to get a peek. The front door was open and I heard a radio inside, but other than that, you couldn't tell who lived there or what they were doing in the house, so I let it go. The only thing of interest was the car in the driveway. It was a '57 Chevy, light green with chrome fenders, and it had a Tulane University sticker on the rear window. It was by far the sharpest car in the neighborhood.

That night at dinner, Pop asked us if we'd met the new family on the block.

"Not yet," I said.

"They're Negroes," Susan said.

"So I've heard," Pop said.

"They have a girl," Susan said.

"Well then, why don't we just invite them over to dinner?" Doreen said.

"Doreen," Pop said.

"No really, Walter, why don't we just get them over here right now?" she said.

"Doreen, please," Pop said.

"Fatback and chitlins?" Doreen said. "Watermelons? I hear Nigroes like them."

That's how Doreen said Negro—"Nigro." It was a southern way of saying it, I'd heard it on the news, sort of a cross between "Negro" and the other word, but just enough on this side of Negro to pass in polite conversation. Except, you always knew Doreen said it that way for a reason.

"Watermelon would be great," Susan said. "What's fatback?"

"Fatback is food, Susan," Doreen said. "Of sorts. And what do you think of it, Walter?"

"I think it's just fine," Pop said. "Just fine."

"Well, good," she said. "Maybe they'll show us how to build a chicken coop in the back yard. And maybe a bean patch in the front?"

"People have the right," Pop said.

"What about our rights, Walter? The neighborhood's rights?"

"What are our rights?" Pop said. "Tell me, Doreen. What rights does a neighborhood have?" He buttered his bread with some force.

"Let's drop it," Doreen said.

"Consider it dropped."

"They have a daughter," Susan repeated.

The next day, I met Ricky Dubois.

Doug had set up a lemonade and old comic books stand on his front lawn, a nickel for a lemonade and a dime for a comic, and was looking to make money he could spend at the circus. I sat with him. Business was slow, but it was the sort of entrepreneurial endeavor that could make a person feel like he's doing something on a lazy, summer day other than sitting around, shooting the bull and drinking lemonade, which was exactly what we were doing.

She came walking up the street by herself, kicking stones in front of her and singing a low tune that I could barely hear. She wore a bright yellow dress and yellow ankle socks, and she was thin, like Susan, and just on the short side of being tall for her age. In other words, about my height. She stopped in front of the stand and looked up as if she'd just noticed it. She stared, sort of nervously, and we stared back, the three of us silent, as if we were passengers on a train.

"Hello," she said after a moment.

"Hi," Doug and I said in unison, too loudly.

Ricky Dubois was caramel brown, and her eyes were bright hazel, like new grass buds in a field of loam. Her hair was also brown and was tied in two braids that sat on the front of her shoulders.

She was, without a doubt, the first girl I'd ever seen in my lifc that I would have called beautiful. Not out loud, of course.

"I see you're selling lemonade," she said. Her voice was light, with a tinge of southern drawl.

"Uhm, sure," Doug said, clearly taken aback.

"A nickel a cup," I said.

"I have a quarter," she said, and reached into her blouse pocket to bring it out. "I'll have a cup."

Doug reached for a cup and, if I'm not mistaken, though he would deny this today, his hands trembled.

Then this extraordinary girl did the most extraordinary thing. She said, "I'd like to buy you boys a cup, too."

"Pardon?" Doug said.

"I said I would like to buy you each a cup of lemonade."

"But, this is my stand," Doug said.

"I know that," she said.

"I mean, I drink it for free."

"I know," she said. "It's a gesture."

"A what?" Doug said.

"A gesture," I said. "She's making a gesture."

"What gesture?" Doug said.

"I mean," the girl said, "we are, after all, neighbors."

"She's making a gesture of friendship," I said to Doug. "You know, to break the ice?"

"What's wrong with the ice?" Doug said, and he looked into his lemonade pitcher.

"Jesus," I said.

"What?" Doug whined.

"Well," the girl said. "That's three cups at a nickel a cup. A dime change, please."

Doug looked at me and raised his eyebrows. I took a cup and said, "Pour."

We sat and she stood, sipping our lemonade.

The girl finished her lemonade and placed the cup on the stand. "That was refreshing," she said.

"Thanks," Doug said.

She stood like she was waiting for something. Finally, with a sigh, she said, "Well, maybe introductions are in order."

"Walter is my name," I said. "Walter Teed, Jr."

"Pleased, Walter," she said. "My name is Rebecca Dubois. My friends and family call me Ricky."

"Dub is what they call me," I said.

"Why's that?" she said.

"It's an idiotic story," I said. "Really."

Ricky smiled, and we both looked at Doug. "Doug," he said with a start. "Hammer."

"Pleased, Doug," Ricky said. "You have a sister, don't you?"

"No, she's my sister," I said. "Susan."

"Oh."

"She's over at the 'Y,' at her swimming lessons."

"Lucky her. I can't swim, really," Ricky said.

"I can swim," Doug said.

"Really?" Ricky said. "It must be something."

"Sure is," Doug said. "I mean, it's better than drowning."

"Of course," she said, and she smiled.

"Uhm, my dad's a musician," Doug said.

"You don't say."

"He plays jazz and rhythm and blues."

"How nice," she said, softly, and looked down the street.

"So," I said. "Where are you from?"

"I was born in New Orleans, Louisiana. That's down south. But we're most recently from New York."

"Wow," Doug said. "New York? And New Orleans?"

"But this is our home, now," she said, softly again.

"You came at a good time," I said. "The circus is coming next month. And the Fourth of July is coming up soon."

"That'll be fun," she said. She cleared her throat. "Have you ever been to the Mardi Gras?"

"I don't even know what that is," I said. I had actually read about the Mardi Gras in a book about New Orleans that I'd taken from the library. And being Catholic I understood the concept of pre-Lenten debauchery and all that, but I wanted to hear it from her lips. I wanted to hear her talk.

"We have it down in Louisiana," she said. "Although I didn't go to the real fun things because I am apparently too young. Besides, we've been living in New York for a long time now. But it's a great ball, lots of fireworks. You know, everything."

"We have fireworks here on the Fourth," Doug said.

"Every town has fireworks on the Fourth," I said.

Doug looked at me with some pain, and I saw that I had just acknowledged a budding rivalry. I was sorry I'd said it.

Ricky offered the dime that was in her hand. "Another lemonade, please. I'd like to buy us all another drink, but I'm short a nickel."

Doug waved her money off. "On me," he said. "Lemonades all around." He poured the drinks.

"Thanks," Ricky said.

"What's your dad do?" I said.

"He's a teacher, in college. Mathematics. He's been at Columbia University, that's in New York, ever since I can remember. But now he's got a position at a college called Trinity—"

"That's in Hartford," I said.

"Yes. That's why we came here," she said.

"Math," I said. "He must be smart."

"He's not here yet," she continued, "but he will be in a couple of days. He's tying up some loose ends."

I liked how she could say things like 'tie up some loose ends' and not sound like some pretentious movie star or a guy who's trying to sound like he's busy all the time. From Ricky, it just sounded like she said it every day.

"I used to go back to New Orleans every summer to stay with my grandmother," Ricky said. "It's such a wonderful place, we'd go walking and go out for ice cream every day. Grandma will be with us soon, here at our new home.

"And my mom is a teacher, too," she continued. "She's going to look for work." She sipped her lemonade, and when the cup left her mouth her lips were wet and she licked them.

"Your mom works?" Doug said.

"Of course," Ricky said. "Doesn't yours?" We both looked at each other.

"Nope," we said.

For a moment, she looked off into the distance. "So, what's it like here?"

I didn't know what to say, and neither did Doug, because he stopped the cup at his mouth and waited.

"I mean I'm new," she said. "And I've never been in the suburbs before. Just cities, my whole life."

Now, that was something we could help her with.

"It's quiet," Doug said.

"Yep, pretty quiet," I said.

"But there are lots of kids," Doug said.

"We go swimming at the lakes sometimes," I said.

"Is there goo at the bottom of a lake?" she said.

"Yeah," I said.

"And turtles and stuff," Doug said.

"I'll have to try it," she said, though it seemed at this point that she was just trying to make conversation. I'm usually good at picking out people who are just trying to make conversation and letting them do just that, but with Ricky I wanted to help her out somehow. To keep her there with us, at Doug's lemonade stand. Just talking. My head was swimming.

So I said the first thing that came to my mind. "Are there a lot of Negroes down south?"

I might as well have said, "What do you think of torturing small animals?" for the way she looked at me. I have said some bonehead things before in my life, but I think this might have been the zenith of my experience in that regard. At least at that point.

"Yes," she said. I felt my face flush.

"I mean," I stammered, "there aren't many around here."

"I've noticed," Ricky said.

"You're the first," I said, sinking deeper into my hole.

"Dub," she said. "That's very interesting, I'm sure."

She didn't sound snippy or mean. She just sounded like that was the last she wanted to hear about being the first Negro in town.

"Well, anyway," I said.

Just then Mrs. Hammer popped her head out the front door and shouted, "Doug, time for you-know-what."

Doug turned to his mother. "Heck. Got to go," he said.

"Heck?" I said.

"Who's your new friend?" Mrs. Hammer asked in a guileless sort of way, as if talking to a black girl was an everyday occurrence on our block.

"Rebecca Dubois, ma'am," Ricky sang out, without hesitation.

"Pleased, Rebecca," Mrs. Hammer said. "Doug!"

Doug left the stand with his shoulders slumped and they both disappeared into the house.

"He'll be a while," I said.

"Well, I really have to go home," Ricky said.

"Why?" I said.

"Pardon?"

I tried to think fast. "Listen, we might be going over to the fireworks together on the Fourth. Do you want to come?"

"Your sister Susan will be there?"

"Of course."

"Well, good, then. Anyway, I really must go," she said. Ricky Dubois waved and turned in the direction from which she came, and disappeared down the street. I was left alone, more or less thunderstruck. I stayed that way for the rest of the day.

The next day Susan took a walk down to the Dubois home to introduce herself to Ricky, only she didn't go down to knock on the door or anything, she went with the hope that Ricky would be out in the yard and she could just stumble upon her as if by accident, much like the way Ricky had just ambled up to our lemonade stand as if by chance. It's sort of maddening the way people have to go out of their way to appear so nonchalant about everything, as if they've always got about a hundred other things to do other than the thing they've specifically set out to accomplish. It usually happens when they're about to place themselves in awkward social situations, like Susan going down to accidentally run into a person of another race.

Well, Susan found Ricky in the yard, and within minutes they'd hit it off like an RC Cola and a Moon Pie. After she'd met Ricky, Susan's report was succinct: "She acts just like a lady." Soon they began to ride and play tennis, and go to the park together, and within a couple of days Susan brought Ricky back around to our place.

Doug and I were still at the lemonade stand, racking up nickels by the dozens, and we drank so much of the stuff I knew I'd never have to worry about scurvy.

They came up on their bikes, out of breath and sort of starry eyed, as if they'd discovered something important.

As an aside, I have said already I wished there were other girls in the neighborhood for Susan to hang around with, and I was happy that Ricky was the one that finally showed up. For Susan's sake, I thought she was perfect, and, on my side, I liked the thought of Ricky being around. I mean, by accident like that.

"Dub," Susan said, "are we going to Grandpa's on the Fourth? What's been decided about that?"

"Good question," I said, and thought about it for the first time since I'd invited Ricky to watch the fireworks with us. "I really don't know."

"Well, you did ask me to come along," Ricky said.

Instinctively, I knew that if the plan was Grandpa's, Ricky would not be welcome.

"Well, yes I did," I stammered. "I guess I forgot about Grandpa."

"So, you don't know what the plan is," Susan said.

"No," I said. "Let's ask Doreen."

"Who's Doreen?" Ricky said.

"Our mother," I said. "Don't ask."

This couldn't possibly turn out well. I worried that Susan wasn't thinking straight, but she was flushed with her new-found friendship, and was acting invincible.

We went over to the house, leaving Doug at his lemonade lode, and walked through the front door. Ricky was behind the two of us.

Doreen was at the kitchen table, cutting coupons from a paper, a glass of wine at her side.

She looked up and her eyelids were heavy.

"Hi," she said, and saw Ricky.

"Mother, are we going to Grandpa's on the Fourth?" Susan said. Her voice was strong.

"What's the question?" Doreen said, keeping her eyes on Ricky.

"What question?" Susan said.

"What's the *alternative*?" Doreen said.

"Well, we want to go to the fireworks with Ricky at Wickham Park if we're not going to Grandpa's."

"This is Ricky?" Doreen said, acting as if Ricky was not in the room, but acting wholly as if she was.

"Ma'am," said Ricky, curtseying slightly.

"What's your mommy's name, Ricky?" Doreen said.

"Mrs. Nancy Dubois," Ricky said. "Of the Baton Rouge Oliphants."

"Fancy that," Doreen said. "And your father?"

"Mr. Herbert Dubois of the Fayetteville Duboises," Ricky said.

"Well, my," Doreen said. "Of the Fayetteville Duboises. Isn't that something."

"Yes, ma'am," said Ricky, without rancor.

"Like it up in our neck of the woods?" Doreen said.

"Yes, ma'am," Ricky said.

"Oh, really?"

Ricky stood rigidly, her two hazel eyes fixed on Doreen. "Yes, ma'am. We've been living in New York, ma'am, for some time now. We sort of know our way around."

"But is it good living *here*?"

"Here?" Ricky flinched, slightly. "Ma'am, if you'll excuse me, I'm not a hundred percent sure what you mean."

"But, you do, don't you," Doreen said. It wasn't a question. She turned to Susan. "It's not clear where we'll be on the Fourth, but you can tell your friend Ricky that we'll be busy nonetheless, and that we hope she has an enjoyable holiday."

"What about Wickham Park?" I said.

"I think it's time to end this conversation. Susan, would you remain here for a moment?" she said. "Walter, why don't you show Ricky to the yard."

And I pulled Ricky out the door.

We walked outside to the lemonade stand, and Doug said. "So, where's it going to be?"

"Hell," I said.

At that moment I had a need to be away, to be far away from the sounds that would soon be heard from my house. Susan would bear the brunt of it this time, and I knew at that moment that her one budding friendship in this town might be lost in the furor of the argument. I looked at Ricky's face, and knew she had lived the situation before.

I got on my bike and said, "C'mon, I'll ride home with you."

We rode down the street silently. I had no idea what to say, and it seemed that Ricky preferred it that way.

When we arrived at her house I saw a man in the driveway, unloading luggage from an old Rambler that was parked behind the '57 Chevy. He was tall and thin, with a wave of brown hair combed back from his forehead and a set of wire-rimmed glasses framing a square face. He looked like a tall James Dean. He looked like a tall James Dean primarily because he was white.

"Daddy!" Ricky said, and jumped off her bike to rush to him.

"Ricky Slick!" He scooped her up in his arms, twirling and kissing her.

"I missed you about three tons," he said. "Maybe four, maybe five, who knows. I'm no good with numbers."

"Me, too," she said as he put her down.

"So, this is our house," he said. "Like it?"

"I like it fine, Daddy. And you?"

"Well, I've hardly been inside yet. So far, it looks like a lily pad on a frog farm. Kind of green, don't you think?"

"We can paint it."

"You mean, I can paint it," he said. "What the heck, it'll get me outside for a while, out into the patrician Connecticut air. We've been living in apartments for too long." The man turned to me. "You must be Dub," he said.

"Yes, sir," I said. His eyes were wide and energetic.

"You're wondering how I know your name. Well, so am I. I think it was a mystical revelation that must have hit me on the road while I was driving up from the city, that's New Orleans, in my fine Rambler rental." He patted the car. "Couldn't say that I knew at the time what it meant, but this morning as I was eating breakfast in a greasy diner south of Virginia, I happened to read the front page of the local rag. There it was, all over the page." He gestured with free hand, the one not holding Ricky's. "The mayor's name was Bud Jones. It was Mayor Bud Jones this and Mayor Bud Jones that. I took it as a sign that I'd meet someone named Bud in my new neighborhood. And, for goodness sake, here you are."

He stretched out his hand. "Pleased to meet you, son. Call me Mr. Dubois."

"But, my name is Dub," I said, and shook his hand.

"Of course it is, son. See, we're north of the Mason-Dixon line now, and you know what *that* does to things. They get reversed. Just like at the equator, where water goes down the drain in the opposite direction and summer is winter and winter is summer and all that."

"Oh," I said. Christ, this guy was corny.

"Good thing the mayor's name wasn't Bob," he said. "Then you'd have to be named Bob, of course. Get it?"

"Got it," I said. "Uhm, I thought you were coming up from New York."

"Well, normally I would have, but I drove south a few days ago to get Ricky's grandmother and move her up here with us. Long drive, both ways. Maybe I've got jet lag or something. Old woman talked my ear off the whole way back. Ricky, did you know that your grandmother was a personal friend of Teddy Roosevelt? Told me herself. Fought at San Juan Hill with him."

"Honestly, you don't believe that baloney, Dub, do you?" Ricky said. "Daddy is a baloney guy."

Mr. Dubois turned to Ricky. "Let's go in and see your mother," he said. "Dub, we must be off, time for tender family moments, you understand. I'm sure we'll be seeing you around. You're welcome anytime, although I'm not so sure I should offer, not having been inside the house yet. Well, if you promise not to tell anyone that the walls are caving in, you can come by and sup with us whenever you want." He winked at me.

Most of the time, when someone winks at you, it is a sure sign that you don't want them to wink at you. It means something bizarre or slightly evil is about to happen. Grandpa Constantine always winks at us. But Mr. Dubois's wink was more like that of, well, a baloney guy.

"He knows your name because I told him on the phone last night," Ricky said, and gave her father a sock in the leg, the type of sock a wife would give a husband who's had a couple of drinks and is telling goofy jokes. They walked into the house, hugging and giggling.

I rode back, but not to the house, because I knew Susan and Doreen might still be in the thick of it. Doug, for sure, would be hearing the row by now, and he and Susan would fill me in later.

Instead, I rode a quarter of a mile down to Zikker's Pond and got off at my rock.

I figure every person has to have some sort of a rock in this world. And my rock is actually a rock, a big boulder that sits by the side of the pond. No one is ever going to move it because it's just too damn big to move. It's smooth and worn to my butt, so I fit in well and can even lean back into it a bit. I generally sit there when I want to be by myself, like when I'm fishing or just tossing pebbles into the pond. Or thinking.

I sat, listening to the bullfrogs and the sound of dragonflies' wings humming over the still pond. So Ricky's father was white. Ricky was lighter in complexion than some Negroes, but darker, I supposed, than others. I hadn't even known that Negroes married whites. I made a mental note to ask Pop about that someday. Not that it mattered. It made her more exotic in a way, even more unique.

Of course, there was Doreen to think about. It was obvious to me and to Susan, and certainly to Ricky, what my mother thought about her. The situation was embarrassing enough, a person making a scene in front of a friend, but it was worse than that. It was my mother.

I stayed at Zikker's for about as long as I thought it would take for the scene to settle down with my mother and Susan, but when I left I didn't go home anyway. I rode around, just looking at things, past the Dubois's home, past the school, past the Gallo's place where I knew that their eight children lived in pretty much a constant state of disarray and confusion. I found myself wondering what it was like to drink wine. I rode around for what seemed like a couple of hours.

When I came home at dusk, Doug had disappeared with his lemonade stand, and our house was quiet. Doreen was napping on the couch and Pop was at work. I looked for Susan and couldn't find her, but when I looked out the window toward the old willow tree, there she was, high up, higher than she'd ever been before. She was snapping branches and dropping them lightly to the ground. It looked real high from down where I was, and I wondered what it looked like to her. I decided not to bother her. She stayed there for a while.

At dinner, Doreen announced that we were going to Grandpa's for the Fourth, no ifs, ands, or buts about it.

Pop didn't to react to that, as if it had been prearranged,

as if they'd talked about it. "Sorry, kids, but I'll be at the newspaper," he said, "you'll have to go by yourselves."

Later that evening I asked Susan how it had gone during her discussion with Doreen. "The usual," she said.

"How usual?" I said.

"She said that Ricky was not permitted in our house and that I wasn't to go into their house to eat, drink, or even think of staying over. But we could still go swimming together and things, if we wanted to."

I was floored. Allowing them to be friends who didn't go into each other's homes was like saying you can drive the car but you can't touch the steering wheel. In our neighborhood, children went into each other's homes as if they owned them.

"I could just spit," she said.

"Does Pop know about all this?"

"Not a clue," she said. "Like always."

But she was wrong, in a way, about what Pop actually knew.

That next day was uneventful. Doug sat out all morning again slogging the lemonade. Ricky came by and met up with Susan, who gently steered her away from the house to go play tennis at the park. We all met later and discussed plans for the Fourth, which was the following day. Susan and I were going, of course, to Grandpa Constantine's, without Pop, and I felt okay about that in an odd sort of way. At least we'd be able to light some fireworks and have some cousins around. Doug was going to Wickham with his mom for the town fireworks display, a partner he considered just this side of embarrassing. He even said, to hide it, "Well, my dad is out on the ocean and everything."

Ricky said she had no idea what they were going to do, as they didn't know the town very well and would get lost even on a simple trip like going to Wickham. Besides, she said, her grandmother was elderly and everything, and you just couldn't drag elderly persons to things like fireworks displays and places where they'd get excited, because who knows when their hearts would give out and on top of it they didn't even know where the hospital was. She reckoned they'd stay in and catch the high altitude bursts from their front yard.

I admired her for that, for her devotion to her grandmother and all, but I caught a hint of sadness during her discussion of it. I leaned over to Doug and whispered, "Invite her to go with you." But he turned and looked at me with some kind of weird horror, as if I'd just suggested he go out and stick his foot under a lawnmower. In retrospect, I know his refusal wasn't because she was black or anything—well, maybe his initial reaction was because of that, it's not something he'd been doing every day of his life—but I suspect it was more because he didn't want to be seen with a girl. Alone. Like that.

Later that night, the third of July, was the start of the whole miserable business for the neighborhood, and I am not proud to say that, in spite of it all, my first concern was how it would affect our day at Grandpa's, at his fireworks.

In the morning, as usual, I awoke early and went about my paper route. I heard Pop in the shower on my way out the door. All was normal until I approached the Dubois's home, and there on the lawn, casting the slightest of shadows in the oncoming dawn, was a charred, wooden cross made of two-by-fours. There was a mucky, gray puddle of ash at its foot. The lights in the house were on. I tossed the newspaper on the front steps, and wondered, for the rest of my route, what in the hell was going on.

When I arrived home Pop was fixing breakfast, as was his custom, and Susan was in the kitchen helping. Doreen would sleep in till about ten or so, as was her custom. To tell the honest truth, I don't think we've had breakfast more than once or twice with Doreen for as long as I can remember.

"Did you see it?" Pop said as I walked in the house. A deep frown crossed his forehead.

"The cross?"

"I was just telling Susan about it," he said. He looked tired, sort of older than he should have looked in the morning.

"Did you see it, Dub?" she said.

"Yes," I said.

"I am truly sorry you had to see something like that in this day and age," Pop said. "Two pancakes or three?"

"Three," I said. "What happened?"

"What did you think when you saw it, Dub?" he said.

"I felt odd, I guess," I said.

"Do you both understand the significance of the cross?"

Without hesitation, Susan said, "Ku Klux Klan."

"Well," Pop said, "cowards, at any rate."

"I thought they were down south," I said.

"They are," he said. "But who knows where else they are? Then again, they may not be up here, they may not be the ones who burned a cross on the Dubois's lawn. The cross is a symbol, mostly. It's associated with the Ku Klux Klan, but anyone can burn a cross."

"Ku Klux Klan," I said slowly, letting the words get jumbled in my mouth. "They hate the Duboises?"

"Who knows?" he said. "Who knows what this is all about. My God, these people have been here less than a week. I expected some bad feelings, but this? So soon, and so vehemently?" He rubbed his forehead, and tugged his ear.

"Maybe it was a prank," I said.

"Yeah, maybe it was just a joke of some kind," Susan said.

"You both—no, we—would like to believe that. But honey, this kind of a thing isn't a joke. If it is, it's the worst kind of joke."

"What are they going to do about it?" I said. "I mean the Duboises?"

"Well, I'll tell you, I just don't know. And I don't know what I'd do if I were in their shoes. You know, I was there last night."

I had forgotten that my father would have had no way of

knowing about the cross any earlier than I did. I'd just assumed that his natural newspaper instincts had sort of dropped the story in his lap.

"I was in my study writing," he said, "and it was late, about two in the morning. I saw a glow in the direction of their house. I've seen fires before, so I rushed down the street and, sure enough, I saw the cross burning on their lawn. Mr. Dubois was out on the lawn in his pajamas with his wife and mother-in-law, and they had the garden hose turned on the thing already. There wasn't any damage."

I thought of the old woman standing out on the lawn, her new world and old heart traumatized by the whole thing, and I wondered where Ricky was during the incident. I asked him.

"She was at the picture window, just watching. Mr. Dubois said he was sorry to have to meet me under the circumstances, but we talked for a while just the same. He hadn't expected it either."

Susan and I were silent, our pancakes gone cold.

"He didn't call the police," Pop said, "or the fire department, because he didn't want any more trouble at the time."

"But shouldn't he?" I said. "I mean, that's what they're there for. They can catch whoever did this."

"Well," Pop said. "That's a call Mr. Dubois has to make, literally. I think he doesn't want to call attention to his family. If the police are involved, so are the newspapers, and once that happens all sorts of people come out of the woodwork."

"But, don't you think there will be more trouble?" Susan said. She was clearly shaken.

"If it was a one-time prank, probably not. If it's outright bigotry, yes, I think so. I'm sorry."

"Is it because Mr. Dubois is white and Mrs. Dubois is a Negro?" she said.

"Maybe, honey. But it all boils down to the same thing: stupid people who are cowards." Pop stretched his arms and yawned. "I never slept last night, neither did Mr. Dubois. We just stayed up talking. I came home just before Dub woke up."

"So, what are they going to do now?" I said.

"What would you do if you were them, Dub?"

"I don't know, directly." I said, and I didn't. "I guess it all boils down to leave or stay."

"That's right," Pop said. "And no one can give that answer unless they walk in their shoes."

He thought for a moment. "But we can help," he said.

"How?" I said.

"Well, we can support them. We can show them some compassion and support. Just be there for them as we would for any neighbor, even more so. Not just because they're Negroes, but because they're people in trouble."

Pop was beginning to sound awfully tired, but I got the gist of what he said. And he hadn't needed to say it, because it was in his eyes. They flickered. Like a fire.

Of course, I also understood that what he was saying about people helping people was fine until we brought Doreen into the equation, and I glanced at Susan to see where she stood on this. It didn't take her but a second.

"Pop," she said, and it was almost a whisper. "Have you talked to Mom about the Duboises?"

"Why?" he said, tugging at his ear. He looked down at his feet.

"Don't you know what she thinks about Ricky?" she said.

"What's that?"

Susan's fist clenched. "You heard her at dinner the other night," she said. "All that about watermelons and bean patches. Don't you think I understood that?"

"You did?"

"Of course. So?" Susan said gently, but with an edge.

"Does that mean she can say those things?"

"Listen, I love your mother, Susan. You love her, too."

And I could've slugged him. I mean it, it was so goddamn frustrating.

Then Susan got to breathing hard through her nose and said, "The way Mom talks about her? And talks to her? That's just not right. Right?"

And when Pop said, "Don't worry, I'll handle it," I excused myself and went to my room. I knew he wouldn't handle it. Pop would handle a lot of things but Doreen wasn't generally one of them. I opened the window and stood in the summer heat, breathing deeply through my nose, until the fury passed.

The Fourth of July festivities were predictably idiotic. I don't know what in the hell I was looking forward to. My cousins tramped around Grandpa's huge and gaudy house whining for this and for that and generally getting what they whined for, and we tossed numbingly powerful fireworks around all afternoon. Doreen drank too much. And Grandpa, he used the word "nigger" twice.

Doug reported later that the Wickham fireworks were the best ever. Pop stayed at work, and the Duboises stayed at home with the lights on all night long, waiting for a repeat performance of the burning cross, which never came.

CHAPTER 4

The cross-burning incident seemed to have less impact on Ricky, at least on the outside, than it did on Susan and me. I certainly hadn't expected something like that to happen. I hadn't expected anything at all.

Of course, afterwards I'd expected fear or anger or something from Ricky, or maybe even rejection. After all, just before the whole thing happened my own mother had kicked her out of our house. But in thinking about it just now, and in thinking about what I knew of Ricky, little as it was at the time, I might have guessed that she'd come out with some quip that downplayed the horror of the whole thing.

"They say charcoal is good for the lawn," she said.

It was a few days after the Fourth, and we were at the YMCA pool during what was known as "town time." This was when the pool opened its doors for a few hours every afternoon, giving free access to the public. Doug was there, as were Susan and I. We had been swimming in the shallow section, while Ricky just sort of sat at the edge of the pool, splashing herself and kicking water. She wouldn't go in, she didn't know how to swim.

"Were you scared?" Susan said, after we'd gotten out of the pool.

Ricky was startled. "Why, yes," she said. "Of course."

"Well I think it stinks," Doug said.

"Thank you," Ricky said.

"Hey, not a problem," Doug said. He smiled broadly as he scored a few points.

We hadn't yet broached the subject with Ricky of why it had happened to her family, of why someone had picked her family's yard to burn a cross on. Of course it was obvious why, but we'd only talked about the fact that it *did* happen, as if midnight cross-burnings were a normal, if unfortunate experience in our neighborhood. My hunch is that we were afraid to mention the racial aspect of it for fear of compounding the issue, as if it reflected on us, as if by our skin color we are as guilty as those who actually poured the gas and lit the match.

I was assuming, of course, that whites had lit the match.

"Who do you think did it?" I said.

"Probably men," she said, which was an odd thing to say. "Women wouldn't burn crosses on lawns."

"Have you met anyone yet who you think would do something like this?"

"Well," she said, "I've only been living here a while, so I guess I'd have to say no." She looked up and her eyes swept the pool. Mine followed hers and I noticed that most of the thirty or so people around the pool were staring at the four of us.

They weren't mean stares. They were empty stares, the type people have when they come across a car wreck on the highway. It occurred to me that people engrossed, really engrossed, in the act of staring take on downright bovine characteristics. They have this dull, slack look about their eyes and mouths, which seem to stay open just a bit. Others slowly chewed sandwiches and candy bars and things, and I really don't have to say what *that* looked like.

"Actually," Ricky said, "it could have been any one of these people sitting right here around the pool, acting normal."

Doug sat up. "No way."

"Why do you say that?" Ricky said.

"Because this *is* Normalville. These aren't the kind of people who burn crosses and things. It was people like Big Farley and them."

"You're wrong, Doug," she said, and he blushed slightly,

probably because she called him Doug. I tasted a small bitterness on my tongue.

"These are exactly the types of people who burn crosses. Why, I'd bet that there are a few people around this pool who wouldn't go into the water if I did. They're ordinary people who just happen to think they are superior and inspired by God or whatever. The thing is, they think they're right. Most racists would no more rob a bank than live next door to a Negro."

"But you're not exactly a Negro," I said, I swear, with about twelve pounds of stupid attached to it. "I mean, your mom is, but your dad is, you know, white."

"Dub," she said, and she sort of rolled her eyes. "What would you call me, then?"

"I don't know."

"Mulatto? Please. One of the worst words I've ever heard. And I've heard it before, from both my grandmothers."

"Yeah, Dub," Doug said, "you blockhead."

Then Ricky reached out and did something no girl had ever done before. She touched my arm lightly, and left her hand there. Her eyes were wide. "Look at me. I'm not white, am I? So I'm black. I'm a Negro."

"Look, Ricky, I'm sorry, I didn't mean anything."

"That's just the point, no one means anything, but they can't help it. The only Negro who knows what to do with me is my Mom, and the only white is my Dad."

"But I think you're real pretty," Susan said, who I think startled herself.

Ricky suddenly seemed self-conscious at being the center of attention, and she dropped her hand from my arm. "Besides," she said, "Mom and Grandma are both full Negroes, so what does it matter what I am. Somebody burned a cross. Perhaps we can change the subject?"

Now it was time for Susan to do the arm-grabbing. "I'm really glad you're a friend," she said.

Ricky smiled and said, "What about your mother?" This took Susan completely by surprise. She slouched a bit.

"Anyway, your father is a nice man," Ricky said. "He helped us at the fire that night. He's a lot like my father, other than being white, I mean."

We sat silently for a moment.

"How often," Ricky said, "does your father go out on the ships, Doug?"

Ricky's smooth skin glistened in the sun, and as she talked I felt a low, pleasant rumble at the base of my brain, the way you feel when you take cough medicine. Relaxed. Humming. Ricky had her brown legs crossed and hands on her lap, and tiny beads of water hugged her scalp. She smelled of chlorine and heat, and she shivered slightly.

"My father?" Doug said. "All the time. But he comes home all the time, too, isn't that right, Dub?"

"Uh, all the time," I said, shifting myself.

"So what are your parents going to do about the cross?" Susan said.

"I don't know," Ricky said. "Do you think they'll come back?"

"No," I blurted out. It was more a wish than knowledge. "Did this ever happen in New York?"

"No," Ricky said. "No one has front lawns in Manhattan." She laughed. "No, really, there are so many Negroes and whites in New York, and so many kids who look like me, it just wouldn't happen. People there are used to it."

"What about New Orleans?"

"I don't remember much about it. I was just a baby when Mom and Dad left. But I know they had some trouble. Just being married was trouble for them. I have been to New Orleans every summer for years, and I've seen plenty of people who are light like me, but I never once saw a white married to a Negro. I think it was once against the law or something. They're like Sammy Davis Junior and Britt Ekland—"

Just then a large shadow spread over us like a gray cloud blocking the sun. It was Mrs. Selwyn, a neighbor and friend of my mother's, an enormous woman who always seemed to breathe through flared nostrils. She had in tow her blue-lipped, shivering toddler, Joey.

She said, "So this is the new girl?"

"Hi, Mrs. Selwyn," Susan said, and she assumed a tense position.

"What's her name?" Mrs. Selwyn said.

God, I was getting annoyed with these people talking right through Ricky. I mean, it was as if she wasn't there, as if her being black also made her invisible. Mrs. Selwyn stood above me, dripping cold water on my back, as the kid sucked in great wads of snot that threatened his upper lip.

"Joey," I said, "tell your mother that her name is Rebecca."

"Huh?" Joey said.

Mrs. Selwyn screwed her eyes to tiny slits, harrumphed, and viciously yanked the poor kid away. They waddled off.

"Dub," Susan said, and shook her head. "Now, who do you think is going to pay for that remark?"

I looked at Ricky, who smiled slightly, politely.

"Jerk," Susan said.

"I'm sorry," I said.

Ricky said, "I think it might be time to go now."

Wc split up for the rest of the afternoon. Doug took off with his mother on some sort of shopping expedition. Susan, who would have preferred to invite Ricky home to listen to her new Elvis records or to ask shadowy questions to her Ouija board, was saved by Ricky's excuse that she had to go and help her grandmother can some fruit. "Negroes do that," Ricky had said, laughing.

I took off to Zikker's Pond. I felt I needed some time at my rock, time to hang out and think about evcrything that had happened, and maybe form a plan or something. Mcn, after all, form plans. It's not quite enough to rail against the inequities of the world, or to wonder if there will ever be an end to things like cross-burnings. My hunch then, and now, is that there will never be an end to them. I figure that good and bad and Heaven and Hell, and hate for that matter, are parts of our lives that we have no hold over, that we can't do a damn thing about because even the big guys, God and the Devil, have no control over them either, when you get right down to it. Or, who knows, hate itself just might be the right emotion to deal with hate.

Running away from it looked like a bad option for the Duboises. It didn't seem that there was any real reason yet to run. After all, it was only one cross-burning, and maybe the guy who did it had since had a heart attack, or maybe choked on a piece of meat or something. It would have been an appropriate way to go. Besides, if it could happen here in East Hartford, where in this United States, home of Richard Nixon and Smokey Robinson, would she not encounter cross-burnings? New York, apparently, except that they'd just moved from there.

Then fighting back it had to be. I wondered if it was really the Ku Klux Klan that burned the cross, but just thinking about that made me shiver.

I had no doubt the bad guys were people like Big Farley and his group, or possibly even them. I actually felt a twinge of remorse for thinking that, for assuming that Big was the one who did it with no other proof than it seemed like the type of thing he'd do. But I needed a villain for my fantasy, and Big was, well, bigger than life. I began to picture the confrontation that would put an end to it.

This is the way it would play out: I would be sitting with Ricky in a field of tall grass behind her house, just gazing at her as she chatted coyly about or something or other. She would be saying something witty and erudite, something about a poem she'd been reading. Maybe she'd be weaving a small wreath of grass stalks. The wreath would be for me. As she talked, she would occasionally look into my eyes and momentarily lose her train of thought, taken aback by the passion of my gaze. "Walter," she would say, "you mustn't look at me that way. It makes my heart fret so." She would at that moment sound like Scarlett O'Hara. She would giggle brightly every once in a while and I would find it necessary to refrain from leaning over to kiss her delicately, but with some passion, straight on the lips. I would burn for her.

Then we would hear noises at the front of the house, sounds of raucous laughter and screams of anguish. I would get up and run to the house to find Big Farley and his thugs in a circle, laughing and viciously pushing Ricky's frail grandmother back and forth like a pinball. Mrs. Oliphant would be terrified and distraught, and every time she fell down, one of the brain-impaired delinquents would kick her with a Nazi jackboot. To the side of the circle would be a burning cross, not unlike the one they'd lit the other night.

"Stop that!" I'd say. I would have preferred to say something brave and clever like, "Avast!" or "Desist!" but would think to myself that the brainless dullards probably wouldn't understand the words.

"Fuck off," Big would grunt with reddened, piggish eyes. I would be maddened by this show of disrespect in front of the old woman, in spite of the fact that he was laying his boots into her ribs as he said it.

"Leave her alone," I would say. Ricky would by now have joined us, wide-eyed at the scene, her delicate hands clasped to her heart.

"Make us," one of the scum would snarl, giggling like a sick weasel. I would consider for a moment about calling out to my trusty and stalwart companion, Simba the elephant, who would race out of the woods and stomp the brutal hoodlums into pools of primal sludge like so much Maypo. Of course, Simba would not exist, so I would be compelled to dispatch the whining brutes myself. This would be my invitation to swashbuckle my way into a bit of fame, and into Ricky's arms.

Magically, a rope would appear on the ground next to me. I would pick it up and quickly fasten a lariat from it, swinging it over my head like the Lone Ranger, shouting, "Glad to oblige, boys!"

I would toss the lariat into the center of the circle with practiced ease, and the laughing would stop. With one swift and sure motion, I would pluck Mrs. Oliphant from the center, depositing her in Ricky's trembling but welcome arms. The bullies would stare aghast at this feat, but I would merely smile knowingly and say, "There's more where that came from, buckos."

I would grab the garden hose and shout to Ricky to turn the water on, which I would train on the burning cross. The fire would die instantly and I would stand there with the hose running, Ricky and Mrs. Oliphant sobbing behind me, the blackened cross smoldering and hissing. The sniveling ferrets would be tongue-tied and mesmerized by my resourcefulness.

"Now, Mr. Beats-an-Old-Woman," I'd say. (No, that sounds too much like my mother.) "Now, Henry," I'd say, "it's your turn."

Big's eyes would suddenly go wide with fear, as he would have by now realized that I was one mean honcho and no one to mess around with. His mouth would drop open, and he would begin to say, "What the—"

But I would have aimed the hose, which would by now have strangely increased in pressure to fire fighter levels, straight into his mouth. This would knock him on his back, and I would advance on him with the stream trained to his mouth, turning him into a frothing, gagging parody of a clown face in one of those circus water pistol games.

"Eat H2O Big," I would calmly say as I bore down on him. When I reached him, I would shove the hose into his mouth, and his eyes and cheeks would bulge larger and larger until he looked like Dizzy Gillespie with a major thyroid problem. He would gag and gurgle for mercy, and I would relentlessly shove the hose further and further into his gullet, force-feeding him water until his belly and arms and legs swelled to grotesque proportions, and his eyes bugged out in fear.

"What's it like, Big?" I'd say, "what's it like to suck Death's hose?"

"Ummmphh," Big would say.

I would hear his skin stretching taut, stiffened and screeching like a rubbed balloon. At this I would laugh mercilessly, and Big would manage to gurgle, "I'm gonna bust!"

"Bust, then, you miserable cur," I'd say.

"Cur?" Big would say, but at that instant he would burst into a thousand fragments, drenching his comrade hooligans with blood and water and the slime of humiliation. Miraculously, I would be untouched. The scum-laden lackeys would scream and stumble and run in all directions, and in a moment the only one left would be me, standing triumphantly, holding a dripping lock of Big's hair. Ricky and her grandmother would swoon with relief and admiration.

Later, I would receive a commendation from the police department, personally handed over by Mr. Officer Bigger Farley, who would say without a trace of irony in his voice, "You did good, son."

Okay, it wasn't exactly a plan, but a man has to start somewhere.

I sat on that rock, sort of rocked by my violent daydream. I watched a couple of frogs locked in the throes of mating, apparently enjoying the whole thing about as much as they could, being frogs and all. The male, the one I assumed was on top, gripped the female as a stranded person might grip a street sign in a hurricane. It was as if he held on for life, and his grip produced ugly little bulges around the female's torso. I couldn't help thinking that she must have been unhappy about that.

The two didn't move a bit, not in the way I imagined it was supposed to be. I searched their dull eyes for some sign that this was what they wanted to be doing, but didn't find it. They seemed resigned to the fact that an ancient hormonal urge had driven them to this ridiculous position, and they were locked into it by a force of nature that would keep them there until they finished what they were doing, or died doing it.

The whole thing made me feel melancholy as hell, but I still managed to be relieved by my daydream about blowing up Big. It was sort of cleansing in a way, deep in my abdomen. I felt I had made some progress.

"You guys want to hear a joke?" I asked the frogs. "You two ought to try and enjoy it just a tad."

Later that night at the dinner table, the old battleground, I encountered Mrs. Selwyn's wrath, as I had expected. Doreen had—imagine my surprise—received a phone call from Mrs. Selwyn about my behavior at the pool. Doreen called me young Mr. Smart Guy and Royal Mr. What's-the-Matter-Your-Friend-Can't-Speak-for-Herself? as well as a couple of other names she was always so creative about. I knew it would be futile to argue with her about having corrected Mrs. Selwyn for an affront Doreen had committed herself.

"You think having a Negro friend makes you something special?" she said.

"No," I said.

"And does your Ricky think she's special because her father is white?" she said, making "white" sound as if it was a pile of dog shit.

"Doreen," Pop said.

She looked as if she was about to say something to him,

then thought better of it. I wondered if some sort of battle had already been fought, and a truce had been drawn between them.

Pop and Susan exchanged glances. I could tell that they were thinking about flying plates and casseroles and things.

"Well, that's that, then," Doreen said. "You will apologize to Mrs. Selwyn tomorrow, do you hear me loud and clear, Mr. Sneer?"

"Yes, ma'am," I said. I wondered how I would do that. "Sorry, Mrs. Selwyn you overweight, mean-mouthed bigot?" No, that didn't sound right. How about: "Sorry, Mrs. Selwyn you squalid, racist snob?" Or, maybe: "Sorry, Mrs. Selwyn, have you burned any crosses lately?"

I glanced at Pop and he glanced around nervously.

"It's the right thing to do, Dub," he said.

"Yes, Pop," I said.

But what I actually did was nothing. Not a goddamn thing. And it all slipped through the cracks somehow, probably because the excitement of the next few weeks made the whole incident about as significant as a pimple on a burn victim. I never approached Mrs. Selwyn about it, and Doreen never once mentioned it again. It was as if God allowed me to slide on this one.

The next few days brought no news, except that Commander Shepard, who had blasted off to over a hundred miles above the Earth in a Mercury space capsule in May, came to Hartford for a public appearance to lecture about U.S. space superiority and all that. There was something about a huge wall going up in Berlin, in Germany. The Russians were predictably sullen about the Bay of Pigs thing, and Pop had taken an unusually conservative stance on the whole issue in his column, saying that even though Communism was not really a major world threat we should be wary about Fidel and the Russians because they can just about spit to Florida. Later he wrote another column saying that perhaps President Kennedy should think about getting a good chiropractor because maybe his back pains were causing him to make ill-informed decisions such as sending small groups of armed exiles back to Cuba to foment revolution and all sorts of mayhem. As I remember, it wasn't a particularly humorous column, but these weren't particularly funny times.

Susan and Ricky began to discover all sorts of ways to spend time together without going to each other's homes, a completely ridiculous situation, but one for which there didn't seem to be an immediate solution. They spent time at the pool, or at the library poring over teen magazines and swooning over Elvis photographs. Ricky's thought about Elvis was that people were afraid of him because of the hip-wiggling and sneering sensuality and all, but they were much more afraid of him because of his links to black music, which, she said, whites thought of as godless and sinister sort of music. Eventually, Ricky lent Susan a record by this New York singer, Bob Dylan, whose music was, in her words, "Not for dancing, but for listening."

So Susan and Ricky played tennis and went riding on their bikes and just enjoyed each other's company, and Susan seemed happy for that.

Meanwhile, Doug and I manned his lemonade stand daily, doing casual business but feeling like fine entrepreneurs and busy people. Neighborhood kids came by and spent a dime here, a quarter there, and talked, of course, about the circus.

"Going to be twelve elephants this year," Lance Cornwall said one day. Lance was one of the neighborhood boys. He, like Doug, shared a predilection for stretching things like the truth beyond reason. Did I say "stretching the truth"? I meant lying. Lying between these two was blood sport.

"I heard fourteen," Doug said.

"Twelve," Lance said.

"Where did you hear that?" I said.

"Paper," Doug said. "It's been all over the newspapers."

"That so? Anyway, I read," Lance said, dropping the elephant question as if on cue, "that the Flying Zalubras are going to have a dog in the act this year, one that does flips and walks the tight wire."

"A dog that walks the tight wire," I said. "Brave dog."

"And he also gets shot out of the cannon," Doug said.

"Get out of town," I said.

"But he lands in a net," Lance said.

"Do you think," I said, "that you can actually train a dog to get into a cannon? And get shot out of it? His ears couldn't take it."

"They stuff cotton in his ears," Lance said.

They were on a roll.

"Actually," Doug said, "this dog is deaf already. He doesn't have to worry about the noise."

"So how do they train him," I said, "you know, give commands and all that, if he's deaf?"

Doug and Lance exchanged glances.

"He reads lips," Lance said. "It said so in the papers."

"I thought you just said they stuff cotton in his ears."

"That's just for added insurance. And to keep the powder out of his ears," Lance said.

"So," I said, "you've got a deaf, lip-reading dog with ears full of cotton which gets willingly into a cannon so that he can get shot out of it. Can I ask why he would do that?"

"Why," said Doug, "would anyone do it?"

"Actually, he doesn't go in willingly," Lance said. "They put a cat in the cannon first, and the dog chases it in. Then they light the cannon, and blast the two of them out."

"And what, pray tell, happens to the cat?"

"Well," Doug said, "it's a sad story. The cat is no more. Good-bye cat. But the crowd doesn't see it happen because by the time the dog comes flying out, the cat is in a million pieces and scatters like a fine mist all over the place. No one is the wiser. You might call it a sacrificial cat."

"My cousin in Trenton," Lance said, "said he got hit by cat fur last week when the circus was in town. Oh, and he's the one who told me they had twelve elephants this year." He shot Doug a stern glance. "He saw it."

"You mean to tell me that they kill a cat every time this dog does his trick?" I said.

"They buy them by the dozen," Lance said. "They just go down to the Humane Society and buy a bunch of strays and use them for the shows."

"So," I said, "the Humane Society sells the circus cats that get blown up every night during the Big Top Show? It seems like a contradiction in terms."

"Of course, they aren't told what they're being used for," Doug said. "I mean, it's not like a clown in makeup walks in and asks for a bunch of cats or anything. Use your head."

"Look, guys," I said, "I don't want to play the Devil's advocate here or anything, but how or why does the cat get blown up while the dog just comes sailing out unharmed, although a little shaken up, I'd bet?"

They exchanged glances again.

"Padding," Doug said. "The cat acts as padding." You have to admit, Doug was good.

"You see, the cat takes the brunt of the explosion," Lance said. "He's in there first, shoved between the explosive charge and the dog. He not only gets the dog in, but saves the dog's life, too. It's a great system."

"Let me get this straight," I said. "Several thousand people are going to sit there while C.D. Lorenzo stuffs a cat down the cannon, then watch as a dog eagerly jumps inside after the cat, and not think anything about it when the dog comes sailing out unharmed and the cat is nowhere to be seen?"

More glances.

"Yeah," Lance said.

"That about sums it up," Doug said.

"They'll think it was a trick or something," Lance said. "They'll think the cat got out the back or something before the cannon went off."

"Because," Doug said, "one of the clowns will have a spare cat stuck in his costume. And after the trick he'll pull the cat out to show the crowd that everything's okay."

"But we'll know the difference, won't we?" I said. "Okay, let me ask you this. Why couldn't they just shove a bunch of milk bones or doggie treats down there instead of the cat? The dog would go in after those, wouldn't it?"

"No padding," Doug said quickly. "The dog would be blown into tiny pieces of puppy chow by the milk bones, and the treats would scatter like buckshot into the crowd, probably killing some old lady or something. It would be a horrible, bloody mess."

"A different horrible, bloody mess than blowing up the cat." I said. I was amazed—they were convincing, in a grotesque sort of way.

"Exactly," Lance said. "Cats are smaller. They disintegrate into atom-sized pieces. A dog would come out in chunks."

"Well, then, it all makes perfectly good sense," I said.

"It's a crowd pleaser," Lance said.

"And the dog loves it," Doug said.

"Which is more than we can say for the cat."

"The dog loves the glory," Doug said.

"And the fame," Lance said.

"Okay," I said, "but just suppose I were to tell you two that it isn't actually an explosive charge that sends the Human Cannonball out of the cannon. It's just a platform on a giant spring inside there, a huge catapult that wings the guy out of the muzzle. The explosion that you see is just a small charge at the back of the cannon, sort of like a giant firecracker, that goes off at the same time they release the spring. In other words, it just looks like the Human Cannonball, and for that matter the dog, is shot out by a powder charge. It's an illusion.

No need for cat padding and all that. Just suppose I were to tell you that."

They looked at each other with astonishment, as if I'd just told them they had zucchinis growing out of their ears.

Lance shook his head. "You are some weird guy."

"Where do you get these things?" Doug said.

"That's what I thought," I said.

Lance helped himself to another lemonade, but I didn't see him make a move to pay for it. Obviously, he felt that the camaraderie fostered by his mutually intimate knowledge of the dog trick exempted him.

Lance was not a great friend, but he was more than an acquaintance. For one thing, his goofy name put him in the same boat with Doug and me, the not-quite-outcast-but-certainly-adrift boat. We hung around together, and he had, in the past, been similarly persecuted by Big Farley, so we had that in common as well. Actually, he was not a bad guy, and he had this great knowledge of cars, when he wasn't lying, which served to make him informative.

"'58 Impala," he'd say authoritatively as a car drove by. "Got a three-forty-eight cubic inch Super Turbo-Thrust and triple carbs. Totally bitchin'." And he'd be right.

The point is, I trusted Lance enough when I knew he wasn't lying. And he only lied about things that would make him seem smart and knowledgeable and everything, which almost always turned back on him and made him look stupid and insecure because they, the lies, were so outrageous that you couldn't help but feel sorry for the situation that produced them.

For instance, Lance once told us that his father, who is about five-five and one hundred-forty pounds, had killed sixteen Japanese soldiers at Guadalcanal *with his feet* as he was escaping from a POW camp. Lance said his father used his feet because he was handcuffed or some damn thing, and had to kick his way to freedom, laying Japs low here and there, crunching larynxes and so on until he made his escape and was freed by the marines. When he told the story we were in a group of about six guys, and everyone fell silent, the story was so goddamn pathetic.

And to make matters worse, when he told that story I came up with one of my own, only mine was true because I'd just read it in a history book. Really. It seems there was this Solomon Islands native, the Solomon Islands being where Guadalcanal is, named Jacob Vusa, who was what they called a coast watcher for the U.S. forces. Solomon Islanders are Melanesians, which means they are Negro South Pacific islanders, and during the war they were mightily oppressed by the Japanese, and understandably irked that their tranquil little island had been overrun by short, sadistic killers. The Solomon Islanders weren't allowed to actually fight alongside the marines, but they helped out as equipment handlers and laborers and the like, and seemed to be happy enough to give any sort of service toward the liberation of their island.

Coast watchers were native men, and some New Zealanders, who camped along the Guadalcanal coastline, where the tropical jungle comes down to the sea. They kept an eye on Japanese ship and troop movements, and sent messages back to the marines about what they were doing and where they were moving to and, according to all sources, were a valuable asset to the allied fight for Guadalcanal.

Well, the Jap soldiers finally caught up to Jacob Vusa at his post one day, and took him prisoner. They tied him to a tree and tortured him, trying to discover where the allied troops were and what their plans were and everything else. They beat him and tortured him for days, even denying him water, but he wouldn't break. Finally, in frustration, they shot him and bayoneted him and left him for dead, still tied up to that tree.

Only Jacob wasn't dead. He had faked it. By his own account, he hung from that tree in a bloody mess for a while, until he was sure the Japs were gone. He then managed to untie himself and crawl back to the U.S. lines. Even though he was bleeding sort of extravagantly and near death, he was not only able to inform the marines that he hadn't talked, but he gave them the latest on Japanese troop movements, including those of the soldiers who had tortured him.

Old Jacob Vusa was one tough nut. Later, after the marines had finally taken Guadalcanal in one of the bloodiest sieges of the Pacific war, he was awarded a Congressional Medal of Honor and became a national hero in the Solomons.

Well, when I told Lance the story in that group of guys, his reaction was, "Yeah, well, my father and him used to play poker together in the hospital, while they were recovering from their wounds." Only he looked a little wounded himself. Actually, he looked pained. That was the only time I ever saw him come close to admitting that he had gone overboard.

His insecurities were a damn shame, but he had a good heart.

"So," Doug asked him, "did you hear about the cross-burning?"

"Who hasn't?" he said. "You're friends with that girl, aren't you?"

Doug and I exchanged glances, but averted our eyes quickly.

"Susan is more her friend than me. Us, I mean," I said. "Her name is Ricky."

"It's really crazy," Lance said. "Do you think there'll be race riots and marches and stuff? Like in Alabama?"

"Don't know," Doug said, somberly.

Lance poured another lemonade.

"I hope not," I said.

"They might have known something would happen," Lance said. "Being Negroes and all."

"What do you mean?" I said.

"I mean they're Negroes, is what I mean," he said. "They should have expected it."

"Yeah? Why should they?" I said. "What if you moved

into a Negro neighborhood, would you expect them to burn a cross on your lawn?"

"That's stupid," Lance said. "Who'd want to move into a Negro neighborhood?"

"But I'm saying, just for the sake of argument, what if you did move into a Negro neighborhood? Would you expect them to burn a cross on your lawn?"

Lance thought for a moment, sipping his lemonade.

"No," he said. "Crosses are for Negroes."

"Bad answer," Doug said.

"Let's say something else," I said. "Let's say the Negroes in the neighborhood broke a window in your new house or something. Or pushed your grandmother around in a circle and kicked her with big boots. Would you have expected it?"

"My grandmother?" Lance said. "What's she got to do with this?"

"We're talking hypothetical, here," I said.

"It's just an example," Doug said, sort of bewildered.

"Well," Lance said, "I'd have to say that, yes, I would have expected something to happen. That's why I'd never live in a Negro neighborhood."

"Now, why would you expect something to happen to you there?" I said, unsure of where I was going with this.

"What do you mean?"

"I mean, why would you be afraid to live in a Negro neighborhood?"

"Wouldn't you?"

Of course I would, I knew that, but I seemed to be doing pretty well with irrationality here, so I pressed on.

"Would they," I said, "kick your grandmother around because she was white and they were black, or because that's something that generally happens in Negro neighborhoods?"

"There he goes with my grandmother again," Lance said, turning to Doug. "What's this all about? Are you nutso, Dub?"

"Indulge me," I said. I was aware that I was getting

slightly abusive with Lance. I was also aware that he didn't deserve it.

"Look," Lance said, "I don't know what they do in Negro neighborhoods except maybe drink and gamble and stuff, but I wouldn't move into one because we're different."

"Of course we're different!" I said. "But why should we kick old ladies and things?"

"Dub, you're cracking up," Doug said.

"Who's kicking old ladies?" Lance said. "For God's sake."

"And the Duboises are even more different, because he's white and she's black." I wasn't handling this well. "Is it their fault?"

"Well, it's not my fault!" Lance said. "I repeat, would you move into a Negro neighborhood?"

"Damn right I would," I lied. "Sure as hell."

"Oh, sure, sure," Lance said. "So go ahead, go ahead and move to the North End and see what you think. Write us a letter."

"Dub, get a grip," Doug said.

"I'd walk right down to the North End and hang out like anybody else and it would be fine," I said. "The Negroes wouldn't break my windows and—"

"So, Negroes don't ever hate anyone?" Lance said, "and whites are the problem?"

"Whites are the problem *here*," I said.

"I didn't burn the cross," Lance said. "I don't know who burned the damn cross, okay? What are you, the sheriff?"

"I didn't say you burned it! It's not fair, is all."

"Fair, Dubby, is a state of mind," Doug said.

We turned to him.

"What's that supposed to mean?" I said.

"I don't know. It just sounded cool."

"Well, get off my back, Dub," Lance said. "All I'm saying is that they might have expected it, moving into this neighborhood. That's all I'm saying. Besides, who do you care about, the family because they're black, or this girl Ricky, because she's a girl?"

Doug seemed interested in the question. "Yeah, Dub, who do you care about?"

I sat with my forehead in my hands. It was not enough to be completely irrational, they had to hit me with some truth as well.

"Justice," I said, seizing the first noble and evasive word that entered my mind. "I care about justice, is all."

"You like her, don't you?" Doug said.

"I like her well enough," I said. "And you?"

"Sure, well enough."

"How well?"

"Well enough. And you?"

"Pretty well."

Lance was lost.

"She's okay," Doug said.

"For a girl," I said.

"Absolutely. For a girl."

"Just another girl."

"I haven't thought much about it," Doug said.

"Neither have I."

"Nope, couldn't care less."

"Same here."

We locked eyes for a split second before Doug averted his. "Well," he said, "Justice it is, then."

"Justice for Negroes," I said.

Lance, whose head had been turning back and forth like a spectator at a tennis match, said, "Sure. Justice."

"What the hell does that mean?" Doug snapped.

"For Christ's sake," Lance said, "You said it first, not me."

"Anyway, what do you think is going to happen next?" Doug said. It was a general question.

"What do you mean?" I said.

"I mean, another cross? Something else? They move away? What?"

"Something else?" I said. I hadn't convinced myself, but in my heart of hearts, I guess at that moment I knew there would be something else.

"Unless it was just a prank or something," Doug said.

"All I can say is they might have expected it," Lance said, seized by his new-found axiom.

"I don't know what's going to happen next," I said.

"It's sort of like waiting for the other shoe to drop," Doug said.

He turned to Lance and said, "You owe me twenty cents for the lemonade."

CHAPTER 5

Over the weekend, Doug was at the front door, knocking like an apoplectic Woody Woodpecker. I got to the door first, and there he was, breathless and beaming.

"Dad's in town," he said.

"Great. What's that on your chin?"

Doug wiped off a gooey, brown glob with his finger and, without looking at it, plunged it into his mouth. Animal, vegetable, or mineral, it was all the same to Doug Hammer. Me, I just hoped it was peanut butter.

"We're going to Boston for the day," he said. "Want to come?"

Now, this was good news. "Sure," I said nonchalantly, as if going to Boston on a regular basis was a normal sort of thing for me. Boston, I thought. City life, squalid degradation, hamburgers. In fact I just assumed that, because I had never in my life been to Boston.

"I haven't been to Boston in years," I said.

"Well, ask your dad, because we're going in about an hour," Doug said.

"What are we going to do? See a game?"

"No," said Doug, and he sounded dejected. "There's a jazz concert on the Commons."

"The common what?" I said.

"I don't know, that's what Dad said."

I was genuinely pleased we weren't going to a baseball game. It's not that I hate baseball. I like it well enough to play once in a while, and I'm not terrible at first base actually. I'm no hitter, and I can't play outfield because my long throw comes off as sort of a sidearm and wild, but I do play the game when it seems appropriate, like, say, when there is absolutely nothing else in the entire world to do.

A jazz concert, though, seemed like a fine idea. Anything other than baseball seemed like a fine idea, and Boston seemed like a superb idea. I went to Pop's study and knocked lightly at the door. It was Saturday, and Pop was at his typewriter.

"Come in," he said.

The room was thick with cigarette smoke and Pop was at his desk, fingers poised over the machine. His eyes were dark and heavy, and his lips were dry.

"Busy?" I said.

"Nope. I mean, yes, sort of. It's that novel. That book." He said it as if the book was a personal enemy. "I've been here for an hour, I've written three sentences."

The novel Pop was writing had something to do with this opium-addicted private detective and Korean War veteran named Kip who's on a case that brings him back to Korea where he has all these bad memories and drug-induced nightmares, and he finally finds himself involved with this Korean woman who's vaguely sinister and related to the case somehow. And even though Kip knows that she's bad business, he can't help himself because he's crazy for her, but he's got a problem because he's got this sweet wife at home who's crazy for him, and, even worse, he's still crazy for her.

I don't know, it made sense to me.

"What do you think would be Kip's motivation for initially getting involved with this woman?" Pop said. "Is it plausible? She's exotic, yes, but he knows she's dangerous. Is it loneliness? Guilt? Physical need? Of course, he's using opium too much. I'm leaning toward physical—"

"How about love?" I said. "Why not just plain old love?"

"Really? Tell me what you know about love."

"Well," I said, "isn't it supposed to be like instant chemistry or something? Some urge?"

"Urge, maybe," he said, "But I don't think real people fall in love at first sight. Who knows, maybe something happens, sort of a spark, that grows until it's some sort of unbearable tide that compels them to do something about it. Of course, then they get married and think they've done something about it. That's their big mistake, getting married and thinking they've done something about it. I'm afraid love is often the last thing that gets figured into the long—what can I do for you, anyway?"

I explained Doug's proposition to him.

"His father is in town?"

"I haven't seen him yet, but that's what Doug said."

Pop let out a long breath. "I don't know," he said. "Boston is pretty far away."

I had no response. I had no idea.

"We'll have to ask your mother," he said. Which, I knew instantly, was like saying, "No way in hell."

"Pop," I said.

"I know what you're thinking, Dub," he said. "You're thinking she'll say no way in hell. Well, we have to learn to have faith in people. You never know."

"But what about *you*?" I said. "What do you think?"

He seemed to wrestle with something. "I don't know. There may be a way in hell. I want to talk to Mr. Hammer first, at any rate."

We looked around the house for Doreen, but couldn't find her. We finally found Susan up in her bedroom, listening to a Buddy Holly record. "Mom went over to Grandpa's," she said.

Pop looked bewildered. "When did she leave?"

Susan looked bewildered, too. "I'm not sure."

"I don't know either," I said.

We came to the realization, simultaneously, that our mother had slipped out of the house and had been gone for some hours, and we hadn't realized it.

"Well," Pop said, "guess it's my call. Let's find Mr. Hammer."

We found Doug at our front door and walked with him to

his house next door. Mr. Hammer was out by his rented Cadillac talking with Mrs. Hammer. His blond hair whipped in the breeze and his shirt was unbuttoned down his chest. He sported a gold chain around his neck.

"Walter," he said when he saw Pop.

"Peter," Pop said, "long time."

"Too long," Mr. Hammer said. "you look great. Tired, but great." He was jovial, though if you ask me it seemed forced in a way.

"You know how it is," Pop said. This was apparently a truism among men. They always know how it is.

"I'm off to Beantown," Mr. Hammer said. "Gonna take Doug here up to an open-air jazz concert at the Commons. Some friends of mine are playing. We thought Dub might like to come along."

"How are things?" Pop said, avoiding the issue at hand for some reason.

Mr. Hammer hesitated. "Never been better," he said. "Real good."

Pop nodded. "Everything fine?"

Mr. Hammer thrust his hands in his pockets. He glanced at Doug. "Just grand. I'm fine, as healthy as a horse."

Pop glanced at me, then Doug.

I hadn't realized Mr. Hammer had been sick. He sure didn't look it.

"Look," Mr. Hammer said, lowering his voice and glancing at Doug. "Doug, why don't you go inside and get your jacket. It might be cold on the way home."

"Go ahead inside, Doug," Mrs. Hammer said.

Doug shrugged his shoulders and walked into the house.

"I couldn't be better," Mr. Hammer continued. He cleared his throat and looked at his ex-wife. She stared straight at him, an unreadable expression on her face.

"I'm counting on that," Mrs. Hammer said.

"Don't worry about it," Mr. Hammer said.

"You're still on the, what is it?" Pop said.

"Queen Beatrice," Mr. Hammer said, happily. "New York to San Juan and the Caribbean every week. Calypso to jazz to rock and roll. Your dancing pleasure in every measure."

"I envy you," Pop said, shaking his head.

"He's got the life, all right," Mrs. Hammer said, with a tinge of irony in her voice.

"You know how it is," Mr. Hammer said.

"I do," Pop said. They, being men, apparently knew how it was all over again.

"I'll have him back by five or six," Mr. Hammer said. "We'll have hot dogs or something at the concert."

Pop looked at me and, for one quick moment, his eyes focused harder than I'd ever seen them focus before. It was as if he looked right through me at the Cadillac. "Well," he said, not turning away, "that's fine. Lunch and a concert would be fine. Home by five."

"Good," Mr. Hammer said. "Dub, you'd better bring your jacket, too. If we've got the top down on the ride home it might be cool."

It would definitely be cool. "Yessir," I said.

Mrs. Hammer turned to her house and shouted, "Doug, don't forget your syringe and insulin." She turned to her ex-husband. "He takes his shot at three," she said.

"We won't forget," Mr. Hammer said.

"Bring him to a restaurant or something and let him use a clean men's room," she said. "Under no circumstances should he have to do it in public."

"I understand, Helen," Mr. Hammer said. "For God's sake."

"Dub," Pop said, "your jacket."

When I came back with the jacket, Pop said, "Dub, you stick with Doug and Mr. Hammer. No walking off on your own, clear?"

"Clear," I said, and his dark, tired eyes bore down on me hard. I don't mind saying that it was pretty damn unnerving, it really was.

We pulled out of the driveway, leaving Mrs. Hammer and Pop waving.

The ride to Boston was, to say the least, the best thing that had ever happened to me, at least at that point. Except for sitting with Ricky by the pool, but that was another sort of feeling entirely. I was alone in the back seat, and the wind whipped my hair around and stung my eyes in a pleasant sort of way. It was highway freedom and energy and the hum of a huge car with tail fins that drove me to blurt this out somewhere near Worcester: "Christ Almighty, Mr. Hammer, thanks for asking me!" It was a truly idiotic thing to blurt out, I know, but I was new at these things.

"No problem, Dub," he said over the radio, which had just started to blast "Chantilly Lace" by the Big Bopper.

Mr. Hammer glanced at Doug and smiled, then chimed in with the Big Bopper about his girlfriend's pretty face.

Doug had shifted in his seat, ready for it, then took over with the pony tail hangin' down part. He was on key, dropping his voice low like the Big Bopper. They nodded to each other, trading lines back and forth, and finished off shouting to the wind about oh baby that's what they like. I was amazed. They were both pretty good, as if they'd sung it before, as if they'd rehearsed it.

Pulling into Boston was like pulling into Oz. The buildings were tall and shimmering gold and green. People were on foot everywhere, nattily dressed and out for that Saturday afternoon walk I'd always heard about. We ended up near a place called Kenmore Square, looking, apparently, for a place to park. I was engrossed with the whole thing, and paid no attention when we pulled up to a brownstone and Mr. Hammer double-parked the Cadillac. He left the engine running.

"I'll be right back, boys," he said. "Just sit here and I'll be right down."

"What's up there?" Doug said.

"Just a friend," Mr. Hammer said. "I promised I'd pick

him up. You'll like him, we play in the band together on the ship. He's a sax player. Just hang in and wait. We'll be down in two shakes."

"Okay, Dad," Doug said, and Mr. Hammer bounded up the steps and was inside the brownstone just like that. Doug turned to me and shrugged.

I said nothing. I was absorbed in the sounds and smells of Boston. Hartford had never been anything like this. Buses screeched everywhere, belching and whining, and taxis and cars used their horns like it was part of the city code. People on bicycles and foot acted as if this type of confusion was commonplace and therefore unworthy of attention. The sound was contained within the brownstone block and echoed off the buildings, as if the noise sat right in your lap, yet was distant and remote.

We waited, talking little. We waited for about five minutes. Then ten minutes, all the time the engine running at a low hum. Doug fiddled with the radio.

"They must be talking to their agent," he said.

We sat for a moment.

"Gets them band jobs," he said.

Finally, Mr. Hammer and another man appeared on the steps. The other man was dressed in a flowered Hawaiian shirt and wore shorts and sandals. He seemed younger than Mr. Hammer, and had a big black mustache. From a distance, it looked like a small bird on his upper lip. They came over to the car.

"Boys," Mr. Hammer said, "this is my friend Johnny. We're on the ship together."

Johnny offered his hand to shake as he leaned over the door. "How ya doin'," he said. It's funny how you can tell when men who have huge mustaches are smiling even though you can't see their mouths. You can tell by their eyes. Johnny's eyes were glazed, but brilliant.

"You gotta be Doug," he said, and took Doug's hand. "I've heard a lot about you."

"Dub," I said, when he turned to me. His handshake was fast and soft and wet, and his fingernails were dirty.

Now, I don't mean to sound prissy or anything, but if there's one thing I hate it's shaking hands with a guy who's got dirt and goo piled up on them like he's forgotten that clean hands are an integral part of personal hygiene. I mean, you shake hands with a guy who's got damp hands and what's the first thing you ask yourself? *Where have those hands been lately?* It's not like you can go ahead and ask him if he's handled a dead dog recently or something like that. And you can't very well pull out a handkerchief and wipe your hands without gravely offending the guy, so you have to sit there like an anal-compulsive case wondering how you can sneak off and run them under scalding water at the nearest restroom or something. In the meantime, you can't eat, you can't touch your face, you can only sit there and look at his hands trying to figure out what that dark stuff is, and hope that whatever it is it isn't all that contagious. It really is a shame and all that, and I hope I never become negligent in this aspect.

Anyway, the truth of the matter is that this guy Johnny was kind of creepy, you know? In a *determined* way. His eyes shifted and then he made this whiny, horsy sort of giggle that, I swear, made my skin tight.

Mr. Hammer and Johnny piled into the car. I sat on my hands, if you want to know the truth. Johnny sat beside me smelling like an ocean of sweet aftershave. I actually caught my breath because of it, and was happy when we took off and the air started to move again.

"To the Commons," Mr. Hammer said.

I could tell by the back of Doug's rigid neck that he was unhappy with this new development, this interloper.

We drove over to the Commons, which is a long village green in the middle of the city, a typical New England thing, only much larger. It was filled with people milling about, waiting for the jazz concert, and we spent about ten minutes looking for a parking space. In the meantime, the radio blasted and Johnny sat in the back seat, drumming on his knees, humming along with the music.

"Come to Boston often?" he said.

"All the time," I said. "I love this town." It was then that Johnny pulled a flask from his hip pocket and took a pull on it. It dribbled, right onto his mustache. No surprise there, I thought.

He looked at me and raised his eyebrows, as if to offer me a drink. Even if it had been a strawberry milkshake I wouldn't have taken it, not after it touched this guy's lips. Still, I glanced into the rearview mirror and caught Mr. Hammer's eyes.

"Johnny," he said, "for Christ's sake."

Johnny shrugged his shoulders and we pulled into a free space.

We grabbed a blanket from the car's trunk and made our way toward the stage, Johnny jabbering on about music and this and that. We walked through crowds of people who wore black berets and small goatees and looked for all the world like the sort of people a town like Boston didn't see very often. We negotiated soda stands and popcorn vendors and people until we found a place to sit. Mr. Hammer threw the blanket down and plopped to the ground like a ripe pumpkin.

"This is the place," he said.

Doug and I plopped next to him. Johnny stood close by with his hands in his pockets and surveyed the scene. The Commons was festive, and smelled like the circus.

"Life is grand, boys," Mr. Hammer said, and he laughed. "Isn't it? Gets better all the time."

"Sure does, Dad," Doug said.

"Oh, yah!" Mr. Hammer said. "We need sodas and beers. Doug, you two guys go and get a couple of Cokes or something." He pulled three dollars from his pocket. "And maybe some hamburgers." He glanced up at Johnny. "Listen, we gotta go to the men's room. We'll meet you two back here."

"Sure, Dad," Doug said and we stood up. Mr. Hammer and Johnny walked off together in search of an outdoor men's room.

When we were twenty feet away, Doug said, "Who is this guy?"

"I thought you might tell me," I said.

"Never heard of him before," Doug said. "It's always been just us."

We found some Cokes and hamburgers. For a moment I had this fleeting thought that I should remind Doug he shouldn't be drinking soda because of his diabetes, but I dropped it because, hell, his own father had suggested it. So we got the stuff and when we arrived back at the blanket, we found the two of them sitting back, sipping a couple of beers. They both stared into the sky, as if there was something up there they really just had to see. Their eyes were huge, like big black moons, and they hardly looked at us as we sat down.

Mr. Hammer nudged Johnny, and pointed up to a cloud. "There," he said. "It's a guy, blowing a horn, something like that."

Doug and I looked up at the sky. Johnny said, "No, it's a woman, big bazooms. I can see her clear as day."

"You always got one thing on your mind," Mr. Hammer said.

"No, two things!"

They both laughed. Mr. Hammer pulled out a handkerchief and wiped his nose. "Jesus," he said.

"I don't see anything," Doug said. "Which cloud?"

"That one!" Mr. Hammer said, and he giggled like a hyena. People around us turned to look. Christ, he almost shouted it out, like it was important or something which damn cloud they were looking at.

"I don't get it," Doug said.

"Well, look," Mr. Hammer said.

"Still don't see it," Doug said.

"What the hell," Mr. Hammer said. "Whatever."

Johnny spasmed with his horsy laughter. "Who cares!" he said. He wiped his nose with his hand and that sealed it for me—the guy was a hygiene refugee.

Mr. Hammer leaned back and took a sip of his beer. "Man, there sure is a crowd here," he said, and he giggled again, this high-pitched giggle that sounded like a kazoo. His eyes were water, almost pure water.

Doug looked at his father, perplexed. "Big crowd," he said.

"Hey, Pete," Johnny said. "Maybe we should go to the men's room one more time before the music starts."

"Good idea!" Mr. Hammer said, with just a whole bunch of enthusiasm. He put his beer down. "You guys just wait right here, we'll be back."

They got up and hurried off. Doug and I continued to stare at the sky.

"I don't get it," Doug said.

"It's the beer, makes them piss a lot," I said.

"No, I mean the clouds."

When they came back, full of jabber and wide-eyed, it was pretty much the same; the clouds, the crowd, this girl over here, that guy over there. They didn't make a whole lot of sense. When the music finally started, it calmed them down a bit, but in an instant they were talking a mile a minute and their faces were red and they were sweating to beat the band, so to speak. It was pretty uncomfortable.

During the show, Mr. Hammer and Johnny made another trip to the men's room and came back the same way, flushed and jumpy. It didn't take a rocket scientist to figure out what was going on in there, although if you asked me then, or now, what precisely it was that Mr. Hammer and Johnny had in their pockets, I couldn't tell you. And it didn't matter, because it was Doug I was thinking about. I mean, what kid wants to witness his own goddamn father laughing and getting goofy all afternoon with a guy who has hands that looked like they've been in a coal mine for Christ's sake? I am sure they thought they were discreet, but they were so *animated* all afternoon, sucking these great wads of snot up their noses every few minutes as if they had hay-fever or something. And giggling like kids. It became almost intolerable when one of the bands came on and Johnny stood up and hooted, "*Whoo! Whoo! Whoo!*" and Doug looked like he wanted to die. It was hell for Doug, and not all that pleasant for me either. Doug finally got up and, without even looking at any of us, walked away. Just like that, he walked away. I figured he wanted to be himself for a while, so I didn't go after him. Neither did Mr. Hammer. Finally, Doug came back with some more Cokes, and we sat and drank them silently.

As well as whatever they were doing in the men's room, they also drank about four beers apiece and were eventually laughing like idiots, though, as I said, they probably thought they were discreet. Then they began to make these loud comments about the bands that were playing, though if you ask me they all sounded pretty good, especially one that had a Negro woman playing drums, of all things. People stared at them—us really—and Doug had this bewildered look on his face the whole time. I didn't envy the poor guy. Finally, Johnny dozed off and that just about killed their little party. I was relieved when we finally pulled up to the brownstone to drop Johnny off.

"Well, boys," Johnny said as he staggered out of the car. "It's been a pleasure." Only I didn't offer my hand for him to shake because, really, that would have been too much.

They went inside together and we sat in the car for another couple of minutes with the engine idling, waiting for Mr. Hammer.

"Weird guy," I said to the back of Doug's head. He said nothing, and didn't even turn around to ask what I'd said. He just stared straight ahead and leaned over to the radio to twist the dial. I caught his eyes in the rearview mirror, and they were stony and empty. Doug Hammer was mortally struck.

"I mean Johnny, not your father," I said.

"I know that," Doug said, quietly.

Just then Mr. Hammer bounded down the brownstone's steps and hopped into the car. "Home, Jeeves," he said in this cheery and fake voice. He flipped the car into gear and we pulled away from the curb.

Doug said nothing and it took Mr. Hammer only but a few minutes before he got the full picture.

"Everything okay?" he said, finally.

Doug's silence spoke volumes.

Mr. Hammer glanced at me in the mirror.

"Whatsa matter, Doug?" Mr. Hammer said.

Doug grunted and sank into his seat. He was aware that his father was about to compound the problem by embarrassing him right there, in front of me. It wasn't going to be a pretty sight, and if I could've jumped out of that convertible right then, I'm telling you, right onto the tarmac of the turnpike at sixty miles an hour, I would have if I thought it could've helped things.

"We had a good time, didn't we?" Mr. Hammer said.

"Sure," Doug said, and turned away from his father. "Real good."

"Oh-oh," Mr. Hammer said.

Well, the ride home was as wretched as the ride up was wonderful, and we didn't say a word, not a single word the whole way. Doug remained turned away from his father, just steaming and staring out the window while the industrial northeast dragged by in all its gray ugliness. I was a little on edge about the driving, but Mr. Hammer managed to hold the road, even though I did notice his eyes turn red and flutter every once in a while.

Finally, we pulled into East Hartford. When we were about five miles from our homes, Doug said, to the window apparently, "I never took my insulin shot."

Mr. Hammer, who by now seemed to have begun a world-class hangover, said, "Jesus Christ, Doug, you're three hours late!"

"I forgot," Doug said, clearly cheered by his rebellion. "It's okay."

"Christ almighty!" Mr. Hammer said.

"I got distracted," Doug said. "We all got distracted. Maybe I'll go into insulin shock or something."

"Great, fine. Well, we're going to pull into a goddamn gas station and you're going to do it right now."

"We're almost home," Doug said.

"I am not going to deliver you to your mother and have her tell me for the rest of my life that I forgot to keep you on your schedule," Mr. Hammer said. "We stop here."

I could have said something about Mr. Hammer's concern that his wife would see a problem in his forgetting about Doug, rather than him worrying about Doug himself. I could have said that Mr. Hammer was negligent in buying Doug soft drinks all afternoon. I could have said something about him and his grimy friend Johnny and their bathroom habit, not that I would have, but I never even got the chance to think about it because at that moment Doug's eyes rolled backward into his head, and he gasped and heaved himself forward onto the dashboard of the car. His forehead hit the padded part of the dash, and he groaned, "Sugar."

Mr. Hammer just about ran the car into a parked truck. He screamed, "Christ in heaven! Doug!"

"Doug?" I said.

No response.

"Dub!" Mr. Hammer said, "What do we do?"

"Sugar," Doug groaned.

"Sugar!" I said. "He said sugar."

"Sugar," Doug murmured.

"What in hell does he mean?" Mr. Hammer said.

"He means sugar!"

"What sugar?" Mr. Hammer said.

"What sugar?" I said to Doug.

"Sugar," Doug groaned.

"He needs sugar," Mr. Hammer said.

"I got that part!" I said.

"Who's got sugar?" Mr. Hammer said.

"Packets in...my…pocket," Doug whispered.

I reached around the side of his seat and searched for his jacket pocket, and while I fumbled, Doug's free hand, the one out of his father's sight, found mine. He squeezed it once, then moved his hand away quickly. "Sugar," he said faintly.

Startled, I slumped back.

"Dub!" Mr. Hammer said, "get the sugar!" The car veered down Main Street, and I caught a glimpse of Mr. Hwan's store as we careened by. Mr. Hwan, I thought, would appreciate this.

"He's almost dead," I said, "Sugar can do no good."

"Sugar," Doug groaned again. I had to admit, he had his line down pat.

"Sorry, Doug," I said. "Try to accept the end with dignity."

"Sugar!" Mr. Hammer shouted, and wrenched the steering wheel wildly to the right. He slammed on the brakes and threw the car in park. He lurched over Doug in the seat and grabbed his coat, searching for sugar in the pockets. Doug was cast back and forth like a rag doll while his father searched in vain for the elusive packets. "Sugar, sugar, where's the *sugar*!"

"It's too late," I said.

"Well you're taking this pretty goddamn lightly!" Mr. Hammer said. He looked up and saw that we were stopped in front of the Waffle Steak, a combination diner and adult book store with a undetermined smell coming from inside.

"Run inside and get some sugar packets," he shouted.

"Sugar," Doug hissed.

"I'm not allowed in there," I said.

"Jesus Christ!" Mr. Hammer said, "I'll go." He bolted out of the car and into the diner.

"We'll talk about this later," Doug said from his slumped position in the front seat.

"Always acting out," I said.

Mr. Hammer ran out from the diner, ripping open packets of sugar and spilling them into his hand. He leaned over Doug's side of the car and yanked him up from the seat, shoving a handful into his gaping mouth. "Sugar," Doug gurgled.

"Christ," was all Mr. Hammer could say. "Doug, Doug, Doug. Should we go to the hospital?"

"Sugar," he murmured.

"He may be okay now," I said. "I've seen him do similar things before."

"I don't know," Mr. Hammer said, "maybe we should go to the hospital. Hold him up, Dub." I leaned forward and gripped Doug's shoulders. As Mr. Hammer hurried around to his side of the car, Doug hunched over and spit a great wad of sugar into the map compartment of the door. Mr. Hammer got in to the idling car.

"Is that you, Mom?" Doug's eyes looped around in his head.

"He's coming around," I said.

"Mom?"

"Doug, it's me," Mr. Hammer said, almost tenderly.

"Is it Christmas, Mom?"

"Christmas?" Mr. Hammer said. "What the hell?"

"Christmas," Doug whispered. His eyes fluttered.

"Better go along with him," I said. "It'll help him come out of his coma."

"Okay," Mr. Hammer said, reverently. "Yes, Doug, it's Christmas."

"Mom?" Doug whispered.

"Yes, Doug, it's Mom."

"Did I get that bicycle for Christmas, Mom?"

"Bicycle?"

"That bike I wanted, Mom?"

"Uh, Doug, son, I'm not your mom."

"Better go along with it," I said. "Really, it'll help."

"The bike, Mom?" Doug said. "Ohhh..."

"Okay," Mr. Hammer whispered. "Yes, son?"

"Please, Mom?" Doug groaned. "The bike?"

"Okay," Mr. Hammer said. "I'll get you a bike, son. Please, come around."

"I want a bike, Mom," Doug whined.

"I'll *get* you the damn bike," Mr. Hammer said. "Now, please, please, come around."

Doug's eyes fluttered open. "Dad? Is that you?"

"I think he'll be much better now," I said.

"Thank God," Mr. Hammer said. "Doug, we almost lost you."

"Dad?" Doug whispered.

"Yeah, I'm here," Mr. Hammer said.

We drove toward home slowly while Mr. Hammer pleaded with Doug not to go into cardiac arrest or something. Meanwhile, Doug groaned and made like he was about to heave all over the car's interior, and every once in a while he grabbed his chest as if wrestling with his shirt. I have to say that I felt sorry for Mr. Hammer, at least for a few minutes. He was so damn *solicitous* and everything, it really was a sight.

"Hold on, Doug, hang on, son, or your mother will kill me," Mr. Hammer repeated.

"Ohhh," Doug groaned.

"Good God Almighty," Mr. Hammer whimpered.

When we pulled into the driveway. Doug shot up like he'd just sat on a cat. "Are we home?"

"You okay, son?" Mr. Hammer said.

"Never been better. Was I asleep?"

"Asleep?" Mr. Hammer said. "You went into a coma! You just had an insulin attack."

"Oh?" Doug said. "Did I forget my insulin?"

"Yeah, but we pumped you full of sugar," I said.

"You look pretty good, a little flushed, but okay," Mr. Hammer said.

"I'm sorry about that," Doug said. "But that's what happens when you forget your insulin."

"Well, you better slip into the bathroom and take it now," Mr. Hammer said. "Okay?"

"Sure," Doug said.

"Listen, I gotta run. There's no need to mention this to your mother, is there?"

"Oh, of course not," said Doug. "I'm as good as gold."

"Then you just say thanks to your mother and tell her I'll be in touch next time I'm in town. Gotta go."

"Dad?" Doug said. "About that bike."

"What's that?"

"The bike."

"You remember that?"

"Vaguely," Doug said. "I mean, I was in the throes of death and all."

Mr. Hammer drummed the steering wheel and searched the backs of his hands for something. "Okay, next time I'm in town, we'll go out and get a bike. Is that all right?"

"Great, Dad!" Doug said. "I'll remember!"

"Gotta go," Mr. Hammer said.

We hopped out of the car and Mr. Hammer threw it in reverse, putting down a little rubber on the driveway.

"Had a great time," he shouted. "We had a few laughs."

"Thanks," I said.

"Say hi to Johnny on the ship," Doug called out, without a trace of irony. Father and son waved to each other.

We watched the car pull away into the summer dusk, and Doug turned to go into his house.

"I don't want to talk about it now," he said with his back to me.

"Okay," I said.

"Remember that men's room on the Commons?" he said. "I took my shot in there."

"That's what I thought," I said.

"Well, that's that," he said, and hesitated for a moment. "See you."

"Sure," I said. And he walked away.

I didn't say a word. I was, basically, speechless, and as I watched his slumped shoulders disappear into the house, I knew that a part of his life had just melted away, changed forever. It lay like the puddle of sugar and spit in the side pocket of that Cadillac. I mean, I had my issues with Doreen, and Pop for that matter, but I knew them cold. I almost always knew what to expect. For Doug, that type of certainty, at least with his father, no longer existed.

I am not ashamed to admit that I have never once talked to Doug Hammer about the whole afternoon, even to this day. Maybe it's enough to say that the next week or so was hell at the old lemonade stand because Doug was all sullen and feisty and loathe to make small talk with me or anyone else, and he even got into a fight with Lance Cornwall when Lance came up to the stand one day and said, "Seen your father lately?"

It's just something we don't talk about, and I think it may be better that way.

I did have a clearer picture of why Pop was hesitant to let me go to Boston with Mr. Hammer, and I wanted to clear a couple of things up with him about the whole thing, but I thought I'd wait until another time so I wouldn't implicate Mr. Hammer in any wrongdoing for this trip. Not that I have any real evidence he actually did anything wrong, but the whole trip was so unseemly and lacking in any subtlety that it had to be the type of thing you don't want to talk about right after it happened unless you wanted to implicate someone.

When I walked into my house, I expected this predictable scene, for what reason I'm not completely sure. It's just that a scene at my house is more or less predictable.

At any rate, Doreen wasn't home yet. Pop met me at the door with these pensive eyes and asked, "Is everything okay?"

"Never been better," I said.

"I'll only ask you this once," he said. "Is everything okay?"

"That's twice, Pop."

"Good," he said, and he let out a quiet sort of sigh.

Pop told me later that Doreen had taken a sabbatical and was staying at her father's place for a couple of days, but she would call every day and see how we were.

It was something Doreen always did when she was beginning to feel, as she called it, "nervy."

Four days later Doreen was home and refreshed and the news came that someone had spray-painted the Dubois's green '57 Chevy with Nazi swastikas in the dead of night.

It was a Wednesday morning. The phone rang and Doreen picked it up, listened for a moment, and said, simply, "Walter."

Pop went to the phone. "Yes?"

"My God," he said to the phone.

"That's insane."

"I am sorry to hear that."

"Did you call the police?"

"Yes, I understand."

"Of course, I'll be right there," he said. And he hung up.

Susan and I were watching cartoons on TV, and Doreen was back in the kitchen.

"There's been another incident," Pop said.

"Where?" we said. We knew, of course.

"At Ricky's house," he said. He shook his head.

"Walter," my mother said from the kitchen. "What was that about?"

Pop stood for a moment, hands in his pocket, and tugged at his ear. "Another incident at the Dubois place," he said. "Their car."

Only heavy silence came from the kitchen. Pop nodded his head.

Then, quietly, he said, "I'm going down there. You two can come if you'd like."

The car was desecrated. That's the only way I can describe it.

Swastikas were sprayed in white paint on each of the side panels, on the trunk, on the hood, and on the windshield. Given any other choice of adornment, the car might have looked festive, as if ready for a parade or something. As it stood, it sickened the heart. Ricky was in the front yard in her pajamas, and Mr. and Mrs. Dubois stood by the car. Mrs. Dubois's mother was nowhere in sight.

I guess I had expected it. Disregarding my idiotic conversation with Lance the week before, I know now that I had been expecting something terrible to happen. The other shoe had dropped.

When I'd last seen Mr. Dubois, he was handsome and tall. Now he paced around the car, his hands in his pockets, and he seemed smaller and disheveled. I realized that he hadn't showered yet, and his manner suggested pain.

Mrs. Dubois had her hair in a tight bun, and her face seemed tight as well. She stood with her hands on Ricky's shoulders.

"Look!" Mr. Dubois said.

We did.

"It's criminal," Pop said.

Mr. Dubois gestured with his hand. "Look what they've done."

Pop was silent for a moment. "Who *are* they, Herbert?" he said.

Mr. Dubois rocked on his heels with his hands still in his pockets. "Other than sons of bitches, I don't know," he said.

"Have you gotten any hints, anything from anyone that would suggest this?" Pop said.

"You know how it is, the looks, the interest," Mr. Dubois said, and looked toward Ricky. "Nothing more than mild disdain. Nothing to suggest this," he said.

"I wonder if it's someone in this neighborhood," Pop said. He thought about that for a moment. "I doubt it. There are people with sick ideas around here, that's for sure, I think you anticipated that. But this and the cross thing...."

"Why do you say that?" Mr. Dubois said.

"I don't know," Pop said. "Do you think it's neighbors?"

"Well, let's just say this, Walter," he said, "I've seen some screwy things in my life, and having neighbors do this is not beyond my experience. You know, since we moved in, do you know how many neighbors I've talked to?"

"How many?"

"One, and that's you. I haven't even met your wife. And the only reason I met you is because you came down to the house that night while the cross was burning in my front yard. Other than that, I haven't even talked to the people next door, on either side. I don't know much about them. I walk out to my car in the morning, and they're walking out to their cars, so we nod hello and they get in their cars and drive. That's it. Why wouldn't it be neighbors?"

Pop thought for a minute and frowned, as if this revelation was both perfectly understandable and hideous at the same time. It was to me.

"You're right, in a way," Pop said. "But it still makes more sense for the perpetrators to be from somewhere else. They'd be less afraid, coming in from somewhere else."

"Maybe you just don't want to believe where they came

from," Mr. Dubois said. At that moment, he seemed completely unlike the baloney guy I'd met a while ago. He was angry, and he glanced quickly in Ricky's direction. Ricky shivered. "Maybe no one could believe that this could happen in their neighborhood. Maybe they don't want to believe that their neighbors are bigots. Just like the perpetrators can't seem to believe that their neighbors are Negroes."

Pop talked slowly and quietly. "Herb, I'm just thinking about the facts. You're right—I don't want to believe anyone I know is a bigot. I don't."

I haven't even met your wife, I thought.

"But we have to consider that maybe it was kids or something, out on a drunk," Pop said, "or maybe someone who has an ax to grind."

"Well, I've got my ax, too," Mr. Dubois said. "I've seen this before. We've all seen it before. I don't care about axes, I've got a family here, and a job and a life, such as it is. I'm not going to see them eaten away by cheap vandalism. These people have no balls."

"Herbert!" Mrs. Dubois said, who, until this point, had remained in the background. "I'm sorry, Mr. Teed."

Pop turned to her. "It's Walter."

"Walter, then," she said.

Mrs. Dubois had a voice that was slightly deep, but not in the bluesy, Negro songstress sort of way you might expect. Rather, it was deep and tired, as if she just wanted to take a hot bath.

"I'm sorry," Mr. Dubois said. He turned back to Pop. "You know, I'm not even sure what *you* think about our marriage, but I can tell you that Nancy and I have seen things like this before. I can tell you this. Down south, racism may be a way of life, but everything is on the line. You know if you move into a certain neighborhood, you'll get a certain reaction, and into another, you'll get another. For God's sake, I grew up like that. I was one of them."

"Does this look like work of the Klan?" Pop said.

"Hell, no," Mr. Dubois said.

"You don't mind me saying so, but this is pretty straightforward. I mean, burning a cross, the Nazi symbols," Pop said.

"They'd be even more open about it," Mr. Dubois said. "They'd leave a calling card, an actual message. 'Get out of town niggers, KKK' it'd say, or something like that." He turned to his wife and daughter with an anguished look. "Nancy, honey, get Ricky in the house, please."

"Daddy," Ricky said, "I've heard the word before."

Mr. Dubois turned to Pop. "There you go."

"And she will hear it again," Mrs. Dubois said. "Don't try to hide it, Herbert. We're a family, and we have our baby to show for it. She'll certainly hear the word again and we can't do anything about it, I know that more than anyone. And this cross-burning business won't stop in our lifetime. As God is my witness, we just have to be stronger than they are."

I was taken off guard by Mrs. Dubois's impassioned speech. Mr. Dubois hesitated for a second, then his eyes twinkled. "So, what do we blame? Love?"

She said, without rancor, "Don't patronize me."

Pop said, "It can't be easy for you two."

"Nancy's right. That's not your problem," Mr. Dubois said. "Now, what the hell do we do about this? Any suggestions?"

"I'd say the first thing," Mrs. Dubois said, "is to clean up this car."

We hung around for a while and talked about how awful the whole thing was and how the people who did it were sick and clearly unbalanced, which would turn out to be an understatement, and we left them with Pop's promise that we'd come back later to help Mr. Dubois clean up the car, as we couldn't have him driving down to the body shop in full daylight with swastikas jumping out at everyone on the road and all, which made perfect sense to me. Pop said we should clean the car in the early evening, in the light of day, when everyone in the neighborhood was out watering their yards and so on. That way it would be visible that we were showing some support for the Dubois family. Besides Pop and Mr. Dubois had work to go to, and we needed to wait until their return.

So Pop drove Mr. Dubois over to the college, and they left that car with swastikas sitting in the driveway all day long for the whole neighborhood to see. And they did see it. People drove back and forth all day, but, I found out later, not one stopped to ask what had happened.

In the evening, we came back to clean the car. I had looked forward to being able to be around Ricky some more, but I did have more than a vague sense that what we did was heroic and all. I got to spray Ricky with water and douse Susan with soap, and the evening turned out to be actually sort of fun, given the circumstances. Doug came along with us, with his mother's blessing, and had a blast flouncing around in the water, soap, and slight melancholy that pervaded the scene, so that was a good thing as well.

I have no proof that Doreen protested though I've got to believe that she and Pop must have had some disagreement about it, because she would have no part in it, and didn't say a word to us as we left the house armed with buckets and sponges. When we came back later she wasn't home, but soon returned from Mrs. Selwyn's place, full of bravado and more than a few glasses of white wine. Again, she said nothing and was sullen and she finally went to bed early.

The next day, Doreen was in this great mood. Who can figure these things? She smiled all morning long, she even baked cookies, for God's sake. Of course, she still had her mind set about things—while she was making up the batter, in the calmest voice, she told Susan and me that we were not allowed to visit Ricky anymore, nor was she allowed to visit us, forget the house-banning business. No more friendship. End of story.

She justified her decision by saying that the situation had become dangerous and she didn't want us getting caught up in the middle of someone else's race war and have people spray-painting *our* car with swastikas, or even worse. I protested, mildly mind you, and she put her foot down as well the bowl of flour she happened to be holding at the time, which caused it to explode across the front of her chest and my face. Given the obvious irony of the situation, us covered in whiteface—I couldn't help myself—and I just about fell to the floor laughing.

The strange thing was, Doreen didn't flinch. She even laughed as she wiped the flour from her eyes, then told us to get lost, but in this calm and almost *peaceful* voice. I mean, she was even smiling.

We went out to the old willow tree in the backyard at the top of which we tried to figure out what in the *hell* was going on. One minute Pop would be providing all this support in the aftermath of these scenes, and the next minute a calm and happy Doreen would simply deny us all friendship privileges, just like that.

"It's as if they didn't live in the same house," I said.

"They don't, really," Susan said.

Susan broke off a small branch and held it above the ground, letting it swing in the breeze, back and forth, back and forth, until it came to a halt between her fingers thirty feet above the green grass of the lawn. Then she let it go, and we watched it bounce and flounder against the other branches of the tree, until it hit the ground.

Well, it had to happen. After a day of not going down to see Ricky, who hadn't ventured out into the neighborhood on account of, in my opinion, the fact that she'd experienced two acts of recent violence on her family's property, I couldn't stand it anymore. Not only was not seeing her wrong for all the wrong reasons, but, well, I just didn't like it. I decided that my mother, short of having her father put out a contract on me, would deal with it in her own way, and I might or might not have Pop to pull for me in my corner.

So, having reconciled myself to some severe punishment, I convinced Susan and Doug to ride down to Ricky's house. Speaking for myself, it was as if I were driven.

When we got to her house, I felt a sonic boom brewing in my chest.

Ricky, in fact, answered the door.

"Hi," she said.

"Hi," Susan said. "Long time no see."

"What's happening?" Ricky said. She was dressed in denim overalls with a yellow ribbon in her hair, and she smelled of soap. "Where have you been?"

"Around," Doug said. "Want to go for a ride?" This was spontaneous. We hadn't discussed a plan for the afternoon.

"Sure," Ricky said.

We decided to ride down to Mr. Hwan's for an ice cream, and we were surprised by the old man's acceptance, instant acceptance, of Ricky. He latched on to her and treated her like British royalty or something. "Yes, Miss Ricky (which sounded like 'Miss Licky')," he said. "I have heard about you. Orange creamsicle? Plenty today, Miss Ricky." It was so out of character for him, but so within her character to respond graciously.

"Well Mr. Hwan," she said, "pleased to make your acquaintance."

And this is what I thought: "Yes, Miss Ricky, Miss Licky, me, too. I want to walk alone with you Miss Ricky and go to the circus and ride the Volcano Mountain together and eat those really bad pretzels Miss Ricky and who knows what else, Miss Ricky."

We all continued on like this for several weeks, visiting Mr. Hwan's, that is, or sometimes meeting at the pool, completely defying my mother's orders to forget our friendship with Ricky. It was a bit of heaven for me, and I began to get the impression that Ricky wasn't all that unhappy about us meeting either. I thought that because, and this is a inane reason for thinking something like this, but I thought this because once or twice she let me buy her ice creams or Malomars, and didn't even make a scene about it.

In the meantime, Susan and Ricky were becoming as close as spots on dice, and they'd often take off by themselves.

I wish I could say that Doug was enjoying our trips to Mr. Hwan's, but it seemed that since our trip to Boston, he had been awfully quiet and thoughtful, and hadn't wanted to talk all that much.

Then one day, standing outside of Mr. Hwan's, Susan asked Ricky if there had been any more incidents at her home.

"I would have told you if there were," Ricky said, slightly hurt.

"Well, were there?" Doug said.

"Well, yes," she said, "as a matter of fact. Little ones, though."

It was Susan who was now slightly hurt.

Ricky went on to explain about the phone calls. They weren't verbally threatening, or obscene or anything. They were hang-up calls. They had started a couple of days after the car incident, at the rate of one or two a day. The caller would wait until someone picked up the phone, and he, or she, would just breathe for a moment, then hang up. Never said a word. It rattled the whole family, until they finally changed their number to an unlisted, and the calls stopped.

"I'd give you our new number," she said, "but I know you're not allowed to call me anyway."

"Who said that?" asked Susan.

"I figured it out," Ricky said. She looked down at the ground.

"What do you mean?" Susan said.

"Well," Ricky said, "you haven't called in weeks, you just show up and we ride around. And we never ride past your house. I'm just putting two and two together."

"Hey, I can call you," Doug said, eagerly.

"You never would," I said, stabbed squarely in the back.

"I would," Doug said.

Susan shook her head. "Just give us the number, I'll see what we can do."

Which is how we got the phone number, and which, when the hang-up calls started again shortly after, was how Doreen came under a very uncomfortable cloud of suspicion.

CHAPTER 6

The following week our family began preparing for the yearly trip to Kelly's Kampground in Stockbridge, Massachusetts. Pop got busy packing tents and the like—Doreen and he would get one tent, Susan and I the other—and Doreen began her annual mope around the house, anticipating her week of sleep disturbed by mosquitoes and constipation from refusing to use those heathen outdoor toilets.

I, on the other hand, was definitely ready for a week of fishing and splashing around in Kelly's Pond. I packed three books to read. Actually, two and a half books. The two were a couple of Hardy Boys mysteries, and the half was the first six chapters of Pop's novel, the one about Kip the Korean War veteran and his dangerous femme fatale. It was a ritual with Pop and me and Susan. Whenever he arrived at the half-way point in a book, he'd give it to us to read on the condition we talk to no one about it, and that we be completely honest in our reactions. It was a privilege, really, the fact that he respected us and let us in on his language, which included words like "crepuscular" and "atavistic" and all that. I never found it a burden, and I always felt Pop took us seriously when we gave him our reactions to his work.

Susan seemed less enthusiastic about our camping trip this year. She packed silently, and didn't seem to get caught up in the anticipation the way she usually does. I noticed, and when I asked about it, she said it was because of Ricky. She said she sure would've liked to ask Ricky to come along with us, and she knew Pop would be fine with that idea, but of course Doreen would be equally not fine with the idea, so she'd never pursued it. I would've been fine with it as well, more than fine, but I also knew that it wasn't my place to ask.

Nevertheless, I did manage to mention it to Pop, in what I believed to be a subtle way. We were out in the backyard, spreading the tents out in the air to get out the musty smell.

"Dub," he said, "there are one or two things in this world of ours better than frying lake trout on a campfire, but for the life of me I can't seem to think of them right now."

"Me, too," I said.

He hesitated for a moment. "You're wallowing in thought."

"I'm thinking about Ricky."

"How's that?"

"I mean, Susan would sure like it if Ricky could come along."

He stopped for a moment. "Susan?" he said. "Susan wants to ask Ricky along?"

"Sure. I think Susan would enjoy it."

"Oh, really. And what about you?"

"I guess I wouldn't mind it either. I could have a tent by myself."

"So, having Ricky along would be a peripheral sort of pleasure for you," he said.

"Sort of. I'm thinking of Susan."

"Ricky's important to you, though, isn't she?"

"Well, only in that I wish these people would stop bothering her family," I said, switching the direction Pop was going in.

"I do too," he said. "It's hard on them, hard on Ricky."

"So," I said, "why are we avoiding her?"

"Who's avoiding her?" he said.

I wanted to say, "Surely, you jest," because I'd just heard someone say it in the movies and it sounded pretty sophisticated, but I just didn't have the heart for it.

"Don't you know Doreen won't let us see Ricky? At all?"

He stood, stunned. "No," he said, "I didn't know that."

Now, really, could you die? Could you just roll over and kick that old bucket to kingdom come? He didn't know. It defies rational thought, it really does. Here these two people are married and living under the same roof, and here I was assuming that Pop had just turned his back on it, had caved in to Doreen and let her rule our comings and goings and who we saw and didn't see *ad infinitum* when, even worse in a perverse sort of way, the truth was that *he didn't know.* I almost choked, I was so frustrated.

"*You didn't know?"* I think I said.

"No, I didn't," he said, calmly, but a dark look crossed his eyes. "Calm down."

"Well," I said. I realized I was sort of wound up. "That's just perfect. How could you *not* know?"

"What are you asking me, Dub? I just didn't know."

"Didn't Doreen tell you?" I said.

"Listen, son, slow down just a bit here. No, your mother didn't tell me and why would I think otherwise? You've been riding down to Mr. Hwan's with Ricky every day. You've been hanging around the pool with her. I haven't seen any break in your routine."

"You know about that?" I said.

"Of course," he said.

"Well, we broke the rule."

Now Pop was in a dilemma. His loyalty to Doreen was on the line.

"Look," I said, "I guess I'm sorry, but the truth is, Doreen's rule doesn't cut it with me." Where that came from, I'll never know.

But Pop just looked down at his toes. "You say that your mother has told you not to visit Ricky?"

"Ricky's not allowed at the house, and we're not allowed over there, and we're not allowed to see her at all, anywhere."

"Did your mother give you any reason for this?" he said, calmly.

"After their car was painted, Doreen said she didn't want us getting involved in anything that would cause people to do the same things to us," I said, truthfully, even though I was beginning to feel like a snitch.

"Well," Pop said, his fingers at the lobe of his ear, "why don't we just think on this for a bit and finish what we're doing. We'll talk later tonight, okay?"

"Pop," I said, "I don't want to get Susan in trouble, because the whole thing about us going out to see Ricky anyway was my idea. I mean, I started it, okay?" Actually, I felt pretty noble having said that, especially after snitching on Doreen and everything.

"But Susan knew the rule and went along with you," Pop said. "And she's older than you."

"Are we in trouble?"

"We'll see," he said. "It was good of you to stick up for Susan, anyway. Now let's get these tents folded up." Pop looked, at that moment, strangely calm.

We folded the tents and he left, and I looked for Susan so I could tell her about the impending destruction of our lives, but couldn't find her. I imagined she was off with Ricky at the tennis courts or the pool. Let it be, I thought. Let her enjoy these last few happy hours.

Later, Pop picked up a pizza for dinner, and Doreen was nowhere in sight. I asked about it, and Pop said, wearily, "Your mother has taken the night off to spend it with her father, and she'll be back tomorrow."

Translation: Doreen was sinking deeper into it, whatever it was this time.

Halfway through a wedge of pizza, Pop looked up nonchalantly. "Susan, how is Ricky these days?"

"Pardon?" she said.

"Look, you've been seeing her, I know that. And I'm not saying that's right or wrong just yet. But your mother has some kind of rule, doesn't she?"

Susan put her fork down and, for a moment, she looked just like Doreen did when she was about to blow her top.

"Yes, she has a rule," she said.

"I take it you don't agree with the rule?"

"No," Susan said, "I do not."

Pop smiled slightly, like a male Mona Lisa, and said, "But aren't there better ways to protest than to simply ignore the rule?"

Susan took a slow, sophisticated sip from her milk, and said, "Such as?"

"Think about it, you tell me."

"Well," she said, "I could talk about it with Mom, but—"

"Okay, that's a start, and we know it doesn't usually work. And then?"

"And then I break the rule," Susan said.

"Hold on. What about before that? Is there someone else you can go to make your feelings known?"

"I don't know," she said.

"Dub?"

"Got me," I said.

"So there's nothing else short of breaking the rules?"

"Can't think of anything," Susan said.

Pop put down his slice of pizza. "What about me?" he said. "What about your *father*?"

Susan and I looked at each other and Susan shrugged. "I don't understand," she said.

Pop took a long breath and shook his head. "Okay. Well, I do understand," was all he said. He finished his slice, and took his plate over to the sink.

"Yessir," he said out of the blue, to a fork apparently, "let's just see about that."

After we finished cleaning up the kitchen, Pop went to his study and I managed to get Susan aside to tell her how this had all come about. She took it, interestingly, in good stride. "About time," she said.

Doreen didn't come back the next day, and I gathered that the two times Pop was on the phone that day there was some intense discussion, because Pop was left both times holding what I took to be a dead phone, as if she'd hung up on him. Or maybe Grandpa Constantine hung up on him, I don't know. I mean, it happened.

Meanwhile, we continued preparing for our trip to Kelly's, and it was beginning to look like a great trip, even though Ricky wasn't coming. The thing was, maybe Doreen wasn't coming either.

I thought about asking Pop if Doug could come, but I didn't, mainly because Doug was back in business at the lemonade stand, saving frantically for the circus. "The Lobster Boy," he'd say, "just wait, Dub, it'll be something."

It seemed that Doug had forgotten pretty much about the whole sordid business with his father, and I figured he had gotten it out of his system by knocking the crap out of Lance, but I'm not sure because, as I said, I really never talked to him about it again. But if it took beating Lance to help get it out of his system, I'd say it was worth it. And besides, sometimes guys like Lance deserved it, in their own way of course.

Finally, Doreen came home. Without a word it seemed, she just breezed back into our lives and asked us how things were and she was sorry but her father was sick and she had to go and take care of him and a bunch of other clearly loaded stuff. But the thing is, I couldn't explain it then and I can't explain it now, it was actually good to see her again. It's a mystery. It really was okay to see her again, and I surprised myself by giving her a hug when she walked back into the house. She hugged me back, a good, old-fashioned mother-hug, and she was sort of weepy as she did it. It didn't look like she'd suffered any ill effects by being in the bosom of her family and all, and I had forgotten for a moment that I was in deep trouble.

And even that didn't pan out in the way I thought it would. She surprised us by asking, "How's Ricky?"

Susan was so stunned she said, "Ricky who?"

"Now, don't be silly, dear," Doreen cooed softly, "how many Rickys do we know?"

"Ricky Dubois?" Susan said. "She's fine."

"And her parents?"

"Fine, I guess," Susan said.

"That's grand," Doreen said. "Tell her I was asking for her, won't you?"

This was taking a weird turn. Pop squinted.

"Tell her?" Susan said.

"Tell her. When you next see her," Doreen said.

"Pardon?" I said.

"Did I forget?" Doreen said. "Well, your father and I have talked the whole thing over. The danger of all that racism business seems to have passed, don't you think?"

We were stunned.

"So, why don't we just have her over for tea or something," Doreen said. "Wouldn't that be nice?"

Susan hesitated. "Sure."

"But as far as inviting her to come to Kelly's with us, I just don't think that would be appropriate just now. I think this is a good time for Ricky to be with her family, don't you think?"

"I guess," Susan said.

"Lovely," Doreen said, "well, I really must get to my housework. A woman's work is never done, don't you know?" She walked to the kitchen, giving Pop a short kiss on the cheek as she passed by.

I never quite sorted out what had happened between her and Pop, but it seemed to have worked well enough and I was happy to let it pass. For the next couple of days Doreen flitted around the house with a weird, inverted smile and scary, sparkling eyes, dripping gushisms all over the place, as if she'd recently discovered some long-lost relatives who hadn't actually died in that plane crash in the Brazilian rainforest or whatever. She seemed slightly sedated, if you want to know the truth.

And, two days later, we went camping.

Kelly's was, as always, more or less a hugely enjoyable

time. Doreen spent a lot of her time sunbathing at the lake beach, or at Kelly's Hotel, drinking wine and talking with other campground mothers who were of similar spirit, which means they detested camping with a passion and would go to great lengths to avoid it even while they were doing it, which translated to drinking and shopping and coming home with sandwiches from Kelly's Deli so that they wouldn't have to cook over a campfire.

That was fine by me. Susan and I swam and fished and did the things we always do at the campground, meaning we pretty much lounged around for a week. Nothing really notable happened except for what Susan and I would later call "The Wrestling Match." That and the bee sting Susan got while playing a quiet game of Monopoly with a couple of girls she'd met. The whole thing was sort of uncanny. While she was sitting there minding her own business, moving her little iron onto Atlantic Avenue, a bee flew up and stung her hand, just like that, for nothing. It was as if the bee didn't want her to buy Atlantic Avenue or something.

Susan screamed and the girls went into a panic and they all ran to the camp's first-aid hut where she was dressed up and calmed down, but it gave Doreen the excuse to suggest that we call off the whole trip and drive home so we could put Susan to bed and nurse the wound—which we of course protested. Actually, Susan protested more vehemently than I, and the funny thing was, Doreen gave in, with hardly a fight. Mysteries were adding up these days.

Anyway, "The Wrestling Match" was really the highlight of the week, and it was so unusual and unseemly that I had Doug in jealous fits for days after we came home, at least about the parts I could tell him. He must have made me tell him the story twice a day for a week, and each time, after I finished, he said, "No way. Get out of town, you didn't see that."

But I did. And so did Susan.

It was just about sunset two or three days into the trip, and we had just eaten the tuna sandwiches Doreen had brought back from Kelly's Deli. After dinner, Pop stayed at the camp with a book, and Doreen sat down with her wine and a magazine. She was still in her nice mode, eccentric but nice, and had been dropping comments all day like, "I just love the muck at the bottom of the lake, don't you? It's so, I don't know, silky," and "You know, Walter, I think the woody flavor in the coffee really improves it. I wish we could do this at home."

Susan and I grabbed our fishing poles and binoculars and went down to the beach to do some evening shore casting and birdwatching.

As we approached the empty beach—most everyone was either eating dinner or preparing to go to the outdoor movie that Kelly's showed every night—we saw a couple of figures out in the water. Actually, at first glance they seemed like one person, because they were close, so close they almost shared a heartbeat.

"Look," Susan said, and motioned for me to slow down. She pointed to a bush, and we scooted behind it.

"It's a guy," she said.

"And a girl," I whispered.

"Good thinking, Dub," Susan said. "Like he'd be necking with a turtle or something."

"They're necking?" One of the figures was, at second glance, the lifeguard that worked at Kelly's Pond all day long. He was the type that had a long, muscular body and the sand-tousled look that girls get dreamy about, the type of guy that they pin pictures of up on their bedroom walls. I caught myself thinking of Ricky.

"Who's the girl?" I whispered.

"I don't know. A conquest, no doubt. Now shush and watch."

"Watch what?"

But Susan already had the binoculars up to her eyes.

From my vantage point I could see that the two were in water just above their waists.

"Man, this sure is something," Susan said.

I felt vaguely uncomfortable. "Big deal," I said.

"Uh, oh," Susan said. "He's got his hand on her strap."

"Let me see."

"Shh! They'll hear us."

"Then let me see!"

"Shut up, Dub!"

"What's happening?"

Susan was silent for a moment.

"God. I can't believe it."

"What?" I whispered.

"Lord, Almighty," Susan said.

I grabbed the binoculars from her hands and pulled it and her to me. The binocular strap was still around her neck. "Dub!" she hissed.

In the binoculars I could see that the girl's hands were under the water, and the lifeguard had his tongue somewhere at the back of her throat, as if he was excavating for gold in there. And best of all, his hand was on her breast.

Susan snatched the glasses back. "We shouldn't watch this," she said. She watched it.

I felt uncomfortable again, yet intrigued. I caught myself looking at Susan's chest, which had sprouted tiny bumps awhile ago, but was nowhere near what I saw in the glasses. She turned to me and I looked away quickly. Susan hesitated for a second, and said, "I think maybe they're doing... something."

I peered through the bush, and barely saw the two-as-one figure in the fading sunset. It moved slightly, rhythmically, up and down in the water. The girl had her arms around the guy's neck, and looked as if she was trying to take a bite out of his face. They looked, for all the world, as if they were wrestling. But gently. A tiny grunt sailed across the water.

"Doing what sort of something?" I whispered.

"I'll bet," Susan said, transfixed, "they're doing *it.* God."

"But they still have their bathing suits on. How can they be doing *it*? Right?"

"How do I know, maybe they're dry-doing it. It's gross, is all I can say."

"Dry-doing it? What's that? They're in a lake for God's sake."

"Dry-doing it is where you…" her voice trailed off. "You are such a moron."

"Let me see."

"No," she spit.

"Let me!"

"I think maybe we should get out of here."

"Give me the binoculars!"

Susan put the binoculars to her eyes again, gasped, and said, "That's it, we have to go."

"What? What happened?"

"Oh…my…God," she whispered.

My heart seemed to be beating pretty fast, and even though the whole scene was pretty vulgar—I mean, they were actually *doing* it, dry or whatever—I had to have another look just the same. Which was pretty damn vulgar in itself.

"Give," I whispered loudly, and grabbed the glasses.

"Dub," she hissed, and grabbed them back.

"It's not fair!"

"Shut up!"

I grabbed the glasses and pushed her to the ground, and when she went back the strap around her neck pulled the glasses, and me, down as well. I tried to right myself, but held onto the glasses, and was pulled down again. In a heartbeat I was squirming on top of Susan, both of us breathing heavily, struggling for the glasses.

We squirmed some more, and as we did, it suddenly—and this is sort of incredible—it suddenly occurred to me that Susan was a girl. I mean, a real girl. She was soft. I don't know why I had never thought of her that way before, and I don't really want to spend the time to analyze the whole thing right now because it was pretty damn embarrassing, to tell the God's honest truth. But whatever it was, it grew beyond my control, and the breathing and smell of Susan's hair made my head spin and I felt nauseated and lightheaded. I squirmed like hell and I guess I was squirming with sort of abandon when I heard Susan hiss, "Dub, what are you *doing*!"

I opened my eyes and saw her beneath me, red-faced. "What?" I said, a little too loudly.

From the water a man's voice bellowed, "Hey, who's there?"

"Holy shit," I said, and let go of the binoculars and rolled off Susan.

"Run!" she hissed. She jumped up and bolted through the bushes. I was up and behind her as we ran like criminals toward our campsite, crashing through the brush, snapping tree twigs, and breathing heavily for all sorts of different reasons. We never looked back to see where the wrestlers were, and escaped cleanly save for the fishing rods we left behind.

We looked at each other with some confusion for the rest of the night, Susan and I, but Doreen and Pop didn't seem to think that anything unseemly had happened, which, I guess, it hadn't. I'm almost sure it hadn't. But I couldn't stop my mind from wandering back to those goddamn frogs at Zikker's Pond, wondering what they were thinking as they gripped each other and sat there blinking, looking as if the world had caught fire around them it wouldn't be any worse hell than they were in at the moment.

At some point Susan announced that she was going to bed, and shot me an ugly glance. I took it as a command. I waited for a while, just sitting by the campfire, until I heard light snoring from inside our tent. I went inside, climbed fully clothed into my sleeping bag, and listened to the sounds of Susan's breathing.

To say I was confused would be to understate it. What I felt was anxiety, the type where you know something is terribly out of whack, but you don't know what the hell really happened. It was actually an exhilarating sort of anxiety—but anxiety nonetheless. It hadn't seemed to really bother Susan, she went out like a light, but, I mean, Christ Almighty, my own sister! Then I started thinking that maybe the thing to do would be to crawl outside and find a quiet place to flog my urges.

I actually don't have a lot of the old Catholic guilt about that. I ought to of course, because Catholics are supposed to feel guilty about everything, especially that, what with Onan spilling his seed against God's will and everything. But somehow I don't. It's not that I do it a lot, or even want to do it a lot, because it's always a sticky mess and you constantly run the risk of getting caught. And I don't believe you can grow hair on the palms of your hands or turn into a raging pervert or whatever, although I have to admit to wondering if it's possible to use up your life's supply of sperm if you do it too often. I do wonder about that sometimes. I mean, I'm not obsessive about it or anything, but I do wonder.

Of course, "masturbate" is the correct word for it. I have this image of walking up to Pop one day and asking him what euphemism he'd use if he were writing a story where some guy masturbates. I have this thought he'd say, "Well, what would you use?"

I'd say, "I think 'choke the chicken' works, don't you?"

"Effective, but overused," he'd say. "It's like 'slam the ham.'"

"How about 'jerk off'?"

"Too obvious. All those 'off' phrases, as in 'whack,' 'jerk,' 'cork,' whatever. Too pedestrian. I think you'd be better off making up your own phrase."

"Like what?"

"Some alliterative or rhyming phrase, something

creative. Something like 'wank the woody' or 'flog the fossil.'"

"Not bad," I'd say. "How about 'clobber the bobber'?"

"Okay. A little violent, but it works."

"Sure, but they're all violent. Like 'beat the meat' or 'bludgeon the banana.' But still popular in the public consciousness."

"That's what makes them so hackneyed. Try something creative. Something like "'jerkin' the gherkin'."

"Cliché," I'd say. "How about 'polish the pistol,' or 'board the train?' Or 'pluck the duck' or 'can the Spam'?"

"'Board the train'?" he'd say. "'Board the train'?"

"Well, it's original."

I'd imagine Pop would think I was pretty clever and he'd probably congratulate me on my use of creative vocabulary. Of course, it's not exactly your average father and son repartee, and I would definitely be embarrassed if he ever brought it up. To tell the truth, I don't think I would talk about it with my own kid either. I mean, it's not like you can ask your own flesh and blood if he's discovered himself recently.

Anyway, as it turns out, while I was thinking about it I fell asleep.

The next morning I snuck off early and found our fishing poles right where we'd dropped them. I looked out over the water, trying to remember where the couple had been the night before, but couldn't quite place the spot. But I looked down and found the crushed grass where Susan and I had scuffled, and I groaned, surprising myself.

For the next day or so Susan and I seemed to go our separate ways, even though we joked around and did this and that together. Susan didn't seem to think less of me for whatever happened, nor did I of her, although I wasn't sure what we were *supposed* to think except that we were, for a moment, involved in something we'd never experienced before. So the whole incident passed, and pretty soon we were talking about the couple in the water as "The Wrestling Match," completely ignoring our own wrestling match, and the irony.

The lifeguard, whose name I later discovered was Bruce—you really had to have seen *that* coming—seemed pretty well pleased with himself for the rest of the week, but that was nothing new. What was new was the girl he'd been with that night, his "conquest" as Susan had suggested, who kept bringing him ice cream cones and things, and who seemed to be hanging around him more than the other girls. She was slightly overweight and used the word "fabulous" as if she'd win a prize if she used it more than the national average. It was always a "*fabulous* day, Bruce," and "*fabulous* breeze for sailing, Bruce," and "Bruce, I've just got this *fabulous* idea." It got to the point where if I heard the words "fabulous" and "Bruce" together in the same sentence once more I would consider eliminating them both from my vocabulary out of spite. Susan considered worse.

"If she says that one more time," she said, "I will assassinate her."

Well, the week finally ended, we drove home, and Doreen made a beeline straight for the bathroom. Pretty soon I was outside, hanging out with Doug at the lemonade stand, turning him all fidgety and green with my story about the wrestling match. "No way," he said, the first of many times. "Get out of town, that didn't happen."

Gradually, though, he began to fill me in on what we'd missed at home.

"I got sixteen dollars and change saved so far," he said, "and we still got twelve days till the circus arrives. I am for sure going to see that woman who twirls the tassels on her hooters—for sure. And the Cyclops Man and all the rest."

"What's been happening around here?" I said. "Big Farley been around?"

"No, but Ralph Schortslee, that kid who's in his gang, he got arrested."

"For what?" I said.

"Well, I think it sort of involves you and me," Doug said slowly, and he smiled.

"What? How?"

"Ralph got caught at Mr. Hwan's place," he said, "writing stuff on the side of the store. I think it was 'Slants Go Home' or something like that."

"'Slants?'" I said. "That's original."

"That's Ralph," Doug said. "Farley and his gang are smart as fish bait."

"So, how does that involve us?" I said, not without apprehension.

"Mr. Hwan thinks Ralph did it because of the time he saved our lives with that fire story, the fire at Big's house that didn't exist."

"So they were getting back at Mr. Hwan?"

"That's what Mr. Hwan thinks."

"What did he say?"

"Well," Doug said, "I went down there one day last week after Ralph spray-painted the place, and Mr. Hwan told me that he'd been expecting something to happen ever since that day he told them about the fire. He said he knew they'd come back one way or another after they found out they'd been had, so he had a plan all along. He'd been sort of waiting for them."

Now I was intrigued, although my instinct told me that if Big tried to get even with Mr. Hwan, things would be doubly worse for us. Particularly since one of his gangsters had been caught.

"What was the plan?" I said.

"Well," Doug said, "Mr. Hwan figured they'd come at night, so he hired his wife's cousin, another Korean guy named Wing, to be sort of a night security guy, to just hang around until midnight or so for a while to make sure things were okay. Sure enough, one night last week Wing hears this bicycle pull up outside. There's Ralph with a can of spray paint writing something on the side of the store."

I was impressed. "So Wing caught him in the act?"

"Better," Doug said. "The official report is that Wing tackled Ralph and tied him up and called the police. But one of the cops who came to take him away was Officer Bigger Farley, and Mr. Hwan said that Bigger cuffed Ralph a few times before tossing him into the cruiser. He said Ralph was bawling like a baby."

"Good deal," I said. "Scared the hell out of him." And, I was beginning to hope, scared away any chance of the Big gang retaliating against me and Doug.

"But," Doug said, and his eyes lit up. I could see that old magic looming behind his pupils. "It gets better. The real story is that Wing had a pistol, and that's how he got Ralph to get down on the ground so he could tie him up. He actually *pulled a gun on him*." This was apparently the best news Doug had heard all summer. He almost drooled, for God's sake.

"And even better," he continued. "After Wing gets Ralph tied up, he takes that gun and shoves it down the front of Ralph's pants—Ralph must have been shitting boulders! And Wing says, 'You botha my uncle again, I pull trigga nes time!'"

"Wow," was all I could say. I imagined Ralph's reaction to the crazed Oriental who had a cold, steel handgun pointed at his crotch. I could also imagine Ralph's thought process, murky as it probably was: "This man will kill me and sell my body parts for opium."

But, remembering it was Doug Hammer talking, I had to express my doubts. "How do you know all this?" I said.

"Mr. Hwan told me," Doug said. "Only you can't tell him that you know, because he swore me to secrecy. I swear."

"You're sure about all this? About the gun?" I said. I was now sure about the doubt.

"I'll eat a dog turd if I'm lying," he said. "It's not on the police report, if that's what you mean. I mean, Ralph isn't going to tell the cops about Wing's gun, because if Ralph rats on Wing, he's a dead kid for sure, you know?"

"Of course. So, did Ralph spend the night in jail?"

"Worse. His old man came and got him and I bet Ralph didn't sit down for two days."

Something clicked in the story. "Did you say Ralph used spray paint?" I said.

"Yeah," Doug said. A knowing look crossed his face. "White spray paint. I saw it on the store the next day."

"Are you thinking what I'm thinking?" I said.

"That someone spray-painted the Dubois's car with white paint?"

"Exactly," I said.

Doug's smile suddenly vanished. "Yeah, and that's the other thing that happened when you were gone."

"What?"

"At Ricky's. They came again, just a couple of nights ago. Only this time, they threw a brick."

I shouldn't have been surprised, yet I was.

"What happened?" I said.

"I heard about it the next day, from Ricky—"

"You were talking to Ricky?" I interrupted.

Doug looked at me as if I'd asked him if he'd managed to eat or sleep once or twice while I'd been gone. It was a deeply stupid question, and one that showed me the depths to which I had fallen. He, justly so, became righteous. "Of course, you idiot. Anyway, it was late at night, or early in the morning, and they hear a smash and a thud, and everyone runs down to the living room and there's a brick on the floor, with a message tied to it. The picture window is smashed."

"Bull. Too much like the movies," I said.

"Except this really did happen," Doug said. "And something else. There was a raccoon's tail tied to the brick."

"A raccoon's tail?" I said.

"Coon, get it?" Doug said.

"You're kidding," I said. "What did the message say?"

"It said 'Nigers Go Home'," Doug said, and he spelled 'Niger' for me.

"Just like 'Slants Go Home'," I said. "It's as if Big Farley is pointing his finger straight at himself. Did anyone hear a car drive away?"

"No, not that Ricky said," Doug said. "But it was a couple of minutes before they were all awake and everything."

"Bikes," I said. "They must have been on bikes. Big Farley. It all fits, it really does."

"But there's another thing," Doug said. "And this doesn't fit. Remember when Ricky gave us her new phone number because they'd been getting crank calls?"

I said I did.

"Well," Doug said, "the calls started again. This week, after the brick."

I couldn't figure it out. "Who else had the numbers?"

"Who knows? Their family back in Louisiana, Mr. Dubois' boss at the college? The police?"

"The police?"

"Mr. Dubois called the police this time."

"You're on the level with this whole story, Doug?" I looked at him hard. This wasn't something I wanted to trifle with. He, apparently, saw that.

"It's all true," he said.

This, of course, threw my theory about Big and company right out the window, so to speak. There was no way Big or any of his gang could have the Dubois's telephone number. The only way to figure it would be that the gang created all the vandalism and mayhem, and someone else made the phone calls.

At any rate, I decided an immediate visit to Ricky's was in order. The mission was to find out about the brick and the phone calls. And I had this vague feeling that I wanted to find out if she'd enjoyed talking to Doug while I was gone.

But before I could find a way to slip off by myself, Pop walked out of the house with Susan in tow.

"Hi, Doug," he said. "I understand there's been a little excitement at the Dubois's house while we were gone."

Doug looked perplexed. Pop said, "I just called Mr. Dubois to see how things held out last week, and he told me the story about the brick."

"I suspect you know about it by now, Dub?" Pop said.

"I just heard," I said.

"Interested in going down there with me?" he said.

Sure, I thought, the gang's all here. And while we're at it, let's invite the Hartford Symphony Orchestra.

As we walked the block over to the Dubois's, Doug whispered to Susan, "So, what about this wrestling match?"

Susan turned to me, and her face was white, then red. "You pig!" she hissed.

"The one in the water, not the other one!" I said.

"What other one?" Doug said.

"What are you kids talking about?" Pop said.

"Nothing," I said.

"There was *no other one,*" Susan hissed at Doug.

"Other one *what*?" Doug said.

"Wrestling match," I said, "There was only one."

"Just the one," Susan said, and she fixed her eyes straight ahead.

"Well, what about it?" Doug said.

"About what?" Pop said.

"Nothing," I said.

"You slime," Susan said to me.

"I didn't mention it!" I said.

"Mention *what*?" Doug said.

"The wrestling match," I said.

"I think I'm going mental," Doug said.

"Let's drop it," Susan said.

"Drop what?" Pop said.

"Yeah, drop what?" Doug said.

"Nothing," I said.

"Nothing," Susan said.

Mr. Dubois came out to meet us as we walked into his driveway.

"Greetings from Hell," he said, almost jovially.

"Hi, Herb," Pop said. "Tell me about it."

Well, I have to say that Mr. Dubois' story was almost identical to Doug's, so I have to give Doug credit for that. The only detail Doug had left out was that the brick was thrown at exactly one-twenty-two in the morning. Mr. Dubois knew that because he had just turned off his reading lamp moments before the brick crashed through the window, and he glanced at the alarm clock by his bed. At first, he said, he'd thought it was a glass that had fallen over, maybe Ricky or his mother-in-law in the kitchen getting a drink or something. But he'd waited a moment and, when he hadn't heard any more movement down there, he'd gone to investigate. And the rest is history. And he added this other small detail: He walked down the stairs with a baseball bat in his hands.

Mr. Dubois described the note. It had said what Doug had said it said, in black crayon, right down to the N-I-G-E-R. Mr. Dubois said the letters were written in a scrawl, as if a right-handed person had held a crayon in his left fist and gouged out the letters on paper.

"And you called the police," Pop said.

"This time I did. It's gone too far."

"I am sorry," Pop said.

"It happens, Walter," Mr. Dubois said. "That's the way it is."

"You gave the police all the evidence? Of all the incidents?" Pop said. "The note, the brick, the tail, the remains of the cross, maybe even a photo of the car before it was cleaned. They might be able to put something together with that."

"I did. Except I threw away the raccoon tail. It was disgusting," Mr. Dubois said. He hesitated. "You still think it's one person, or the same group of people, don't you?"

"I do," Pop said.

"Well," Mr. Dubois said slowly, "what if it isn't? What if it's more, say a conspiracy? Think about it. Not an organized conspiracy, but more a conspiracy of thought, of philosophy. Say a large group of people hate you, for whatever reason, but they don't necessarily know each other. Say this whole group of people wants to drive you away. One night, a person or a couple of people come and burn a cross. Another night some others paint your car. Another night they do this." He held up the paper. "The police arrest one of them, so what? Another one is there to take his place, to take up the mantle and run with it. Another person or group, Walter, is always there. Even if these are all just random crimes, someone will always be there to do it." Mr. Dubois was clearly exasperated, tired, and angry. And saddened.

"So, Herbert, what are you going to do? You're going to roll over?" Pop was also exasperated.

"What can I do, except guard my house?" Mr. Dubois said. "There is a theory, you know, that says if you don't react violently, if they can't get a rise out of you, they go away, they give up."

"Non-violent resistance? If you're talking about Gandhi's world, it was the majority, the masses, that resisted a minority colonial government. The government simply couldn't kill or beat that many people. You're a family. You've got a kid."

At that, my heart took a small but significant leap. "Where's Ricky?" I blurted out.

"Shopping with her mother," Mr. Dubois said. "But I'll tell her you were asking for her." Then he did the most incredible thing, possibly the most embarrassing thing that had ever happened to me aside from my most recent and confusing encounter with Susan. He winked. Plain as day, in front of Doug and Susan, he winked at me.

But, determined to take it like a man, I had to say a manly sort of thing. "Women and shopping," I said, and shook my head.

Pop and Mr. Dubois just stared for a moment, then resumed their conversation.

"Okay, so I've got a kid," Mr. Dubois said. "And that certainly doesn't make this any easier. I've considered that, believe me, I've considered it. I thought about sending them all home until this blows over."

"No!" Susan said, startling herself.

"Honey, I just said I considered it," Mr. Dubois said. "I'm not doing it, not yet anyway."

"But wouldn't it be better to stand and fight—to nip this in the bud?" Pop said. His face began to turn red. "Otherwise, what happens? You move to another town, they throw bricks again. Then another town, more burned crosses, and so on. You could keep running and sending Ricky back home for the rest of your lives."

"Of course it would be better to fight, for Christ's sake. But dangerous. I'm not in this alone," Mr. Dubois said. He seemed to be getting a little steamed at Pop.

"And the next black family that moves in, what legacy do they have? There's nothing to build on, no hope. The goons start in right away with the paint and bricks. You see what happens? Nothing will ever change if we don't change it." Pop was almost out of breath.

"*We*, Walter? Watch what you're saying here. It's my fight, not yours."

"Look, Herb, I've thought a lot about this, and I'm not talking off the top of my head. I am willing to commit to helping you through this in any way I can. If you need advice, a good lawyer, if you need a support, if you need somewhere to stay, I want to say that I'll be here for you and your family. If you want, call the police and get them down here again, and I'll tell them my side of the story, the night I came to your place when the cross was burning. It's not much, but it'll get them down here again, and it is more evidence, such as it is."

Mr. Dubois stared intently at Pop. They were both being

so goddamn noble and everything, I just wondered how this could end.

"Walter, are you sure you've thought this through? I mean, say we do need somewhere to stay, say they burn our house right down to the ground. Say we move into your place for a while. What's your wife going to think about that?"

"I'll handle that," Pop said without hesitation, as if he had indeed thought this out.

Mr. Dubois stared at him intently.

Pop glanced at us, and tugged his ear. "I said I'd handle it, Herb. I mean that."

Well, I was pretty proud of Pop for that, and I remain so today, no matter what the eventual outcome was. It was, first and foremost, a good feeling to hear him declare himself that way. And it was sort of new to me.

Mr. Dubois hesitated for a moment. A look of relief crossed his face, and I took that to mean he was beginning to see it Pop's way. And he was, but in fact the look was directed over Pop's shoulder, where he could see his car and Mrs. Dubois and Ricky coming back from their shopping trip.

We all made a space in the driveway, and they sounded the horn as they pulled in. Ricky jumped out and said, "Hey, there."

"Hey," we said.

God, she was pretty. Her hair was combed straight back and her skin glistened. She was bright as a headlight, and I was truly happy to see her.

"I want to hear all about your trip, you look so grand," she said in a bubbly sort of way, mostly to Susan. "Come on in, you've never been in my house before. We'll have tea."

Mrs. Dubois came around the car and kissed her husband lightly on the cheek. It was the first time I'd ever seen a black person kiss a white person, and it was startling, for a moment.

I looked at Pop and I was torn. Stay outside with the men and finish the business at hand, or go inside with Ricky? The tea business felt distinctly uncomfortable. I glanced at Doug. His look said stay outside, and I had to agree.

Susan and Ricky started toward the door, and Ricky turned and said, "Dub, Doug, aren't you coming in?"

"Uh, maybe later," I said.

"Yeah, later," Doug said.

The women, including Mrs. Dubois, gathered some packages and walked into the house.

"So," Pop said, "my thought is that you are at a nexus here. They're running out of things to do to your house and property, short of threatening your family with physical harm. You've called the police, and that's a first step. What next?"

"Well," Mr. Dubois said, "the police came to the house, and that was a good show of force. Maybe that's enough for now."

"Can I say something?" I said. The two men looked at me, and Mr. Dubois nodded.

I started in on my theory, with Doug adding this and that, about the similarity in the white spray paint and spelling mistakes made in the acts of vandalism here and at Mr. Hwan's. And how no one heard a car pulling away the night of the brick, so it could've been someone on a bike. We did this without mentioning Big Farley by name, but we did mention that Ralph, the perpetrator at Mr. Hwan's, was part of a street gang of kids in the area.

"You mean Henry Farley's gang," Pop said.

"Well, yeah," I said.

"It's not a bad theory, Dub," Pop said, "and it's well thought out. But I think it's got some holes. First, I don't know if Henry Farley is sophisticated enough for the symbolism of a burning cross. I'm just not sure he knows enough history for that. The spray paint I could see, and maybe the brick, but the raccoon tail might be a bit obscure as well. It'd be beyond a lot of people older than he is. Aren't you giving the gang some credit here they don't quite deserve?"

I had to admit Pop had a point. Big Farley was, above all things, another kid. The burning cross did seem beyond him.

"Unless someone put him up to it," I said.

"Well, yes. Now, why do you think the Farley gang has singled out Mr. Hwan and the Duboises for their wrath, if it's true that they did this?"

"Good point," Mr. Dubois said, "there are other ethnic families around, and Hwan has been in his store for, what, years I assume. We're new here. But why him?"

Then Doug blurted our story about the bicycle chase that ended at Mr. Hwan's that afternoon, and how Mr. Hwan quickly thought up a lie that most likely saved our skins. Doug, of course, left out some details. The way he told it, we were innocent and merely set upon by a gang of salivating thugs who had nothing but mayhem on their minds. But it wasn't a bad story, nonetheless.

Mr. Dubois and Pop took it in slowly. Pop stared at me to see if the truth was coming out, but I looked up, noting the cumulus clouds that had gathered over the area, it seemed, all of a sudden.

"So, there may be a vendetta angle," said Mr. Dubois. "They're getting back at you boys through Mr. Hwan, and through Ricky as well. They have to know by now that you've become friends."

"Seems far-fetched," Pop said, "but plausible. It also seems like you boys had better keep your eyes over your shoulders for a while. The thing is, why beat around the bush to get at Dub and Doug? Why not go straight for the jugular?"

I didn't care for Pop's analogy, if you want to know the honest truth. I felt this sort of twinge at the base of my neck.

"No," Pop continued, "Henry Farley is not capable of that type of subtlety. I could see the Mr. Hwan incident, perhaps, because they'd be punishing him directly for the lie, and a pretty damn interesting lie it was, if you ask me. But if I know young Farley like I think I know him, he'd come straight at the boys like a bulldozer before resorting to throwing bricks through your windows."

"Like a bulldozer?" I said.

"Just a comparison," Pop said.

"At any rate," Mr. Dubois said, "I think we'll go with your idea Walter. This sort of thing is for the police to figure out. Wait—"

"What's that?" asked Pop.

"There's one more thing—the phone calls," he said. "They've started again, just this week, after the brick business." He went on to explain how it would happen once or twice per day, just a call and a hang-up. Just like it had happened before they had their number changed and unlisted.

"And who has the number?" Pop said.

"Well, aside from you, there's my family and Nancy's family in Louisiana. A couple of instructors at the college. And Ricky said she gave it to the kids, here. Of course, now the police have it. That's it, as far as I know. I can't figure that one out to save my life."

"Did you kids give anyone else the number?" Pop said.

"No," Doug and I said, in unison.

"Anyway," Mr. Dubois said, "I'll call the police again tomorrow and tell them you want to give them your account about the cross-burning business. And if they recommend it, I'll probably have to change the number again."

Pop and Mr. Dubois said their good-byes and parted with the promise that Pop would come down the next day when the police were there.

Doug and I went home with Pop, deciding that the proper thing to do was let Ricky and Susan have their tea time together.

The police came the next day, Sunday, and Pop went down to the Duboises to help fill in the story. Doreen refused to let us have anything to do with that side of the whole thing, and wouldn't let us go with Pop. In a bizarre way it was heartening to see that she'd gotten some of her edge back—she called Pop "Mr. Dick Tracy" when they had the expected argument about going to the police and all in the first place. "Well, Mr. Dick Tracy," she said, "I guess this puts us out in the foxholes of the race wars of East Hartford, doesn't it? Well, isn't that nice? Kids, how would you like our house, medium or well-done?" To which Pop had responded, "Doreen, it's bad enough without scaring them."

To tell the truth, it wasn't that I was scared about race wars or anything, I was just scared that Pop would start caving in to Doreen again just because she was getting her own energy back.

I was wrong, though, because that week Pop did something completely unexpected, and completely without hesitation, that put us even closer to the 'race wars' of East Hartford than she expected. It actually put us out on the front line, almost ahead of Mr. Dubois.

The only interesting thing to say about the visit from the police was that they were very sympathetic and seemed concerned about the incidents. They hadn't yet made any progress on the case, but felt they could soon, now that more information was coming in. They did promise to assign a patrol car to drive by at regular intervals during the night to, at the very least, give the message that they were on to what was happening at the Dubois home. This was the good news.

The bad news was that while Pop and Doug and I had been conversing with Mr. Dubois in the driveway the day before, and while Susan and Ricky had their tea up in the bedroom, the phone had rung and Mrs. Dubois picked it up. The caller had hung up.

CHAPTER 7

What Pop did that was shocking was also simple. He wrote a column for the Monday edition of the newspaper devoted to the incidents brewing in our neighborhood.

What was equally shocking, I'll bet to his editor and I suspect to some of his readers, myself included, was that the column had nothing to do with humor or satire. It was a contrary sort of column for Pop.

After meeting with the police and Mr. Dubois on Sunday, Pop had gone quietly into his office for about five hours, and when he came out he'd said he was going to the newspaper for a while. He came back late that night, and in the morning, as I read it after completing my paper route, this is what appeared under his byline:

"I find it hard to place myself in the shoes and heart of another man, more so when that man's life is so utterly unlike my own. Yet among men there are certain universals that strike at the core of our nature, for which walking in another's shoes would provide no special insight.

The strongest universal among men is perhaps the need to provide for our families, to provide material comfort and paternal love for our children—those whom we see, in some ways, as weaker than ourselves. It is, for men, a need as old as time itself.

It is, for the most part, a simple exercise to wake up, go to work, make some money, and come home to dinner and conversation with the family, and feel as if you've had a complete day, a worthwhile day.

Yet this scenario is not easy for a neighbor of mine, a man who shall remain nameless, because, as you will see, it would be imprudent for me to reveal his identity. His life and the lives of his family have been threatened.

The reason for the threats is simple: He is a victim of racism. The racism results from the fact that the family is Negro.

Let me reiterate: The threats stem from racism, not from the fact that Negroes live in a neighborhood which has been, until recently, a neighborhood of whites. Negroes have nothing to do with white racial prejudice, other than acting as a catalyst for an anger that has no rational basis.

Please allow me to reiterate again: Racism is simply wild anger, and has no rational basis. This man's family has been threatened for no other reason than that they are not white. They have not hurt anyone, nor have they intruded upon anyone's property, lifestyles, or ethics. They have not hated anyone and have not kept suspiciously to themselves. They have simply had the temerity to buy a house with hard-earned money and move into it. They have merely tried to live the American dream.

The nature of the threats is particularly unsettling. The family has received crank phone calls, and a car was spray-painted with Nazi swastikas, a genuinely horrifying and cowardly act. A brick with a racist message has been thrown through their window. But perhaps the most heinous, the most tormenting threat came in the form of a burning cross left on their front lawn in the dead of night. For any Negro in America, this symbol epitomizes the viciousness of racial prejudice in all its historical context. It is the oldest, most dastardly call to violence against Negroes that we know. It is tantamount to saying, "Get out of town, or a lynching follows." It pains me that the word "lynch" is applicable in 1961.

Earlier this year President Kennedy launched a new government organization, the Peace Corps of Young Americans, with the mission to travel to developing countries to impart knowledge and peace. Many of these young people will be traveling to black African countries with that lofty goal in tow. Yet, in our own country, the "Freedom Riders" of Birmingham, Alabama, demonstrators for civil rights, have recently been attacked by mobs of whites, police, and dogs.

Sit-ins for civil rights have become part and parcel of our nation's identity, yet black men are still being lynched, hung by the neck, for no crime at all. They were simply born Negro.

It is a gross understatement to have to say that this is wrong. It is an embarrassment to have to ask this question: Where are our priorities?

For the racially prejudiced, their priorities are entirely with themselves. Racism is perhaps the world's most supremely selfish act, based on lack of understanding and extreme xenophobia. Negroes do not threaten the lives of whites, either locally, or globally. Yet we seem to be able to ascribe a set of behaviors to Negroes, and other groups for that matter, which feed our fears and allow us to act against Negroes with the impunity of the righteous, with no fear of reprisal. We've all heard, perhaps used, the stereotypes: lazy, unclean, sexually promiscuous. The list goes on.

What follows is that we go beyond the mere hate crime, beyond the mere act of malevolence toward another human being. We use stereotypes to rationalize the crime and reduce the victim to a subhuman level. We treat the crime much like one would treat the beating of a dog. We say to ourselves, in essence, "It doesn't matter, he's only a Negro."

But it does matter. It matters a great deal. Negroes serve in our armies, pay taxes, vote, send their children to schools, and share our common heritage. In short, aside from that which engenders all the pain, their skin color, they are the same as any American who simply wants to live a life.

The Negro family in my neighborhood wants just that. They cannot understand the cross, the brick through the window. Nor can I or my children understand it. It just is, for now, and it is something that shames me deeply.

Today, as this column goes to press, a wall is being erected between communist East Berlin and West Berlin. That wall is both symbolic and real, and epitomizes the world order today. Fidel Castro has made communism in Cuba a state tool, and our own government made a ridiculous effort to oust him earlier this year. Vietnam is in turmoil over communism, and we seem destined to continue a rescue effort there with all our nation's vitality. The world is polarized over the Cold War.

Yet I will contend that the greater threat sits with us here, at home.

We are a nation, a melting pot, if I might invoke one of our favorite sentiments. Our Constitution is founded on freedoms of all types and import, including the freedom to own property and live in the place of our choice. It is not just our *right*, as Americans white or black, to participate in those freedoms, it is our *duty*. It is our duty because one man's racism is another man's religious intolerance which is another man's call to tell you how you may not dress, think, or what you may not read. They are all connected, our freedoms, and as one falls, so do the rest, for all Americans, of any color. The obviation of our freedoms could become, to coin another popular phrase, a domino effect—as one falls, so falls another, and on. It is something about which we should worry mightily.

And more—it is not only our duty to participate in our freedoms, but it is our duty to protect those freedoms, and to rally to protect our neighbors' freedoms when threatened. That will begin, in my case, right now, in my own neighborhood."

I just about dropped my glass of juice.

At breakfast, Susan read it and told Pop that it really made her proud, and I said as much.

Pop's answered that it was all well and good to write something, to take a stand, but that was only the beginning and the smallest part of the battle. He asked us if we understood that, and we did, and we said we did.

Pop also said that we should expect some reactions from neighborhood people or others who might have read the column. This would turn out to be an understatement.

Doreen came down to breakfast for one of her rare appearances at that meal, bleary and full of phlegm—she seemed to be having a summer cold. She sat down with the column and her coffee. She never reads the paper, and usually reads only the first couple of lines from Pop's columns and says, "Very funny" or something, before she gets busy around the house.

But this time she became interested, real fast. The lines on her forehead started to deepen as she read on. Pop and Susan and I sat there eating toast and sort of nonchalantly waiting for a reaction, which we got.

"Well?" Pop said as she slowly put down the paper.

Doreen glanced from Pop to me to Susan, then back to Pop. She worked up a strained smile. "I really don't have much to say Walter. It's written well, and says important things. I think you knew what you wanted to say, and you said it."

"That's all?" Pop said.

"What else would you have me say?"

"I'm not sure," Pop said.

"I mean, did you write this for *me*? Did you write it so you could get a reaction from *me?*"

"No, Doreen, I suspect I wrote it for myself more than anyone. I just wanted to know, from you, what you thought of it."

"Well, Mr. Go-Tell-It-On-The-Mountain, since you asked," Doreen said, "do you think possibly, just maybe, you have put this family, your family, in danger with your preaching? Any chance of putting your loved ones first just once before you start spewing your treacly *dogma?*"

I moved a glass of orange juice away from her hand.

"Treacly?" Pop said.

"Yes, treacly!" Doreen said.

"It's not what I would call treacly," Pop said. "I thought it was pretty serious, actually. At least, I felt serious about it."

"Well, I say it's treacly. I know treacly when I see treacly. I don't have an opinion?"

"Of course you do. Anyway, Doreen, this is the first time I've ever written something like this. It's not like I jump on a soapbox every week."

"No, but you had to pick the *biggest* issue in this neighborhood to bring to that soapbox, didn't you? You picked the one issue that's going to get our house burned down, Mr. Martin Luther King. My God, Walter!"

"No one is going to burn the house down," Pop said, evenly.

"I should never have listened to you. 'Don't worry, Doreen,' you said. 'It's better that the kids get to know Ricky,' you said. 'It's part of growing up,' you said. 'No matter how you feel about Nigroes it's best to show tolerance,' you said. Then you go and write *this?"* She shook the newspaper in Pop's face. "I should have stayed at Papa's."

"Do you mean last week, or in general?" Pop said.

Susan stood up quickly and knocked her chair over in the process. She glared at Doreen, turned, and walked out of the room. She had just, in my way of thinking, committed suicide. The chair remained on its side on the floor. Doreen watched, dumbfounded, as Susan left the room.

"There, it's done," Doreen said. "You've succeeded in turning my own daughter against me!"

"Dub," Pop said, "go and join your sister.

"You did this just to get at me, didn't you?" Doreen said.

"Of course not. With all due respect, Doreen, I don't use my column to exorcise family demons. Dub, leave."

"Family demons? *Family demons*?" she said.

"Dub!" Pop said. I excused myself and took off.

They fought of course, and it was more or less a blowout. I can't say that Pop was without fault either, in this one. I mean, he'd had this look in his eye as he waited for Doreen's reaction, as if he'd wanted to see her fly off the handle, as if that would somehow justify his nobility even more. Don't ask me how, but he had the look.

Later Pop came and apologized to Susan and me, and said that maybe Doreen did have some relevant points after all, and he started tugging at that ear. He asked us to excuse her, and said that he might have acted too quickly on the whole thing, which caused my heart to sink an inch or two until he said, "But the column is out, and I stand by it. You two will have to make up your own minds."

He needn't have said that because, as far as we were concerned, our minds had been made up a long time ago.

Doreen hadn't gone after Susan, and I figure she'd pretty much seen that she'd have to give up on us and either, as she said, go back to Grandpa Constantine's or resign herself to Pop's stand on the Dubois issue. I mean, she had begun to resign herself to Ricky's presence before we went to Kelly's, and things had been more or less better up until now. But the point was that the incidents weren't going to stop, and the situation was just going to get thicker. Maybe Doreen needed to make a decision.

As we expected, the phone rang later that morning, and it was Mr. Dubois calling from work. Pop picked up the phone and said, "Yes? Herb, how are you?"

"I appreciate that, Herb," he said.

"Yes, perhaps we should," he said. "What time do you get home from work?"

"Fine," he said, "I'll be there at about five-thirty."

And I knew that that's where I'd be at five-thirty as well.

Later, Susan called Ricky and they went to the pool for a while, and I went over and knocked at Doug's door, wondering why he wasn't out at the lemonade stand. Mrs. Hammer came to the door and said, "Dub, I saw your father's column today."

"Yes, ma'am," I said.

"He's a brave man," she said, smiling.

"Yes, ma'am."

"But you watch yourself. There will be people who know who he's talking about."

"Yes, ma'am," I said.

"Even the people who've done those terrible things to the Duboises, they might cause trouble again."

"I expect they might," I said.

"You don't seem worried," she said. "That's good."

"We've got nothing to fear but fear itself," I said.

"You've been waiting for a chance to say that, haven't you?" she said.

"Yes ma'am," I said.

"Doug," she shouted to the back of the house.

Doug came to the door and Mrs. Hammer said, "Now I want you two boys to listen. I have a good feeling and a bad feeling about today. You just keep your heads above water and don't get into any situations with anyone. If someone mentions something about the column or the Dubois family, you just let it be. Doug, do you understand?"

Doug looked confused. "Who's going to say anything about the column?"

"You just be careful. This whole thing will play itself out in time, and you don't need to go looking for trouble, hear?"

"Okay," Doug said, but he still looked confused.

"What I mean, Doug," she said as if speaking to a retard, which Doug could be sometimes, he really could, "is you should try extra hard not to get into any confrontations today."

"Okay, okay," Doug said

We left her and decided to go for a bike ride, with no particular destination in mind. It was a damn near perfect summer day.

"What happened to the lemonade stand?" I said as we got on our bikes.

"Called it quits for a while," Doug said. "I got thirty-six dollars saved up for the circus and that should last me the week. It comes in just a few days, Dub."

"You going to go every day?" I said.

"Sure, aren't you?" he said. "At a week, that's about five dollars a day. The rides are a quarter, and the freak shows are fifty cents, so I figure that's about twelve rides plus two shows a day, plus hot dogs and something left over for games and stuff. Piece of cake."

"What about the Big Top Show, that's a buck admission," I said.

"My mother will spring for that," he said. "She's good for it, because she likes to go with me sometimes. She'll say that my Dad sent the money or something like that." A dark look crossed his face. "Anyway, I'm going every day, that's for sure."

"So am I," I said. I took a momentary sojourn as my thoughts switched to the smells, sounds, and heat of the circus.

"The Dog-Faced Boy, Dub. It'll be great."

"It will," I agreed.

We took off and ended up heading toward the old Nike Site.

The Nike Site is about as odd and peculiar a place as you'll find in the state of Connecticut. It's actually a small, abandoned military installation—one of many, apparently, that were set up in New England during the early '50s—that was responsible, primarily, for pointing missiles at Russia. Or maybe it was there just to give the *illusion* of pointing missiles at Russia—I don't know because ever since I've been aware of the Nike Site it's been abandoned, and I've never seen a missile there to save my life. So to speak.

The Nike Site sits up on a hill, in a non-residential section of town, near the high school and the town dump. The entire thing is underground. You get to it by passing through some gates and riding a crumbling road up a long hill to the doorways. Then you head down a set of stairs behind a metal door that has long been pried open. It's dark underground, and the damp passageway smells of mud, candles, and cigarette butts, because this is the cool place for the kids to hang out. In fact, many, including Big Farley and his crew, regard the Nike Site as their own personal clubhouse, and post signs in and around the area to that effect. "Don't Tread On Me" a painted cardboard sign says. Another says "Home Of The East Hartford Vipers. Trespassers Beware." One, which I think is Big Farley's sign, says, succinctly, "Get Out."

At the bottom of the stairs is a long, thin corridor, and off to the sides of the corridor are small rooms, which were probably used for offices at one time.

Then, of course, there are the rats.

If there's one thing I hate, other than dirty hands, it's rats. I suspect the two are related, at any rate. I can take furry animals and mice and hamsters and the like, but rats have got a hold on me I've never been able to explain. It's not just that they're dirty and ugly and that they caused the Black Plague, or that their tiny pink eyes and twitching noses practically define stupidity and banality and evil and all that. It's mostly that they represent natural selection out of control. I mean, they breed like rats. They're everywhere, or could be everywhere, and I have this image of them taking over the world someday if we don't poison them all pretty much instantly. The image isn't a pretty one, but I can't help thinking that *because* they're so stupid and evil that they really just *have* to win in the end. That's just the way life is, most of the time. I'd read *1984* a while back, and I don't mind telling you that the rat scene was pretty chilling and grim. I tried a couple of times to read it without breaking out in a cold sweat, but I only managed to get through it after putting the book down about a hundred times. I mean it, I really get unnerved about rats. And they're all over the Nike Site. You can't see them all the time, but I know they're there.

Anyway, at the end of the Nike Site corridor is another door, and behind that door is a short railroad track that runs at right angles to the corridor. This is where the real stink is. It smells like a vat of diesel fuel and cat turds, and it burns your eyes to walk through the place. Kids are always lighting matches in there to see if anything blows up, because if there's anywhere in the world that seems like it'll blow up, it's that underground railroad track. Which makes lighting matches in there about as smart as getting down and licking the track, but that's the way kids seem to think, anyway. I've lit a match or two in there myself, come to think of it.

The railroad track is about fifty yards long and leads from a gigantic metal door, almost like a vault door, to a huge trap door at the other end, which leads to ground level. There's some kind of hydraulic lift at the bottom of the trap door, and the nearest I can figure is, in the event of a Russian attack, they were supposed to wheel the missiles, which were called Nikes, from that vault along the track and onto the lift, where the trap door would open and the missiles would take their position, pointed at Moscow or someplace.

Only, we never saw any missiles, and we were never able to open that vault though God knows we tried with everything we had, including M-80s, rocks, and loose gunpowder, which is why the track smelled like a battle field.

As far as the missiles go, I truly doubt that the military actually left any behind anyway. I mean, *that* would have been beyond irresponsible, even for the government. At any rate, the whole installation was apparently pretty much discarded when Nike missiles became obsolete, and newer, larger missiles required newer, larger bases. When the Army shut down the Nike Site and thought they'd sealed it off, they had made plans to dismantle the underground buildings and fill in the whole business with dirt. But it hadn't happened yet, much to the town's dismay.

I have to admit that even though it was fun to hang around at the Nike Site, rats aside, the thought of missiles being launched from our backyard into the plumes of an atomic war was not the most settling of thoughts. It was a contrary sort of logic, actually. I agreed with Pop when he said, "They set up an installation for our protection and it turns us into a target."

Doug and I made our way toward the site, through side streets and woods, until we came to the gate with the official sign that said "Stay Out Per Order of the United States Army. Trespassers Will Be Prosecuted to the Fullest Extent of the Law." Which was a hoot. Isn't it always true that the bigger the threat, the easier it is to break the rule? The gate was wide open and had been for years. I always thought that the Army should, at the very least, remove the sign just to save a little face.

We rode past the sign and up the hundred feet or so to the top of the hill where the Nike Site's underground passages began. From this vantage point we could see row upon row of gray, tiny track houses—our neighborhoods. The whole panorama looked like the crowded squares of a massive Monopoly game, and I don't mind saying it was always awful depressing to look at it. The towers and stacks of Pratt rose in the background, idle now, and for the next week, while the factory took its annual summer break.

No bikes sat outside the main building, so we figured it was safe to go down the stairs and explore a little. The great irony was that it wasn't the Army you had to worry about when exploring the Nike Site, it was other gangs of kids. Gangs like Big and his thugs, who claimed it as their own turf. The real danger was going down inside, and having another group come along after you, through the one and only opening to the tunnel. Then you'd be trapped, and trouble would follow. To tell the truth, it really didn't make much sense going to the Nike Site, but because it was there, it didn't make much sense not to go.

The thing is, this time we'd come unprepared—I'd never gone into the corridor without a flashlight or candles before, so I wasn't sure what we'd be able to see. Or, for that matter, what we'd not be able to see.

We opened the door and Doug immediately stepped on what first appeared to be a deflated balloon on the steps. But taking a closer look it turned out to be, I swear this is true, a used rubber. Which is possibly the most disgusting thing in the galaxy.

Of course, that type of thing didn't matter to Doug Hammer. He picked it up.

"Jesus, you've got to be insane," I said. "That has *sperm* in it."

"And a lot of it, too," he said, proudly. "Look," and he thrust it in my face. One or two tiny pubic hairs adhered to the crusty outside of the translucent, sagging receptacle.

"Doug," I said, and flinched. "Just take it out of my face."

"Besides," he said. "This isn't exactly sperm, or spermatozoa as it's known in the scientific community. Spermatozoa, you might be interested to know, is the plural of spermatozoon. No Dub, this is spermatic *fluid,* or semen, the liquid medium of spermatozoa."

"Where'd you learn this?" I said.

"What, a guy can't be smart? I read up on things that are important."

"Yeah? Since when?"

"Dub, does one have to have a specific time for self-improvement? It's never too late to start educating yourself. We have so little time and so much to know. Repeat after me: encyclopedias."

I was dumbfounded, in a way. So I repeated it. "Encyclopedias."

"Besides," he said, "admit it. This is keen. Admit it."

"Okay, okay. What are you going to do with it, take it home?"

"Yeah, I'll show it to Lance, he'll think it's keen." Lance

was apparently Doug's best buddy now, even though he'd been beaten to a pulp within that week's time by the very hands that were now holding the slimy thing.

He took his handkerchief from his hip pocket, folded the grimy rubber carefully, and wrapped it up. He put the handkerchief back in his hip pocket.

This took the cake. "Remind me, please, never to shake hands with you again," I said. "You know when you sit down that's going to leak all over the place."

"That's why I wrapped it."

"You're carrying a leaky, used rubber around in a handkerchief. If it wasn't so unbelievable it'd be nauseating."

"Hey, it's in my pocket, not yours."

"You're carrying *spermatic fluid* in your back pocket for Christ's sake."

"Very good. Now stop whining and let's go."

We walked down the dank, concrete stairway to the bottom floor. The only light we had was from the open doorway above, and that dissipated as we made our way along the hollow corridor. In the distance I heard rats scuttle and scratch as they got out of our way.

Our voices echoed off the walls and I thought I could hear water dripping somewhere ahead of us. The walls themselves were damp and gooey, as if they'd grown wet fur. My heart was beating to break my ribs, and the whole thing was a horrible movie cliché, it really was.

"I wish I brought my flashlight," I said.

"For what?" Doug said. "It's more fun this way."

"Sure is," I said to the back of his head, which I couldn't see.

"Well, maybe we'll find some more good stuff," he said.

"Not without a flashlight," I said. "Rats are everywhere anyway. I don't know what's worse, not seeing them, or catching their diseased little eyes in a beam of light."

"We can go back home," Doug said, "and get our flashlights."

Or, I thought, we can just go back home. There didn't seem to be much happening at the Nike Site at any rate. The rats be damned, let them win again.

"Okay," I said.

From behind us, from the top of the stairs, a singsong voice drifted through the corridor.

"Well, hello, Dub," it hissed, "Hello, Doug Fatbutt. Guess what? You're dead, D-E-D." High-pitched, screeching laughter followed.

A beam of sunlight and a long, human shadow loomed from the door on top and ended in a splash at the bottom of the stairs. Without being able to see Doug, I could feel his eyes stretch wide open, as did mine.

"It's Big," Doug hissed.

"We're dead," I whispered.

"Shit," Doug said.

"Hello, boys," Big sang from the top of the stairs. "Come out, come out, wherever you are."

"He wants to kill us," I whispered. "And do you know why he wants to kill us?"

"Because we're alive?" Doug said. His voice trembled, but only slightly.

"No, because you called him a monkey that day," I said. "If we die, it's you who killed us."

"Shut up," Doug said. I heard him breath deeply through his nose. "Rage confuses the heart of the beast," he said. "Not to worry."

"Oh, boys," Big snarled in a nasal voice. "Afraid to show your scaggy faces?"

"'Rage confuses the heart of the beast'?" I whispered.

"What, it's a crime to be poetic once in a while?" Doug said. "You're the only one who can be smart? You only do it to impress Rick—"

"We don't have all day, dickheads," Big sung out.

"We are dead meat," I said. "No, make that *confused* dead meat."

"He's bluffing," Doug said. "He won't come down after us."

"How do you know that?" I said.

"Because if they had a flashlight, they'd have come down here and beat the piss out of us by now. But they don't, so he knows we have the advantage down here. Our eyes have adjusted to the dark. They'd be walking into an ambush, blind."

I had to admit, Doug's reasoning was good. Big would have to fight us on top if he was going to fight us at all.

"I wonder if Big read Pop's article?" Why I said that I'll never know.

"Big can't even read his own name," Doug said.

"Oh faggots," Big sang. His gang cackled ruthlessly. They apparently didn't see the irony in a bunch of guys who hang around together every single minute of the waking day calling us faggots. "Come up and die!"

Doug took in a sharp breath. "Well, we've got to do something," he whispered. "And I know what it is. Carpe diem." He shouted, "Big, is that you?"

"Who'd you think it was, wanker, the milkman?" Yuks all around up there signaled another hugely successful joke.

"No, but from the smell that's coming from the top of the stairs," Doug said, "I thought you were a great big *enema bag!"*

Complete silence stopped time for a moment. It was a long moment, sort of like a couple of days on death row. Big, however, rallied, as we knew he would.

"A what?" Big said.

"Okay, then, a *douche bag!"* Doug said.

"Now we are truly dead," I whispered.

"You *die!"* Big growled.

"I told you," I whispered.

"Don't worry," Doug whispered.

"Come up here and say that, fuck-face," Big said.

"Yeah," echoed the whiny voice of a lackey.

"Don't worry?" I said. The beam of light from the top of the stairs shifted. Big moved around up there, pacing like an animal, punching one fist into the other.

"Yeah, don't worry," Doug whispered. "It's under control."

"Remember Mr. *Hwan?*" Big said. "You lied to me, assholes, and I don't like that."

"Come down here and we'll talk it over," Doug shouted at the stairs.

"Doug," I said, "I think I need to advise you that that's a bad idea."

"He'll never come down," Doug whispered.

"You're dead, *chumps,*" Big said. "We can wait all day."

A voice from the lackeys said, "All day? I can't wait all day. I got a Little League game—"

His voice was cut off by a slap. "Shut up!" Big snapped.

I had to admit that Big had a point. He probably would wait all day to kill us, and even into the night. Big was nothing if not determined. And he had a major score to settle with us.

"What, you're scared to come down here, *dork?"* Doug said.

"Like I said, we can wait all day." Big's voice echoed down the dark corridor like a bad wind. Then, we heard him say softly to one of the gang, "Ride home and get a flashlight."

"That's it, we've got to go up now," Doug said. "Otherwise, we die like rats down here."

"No way," I said. "We wait."

"Don't worry," Doug said. "I said I got it under control."

"You guys down there with your jigaboo friend?" Big said.

That was it. I felt my face turn red. And I was dead anyway, so why not let Big enjoy a bit of overkill? "At least we got friends who aren't *retarded*," I said.

"Wow," Doug said, and he actually laughed.

"What are you going to do about it, queer," Big said.

"It's time," Doug said.

"We're in for a huge fight up there," I said. I imagined what I would look like with a broken nose. I imagined what I'd feel like with a broken nose.

"I said don't worry," Doug said. "Just stay behind me, and do what I do. Grab my shirt."

Doug moved toward the sunbeam, quietly, and I held on to the back of his shirt, psyching myself for the fight. I tried to focus on Ricky. I whispered, "Jigaboo, eh? So it's jigaboo, is it?" Inside, I thought, "Oh God, oh God, oh God."

At the bottom of the stairs, Doug said, "Big, if you're a man, you'll let us get to the top of the stairs before you jump us." He paused for effect, and to let Big take it in.

At the top of the stairs, Big was huger than usual. He had on a pair of overalls and no shirt, and looked, for the life of me, like Lil' Abner with a bad attitude.

"Okay, shit-for-brains," he snarled. "Come on up."

"Don't trust him," I whispered to Doug.

When we stepped onto the stairs, the sunlight momentarily blinded us, and I could feel Doug, just for a moment, lose control. He hesitated, then started slowly up, one step at a time.

Big burst into laughter. "Well, Dub, looks like you got your faggot friend to protect you again." The gang laughed like half-witted lemurs.

"Don't let go," Doug hissed under his breath. He rubbed his eyes.

We reached the top step, and the gang took a step back to let us emerge. Their faces were tight and fists were balled, and two of them had baseball bats. They had that smug look of the courageous. We had that tense look of the hopelessly outnumbered. Big had a sickening, ugly smile on his face.

Doug looked left and right, then made a quick movement and whipped his hand around to his back pocket, as if going for a knife. The gang reacted appropriately, springing back a couple of steps.

Doug whipped the handkerchief from behind, flipped it open, and yanked out the used rubber with his right hand. He held it up.

"What the-" Big said.

"You know what this is, don't you?" Doug said.

The boys stared, dumbfounded.

"This is spermatic fluid, more commonly known as semen. One step closer, and you get it in the face!"

"Jesus Christ," one of the boys said, "it's full!"

"You got that right," Doug said, and thrust it out at the boy. The whole gang jumped back another step. Doug held the used rubber out like a wooden cross and turned slowly toward our bikes, which were parked against a tree. I turned with him. "One move and your name is Spermatozoa Face," he said.

One of the gang turned and leaned against a tree, green around the eyes.

"Jump him!" Big said, to no one in particular. No one moved. We continued to circle toward our bikes.

"Sure, jump me," Doug said, "get a good taste of it." The boy against the tree threw his hands to his mouth.

"Throw the bat at him!" Big yelled.

"Go ahead," I said, "then we ride off with your bat, too."

"Now, we're going to walk over to our bikes real slow," Doug said, "and you are going to let us ride away, because if you don't, someone's going to get this prophylactic, more commonly known as a rubber, stuck right on his forehead."

"Someone jump him!" Big yelled again.

"Come on Big, you jump me," Doug said. "Did you know that seminal fluid, more commonly known as jizz, makes you blind, and then you turn into a homosexual?"

"Bullshit," Big hissed.

"Try it, then," I said. I had begun to enjoy this.

"Don't make you into no homo," one of the boys said.

"Yeah? Have you ever spilled any of it on yourself?" Doug said. "You could be one right now."

The boy held up his hand and stared at it in horror.

Doug turned violently to another boy, who jumped back three feet. "Or you, you try it," he said. "Go ahead. But just make sure you stay away from your sister's dresses, because you're going to be wearing them real soon."

"Goddamnit, throw a rock at him!" Big said.

The boys stood still, mesmerized by the sagging rubber and its apparently toxic contents. And they knew it was Doug Hammer they were dealing with, a reputedly very crazy person.

Doug and I moved quickly toward our bikes, still facing the circled boys. No one made a move toward us. We reached the bikes with Doug still thrusting the rubber like a sword.

"Now, we're going to get on these bikes and ride away, and if anyone follows, I'll make sure this ends up in their ear," Doug said. "And there's more where this came from." He patted his hip pocket.

"Christ," one of the boys whispered, awestruck.

Big was purple with rage, and spittle formed at the corners of his mouth. He shook his fist in the clichéd motion of a beaten bully, which he was. "I'll get you later, I'll get you good," he screamed. "Big time!"

We mounted our bikes and backed away, the rubber acting as a beacon in front of us. Doug rode one-handed, thrusting the vile condom as he would a spear, and I stuck close behind. We rode past them, their jaws slack with wonder, as they remained silent, impotent, and defeated.

As we wheeled down the hill, I looked back over my shoulder just in time to see a rock sail through the air. It missed by at least five feet, and I let out a stupid laugh, loud enough for Big to hear.

We pedaled like rats out of hell. Which we were, in a way.

Doug tossed the condom to the side within minutes after leaving the Nike Site.

"Served its purpose," he said over his shoulder.

When we arrived home, breathless, it was clear that the Farley gang hadn't followed. But we knew that situation would be short-lived. They were bound, by honor and pride now, to follow. Maybe not physically follow us that day, but they would always be there, somewhere, ready to take us on.

Doug's mother's car was gone, and we walked into his house.

"I need to wash my hands," Doug said.

"There's a switch," I said.

When Doug came out of the bathroom, he did something he'd never done before. He threw his arms around me and gave me a hug, a big hug. "Dub, did you see the look on their faces? It was like I was holding a piece of radiation or something. Damn!"

"You did a great job," I said. "I'm impressed. I thought we were dead."

"Big Farley, you mean, stupid, son of a bitch," Doug shouted to the ceiling. "We got you *good*."

"But, maybe not for long," I said, looking out the window.

"Are they out there?"

"No, but they will be," I said. "Look, Doug, we both know they'll be back, somehow, someday. We'd better think about this."

"So, we'll get by on our wits. We did it before, we'll do it again."

"You did it, and it was good work. But we'd better prepare for the worst."

"Such as?"

"Well, you saw what they did to Ricky's family. They might do the same to us, to our houses. For different reasons."

"You still think it was them?" he said.

"Who knows? You heard what Big called Ricky."

"Yeah, but everybody says that," Doug said.

"You don't think he did it?" I said.

"Well, I mean he's scum and everything, but I don't know.

He still seems too dumb to have done it. And what about the phone calls? Remember, Big doesn't have the number."

Suddenly, I remembered Pop's meeting with Mr. Dubois at five-thirty. "Hey," I said, and I told Doug the story of the phone call that morning. "Want to come?"

"I don't know where Mom is," he said, "I should probably wait around for her."

"There's a note on the fridge. You walked right by it."

The note said, "'Out shopping, I'll be back at five-thirty, dinner at six, Love, Mom.'"

"What time is it now?" Doug said. We looked at the clock above the kitchen table. It was four-thirty. We decided to go over to Ricky's place right away, partially to be able to tell the story of our second defeat of Big Farley, and partially to just hang out with her for a while and all. I mean, that was my intent, anyway, and I'm sure it was Doug's as well.

Susan was there, and Ricky greeted us at the door in her usual way.

"Why, Doug and Dub, what a pleasure. Come in."

They'd been in Ricky's room talking with a Ouija board, and Susan flipped her hair in recognition as we came in.

Immediately, Doug started to blurt out our story with typical enthusiasm and abandon. And, I don't know what had got into me, but I suddenly remembered and realized with horror that he would have to talk about the condom, the *used* condom, in order to get the story straight. *In front of Ricky.* This was not only going to be disgusting, it would be embarrassing as well.

"Uh, Doug," I interrupted.

"Not to worry," he said, hardly missing a beat.

There was no need to worry. Doug's prowess at the story board shone through again. He conveniently changed the condom to a stinking, dead rat, which was still disgusting, but not nearly as horrendous as the alternative. And he added a few details as well. He said that he'd managed to get in a swing on Big, and knocked him flat on his butt, and managed to produce a skinned knuckle to prove it. Where he got the skinned knuckle I'll never know, but it was there and served its purpose.

He also said that I was the one who found the rat in the first place, although he'd carried it, and that it was my idea to use it as a shield. It was a nice gesture, and I believe he felt he was doing me a favor in a perverse sort of way, but I caught Ricky looking at me with a wrinkled nose and it made me sort of shudder.

We left out the "jigaboo" part out of the story, although I'm not sure it wasn't because we wouldn't have been able to get the word out anyway. At least in front of Ricky. And we didn't talk about the future of our lives on this planet, because I could see in Susan's eyes that she understood the grave consequences of having crossed Big Farley—not once, but twice, in recent months.

In fact, later that night before we went to bed, she would say, "Aren't you afraid of Big?"

"Of course," I would say. "I'm numbed with fear."

"See, you're being sarcastic again," she said. "That's what always gets you in trouble. Next time you see him, you'll mouth off as usual and get your head bashed in. You do the same thing with Mom, Mr. Wise Guy."

"Mr. Wise Guy?"

Of course, Susan would be right. I do have this problem with running off at the mouth sometimes, and I've always known deep inside that it is a coward's way out. Really, when you think about it, Doreen and Big Farley are sort of easy targets for sarcasm, so there's no percentage in making fun of them. I mean, Doug is always mouthing off as well, but he's got the goods to back it up, meaning no rational fear of anyone or anything.

Me, I'd just been lucky, at least as far as Big Farley is concerned. But I have always known that being a wise guy takes very little intelligence, and, in the end, very little courage.

The girls were impressed by the story, at least they indicated they were. Ricky's comment was, "That's very brave and all, but have you washed your hands, Doug?"

I *knew* we had something in common.

We hung around in Ricky's bedroom until we heard Mr. Dubois's car pull up. Ricky jumped up and ran down to give him that old hug and all. Within a minute or so Pop came walking up the driveway. We all came down to the living room, where we were joined by Mrs. Dubois and her mother, who seemed tired and moved slowly. This was apparently going to be some sort of meeting to deal with the ordeal of the family Dubois.

"So, the war tribune convenes," Mr. Dubois said, in a forced-cheery sort of way.

"Let's hope it never comes to that," Pop said.

"Walter, I'd like to say that I appreciate your not mentioning our name in your column this morning," Mr. Dubois said.

"It would have served no purpose," Pop said. "It might have even brought more incidents."

Mrs. Dubois stood up and asked, "And we appreciate the sentiment as well. Now, would anyone like tea or coffee?"

"Beer, Walter?" Mr. Dubois said.

"Tea is fine," Pop said.

"What about the kids?" Mr. Dubois said.

"I'll get some Cokes for them," Mrs. Dubois said.

"I mean, what about the kids being here?" Mr. Dubois said.

"Ricky will stay," Mrs. Dubois said. "She's already part of it."

Ricky said, "Please?"

"Sure, sugar," Mr. Dubois said, "it's okay."

Pop shot us a questioning glance. "I'd like to stay, too, if it's okay," I said. Susan and Doug nodded.

"Okay, then, a committee it is," Pop said.

Mrs. Dubois turned to get the drinks when her mother, Mrs. Oliphant, slowly stood up. When she reached her height, which was about five feet, she sighed slightly.

"I would like to say something," she said. I had never heard her voice before. It was heavy, and had the thickness of age. "If you would indulge me." We all stopped and stared.

She cleared her throat. "I'm not an educated person, Mr. Teed, but I have seen some things."

"Please, call me Walter," Pop said.

"I suppose you know that a Negro woman my age never calls a white man by his first name," she said. "It don't matter, really, I'd rather call you Mr. Teed anyway."

Pop didn't quite know what to make of this. "Sure," he said, tugging at his ear.

"Now, this is what I think, and I'll say this and take my leave because I'm not much for meetings and I have been in these kinds of things all too often, when I was younger. Secret meetings. Secret meetings to help someone out, usually to help a woman whose husband was beat, taken away, or dead. Harsh meetings they were, too. About how to make it right with the whites and the police for what they done. Although we never got a good answer for that, never."

She shifted her stance, but kept her hands clasped in front of her, as if addressing an audience, which she was.

"I think you done a brave thing by writing in the newspaper," she continued, "and I think you think you done a good thing. You said it well, and that's commendable. But I wonder, mind you I'm just wondering, what you meant by 'protect our neighbors' freedoms?' I wonder how you going to do that with this family, Mr. Teed. Who you going to protect?

"I was born in 1889. My mother was born to freed slaves. So was my father. Back then no white man ever married a Negro. Oh, they had kids all the time, going back to slave days, but no whites and blacks ever got married. Just wasn't the thing to do back then. Still isn't today. Besides, where would they live, who going to be their friends? Whites or blacks? How their kids going to be treated, white or black?

"We all know the answer to that. Black. When a white marries a black, he's a black man and that's a fact. Kids, too. I'm not saying good or bad, but people got to put a man somewhere, so they put him black, simple as that. That's part of what happening in this neighborhood.

"At first, I didn't want Herbert for my girl," she said and pointed to Mr. Dubois. He said nothing, as if he'd expected this, as if it was part of the meeting. "I opposed it, and my daughter and him can tell you that is true as the day I was born. I knew something like this going to happen someday. I knew that someday all hell going to break loose.

"But then I see that he's a good man, and I see that my girl and him got a love, a hard love, between them. And I got to keep my peace because I know that how the Lord intended it to be. And when I see my baby granddaughter here, Ricky, I know they done the right thing, and we just got to live with the rest."

At this, Mrs. Oliphant swept the room with her eyes.

"So, I'm not blaming you for our troubles, or even whites in general, and I'm not blaming this marriage. We made our bed here and we got to lie in it. Besides, I'm too old to set blame, maybe even too old to fight. But I still got to wonder something. Do you understand yourself what you getting in to?

"Maybe you even got to ask yourself this: If my son-in-law was a Negro man, if we was all black in this family, would you have come to us? Would you have written that column? And if it happened across town in some other neighborhood, would you make the same promise, would you do the same thing?"

She paused, and Pop looked at her in wonderment.

"In my day, Mr. Teed, we got used to whites helping us fight our fights. We got used to whites making waves for us and then patting us on the head and sending us back to darkie-town, as if we was all poor, helpless children. I'm sure you understand. I don't know about how you think, but maybe you need to question this yourself.

"In the old days they taught us never to look a white man direct in the eye, or he going to make trouble for you. But I got to look you straight in the eye right now, Mr. Teed. I got to ask you this for your own good, and for the good of this family here. Do you understand what you saying when you promise to help us fight? It mean you got to look at yourself and wonder why *you* doing it, why *you* feel this need. Forget these human rights you been talking about. What is it makes *you* want to be here right now?"

She breathed heavily, and nodded her head. It was amazing. I wondered how I ever could have had that fantasy about Big and his gang pushing her around and kicking her and all. It seemed impossible now.

Everyone in the room, save Mrs. Oliphant, was dumbfounded.

"Mama," Mrs. Dubois said, softly. "I'm sure Mr. Teed has good intentions."

"I'm not saying they're bad intentions," Mrs. Oliphant said. "I'm only asking Mr. Teed, and the rest of you, what you think you can do about these crosses and bricks and things. And," she turned again to Pop, "*why.*"

"But," she continued, "no need to convince me. What going to happen going to happen, and nothing I can say going to change that. I just think you all got to be clear with one another. Because it going to get worse."

Pop cleared his throat. "They're good questions, Mrs. Oliphant," he said.

"I don't mean to scare these children," Mrs. Oliphant said, "but the truth is the truth, and you got to get the truth straight in yourselves first.

"Now, I'm going to lay me down for a bit. These bones are older than that Constitution you mentioned, Mr. Teed."

She turned and walked slowly up the stairs, a bent, white-haired old woman with much on her mind. We all watched her struggle, silently, step by step. Then she was gone.

"She's outspoken, she's always been that way," Mrs. Dubois said. "I hope—"

"But she's right," Pop interrupted. He drummed his fingers on his knee. He thought for a moment. "The truth of the matter is, I don't know why I want to help you. I don't know why I wrote that column, and I don't know if Herb's being white has anything to do with it. I don't. I mean, for whatever reasons, I consider us friends now."

Mr. Dubois regarded Pop for a moment. "That's good enough for me," he said. "But I want you to know that I am prepared to fight my own fight, if it comes to that. And I am also prepared to send my family home to Louisiana, if it comes to that."

Ricky took a sharp breath.

"And our kids are friends," Pop said.

Mr. Dubois hesitated. "Well. Do you think this column is going to do good or bad?" he said.

Pop was deep in a private thought, staring at the floor.

Mr. Dubois cleared his throat.

"Pop," Susan said.

"Pardon?" Pop said.

"Do you think the column is going to help?" Mr. Dubois said, softly.

"I am hoping it will shame them into rethinking their actions," Pop said, "but perhaps that's my own hubris talking. And I'm also hoping it will be a call to arms, of sorts, for this neighborhood. What we need here is some community action, some solidarity that will send a message to the vandals to stop it."

"That would be nice," Mrs. Dubois said, "but personally I don't see myself canvassing the neighborhood asking for their support."

"I agree, Nancy," Mr. Dubois said. "We don't even know these people. And they don't know us. Not yet, anyway."

"No, asking for help wouldn't work," Pop said. "That would be beneath you, all of you. Besides, who knows who in the neighborhood might be involved."

Mr. Dubois raised his eyebrows.

"I've changed my thinking about that, Herb," Pop said. "I have to agree with you that it could be anyone, unfortunately. God knows."

I thought that was an interesting twist on Pop's previous idealism. I wondered who brought him around to the realization. I had a hunch it could've been someone close to home.

"But it wouldn't be beneath me to ask," Pop said.

"What do you mean?" Mr. Dubois said.

"I mean that I could canvas the neighborhood myself. I could make the rounds, learn a few things. I could call a meeting."

"What sort of meeting?"

"I could call a meeting of anyone interested in pitching in to help watch your house," Pop said. He paused to let the idea sink in. "It's a long shot, but maybe worth a try. The incidents happen at night, and even though the police have promised to step up their patrols around here, I'll bet that if someone was outside of your house, parked, let's say, from about midnight until five or so in the morning, that would deter the vandals. They're cowards, we know that. They wouldn't try anything with someone parked outside the house."

Mr. Dubois considered the plan slowly. "You'd call a neighborhood meeting to see if anyone will help us stand guard over the house?"

"Yes."

"And what will you do when no one shows up?"

"What if some do show up?"

"That's asking a lot in the name of idealism," Mr. Dubois said. "Walter, I don't know anyone here except you."

"It's worth a try, Herb."

"And let's say one or two people agree to help us do that. How do we treat the others who don't show up at the meeting. Like suspects?"

Pop contemplated that.

"No, Walter," Mr. Dubois continued, "it's noble, but unworkable. Besides, what are we going to do, stand guard over the house every night for the rest of our lives?"

Pop sat back in his chair. "Okay," he said, "then please accept my help in watching the house, at least for a while. Maybe we can catch them in the act and stop this madness."

Mr. Dubois smiled. "Well, I can do that. You and I can stand guard over the house. But only for a while. We could hide in the bushes and—"

"No bushes," Mrs. Dubois said. "There will be no war games on my property. Sit in the car in front, with the doors locked, that's fine. Take note of strange cars driving by at three in the morning, that's okay. But no skulking in the bushes."

Both Pop and Mr. Dubois nodded, as if they shared some secret joke. I thought it wasn't so much a joke as it was a couple of older guys sitting around remembering things they did when they were kids.

"Can I help?" I said.

"Yeah, can I help, too?" Doug said.

Both men said, in unison, "No."

They talked for a while longer, and finally Doug had to excuse himself to go home for dinner. Pop and Mr. Dubois sat for a few minutes longer to make up a night watch schedule. Pop would take the first shift, from midnight to three, Mr. Dubois would take the next shift, from three to six in the morning, and they would alternate daily. They decided to do it for two weeks, and then take a look at the situation later to see if there was any reason to continue or change the hours.

They agreed that they would sit in their cars in front of the house. Mr. Dubois would even move his car from the driveway to the street on his shift. They would take note of any strange cars in the neighborhood. This would be especially easy for Pop, since he knew every car, and they figured they would begin to sort out the familiar cars soon enough. Like Mr. Swan's car, which would pass by every weekday morning at about two, when he began his shift at the Wonder Bread Bakery.

Mr. Dubois volunteered to call the police to tell them about the arrangement, so that the police wouldn't be surprised when they started to see cars parked outside the house at all hours during their patrols.

Also, they agreed that, in the event of any danger, they would use their horns to alert the household. Ricky suggested a code, something like one if by car and two if by bike or that type of thing, but her father said if it got to the point of horn blowing, it wouldn't matter how the hell someone got there. Ricky seemed to get real quiet after that, as if she were about to burst out crying, and to tell the truth, I wouldn't have blamed her if she did. I sort of felt uneasy myself.

They decided they would not carry weapons; neither of them owned pistols or rifles anyway, but they figured weapons would defeat the purpose of the vigil anyway. Besides, they didn't know a damn thing about weapons at any rate, and were more likely to shoot off their own feet before deterring any vandals. I said hey what about a baseball bat at least, thinking about Big and his bat-wielding thugs, and they said maybe, they'd think about it.

It was time to go, and I knew Pop faced a much bigger challenge at home trying to explain the whole arrangement to Doreen. I preferred not to think about it.

I said good-bye to Ricky, who seemed subdued and not at all herself.

On the way out the door, Pop turned to Mr. Dubois and said, "What about those phone calls? Any more?"

"As a matter of fact, yes," Mrs. Dubois said. "One this morning."

Pop shook his head. "Maybe it's time to think about changing the number again. This time, don't give it to anyone."

"What about you?"

"No one," Pop said.

Who was it? We had the number, Mr. Dubois's boss had the number, and Doug, he also had it. And, as Doug had pointed out, Big Farley did not have the number. Go figure, I thought.

CHAPTER 8

The next morning I awoke with this thought: The circus would be in town in four days.

It had sort of snuck up on me, with the events around the neighborhood and everything, even though it seemed like Doug had been reminding me of it every day for the last twenty years.

Still, it was an exhilarating feeling, sort of like the arrival of Christmas—but better. Christmas is, after all, only one day, and even though its arrival is supposed to be inspiring and full of the wonderment of the baby Jesus and all that, Christmas itself has always been pretty annoying for me. I think it has to do with the way my mother gets frantic about the whole thing. Also, my cousins have this irritating habit of telling everyone and their brother twelve times in a row about the *spectacular* gifts they got.

The circus was different. It would be in town for a full week of Big Top shows, no guilt, no religious undertones, and no gifts.

Part of the circus' attraction was the side-show atmosphere, the games and rides and Flying Zalubras—the cliché stuff—and the crowds. You could always count on seeing the same type of people, year after year—gangs of teenagers roaming around in Marlon Brando jeans and Little Richard hairdos, holding hands, laying their faces in cotton candy; groups of old men with puffy faces and Pall Malls hanging loosely from their lips, waiting for the strip shows to start. Everything and everyone was loud and full of energy or drink, and when you get right down to it, the whole spectacle was tawdry as sin. And I couldn't wait.

Anyway, I got up that next morning with the circus on my mind, and another thing. Big Farley. The Big Farley part was inevitable. I was sure Big would be on his way soon to exact retribution for the Nike Site incident. I knew I'd have to be on my toes for a while. I felt like a guy with a noose around his neck—I was right up on those old toes.

It was still dark when I grabbed the newspapers and bike and hit my paper route. Actually, now that I think about it, my paper route would have been a good time and place for Big and his thugs to ambush me. No one would have been around to see or help, and they could easily have jumped out from behind a bush or tree and pummeled the hell out of me before anyone got up for their morning coffee. I'd be left in a pool of newsprint and blood on some poor guy's front lawn for him to discover on his way to work.

When I got down to the Dubois's home, Mr. Dubois was sitting in front of the house in that old Chevy, now minus its swastikas, snoring away. I decided not to wake him up. Given the circumstances after all, it seemed like it would have been a pretty foolish thing to do.

The house didn't look like it had been touched during the night, and that gave me confidence, at least for the moment, that the nightly vigil plan just might work out.

I looked up at Ricky's bedroom window and saw that the light was on. It was about the only light in the whole neighborhood that was on. I wondered what she was doing up there. Maybe she left the light on to give the illusion someone had been awake throughout the night. Or maybe she was awake, worried and restless. She certainly hadn't looked very settled when we'd left her the night before.

I stared for a moment, hoping she'd step over to the window and wave or something, or maybe invite me up. To tell the truth, I could have gone on with that fantasy for a long time. A hell of a long time. It just seemed like the moment for it. But I moved on. I had work to do. I mean, if these people don't get their newspapers exactly on time they get awfully testy, as if the world needs their approval to keep turning for God's sake.

You're probably wondering how Doreen reacted to the plan, I mean to Pop getting up in the middle of the night to sit in a car in front of the Dubois's house. To tell the truth, I wondered too. She hadn't come down the stairs from her bedroom pretty much at all that previous day, and Pop had even brought dinner, macaroni and cheese, up to her so she could eat in bed. We hadn't heard any noise or arguing from up there, so I had to assume that she took it well. Or that Pop hadn't told her, although you've got to wonder how he was going to pull off getting up in the night and disappearing for three hours without telling Doreen. I began to see the pattern with Doreen and this whole Dubois thing—she's hot, she's cold, she has an opinion, she doesn't. Not that I understood it, I just saw it. It was unsettling, to tell the truth.

When I arrived home after my route, Pop and Susan were just waking up. We had breakfast together. Pop said that his shift at the Dubois's house had gone well, and that he hadn't seen anything out of the ordinary. He said the police had driven by once, and he'd stepped out of the car to talk to them and to make sure that they knew what he and Mr. Dubois were doing, and they said, yes, they'd been told about it all and was everything okay? Pop said they seemed to want to be helpful.

Pop hummed and seemed almost cheery about the whole thing, as if the whole controversy had done something that, in a contrary way, actually made him happy. I asked about it, and he said, "It's just that it has been a long time, Dub."

Whatever the hell he meant by that, I don't know, but it was sort of a pleasure to see him in a good mood anyway.

As he poured some orange juice, he got serious for a moment.

"About those phone calls," he said. "You two want to play detective for a while?"

"Sure," Susan said. I did as well.

"Look, we know it's not any of us," he said. "So that leaves—and I'm not pointing a finger here—but that leaves

Doug and his mom, because I'm assuming they both have access to the telephone number. It also leaves the police, Mr. Dubois's colleagues at the college, and some of their relatives back in Louisiana. We can rule out the police and the relatives, don't you think?"

We agreed.

"Now, where do we go from there?" he said.

"It's not Doug," I said.

"I'm prepared to believe that," Pop said. "But let's just say I was a judge or jury. How would you convince me of that?"

"Because," Susan said, "he just wouldn't do something like that."

"And because," I said, "if you were a judge or jury, he'd be innocent until proven guilty."

"I know that," Pop said. "Good call. But convince me, nonetheless."

"Well," I said, "whoever is making the phone calls is probably the same one who burned the cross and threw the brick and painted the car."

"Okay," Pop said, "we can start with that assumption."

"So then Doug would have had to have done all those things," Susan said.

"Only, he didn't," I said. Pop raised his eyebrows.

"I mean," I said, "take the brick, for instance. The person who threw it wrote, 'Nigers Go Home' and they spelled it wrong. Doug knows how to spell 'nigger.'"

"What if he faked it?" Pop said. "Just to throw off the trail?"

"Well," Susan said, "what about the cross? He would have had to build it, carry it down to the Dubois's, and burn it all by himself? It doesn't seem likely."

"Now, that is pretty solid evidence," Pop said. "He couldn't have carried it all by himself. But say he got a friend to help him, someone like, I don't know, Lance Cornwall. What do you think about that?"

"Lance?" I said. "Impossible. He hasn't got it in him."

"You mean the hate? He hasn't got that kind of hate in him?" Pop said.

"No," I said, "I mean the wherewithal, the...something. I just can't see it."

"You'd be surprised what people can do once they set their minds to it," Pop said. "But, okay, I'll grant him that. So, Doug and Lance are off the hook. Who does that leave?"

"The college people," I said.

"And Mom," Susan said.

Pop shot her a confused sort of glance.

"Just playing detective," she said.

"It's okay," Pop said, "that's what we're doing here." He glanced at his watch and jumped up, startled. "Oops, I've got to run," he said, "I've got an early interview today down at the Hartford Hotel."

"Who's that?" I said.

"His name is Baldwin, James Baldwin," Pop said. "A writer. He's in town to make a speech. If you'd like to come along and listen, you're welcome."

A speech didn't exactly sound all *that* interesting to me, and I declined, as did Susan.

"Well, try not to bother your mother much today," Pop said, and he tugged slightly at his ear, "she's feeling a little under the weather with all that's happening. You know how things upset her. Okay?"

"Sure," we said.

"Hey, Pop," Susan said. "What about the college people?"

"What's that?" he said.

"The college people," she said. "They have the phone number, too."

He nodded, and said, "Well, school isn't in session yet, so there aren't many instructors around. I don't know, it just doesn't seem like they'd be the types to do that. You never know, though. Good point, let's keep it in mind. I've got to go."

Pop left for his interview, and I decided to spend a few hours that day at Raymond Library, in town, picking up a few books or something. I though I might pick up a book by this guy Baldwin, since Pop was meeting him, so I could talk more intelligently later about the whole thing. Or at least so I could see if the guy was famous or anything.

I asked Susan if she wanted to go with me, not just because I wanted *her* to go with me, but because I wanted her to ask Ricky to come along with us and make sort of a little excursion out of the trip. And, it would have been nice to have people along because I thought that Big Farley might be lurking somewhere. I decided to ask Doug if he'd come along as well.

I mentioned to Susan that I thought Big Farley might be out to get us that day.

"But you knew that would happen," she said. "It's no surprise, is it?"

"No," I said, "but we couldn't have let him kill us at the Nike Site, could we? I mean, to die in a rat-filled, underground hallway? Where's your sense of nobility?"

"So, what are you saying, you're not scared, or you are scared?"

"I'm saying that it's going to happen," I said. "Sometime. I know I'll be scared when it happens." The truth was, I was scared right then and there, right out of my wits, and I couldn't see any way around it. I figured I had two choices: Either stay in the house for the rest of my natural life, or go out and let Big Farley find me and do the deed and hope that I survived with my limbs and my dignity intact. Besides, the way I saw it, Doug and I had beat Big in his own game a couple of times this summer alone, and the odds were definitely against us. Big had to win sometime.

"Better go upstairs and tell Mom we're going to the library," Susan said.

"Me go upstairs?" I said. "What about you?"

"It was your idea to go to the library," she said, with perfect logic.

"Do you think Pop told her about the guard duty he and Mr. Dubois are doing?"

"He had to," she said, "he couldn't just disappear in the middle of the night otherwise."

"But, she didn't say anything about it."

"Maybe she just doesn't care anymore," Susan said. She sighed. "I sort of wish she wouldn't care anymore, about anything."

I walked upstairs, sure that I did not want to see my mother and tell her we were going to the library with Ricky. In fact, I was sure that I did not want to see my mother at all. Doreen's bedroom door was open. I stepped in and she was sitting, propped up against her pillows, with the telephone to her ear. She had her hand on the hook. As I walked in, her eyes widened and she hit the button with her finger. A haze of cigarette smoke hung close to the ceiling, and an empty wine bottle sat on the nightstand.

She cleared her throat. "You're home," she said.

"Sorry. The door was open." The bags under her eyes were dark and heavy and her lips were dry, but her eyes shone brightly.

"I thought you would have wanted to go with your father," she said.

"Nope," I said.

"Darn doctor," she said, and she placed the phone back on the hook. "His line is always busy."

"You feeling okay?" I said. I looked at the clock on her nightstand and noted that it was ten thirty-five, and I filed that fact away, with some confusion.

"Maybe just the flu or something," she said. "I'll be fine."

"Susan and I are going down to Raymond Library," I said. "Maybe with Doug. And Ricky."

She smiled. "Well, that's fine," she said. "What about lunch?"

"We'll get something at Mr. Hwan's or somewhere," I said. "There's this new place, McDonald's, maybe we'll have a hamburger."

"Or, maybe you can eat at Ricky's," she said, and slipped a cigarette between her lips.

"Maybe. Sure, Doreen." I prepared to leave.

"Dub," she said, a little too loudly.

I turned back to her. Doreen had called me Dub about twice in my whole life.

"You hate me, don't you."

I was startled, and had this sudden urge to tug at my ear.

"I'm not saying in general," she said, "or even all the time. I'm saying as of recently. As of about the time Ricky moved into town. I can see it in your eyes."

"No, Doreen," I said, and then I actually did it, I tugged at my goddamn ear. If I could've done a stupider thing just then, I can't imagine what it might have been.

"Admit it, you think I've been harsh." Her voice was steady, almost teasing, as if she'd rehearsed this.

"I don't know."

She shook her head slowly and said, "You're just like your father."

I dropped my hand from my ear.

"You always want to be so good to people," she said, "to be so good *for* people. You want everyone to like you. You can't see the truth for the fog you walk around in."

"What truth?" I said. I don't know why I asked. I just wanted to get the hell out of that room with its stale cigarette and stale wine smells, and, I noticed for the first time, its ugly, ugly curtains.

"The truth that the Duboises shouldn't be here," she said. "They don't belong here. That truth."

"Where should they be?"

"Not here."

"But, they are here."

"Then they should leave," Doreen said. "What do you think about that?" She lit her cigarette.

"I don't know. I'd say I think the whole thing is real sad."

"You *are* just like your father." She sighed. "You know, you could have been different."

"Different from Pop?"

"Yes, different from *Pop*," she said, though she spit out the word "Pop" as if it was a bad tooth. "Does it bother you that I think they shouldn't be here?"

"I guess I've known it all along."

"You're not answering the question."

I had no idea what to say, so I said, "We'll be back later."

"*Now* you're answering the question," she said. "And be careful out in the neighborhood. Who knows what that column will do."

I flashed back to her finger on the receiver. "Are you going to the doctor today?" I said.

She looked blank for a moment. "Oh, probably not," she said. "It'll pass."

"I'll see you," I said.

"Okay."

I walked out of the bedroom, my mind on that phone.

It made sense, really. Awful sense. Everyone else who had the Dubois's phone numbers was not likely to make prank calls, and Doreen had just demonstrated she had the opportunity. And the motive.

But it was such a juvenile thing to do, such a petty prank, I just couldn't believe it. It was the type of thing I used to do for Christ's sake, calling up hardware stores and asking if they had size "S" batteries, or size "H," "I," or "T."

To tell the God's honest truth, the thought of Doreen actually doing something like that made me sick to my stomach. I mean, what do you do in a situation like that? Turn your own *mother* in? To whom? What do you say? "Hello, officer, I'd like to report a case of telephone fraud.

Who? Why, my goddamn mother, for God's sake." Of course not. This is where Pop would say, "We deal with it in the family. We take care of ourselves. We have to help her."

And I would agree with him. The police are for other people, for bad guys. Not for family.

I don't mind telling you that it was starting out to be a exceptionally bad day. What with Big Farley on the warpath, and now Doreen and the phone, I was sure my birth stars were aligned with some wayward comet or something.

I went downstairs and found Susan. "Doreen says to be back by the afternoon," I said.

"She said nothing of the sort," Susan said. "She probably said that her life stinks and why can't anyone ever listen to her. And she probably called you Mr. Vigilante or something. Am I right?"

"Close," I said.

"You don't look so hot," she said.

"Let's go," I said.

We went outside and found Doug working on his bike, sticking baseball cards in the spokes.

"You shouldn't do that," I said. "They say those cards are going to be worth a lot of money some day, you should save them."

"Bull," he said. "They're just cards. Who's going to care about Sandy Kaufax in twenty years?"

We explained our trip to the library.

"What about Big?" he said, but it wasn't a question, it was more like a taunt. He was still feeling cocky about the condom caper.

"I guess we'll have to play it out when it comes," I said. "There's strength in numbers, anyway."

"No prob," Doug said. "We escaped him before, we'll do it again."

"Pushing that old luck, aren't we Doug?" Susan said.

We cycled down to Ricky's place and found her

grandmother and mother in the front yard, weeding the flower garden.

Mrs. Dubois stood up and wiped some sweat from her forehead. Then, I hate to admit this, I really do, but I leaned in just a little closer to see if she smelled any different. I mean, everyone always says how black people smell different, but I really didn't mean to do it like that because it was more of an impulse, which is not to say it wasn't horrendously stupid. But there I went—I leaned in toward her and took a small whiff. She stiffened slightly, almost imperceptibly, and I leaned back as if nothing had happened. And I surely wished it hadn't.

I guess I don't have to tell you that she smelled a lot like a person who had been working in a garden on a hot summer morning, nothing more, nothing less. God, I can be an total idiot sometimes.

"Well, looks like you're all prepared for an expedition," she said, cheerily. Even Mrs. Oliphant smiled at us.

"Ricky is in the house somewhere, I'm sure," Mrs. Dubois said. "Just go on in and give her a shout."

"Excuse me, ma'am, but did everything go well last night?" Susan said.

"Yes, I suppose it did," she said, and shook her head. "I cannot figure this neighborhood out. Not a peep from anyone, not a 'yea' or a 'nay' to be heard anywhere. These people are positively quiet. We're never sure about them. I swear it's a mystery."

"It's the north," said Mrs. Oliphant, as she bent over some flowers.

"Any more of those phone calls?" I said. I didn't want to hear the answer.

"As a matter of fact, I just got one about half an hour ago," Mrs. Dubois said. "At about ten-thirty."

"Jesus," I said, stupidly.

Mrs. Dubois tilted her head. "What's that, Dub?"

"Oh, nothing," I said, recovering. Doug and Susan both stared at me. I mean it, I can be *positively* half-witted sometimes.

"Well, we're changing the number again very soon. Anyway, Ricky is in the house."

"I'll get her," Susan said. She disappeared through the front door.

Doug and I hung around, waiting, watching Mrs. Oliphant and Mrs. Dubois, mother and daughter, weeding their small flower garden in the small yard of their suburban dream home. They worked steadily, pulling weeds and tossing them onto a small canvas tarp they'd laid out on the ground, talking little. I don't know about Doug, but I began to feel out of place, sort of like a refrigerator in an igloo, and I wished Ricky and Susan would hurry up.

They finally came out, laughing about something or other, that pleasant laugh good friends have. Ricky was almost glowing, and I caught her eye as they stepped out the door. She caught mine, and looked away quickly. She looked a whole lot better than she had the evening before, when Pop and her father had worked out the "nightly vigil" plan. Her hair was pulled back in one braid, the color of a brown paper shopping bag—I know the comparison lacks something in the telling, but that's the first thing I thought.

"Doug, Dub," she said, a matter-of-factly. "Nice to see you."

We explained our trip to the library, and Mrs. Dubois gave Ricky a couple of quarters so we could get a sandwich somewhere along the way. We jumped on our bikes, and then something curious happened. Doug, who had been pretty quiet since we arrived at the house, suggested that he ride at the end, and that the two girls ride in front. This, coming from a guy whose main thrill in life was to be first, go first, see everything first. He caught my look.

"Bringing up the rear," he said, and bobbed his head in a determined sort of John Wayne nod. "Keeping an eye out."

We took off toward Raymond Library, which was about half-way to Mr. Hwan's, and about a mile from the circus site. "Let's go to the circus grounds after the library," Susan said.

"I think that might be a problem," I said.

We stopped our bikes to discuss this.

"Is it a place where Big's gang gathers?" Ricky said.

"Well, sometimes," Doug said.

"I'm afraid of them, aren't you?" Ricky said. "Anyone with sense should be afraid of them."

"We're not exactly afraid," I said. "Just terrified out of our gourds." I glanced at Doug. "Speaking for myself, of course."

"Please, let's not go there," Ricky said. "You've heard 'discretion is the better part of valor'?"

"Discretion is the better..." Doug said, filing the phrase away.

"She means," Susan said, "that it's better to avoid trouble than to go looking for it. Okay, so we forget the circus grounds."

"We're not the ones looking for trouble," Doug said, "they are."

"Just the same," Ricky said. "I don't want any more trouble. No fighting. Please?"

"What else is there?" Doug said.

Susan jumped in. "Shut up, Doug. Just no fighting, no looking for it. Okay?"

"I'm not looking for anything," Doug said.

Ricky looked down, biting her lip.

Susan spoke softly. "No one's going to get hurt, Ricky," she said.

"But Dub suggested they carry baseball bats," She put the balls of her palms to her face.

"Who are we talking about here?" Doug said.

"God!" Susan said.

I, of course, felt about as small as a pimple on the moon.

I hadn't meant to suggest violence when I mentioned that Pop and Mr. Dubois might keep baseball bats in their cars, I thought I was being practical. I just thought I was being a guy.

"It'll be okay," Susan said, and she put her arm around Ricky. It was a gesture so right, so perfect, it was something I wanted to do myself.

"I'm sorry about the bats, Ricky," I said.

"It's not your fault," she said. "Sorry."

Doug shrugged his shoulders and I shrugged, I guess, my conscience. I felt helpless, but more important, angry. I thought about Doreen and the telephone, and I about bit my tongue.

"Something will give soon," Susan said. "It'll be okay real soon."

"I'm sorry," Ricky said. "Really. Come on, let's go to the library." She wiped her face with her hands.

We started off again, slowly, into the humid morning. As I said before, this was turning out to be an odd day.

We spent a good hour in the library, partly because we like libraries, and partly because it was air-conditioned. I picked up a couple of new Hardy Boys mysteries, and I found a book by James Baldwin, who, it turns out, is a Negro and who writes about the Negro experience. The book was called *Go Tell It on the Mountain,* and from what I could gather by reading the first page of the novel, it was not going to be an easy book, for a lot of reasons. But since Pop had recommended him and, let's face it, it seemed like an apropos sort of book given recent events, I decided to give it a try.

Susan picked out a couple of those Nancy Drew things for herself and two more for Ricky, who hadn't yet managed to get a library card. Doug spent about twenty minutes thumbing through the "D" section of the encyclopedia before going over to the car magazines. He didn't take anything out, because, he said, he had an encyclopedia collection at home and otherwise he read about as much as his grandfather, who is dead.

We decided to go down to Mr. Hwan's for some candy and cokes for lunch. "But apples for you," Susan said to Doug.

"I know, I know," Doug said, looking nervously at Ricky. "God, I got another mother?"

Susan contemplated that for a moment. "Yes," she said.

But, when we walked out the door, the pace of our lives accelerated considerably.

Leaning on some bikes was Big Farley and several of his hoodlums, chewing gum and smirking as if they'd just seen a guy with his pants down. And that's what I felt like. I immediately looked for exit paths, even thought about running back into the library where we'd be safe until it closed. But I knew Big would rip our bikes to shreds while we hid out, and, frankly, for me there was a small bit of relief involved in seeing him. Not that he was a great old friend or anything, but because I knew what must come to pass was about to pass. There would be some relief in getting it over with.

"Hello, boys and girls," Big said.

Ricky froze and Susan sighed, or maybe hissed, I don't know which.

"Hello, Big," Doug said, "long time no see."

"Got anything in your back pocket?" Big said, and let out this sort of hideous, nervous laugh.

"Only a magnifying glass this time," Doug said.

"Yeah? What for, scumbucket?"

"So when this is over, we can find your brains on the sidewalk."

I want to pause for another, very small moment, and remind you that Doug Hammer is a guy whose mind, while quick, was not altogether attached to reality. This, coupled with the recent success of the condom adventure, was a deadly combination. Doug Hammer smiled.

Big hesitated a moment.

"Well, I got something in my back pocket, too," he said. "Have a look." He pulled a large, glistening hunting knife from his hip pocket and whipped it in front of him, cutting an audible swath as it slashed the air. Ricky gasped, as did the rest of us, even the thugs.

"And you're going nowhere," he hissed, and plunged the knife into the front tire of the bicycle he was leaning on. The tire popped like a small balloon, and its air wheezed out.

"Big," one of the thugs said. "That's *my* bike!"

"Wha-?" Big said.

This was no time for banter. Big had a knife, and this had changed the equation considerably. Even Doug Hammer knew this. And there was no telling what the other thugs had in their back pockets. I believe now that Doug and I both sensed this instantly, because we both acted at the same time.

"Run!" we shouted.

"Surround them!" Big said, and, as if it were a plan, the boys jumped to action and were around us, menacing and evil. Except, of course, for the unfortunate guy whose bicycle tire was hissing in the wind.

"Jesus, Big," he said, "that was my bike."

"Shut up," Big said. "You can take the fat one's tire, or maybe *her* tire." He pointed to Ricky.

"Yeah," he repeated, "take the coon's tire."

"You shit!" Susan spit.

The boys stood wide-eyed, amazed by Susan's venom. For that matter, so did I. Even Doug turned his head. Ricky, whose fists were clenched, stood firmly, feet planted wide apart. "Take that back," she said.

Big said, "What you going to do about it?"

"Leave them alone," I said. "You got a beef with me and Doug, not with them."

"Any friends of yours are friends of mine," Big said.

I heard Doug take a deep breath and exhale through his nose. His face was beginning to turn red.

"Yeah," Big said, "*any* friend of yours. Even a spook."

Ricky exhaled.

Doug raised his arms high, threw his head back, and whooped a blood-boiling scream. He threw himself forward like a cannon ball and hit Big full in the chest. Big let out a great whoof and spilled backward over the wounded bike like a sack of cornmeal. I turned and kicked the boy closest to me directly in the groin, which, as far as I was able to determine, put him on the ground for the rest of the fight. I then grabbed my book bag and swung it wildly, clipping another thug on the side of the head. He went down with a groan, scoring one, marginally, for James Baldwin.

Susan jumped another boy's back, and Ricky was right there on his face with her nails slicing his cheek, like she had a small cheese grater in her hand. Then Doug was up again. He kicked the knife from Big's hand, while I took another swing with my book bag at anyone close. The knife spun into the air.

I heard another bone-rattling scream, and saw a thug jump Doug from behind. I jumped them both, and the three of us went down in a heap, spitting and cursing and grabbing. Big got up and kicked me square in the back, and the next thing I saw was Susan in Big Farley's face, landing what sounded like a mighty slap across his ear. His eyes went buggy, and he grabbed at the popped ear as if to take it off and repair it. I stayed on the ground, sure that my spine was severed. The guy at Ricky's nails was on his knees, pawing at his eyes. There seemed to be blood coming from between his fingers, and he reached up blindly and socked Ricky right in the chest. She fell like an old blanket.

Doug kneed his guy somewhere, I couldn't tell where, but the boy groaned, went limp, and rolled over. Another thug was instantly on Doug's back, and I saw Big staggering over toward the knife, clutching his ear, his eyes blinking. Susan rushed to Doug, and I went over to Ricky, thought a second about it, and kicked the kid who was on his knees directly in the side. He let out a yelp and fell right over, and I saw that his face was, indeed, a bloody mess. Ricky remained on the ground, gasping for breath.

Someone grabbed Susan from behind. Doug recovered, stood up, and head-butted the thug. The guy's nose split, and a wild spray of blood doused the front of his shirt. Big staggered, losing his balance, while groping the ground for the knife. Suddenly, something like a screaming wildebeest hit me square in the back, between my shoulders, and I went down, having sustained the second back injury within minutes. I was sure I would never walk again. In fact, at that moment, I couldn't. I was horizontal next to Ricky, the both of us gasping away, as if we were emphysema patients or something. It was uncanny, it really was. Here might have been our first intimate moment together, lying next to each other, and both of us were wheezing as if we'd just done something wonderful. Which we hadn't.

I turned my head and saw that the thing that had hit me was a rock, a jagged rock about the size of a baseball. The guy who threw it was coming toward me. Ricky was still down, although I noted with some pride, in another uncanny moment, that she had made a good showing for someone who had hours earlier lamented the growing violence around her.

The rock-thrower raised his shoe to kick me, and there was little I could do about it. I remember thinking that, since he was wearing a rubber-soled sneaker, my head would bounce a little before it came off at the neck. But just as he was about to deliver the kick, Ricky screamed and rolled over, diverting his attention. When she came up it was with a fistful of sand, which she delivered squarely into the guy's eyes and mouth. He went down, and I thrashed about on the ground, kicking at what I could find of him.

Doug had locked himself in a choking contest with one of the thugs, and Susan was on the back of another, screaming and slapping. Ricky recovered and ran toward Susan and her fight-mate, and out of the corner of my eye, I saw Big loping unsteadily toward Doug.

With the knife in his hand.

Big raised the knife—he raised it as if he were about to plunge it into Doug's neck. "*Doug*!" I said, and propped myself up. My shoulders felt as if someone had run a power drill between them.

Doug saw Big out of the corner of his eye, but couldn't break loose from the choke-hold. I pulled myself up, grabbed the rock that had hit my back, and gauged the distance between Big and myself. "*Big*!"

Big looked around, loopy-eyed, and seemed to focus on me. He pawed at his ear. I lunged forward as Big continued on his run toward Doug. I shouted, "Big, *no*!"

Big reached Doug and stopped dead. Out of the corner of my eye, I saw Susan and Ricky and the thug, grunting, locked in a hair-gripping, shin-kicking contest. Doug and his choking partner were both purple in the face, and neither would budge. The other guys were on the ground, holding various body regions, groaning.

Big leered at me, and slowly raised the knife. Doug, bug-eyed by now, saw the flash of the blade and let out a stifled groan.

"Fuck you, Hammer," Big said.

"No!" I yelled, and heaved the rock as hard as I could, more out of frustration than a need to be accurate.

The whole thing happened in slow motion. The blade came down as I watched the rock sail from my arm, direct, dead center toward Big Farley. Blade, rock, blade, rock, blade was all I could see. It was as if the world had turned into a vacuum, and the only sound I could hear was my own breathing and the slice of the blade and the whoosh of the rock.

The rock rolled and sailed, arching upward, sort of like a curve ball on its side, or a ballet dancer floating toward a partner, and smacked solidly, heavily, into the side of Big

Farley's head. Big turned to me with a look of surprise, and then his eyes rolled back. The knife slipped from his hand, and Big, the rock, and the knife hit the ground at the same time. Big groaned, and then let out a short cough.

The thug choking Doug dropped his arms and let Doug fall backward on his butt. Susan and Ricky dropped their guy and he fell down to the ground quickly, as if he had an important meeting at ant level.

We all turned our attention to Big.

"Holy shit," a boy said. "You killed him."

"He was about to stab Doug," I said.

At the word "kill," the remaining thugs started to stir and get up from the ground. The guy with the split nose crawled over on his knees, his face an ugly, contorted mess.

"Jesus Christ almighty," he said.

"Wow, Dub," Doug croaked, rubbing his neck.

Big Farley was inert on the ground. A small river of blood streamed from his temple, creating a viscous goo in the dirt next to his nose.

"I killed him," I said.

"Jesus," a boy said.

"He had a *knife*," Susan said.

Ricky, her chest heaving, turned to me and whispered, "Dub, you better go."

"We should call an ambulance," Susan said.

"He's *dead*," the boy said. "We're all going to get arrested!"

"Oh, shut up," Doug said. "Let's think about this."

"*Think*?" another thug said. "What's to think? We got a dead kid on our hands. Holy shit oh Christ!"

"I said *shut up*," Doug growled. "What do you think he was going to do with that knife? Give a carving demonstration?"

"*I* didn't know he had a knife," the boy wailed. "None of us knew he had a knife!" The others nodded, and old split-nose groaned from behind us.

"And you, *definitely* shut up," Doug said.

"I killed Big Farley," I said.

"No, you didn't," Susan said. "He's breathing."

We all looked at Big. A faint puff came from his lips and raised a little dust on the ground next to the growing blood puddle.

"Yeah, but he's dying," the choker said.

"So?" Doug said. "Like, we're supposed to give him mouth-to-mouth or something? *Like he's our best buddy?* What would you have done if that knife was in my throat?"

The kid looked down and started to cry, big tears that messed up the grime on his face.

"We should call an ambulance," Ricky said. "That's that."

"I'll go into the library," Susan said, "and use their phone."

"Dub," Ricky said, "pardon me for saying this, but I think it's time for you to go," and she breathed heavily.

Susan smoothed her jeans and shirt, and turned to Ricky. "How do I look?" she said.

"Fine," Ricky said.

"I'm not going anywhere," I said. "I killed a kid."

I was in a state of shock. My back screamed pain, but my mind was numb. It was like being on an operating table at the moment before the anesthesia takes over.

Susan turned to go into the library.

"Wait," Doug said. "We have to have a plan. Okay, Dub, you have to make a choice here. Either you stay and we handle this, or you take off—"

"I killed Big Farley," I said.

"Or you take off," Doug continued, squinting hard at the boys gathered around the body, "and we think about the fact that Big Farley tripped and hit his head on this rock as he was moving in *to stab me!*" Doug glared at the thugs, one by one.

"Got it?" he said. "Big Farley tripped and hit his head on

a rock. He came at me with a knife and he tripped." His eyes never left the boys.

"Okay," said the guy with the split nose.

"Sure, sure," another said.

The others nodded.

Loyalty was apparently not a requirement to join Big's gang.

"Ricky?" Doug said. "Susan?"

"Well," Ricky said, "what I think happened is that Big tripped and hit his head on the rock, and Dub might not even have been here. I'm pretty sure it happened that way. Is that too extreme?"

"Ricky!" Susan said. Then, hastily, she added, "No, actually, it's okay."

"Okay, Susan," Doug said, "go and get the ambulance. And Dub, you're gone."

Behind us, Big groaned and snuffed into the ground.

"He's dying," I said.

"Maybe," Doug said. "Just maybe he is."

Doug led me, zombie-like, to my bike. He helped me get on, and pushed me in the general direction of home. As I pedaled slowly away, sharp pains reached across my back, and I had the vague sensation I should stay around. But I also had the vague sensation that going would be a major relief. I rationalized it by thinking this: maybe Big wouldn't die. No matter how many times in the future he would try to beat me up, I didn't want him dead. Actually, more important, I didn't want to be the one who killed him.

Yet, even at that, I knew I had no right to leave Susan and Doug behind. And Ricky. Even saving Doug's life, which I apparently did somehow, was not enough to justify the flight. But fly I did, somehow burying my anxiety. I was willing to follow my shocked state wherever it would lead me. And it did lead me places.

CHAPTER 9

Where my shocked state led me, in a roundabout way, was to Zikker's Pond. Immediately after I'd left Big Farley lying there with his brains oozing out of his head, I actually had no idea where I would go. I let my legs lead. I pedaled and navigated streets and paths without an inkling of where I might end up, sort of like a zombie without a mission, with no heads to devour or no living souls to carry to the tombs of the dead. I must have looked the part, anyway. To this day I am surprised I didn't get hit by an ice cream truck, or end up in Vermont or some other God-forsaken place.

Only twice during my ride was my consciousness jogged to the point where I became aware of my surroundings. Once was when, in the distance, I thought I heard sirens. They sounded like the wail of a ambulance plus several police cars. I knew they had to be heading over to the library, or, as I was beginning to think of it, the scene of the crime.

As I rode, I remembered something about Doug telling everyone that Big was supposed to have tripped and smacked his head on the rock, thereby causing him to lose his mind, but I wasn't exactly clear on that. It didn't matter, the sirens jogged my memory, and at that instant I knew I had thrown the rock. I saw it again, sailing straight and true, directly at Big's temple. If I were big on irony, I would've thought that, given a million years and a million bucks, I would never have been able to throw that kind of a pitch in a baseball game.

The other time I was snapped from my dream-like state was when the front wheel of my bike got caught in a sewer grating—it wrenched me forward over the handlebars. I almost fell, but that wasn't the half of it. The strain caused my aching back to spasm, which made me want to puke right there on the street, and, if I'm not mistaken, caused me to scream outright.

After that, I just pedaled aimlessly, and the dead smokestacks of the Pratt and Whitney plant stood in the background. Pratt-rats on vacation drove idly up and down the streets of our little town, drinking beer, sneering at their lives. And I was sure they were whispering, "See that boy? He just killed Big Farley." But I wasn't afraid. It was as if I'd taken a drug, the kind they handed out to people in *Brave New World,* that made me, if not happy, at least not sad. I was perfectly calm, and perfectly out of it.

Somehow I circled through the back streets and the next thing I knew I was staring at the still, fetid water of Zikker's Pond. No one else was around, which was good—I didn't want to have to tell anyone to leave me alone while I contemplated the existence of God, sin, and eternal damnation. I didn't want to have to tell anyone to buzz off or I would very probably kill them and don't push me because I have some excellent credentials in that department. I didn't want to have to tell anyone that I had recently discovered the meaning of life, which was this: to like someone, even slightly and from afar, and even someone who isn't the same race as you, is much, much easier to take than a fight to the death with a neighborhood bully.

I found my way to the rock and sat down for what I knew would be a long time. I was going to pick up some pebbles to toss into the water—I often do some great thinking while watching the ripples disappear to the outer edges of the pond—but I thought differently as I picked a few stones out of the mud. All of a sudden, I just didn't have the heart for it.

I took a long look at that water and wondered how deep it was. I had never actually taken a swim in Zikker's—it was muddy and smelly and rumored to be chock-full of snapping turtles. Which, I'm told, are able to take hold of a guy like me and pull him down to the bottom of the pond to drown him and then stuff him under some rock until his skin goes all mushy and he's easier to digest.

It occurred to me for a moment, it really did, that I ought to hurl myself into the pond and let the snappers have their way with me. But instead of thinking about my actual death, all I could focus on was how great my funeral would be, with everyone sobbing and Pop delivering a great eulogy, and maybe Ricky breaking down as she threw a red rose onto my casket, which, of course, would be empty because they never would have found my body. Not unless they opened the bellies of about two dozen snapping turtles from Zikker's Pond.

But after a while I realized that the whole fantasy was just another coward's dream. And I was King Coward, Mr. Spineless. I'd run out after the fight, I'd hung on to Doug's shirt tail at the Nike Site. I wasn't about to throw myself into the pond, and I really didn't want to die. All I wanted was the sympathy, when, in fact, we already had a guy lying over there whose head was split open. Big Farley was where the sympathy should go. I knew that suicide was not for me, not in this life anyway.

So I just sat on that rock for the longest time, and after a while I didn't even feel my back anymore. I didn't feel much of anything until the mosquitoes began to come out and I realized it must be close to dusk. I didn't feel hungry, thirsty, and I certainly didn't feel much alive. I just sat and listened to the sounds of birds flitting in and out of the water.

Finally, I fell asleep. I don't know how long it was, or when it happened exactly, but all of a sudden I woke up on my rock at Zikker's pond with the croaking sounds of about a zillion fornicating frogs and my ankles and face full of mosquito bites. And my body, particularly my back, was one big throb of pain. I must have been exhausted from the fight, or from the ride, or whatever, but I surely was tired.

I hadn't contemplated the next move. I hadn't even contemplated going to Zikker's, but here I was and I had no idea what time it was or what I should do next. Turn myself in? Go home and hope that Big hadn't died?

Join the French Foreign Legion?

Who knew? I was inexperienced in this, in evading the law or whatever. But the pond was spooky, and I heard a splash out on the water that convinced me that this was not the place to be.

I got on my bike and rode quickly through the dark toward home. When I got out to the road, some streetlights glowed hazily in the dark. But the streets were quiet, there were no cars about. I figured it must be pretty late. Suddenly, going home seemed like a bad idea. I could imagine arriving home and stepping through the front door to be greeted by a flying plate of melon balls or something, Doreen on the delivering end shouting, "Your sister's in jail, Mr. Nonchalantly-Commits-a-Felony! What do you think about that?"

No, home was out.

I thought: Ricky's place. I'd sneak by there and see who was out on guard, Pop or Mr. Dubois, and I'd be able to get an idea of how late it was.

I cycled slowly up our street until I saw Ricky's house from a distance. No cars were parked out front. It told me nothing. Only one light was on inside the house—Ricky's light upstairs, which told me nothing as well. I remembered that morning, when I'd delivered the paper. Her light had been on and for all I knew she kept in on all the time, which wouldn't have surprised me, given the situation.

The surrounding houses were dark. Another bad sign. Flying melon balls would be the first and least significant of my problems later on, I thought.

Then, I saw a shadow behind Ricky's curtain. Someone was awake and moving around. I watched for a while, and the shadow moved back and forth and back again, pacing. Whoever it was seemed to be alone, and I decided then and there that my destiny that night was to talk to Ricky, alone.

About something. To tell the truth, I had no idea what it might be, but, I knew I would do it. All of a sudden it became a burning thing, a rush. I was, literally, overcome, and I had to step off my bike and take a deep breath before thinking about it.

How I would talk to her was the problem. She in her room, and I was out on the street. And her family was on edge about things happening around their house at night, so I couldn't just start shouting or anything. I couldn't sort of walk up to the front door and knock at this time of night. Or morning.

So I walked my bike quietly around to the back of the house until I could see Ricky's back window. It was open, with a screen. I saw the shadow pacing back and forth. I had a scare for a second, thinking the shadow might be her mother or someone lecturing her. But I was on a roll, and I don't think now I could have stopped myself if I'd wanted to. I positioned myself in the dark, and I decided to try a trick I'd seen in the movies.

I picked up a small pebble—it seemed to be my destiny to throw stones that day—and tossed it lightly at her window. It clicked against the ledge and dropped back to the ground. The shadow continued to pace.

I picked it up again, the same pebble for good luck, and tossed it. It hit the screen, and the shadow stopped. "Ricky," I hissed.

The shadow moved to the screen. It was Ricky, I could tell by her braids. "Ricky," I hissed again.

"Dub?" she whispered.

"It's me."

"Thank God," she said, almost aloud.

"Shh!"

"What are you doing here?" she whispered.

"I don't know."

"It's two-thirty in the morning."

Great, I thought. Splendid.

"Can you come down and talk?"

She hesitated for a moment. "Stay there and be quiet," she whispered.

The light went out in her room, and after two or three minutes the back door opened, and out stepped Ricky in her bathrobe.

"Over here," I whispered.

"Shh!"

Ricky walked over to me, put her finger to her lips, and grabbed my hand. She led me away from the house, about ten yards into the darkness of the back yard. I could barely see her by the light of the half-moon.

She turned to me and smiled, grabbed both my arms, and, I swear this is true, hugged me. Her arms were full around my neck and back, and Ricky Dubois buried her head in my shoulder. Her hair and her neck smelled like rose water and her bathrobe smelled faintly of bleach, and if I'd had a heart seizure right then and there I would have died with the positive knowledge that life can be strangely wondrous and good.

I picked up my arms and put them around her back, and then, only then, noticed she was crying. So I started in, and in a moment we were both full-tears sobbing in each other's arms and I had this feeling that I could cry with Ricky forever and ever and ever in the heat of a summer night under a half-moon's light.

She picked her head up and stepped back. "I've been so worried," she said. "Where have you been?"

"I don't know," I said. "I just rode away and ended up at Zikker's Pond."

"They're all out looking for you," she said. "Your father and my father, even the police."

"The police? Then Big is dead? Jesus, I knew killed him."

She giggled. "Hardly. Just badly bruised."

"So what happened?"

"Just after you left, Big's gang ran away, each and every one of them. The three of us waited for the ambulance. Then the library people came out and Doug told them the story of how Big started the fight and pulled a knife and tripped and fell on the rock, and you know what? They believed every word, in an instant. One of the library ladies even said, 'Henry's been a problem ever since he was born. Not an ounce of decency in that kid.'"

"Holy Moly," I said. "What about the ambulance?"

And this is what Ricky told me: While they were all standing around waiting for the ambulance, one of the library ladies was tending to Big's head with a first-aid kit. All of a sudden, he woke up, rolled over, and socked her right on the chin. You can imagine how that went over. He didn't even apologize, he just grabbed his head and told her to get the "blank" (Ricky's word) away from him, and all the library ladies stood back in disgust, like he was a wild animal or something. They left him alone until the ambulance arrived.

The ambulance arrived with one police cruiser close behind, and who should get out of the cop car but Mr. Officer Bigger Farley, and another officer. The ambulance men ran up to Big, and when Big saw his father walking toward him, he stood right up and tried to smile and say something, but he sort of fell back down.

Then Doug and Susan told Office Bigger Farley the falling-on-the-rock story while the ambulance guys examined Big's head. The library ladies were happy to chime in with comments like, "Why don't you wash this kid's mouth out with soap, Henry Farley" and "He hit me, he's a menace to society," and all that sort of thing while shaking their fingers all over the place. This was not a happy moment for Officer Bigger Farley, and he glared at his son the whole time.

When Doug pulled out the knife and told Officer Bigger how Big had tried to attack him with it, Officer Bigger's eyes just about bugged out of his skull. "That's my hunting knife, Henry," Officer Bigger said, and from there on in it was gravy.

Big then apparently tried to give his own version of the fight, how *we* had started it, and how *we* had attacked him with a rock. But the library ladies would have none of that and kept berating Officer Bigger with remarks like, "You should have this kid's head examined, and we don't mean because he fell on a rock," and, "We never want to see him around this library again."

You can imagine that the evidence was stacked pretty heavily against Big, and anything he said after that had about as much significance as, in Ricky's words, a fly on a horse. Big tried to protest and told everyone that I had thrown the rock at him, but it didn't fly. The knife apparently clinched it. Officer Bigger pocketed it and told Big to shut up, and then asked the ambulance guys how bad Big's wound was. They said it wasn't too bad, but it should have some stitches, and he ought to go to a doctor to see if there's any clotting or something like that. Then Officer Bigger grabbed Big's arm and repeated, "That was my damn knife, Henry. Get in the car and I'll deal with you later."

He threw Big in the police car, and went to the ambulance guys and apparently told them that he could handle things on his own, that everything was fine here, because they just packed up and left without Big. Then Officer Bigger returned to the library ladies and apologized. He said that everything would be okay and he was sorry there was this "commotion," but since he was the boy's father he felt he could deal with it best at home. The library ladies, dumbfounded, threw up their hands in disgust as if to say, "What can we say but what we've said?"

Ricky said that later Doug wondered if he should have asked to press charges, but he kept quiet, not wanting to push his luck about the whole thing. Finally, Officer Bigger and the other officer and the now-doomed Big took off in the police car. Ricky didn't know what then happened to Big, except she was sure his father had taken him home and given him the licking of his life. But she said a strange thing had happened just as things were breaking up. Just before the police car pulled away, Officer Bigger Farley had looked out his window and given them all the nastiest look she'd ever seen, as if he'd just swallowed an anchovy. Even when she told the story, she shuddered.

By the time Ricky finished her story, she was almost breathless. I don't know if you've ever whispered hard for five minutes or so, but I can tell you this, it leaves a person breathless.

"Then what happened?" I said.

Well, then Doug and Ricky and Susan had gone home and hung around, discussing the battle, laughing about how they'd won it as they cleaned off the grime and blood at Doug's garden hose.

They had waited for me, but when I didn't show up during the afternoon, they'd begun to get worried. Finally, they'd had to break up and go home for dinner, and when I didn't show up for that, Pop had called Doug, and Doug had sort of explained what had happened, at least the official version. Doug told Pop that I had taken off to look for help after Big had fallen on the rock. This was a pretty lame excuse, but apparently Doug hadn't thought that far ahead about the whole thing, and he'd just said what came off the top of his head.

Then Pop got on the phone to Mr. Dubois (which is how Ricky knew about his phone call to Doug), and they had decided to go out and look for me, and, as far as Ricky knew, they were still out looking for me. They had called the police, who had joined in the search, and the way Ricky told it, just about everyone in the world was out looking. She said she wasn't sure what was happening at my house, but here at home everyone had gone to sleep at midnight—everyone except her. She'd been so worried about me—that's *me* by the way—that she had been on the phone with Susan for about an hour discussing the whole thing, and had stayed awake in her room until now. She said she'd also stayed awake to help stand guard, since her father and Pop were out looking for me and not able to keep their watch. All in all, it sounded like a pretty rough way to spend the night.

At this point I noticed, not that I had been completely unaware, that Ricky was still hanging onto my arms. Her hands were warm and strong, and I sure did think it would be nice to hug her again. "I'm sorry about all this," I said. "It was our fight, not yours."

"He called me a spook," she said, softly.

"Maybe that's because you were with me and Doug."

"Dub, do you think I stop being black when you're not around? To tell the truth, I felt good about it afterward. I was angry, and now I'm not so angry. I don't know."

"'Cause you got to belt someone," I said.

"Maybe. I didn't want to. But at least I finally saw their faces, up front."

"You were great in there," I said.

"I've been told I have my moments," she said, softly again.

From our vantage point at the back of the house, I saw pair of headlights turn slowly around the corner. "It's Pop and your father," I whispered.

"They shouldn't see you here," Ricky said.

We crouched.

The headlights went dim, and the car slowed down out front. I slipped around to the back corner of the house, leaving Ricky behind, and watched the car as it stopped in front of the Dubois's house, its engine idling. It wasn't Pop's car, and it wasn't Mr. Dubois's Chevy. A man sat alone in the front seat. "It's not them," I whispered. Ricky trotted over and stood behind me.

"Who is it?" she said.

"I don't know," I said. "But I'm thinking we're going to find out soon."

"What's he doing?" she said.

The man opened the front door of his car and the interior light shone on his face for a moment. My eyes worked hard at focusing. He looked around briefly, and stepped out. He was a big guy, a huge guy. He was Officer Bigger Farley.

Pop has always told me that your first reaction to a situation is often the truest. Well, I am here to tell you that my first reaction failed me that night, failed me miserably. At first I thought Officer Bigger was at the house because he was checking up on it, and he was out of uniform because he had just gotten off his shift and was dropping by like a good neighbor and conscientious law enforcement officer. "Just stopping by on my way home," is what he would say, "wanted to see how the little family was doing, is all."

My second instinct was that he was looking for me. I was on the lam after all, and I figured he'd dropped by to see if I was around the house. That, coupled with the fact that it was his own son whom I had beaned with a rock, caused me to hold back for a moment.

As it turns out, I was wrong on that count as well.

Bigger Farley surveyed the front of the house quickly, and turned and opened the back door of his car. He leaned in and pulled out what appeared to be a baseball bat, and held it at hip level, pointed at the house. Only it wasn't a bat. I saw the flash first. It came from the tip of the shotgun, and was followed by an explosion I can only compare to the biggest firecracker Grandpa Constantine has ever let me light. It was a thudding roar, followed by a smash and an echo ricocheting off the tiny houses on the empty street of our neighborhood. The acrid smell of gunpowder blew past my face.

Ricky screamed as if she'd stepped on fire, and fell backward, her fingers deep into my back. I screamed at her scream, and we both pitched back into the shadows of the side of the house.

Officer Bigger snapped his head in our direction and said, "Shit! What the—" But he was cut off by our screams.

He tossed the shotgun into the back seat and jumped into the car, screeching and peeling rubber down the street until I saw his headlights flip on. Then the car was gone.

And, in a heartbeat, the whole world became quiet.

Then all hell broke loose. The lights in the Dubois house flipped on one by one, and Mrs. Dubois's scream reverberated through the house, "Ricky! Ricky!"

Lights in adjacent houses went on, flick by flick, as if it were a synchronized light show. Ricky rolled off my back, sobbing, and for a terrified moment I thought she'd been hit. Light streamed through the front door of the Dubois home, little pinhole beams and one large, jagged stream that threw an eerie pattern across the front lawn. "Ricky," Mrs. Dubois shouted.

Neighbors in bathrobes began to emerge from their front doors, tentatively, peering around corners. My back started to throb like hell.

The front door swung open, and Mrs. Dubois charged out. "Ricky!" she said.

"Over here, Mama!" Ricky sobbed.

"My God, what *is* this, what *happened*!" Mrs. Dubois yelled and rushed over to her daughter, picked her up, and slammed Ricky's head into her chest.

"Dub, what are you doing here, *what* is going on here? My God, my God, my God." She held Ricky and rocked back and forth. "Are you okay baby?" she said softly.

She turned to me and about spit in my face. Her eyes were small slits and she shook with fear and rage. "Explain this and explain it quickly."

Well, I tried to. But between Ricky's sobbing and the neighbors rushing over and Mrs. Oliphant showing up and wailing, "This is the truth of our lives, the God's truth," I really didn't get to say much at all.

It all happened so fast that I wasn't sure if what I

managed to say made any sense anyway. The whole atmosphere took on a charged craziness, and before I knew it, neighbors were everywhere. Apparently, a brick and a painted car were one thing; a shotgun blast in the middle of the night was something entirely different. Mr. Hubbard, who owned a gas station over in Manchester, examined the shotgun holes in the front door, and old Mrs. Bedford, who was a widow, rushed up to me and Ricky asking if we were okay. Others were saying, "Looks like buckshot," "Did someone call the cops yet?" and "Which way did they go?" and things like that. Ricky got control of her sobbing, more or less, as her mother stroked her head, and off in the distance I heard the wail of a police siren.

"What were you two doing out here?" Mrs. Dubois said. "Were they shooting *at you?* Dub, where have you *been?*" But she didn't wait for answers; it was as if the mere act of asking gave her strength.

Somewhere during the commotion, someone managed to call my mother, and then Mr. Dubois and Pop showed up in what I had to attribute as a huge coincidence of timing. Even Doug and his mother pitched up out of nowhere. Yet amid all the yelling and confusion and anger, which was understandable I guess, all I could think about was Officer Bigger Farley and the pain in my back and all the violence I had seen.

Mr. Dubois made heroic efforts to calm his wife down while Mrs. Oliphant hung on to Ricky. While Pop asked me questions about where I'd been and what had happened and thank God you're okay and I tried, in vain as it turned out, to answer him, Susan and Doreen showed up. Doreen, who was wild-eyed, staggered into the fray and immediately called me Mr. Now-You-See-Him-Now-You-Don't. She was about to slap me when Pop grabbed her arm and said, "Doreen, there's been a shooting."

"I know there's been a shooting," she said, almost hysterical. "They could hear it in Timbuktu for God's sake!"

Susan grabbed me aside and asked what in the hell I was doing over here when people were shooting the place up. Pop was navigating the crowd, looking for me again, and someone's baby started to cry and it all went on like that for a couple of minutes until the police showed up. The two officers arrived with sirens blaring and lights twirling, and it was getting to be a real circus scene—it was a madhouse, it really was—when I saw, out of the corner of my eye, Doreen walk up to Mrs. Dubois.

"It comes to this," Doreen spat out, and smiled.

"I don't believe we've met," Mrs. Dubois said, although I got the impression she knew exactly who she was talking to.

"I am Doreen Teed."

"And you are drunk, Mrs. Teed."

Doreen's mouth flew open like a catcher's mitt.

"Please, leave us alone," Mrs. Dubois said, and she walked off.

I had no time to worry about that, at least not now, so I reached Pop, who was wide-eyed at the exchange, and said, whispered really, "Pop, it's Officer Farley."

"No, he said, distracted, "I believe this is Officer Dwyer, and I don't know the other one's name."

"No, Pop," I said, and yanked his sleeve, probably a little too hard. "I mean the guy who shot the door. It was him, Officer Farley."

His head jerked around and his eyes bored straight into mine. "What?" he whispered.

"The guy who shot the gun, I saw him. Ricky did, too."

"Officer Farley? Henry Farley? Are you sure of that?"

I tried to think of something clever to say, some witty retort that would drive it home like, "I'm as sure as the stinger on a bee's ass." But all I could do was nod my head, and even that hurt, then he cocked his head and I swear he looked as if he was hurting, too.

One of the officers said, "Okay, now, everyone go on

home, there's nothing more to be seen here. Who is Mr."—he referred to a piece of paper—"Herbert Dubois?"

Mr. Dubois stepped forward, and the other officer started to circulate through the crowd, holding people back, asking them to go home because they might be stepping on pieces of evidence or something else important. Pop told me to wait for a minute, then walked over to the cop and told him who he was and told him that his son was one of the witnesses and perhaps we should stay, and it went on like that until everyone started to drift home, or at least to the edge of the property where they could stay in on the action.

As people shuffled to the curb, several neighbors came up to Mr. and Mrs. Dubois and offered their help, was there anything they could do, just call me if you need a hand, that type of thing. If the whole thing wasn't so goddamn absurd, it would have been heart-wrenching, honest to God.

Doreen, who hadn't moved, stared slack-jawed at Mrs. Dubois busy with Ricky and Mrs. Oliphant.

Then came the questions about the shooting and were we okay and where I had been all night and why I had run away and that type of thing. When the policeman, whose badge identified him as Officer William Dwyer, asked us if we'd seen who'd done this, Pop gently put his hand on my shoulder and I could tell by his touch that he was confused as hell, and I don't blame him for that because I was confused as hell myself, but I plowed on.

"Well," I said, "this is probably going to surprise you, I mean who wouldn't be surprised, I guess. But the guy, the one who shot the door I mean, it was Officer Farley."

Officer Dwyer's pen stopped over his notebook, and he looked up with a half smile, as if he hadn't quite heard me.

"What's that, son?"

In a flash, I had this horrible thought: I had no idea that these police officers, who were definitely connected with Officer Bigger Farley on a professional and God knows what else level, were not involved in the whole thing. I mean, wasn't it true that the nightly police patrol was conveniently *not there*?

But I also knew I couldn't slam on the brakes, not now. "It was Officer Farley."

Ricky piped in from the side. "We *saw* him," she said.

"Shooting at you? Henry Farley? That's a very serious allegation," Officer Dwyer said. He wasn't smiling anymore. "He's a policeman, you know."

Upholder of the law.

"Ricky, are you sure?" Mr. Dubois said, and Ricky nodded, hard.

Just then the radio in the police car crackled, and the other cop went over to pick up the mike.

"He wasn't shooting at us," I said. "He shot at the door, then he turned and ran."

"Do you know Officer Farley?" Officer Dwyer said. "What makes you think it was him?"

"I recognized him," I said. "I know his son."

"Right," Dwyer said. "The library. Is that how you two kids ended up in the back yard?"

"Sort of," I said.

At that, both Doreen and Mrs. Dubois harrumphed and turned their backs to each other. A large shape moved in from the shadows and put her arms around Doreen. It was Mrs. Selwyn.

"This wouldn't have anything to do with that fight you had with Henry's son, would it?" Dwyer said. "You wouldn't be trying try to get back at anyone, would you?"

"No!" I said.

"Dub doesn't make a habit of lying," Pop said, and I silently thanked him for it.

Officer Dwyer glanced at Pop. "I'm just covering all the angles, Mr. Teed." He turned back to me and Ricky. "Look, kids, it's dark, shadows everywhere, and you've just had the shock of your lives, with that gun and everything. You're both absolutely sure it was him?" He was right about that, but it wasn't the gun that gave me the shock of my life. It was seeing Officer Farley behind it.

I looked at Ricky, and she slipped me this encouraging sort of nod, so I said, "Yes."

"Listen," Officer Dwyer said, "I have to tell you that this is a strange story. I mean—"

Just then the other cop, over by the police car with the radio mike in his hand, interrupted with, "Bill, this is important."

Officer Dwyer went over and the two talked, occasionally handing the mike back and forth, while Pop continued to squeeze my shoulder and Mr. Dubois went to his wife and Ricky. My thoughts were a mess, and I glanced over at Doug by the curb. He was beaming, as if he couldn't wait to tell the story to Lance and to just about anyone who would listen, as if it confirmed that Big Farley was not only a criminal, but a member of a completely deranged family and from now on deserved everything he ever got. He was also jealous, I knew that, what with me and Ricky in the back yard, but I had no time to think about it because Officer Dwyer returned from his conference at the police car.

"That was the front desk of the station," he said, to all of us. "Henry Farley, Officer Farley, is down there right now." My eyes must have gone wide, because Officer Dwyer smiled at me. He seemed to be relieved.

"No, he isn't turning himself in," he said, and chuckled. "He's there reporting the same thing you're reporting. Officer Farley was, in fact, here tonight. So I guess you kids did see him."

"What?" Mr. Dubois said.

"Well, he'd just knocked off duty and he knew that most of us on the force were out on a special mission, so he thought he'd swing by the house to check in and make sure everything was okay."

"What special mission?" I said.

"Looking for you," he said, and laughed and slapped me

on the back. Jesus, that hurt. "And he said when he was nearing your road he saw a flash and heard the blast, and just as he swung around the corner over there," and here Officer Dwyer pointed down the street, "he saw someone jump in a car and take off. So he stopped and got out real quick and saw the holes in the door and put it all together, and took off in pursuit of the guy. The kids must have seen him on the street jumping back into his car to chase the bad guy."

I went cold, as if someone had dragged a feather up my spine. Ricky's face told the same story.

"So you see," he continued, "the kids did see him, but they made a mistake. An honest mistake, I might add. They heard a shotgun blast and then saw Officer Farley in his car taking off, so naturally they got it jumbled up."

The other officer walked up with an empty shell which he then placed in a plastic bag. "Buckshot," he said to Officer Dwyer. Dwyer nodded, as if this confirmed Officer Bigger's story.

"No," I shouted, more out of frustration than anything else. "We didn't see him *after* the gunshot. We saw him stop his car on the road, we saw him pull up, for God's sake. He got out and shot the door, and then he peeled the hell out of here. That's what we saw."

Ricky went right along with it, nodding pretty vigorously. She added that Officer Farley must have heard us scream, and had muttered an obscenity as he sped away in the car. But that he didn't really see us. Apparently, the cursing business had frosted her as much as anything.

Officer Dwyer took a deep breath, his equivalent of rolling his eyes. "Kids," he said. "I know you believe you're telling us what happened. But it doesn't add up, see? Officer Farley chased the guy, he—"

"Did he catch him?" Mr. Dubois said.

"And wait just one minute," his wife added. "You say that Officer Farley stopped and stepped out of his car and saw the holes in the door? Didn't he hear the children screaming? Because I certainly did! Didn't he think to stop to see if everyone was okay?"

"Ma'am, that's a decision he made, I can't speak for him. Maybe he should have stayed to secure the scene, but in the heat of the moment he decided to pursue the suspect. And he did get a partial on the license plate and a make on the car. Still, the guy got away. He's filed it in his report. He was in his civilian car, with no radio. Otherwise he could have called for some backup, and we might not be having this conversation."

Great, lovely. He got a partial on the license plate.

"Wait," I said. "How about the shotgun? He threw the shotgun into his car, maybe it's there now. I mean, shouldn't you check it, see if it's been fired recently?"

"Walter," Doreen said from the shadows, "I think *that* is enough of *that*." Her words ran together, thick like cold syrup, and it seemed to snap Pop back into the scene.

Behind me, he squeezed my shoulder and said, "Everyone is tired, Dub, and shaken up. And you're tired, too. No one is saying that you're wrong, but maybe," and he addressed Officer Dwyer, "maybe we should all sleep on this, think about it and get back to the police if we have more to say."

"My God," Mr. Dubois said, vacantly. He shook his head, as if to clear it, and said it again. "My God."

"That would be fine," Officer Dwyer said. "Look, Dub, Ricky, it's been a long night, and you've seen some things, some bad things. I understand what's going through your minds. Maybe a good night's sleep would help. I think to be fair to yourselves, and to Officer Farley, that would be the best idea."

"Dub?" Pop said.

I looked at Officer Dwyer. "Did you tell Officer Farley we saw him?"

"Sure, son, I mentioned it, and it'll be on my report. But he knows it was just a mix-up. Don't worry, he said he understands. He's got kids, too."

Nice touch. He's got kids, too. I had no idea what else to say. I'd just said it all. I saw what I saw, I'd tried to kill a kid, and my back was screaming in pain. Everything, all of a sudden, made no sense whatever.

The bad guy was a good guy.

But I did have one more thing to say, and it had to be to Ricky. I turned to her. "Do you think we're telling the truth?"

She was near to tears, wrapped in her mother's arms, but she choked it out. "Yes."

"Then that *is* that," I said.

The other officer, who'd been out on the street, turned and said, "There're some tire tracks here. Looks like the guy might have put down a little rubber when he took off. Or they could be Farley's tires. Radio the lab and have them come down with a camera." He turned to Mr. Dubois. "Let's try not to walk or park on this area until the lab people have examined it. They should be here within an hour."

Then Pop took Mr. Dubois aside and they had a long conversation in private, and I could see Mr. Dubois shaking his head and cursing under his breath, and he finally threw up his hands in disgust and said, loudly, "But they tried to kill us this time. It's final, we're on our way south, Walter. End of the story."

"I can understand that," Pop said. "But right now, we've got to do something about that front door."

"Front door! Front door? They're using weapons now. What good is a front door, for Christ's sake?"

One of the men from the crowd at the periphery said, "Walter, uh, Mr. Dubois? I've got an old door in my garage. It's not pretty, but it'll work for the time being. These houses are all standard. You're welcome to it."

Pop turned to the man, "Thanks, Ed. Why don't you go

over and get it and we'll put it up right away." He turned to Mr. Dubois. "Is that okay, Herbert?"

Mr. Dubois said, "Thanks, Mr.—"

"Selwyn," the man said. "I live up the street."

"Selwyn," Mr. Dubois said. "Much obliged."

"And I want your family to come to my place for some hot coffee and doughnuts," Mrs. Hammer piped in. Some heads turned.

Mrs. Dubois turned to her.

"Helen Hammer. Doug's mom."

"Mrs. Hammer. Thank you. It would be good to get away from the house. I think that would be splendid."

Under her breath, Mrs. Oliphant muttered, "Coffee and doughnuts in a white lady's home. This world just keeps turning, don' it?" Then, incredibly, she chuckled to herself and nudged Ricky. "'Don' it?' Doughnut? Get it?"

Everyone started to get busy, fetching doors, going home to make coffee, and light started to creep over the tops of the houses as morning arrived.

"I'll do your paper route for three bucks," Doug said.

"One," I said.

"Two."

"Done."

Mrs. Selwyn led Doreen slowly home with her arm around her shoulders. The Dubois women, including Ricky, followed Mrs. Hammer home, and pretty soon it was just the policemen, me, Pop, and Mr. Dubois. In a few minutes Mr. Selwyn came by with his door and some tools.

Eventually the lab guys arrived and dusted this and photographed that, and by early morning the door was in and we acknowledged that damage to the inside of the house was limited to a few small buckshot holes in the walls. Apparently, the door took the brunt of the blast.

Everything then drifted slowly back to normal. Everything except what I now knew about Mr. Officer Bigger

Farley, that is. The police left with promises to get back in touch with any leads (which, I guessed, would have to be professionally supplied by Officer Farley), and Pop told Mr. Dubois that he'd do his best to keep the newspaper guys from mentioning anything about us accusing Officer Farley, which, when I thought about it, was a good idea. I mean, I now knew that Officer Bigger was a lunatic, but a shrewd lunatic—there'd be nothing to gain by sending him completely over the edge with publicity. Then Pop, Mr. Dubois, and I decided to go over to the Hammer house for some of those doughnuts.

"You know you're in trouble, Dub," Pop said.

You don't know the half of it, I thought.

"I know," I said.

"You had your mother up all night, and Herbert and I drove all over town looking for you."

"I know, Pop."

"Makes a man crazy when his son is missing like that."

"I'm sorry."

"You want to explain it now, or later?"

"Later," I said, "if it's all the same."

"Just one thing, though," Mr. Dubois said, not unkindly. "How did you and Ricky end up in the backyard?"

I stopped in my tracks. "Our luck, I guess."

The thing is, they both seemed satisfied with that.

By mid-morning, Doreen had retreated to Mrs. Selwyn's house and God knows what they were doing over there. Mrs. Dubois's remark to Doreen about being drunk did about as much for whatever friendship they might ever have had as the Bataan Death March did for us and the Japanese. But I didn't blame Mrs. Dubois. The plain truth is, Doreen was drunk. And it's clear to me now that if there's one rule in life that should be absolute, it's that a guy shouldn't ever have to see his mother drunk in public. Or anywhere. It's just a wrong thing to see.

Pop just kind of walked around the house pretending he

was thinking about his novel, when really all he was doing was waiting for me to come to him with the story of why and how I disappeared for the night, and why I ended up at Ricky Dubois' place just in time to witness the shooting.

I was beat, literally in fact, and I eventually went upstairs to take a long nap. It was a strange nap filled with vivid dreams. Most of them involved fights and condoms and all kinds of shouting and mayhem, and I couldn't tell who was involved in the dreams except whoever they were, they bled a lot and cried even more. I did have one dream where I could identify the people. That was the one where I stood with Ricky Dubois in an aisle in Woolworth's, looking at things to buy, doughnuts I think they were, while during the whole time Ricky had her hand on my arm. That's it, that was pretty much the whole dream. Ricky had her hand on my arm.

I awoke during that one. I stayed in bed for a while, thinking about the dream, wondering what to do about Officer Bigger Farley. Then I got to thinking about that great hug Ricky had given me, but the thought was interrupted by Bigger Farley once again. It went back and forth like that—Ricky, then Officer Farley, back to Ricky. Finally, my back spasmed a few times and that was enough to make any guy forget about hugging Ricky Dubois. I gave up and got out of bed.

It was afternoon, and the house was quiet. It could have been the next day, for all I knew. I walked downstairs, and found Pop sitting in a chair smoking a cigarette. He was by himself, no book, no notes, no magazine, nothing.

"Feeling better, Dub?" he said.

I nodded.

Pop exhaled a long sigh. "You know that I love you very much."

It was going to be that kind of a talk.

"I've always wanted to be here for you," he said. "I mean, if you ever need to talk or confide in me, I've always wanted to be here for you."

I nodded again.

"So, want to tell me why you took off?"

"I don't know why, Pop," I said. "I was in a daze, I guess I went to look for help."

"Please remember what I just told you," he said. He stubbed out the cigarette. "I want to be here for you."

"Well, I guess I got scared," I said.

"And?"

"And, I ran."

"I believe you were scared," he said. "I would have been scared too if I'd just knocked a boy unconscious with a rock. I might have run too, come to think of it."

I guess my startled reaction was none too subtle.

"Look," he continued, "Doug and Susan and Ricky are loyal friends, but their story about Big tripping and falling on the rock doesn't hold very well, does it. Now, I'm listening."

I hesitated for a second, and started to shake. I hadn't wanted to cry, and thank God Susan and Doreen weren't around, because it would have been pretty damn embarrassing to have to sit there and tell a long, involved thing like that while sobbing for an audience.

Anyway, I told Pop pretty much everything, from the Nike Site incident and the rubber to the fight and the rock and knife and how I ended up at Zikker's and later at Ricky's, and how I got her to come down from her bedroom and pretty much the whole caboodle. Pretty much, but not all.

I didn't tell him about Ricky hugging me, and I didn't tell him about this thought, this fear I'd been having since the shooting, still unstated between Ricky and me, that others in the police department might actually be involved. I mean, why not? It's a crazy world. If Officer Bigger was involved, who's to say that he wasn't part of some larger group of racist cops? It made sense, really, or at least as much sense as Officer Bigger acting alone.

"Dub," Pop said. "I just wish you'd have come to me instead of running away."

"I wish I hadn't run away," I said, still kind of shaking.

"I know that."

"Did Mr. Dubois mean it when he said he was sending his family down south?"

"What he said was that he wanted to send them away until this thing blows over, until they find the perpetrators."

"But, he didn't mean for good, that he was sending them away forever, did he?"

"I don't know. I think he just wants to protect his family until things get better for them here. I think we'll just have to wait until the police catch these people. What they did last night was a serious crime."

"He," I said. "What he did. Officer Farley."

"He, then," Pop said, and he managed to get even more serious. "Which brings up another point. Now that you've had a chance to rest and think, has anything else come to mind about last night, anything that would help the police?"

"Pop," I said, "we saw him do it, Officer Farley. There was no other guy. It was him."

"Look, Dub," Pop said, and he leaned back a bit. He seemed to take me in for a moment. "I know you're not lying, but Bill Dwyer had a point. It was a chaotic night, and it happened so fast. Officer Farley was there, at least at some point, and you did see him. Isn't it possible things got muddled in your memory? I mean whom you saw, and when? I mean, Mr. Farley is a policeman."

Thank God he didn't tug on his goddamn ear because I was ready to say something this time, I really was. Instead, I just shrugged my shoulders. Farley was a man with a badge and an iron-clad alibi, and I couldn't even get my own father to believe me. It was clear to me that Ricky and I would have no allies.

We were on our own.

"Sure, Pop," I said. "Anything's possible."

"Well, thank God he didn't shoot at you two," Pop said.

I had a thought, though a desperate one. "Now that he knows he's been seen, maybe he won't come back." The irony, of course, was that Pop and I were talking about two different people.

"Possibly," Pop said. "Or, it might drive him to come back in desperation, to finish off the job. This man is clearly an unbalanced person. We're not talking bricks anymore, Dub."

"So," he continued, "Henry Farley tried to stab Doug with a knife. We're living in a changing world." He slapped his hand on his thigh. "But that doesn't mean we have to change, Dub."

"Pardon?"

"You know we have to take some steps about your disappearance," he said. "We have to make it right."

"How?"

"First, we make peace with your mother. She was out of her mind with worry last night. And I'm afraid what Mrs. Dubois said to her isn't going to make it any better."

"You heard that?" I said.

"Yes," he said.

"But it's true."

Pop looked off into the distance for a moment. "She's having a tough time," he said, and then reached for his ear. But I must have sucked in my breath, because he retracted his hand in a smooth movement.

"Next," he continued, "you're going to write a letter to the Chief of Police and apologize for sending the police all over hell last night."

I began to protest, but he held up his hand.

"Last," he said, "you'll apologize to Big Farley."

"What?"

"You heard me. You hit him with a rock."

"But, he had the knife."

"I know it sounds like a lot, and it is, but you'll be a better man for it. Believe me."

"But, Pop," I said.

"We can do it right now and I'll go over with you," Pop said. "Or we can do it tomorrow. Your choice."

"Over to where, the Farley house? With Mr. Farley there?" I said. Just absolutely peachy wonderful, I thought. Let's just march on into the den of knives and shotguns. Let's just drive right on over there and say, "Jeez Officer Bigger, how ya doing today? Well, here I am, Dub Teed at your service. How do you want to do this? Want me to stand outside so you won't splatter blood and intestines all over the kitchen wall? Fine, glad to oblige."

"Dub, it's the right thing to do," Pop said.

No, I thought, it's not the right thing to do. It's the suicidal thing to do.

"Why is it the right thing to do?" I said. "Big was the one who came after Doug, *with a knife.*"

"Because you will rise above that, that's why. You'll be a man, and Big will still be Big."

"Big, he'll think he won if I go over there and apologize."

"Then let him think he won. You'll know in your heart that you won, on both counts. You saved Doug's life, and you confronted Big later."

"Pop," I said, exasperated, "what about the knife? He was going to *kill* someone."

"Well, that's a problem. And I intend to take that up with Mr. Farley. I'll talk to him about it. I think Big should get some help."

Big should get some help. Tremendous. From whom? *From Officer Bigger Farley?* What's he going to help him with, his shotgun techniques?

"I'm not doing it, Pop," I said.

"It's the single most difficult thing you've ever dealt with, I know. That's why you have to do it."

"No."

"I'm afraid so."

"Nope."

"Like I said, today or tomorrow."

"It doesn't make sense," I said.

"For God's sake, Dub, you've got to rise above Big."

"You should talk!" I blurted out. "Doreen's over here calling people *nigroes* and everything and talking about watermelon patches and she sits up in her stupid room all day with a bottle of wine making phone—" I stopped myself.

"Making what?" Pop said.

"Nothing," I said. "I'm sorry."

"Phone calls? Your mother?"

"I don't know," I said.

"Why do you say that?"

"I don't know," I said, which was true because I didn't have any proof, per se. And, just at that moment—I mean I hadn't had a chance to work it all out—it occurred to me that there was a good chance she *didn't* make the calls. Maybe Officer Bigger was on that pleasant little task, too.

But then he seemed like more of the action type, a cross-burning, brick-throwing, shotgun-firing type of guy. I hate to say it, but the phone calls seemed more like a thing that, well, my mother would do.

I had no time to sort it out. But I hoped it wasn't her. It was enough of a hope to drop a bright spot in this otherwise horrible couple of days. No matter how I felt about Ricky, and no matter how I felt about Doreen for that matter, maybe it wasn't my goddamn mother.

"Dub, you're smiling, and that's weird. Do you know something I don't know?"

"No, Pop," I said, "I'm just saying, what if there was proof, what would you do about it? If it was Doreen, for God's sake. What would you do? Make me apologize to her, too?"

"Dub," he said, harshly. "That's uncalled for. I would cross that bridge if I came to it. Now, have I come to it? Do you have proof that your mother made those calls?"

"No, I don't."

"Feeling the way she feels is one thing," he said, "but

making crank phone calls is another. She still loves you. Us. All of us." But his shaky voice made it clear: He'd been rattled by it. He knew she had it in her.

"I know," I said.

Pop remained silent for a while, gave the old ear a tiny tug. Finally, he said, "I don't know what else to say." He really looked like a guy who didn't know what to say, I'd have to give him that.

"I didn't want to talk about it in the first place," I said.

"Let's drop it, then," he said.

I hesitated. "Okay, today."

"Today?"

"I'll go to see Big Farley today," I said, "and get this over with." This ought to be a real honey of a trip, I thought. But at the same time, I began to have this sort of perverse attraction to confronting Officer Bigger, to see him up close. To share our little secret. After that, it was out of my hands.

"Good choice," he said.

"Where's Susan?" I said.

"She's sitting up in the willow tree in back," Pop said. "I'll call Mr. Farley and tell him why we want to go over. I'll come and get you."

I went outside and saw Susan perched up in the tree, reading a book.

"Hey," I called.

She put the book down and gestured for me to come on up.

I climbed the tree, no small feat given that I had to use my legs to climb, and they were attached to my screaming back. I sat next to her.

"So, what were you doing over at Ricky's at three in the morning?" she said.

"Two-thirty," I said.

"Close enough."

"Well, I was riding around and I saw her light on in the

bedroom, so I threw some stones to get her attention, and the rest is, as they say, history. And, by the way, so am I."

"Why's that?"

I explained to her how I was about to go over to Big Farley's place to apologize for throwing a rock at his thick skull.

Susan's reaction was predictable. "What?"

"You heard it here first," I said.

"I don't get it," she said. "You know, I'll never get these people, Pop included. Apologize to a psychopathic killer." Her eyes went wide. "Dub, what if Officer Farley is there?"

"Susan—you believe me, me and Ricky?"

"Well sure. Like father, like son, like son, like father. Something like that. Doug believes you, too. But aren't you worried that he'll try to do something? You turned him in. Pop *can't* bring you over there."

"It's okay. Officer Bigger thinks he has it licked. He knows no one will ever believe a couple of kids over a cop's word. And no one does, not Pop, not Mr. Dubois. Officer Bigger was *chasing* the bad guy, remember?"

"Wait'll Doug hears this. This is rich. Wait a minute, how does Pop know that you threw the rock and that Big didn't fall on it?"

"I told him," I said.

"Nice," she said. "So now we're liars."

"It doesn't matter," I said. "As far as Pop is concerned, that part is over. He just wants me to be a man, or something like that. A dead man, I guess."

"But Big will think you're a patsy for going over there like that."

"Pansy," I said. "Big will think I'm a pansy."

"Whatever. These are strange days."

"And they're going to get stranger."

Susan cast me a sidelong glance. "So what were you and Ricky talking about in the backyard at two-thirty?"

"Nothing," I said. It was clear Susan felt strange about it.

"We hardly had time to talk. We just said this and that about the fight with Big and his gang." I decided a small lie would be politic about now. "She said you saved her from a beating."

Susan took it in. "I suppose I did," she said, "not that it matters much in real life. Being a good fighter is not going to get me very far."

"Hell, look where it got me," I said. "I'm apologizing to Big Farley."

"We'll probably have to apologize to Mom about the whole thing, too," she said, echoing my earlier sentiment. "I just don't get it. I mean, did you see her last night? And where is she today? Over at Mrs. Selwyn's, drinking again. I don't get it. I don't get anything."

"Me, too," I said.

"I mean it," she said, "and Pop just sits there tugging at his ear, and Big Farley gets an apology."

Susan was disgusted, I could feel it deep in her voice, beyond what she was saying. But to tell the truth, I beginning to feel sort of sedated. It was the sweet sedation of exhaustion, of beyond caring, at least for the time being. I felt as if I could sleep for a year.

In a couple of minutes, Pop came from the house. "Dub," he shouted, "let's go, pal."

"Pal?" Susan said.

"He's pretty goddamn exhilarated." I said, "It's all this honesty and father-son relationship stuff."

"Pal?" Susan repeated. She chuckled to herself. "Anyway, you cuss too much," she said.

"It's a cussing time," I said.

I climbed down the tree and met Pop at the top of the hill. We piled into his car, and started to make our way to Big Farley's place for the showdown.

"What did Mr. Farley say?" I said.

"He said that if you wanted to talk to his son, that was okay by him, though he'd already made his peace with the boy."

"Meaning what?"

"Whatever it was, I'm guessing 'peace' is exactly the opposite of what he did. Poor kid."

"Poor kid?"

"Look, Dub, something made him the way he is. You are not born with a knife in your hand."

"Pop," I said. "If Mr. Farley, you know, sort of goes berserk, remember me in your next novel."

"If you're worried about having mentioned him in your police report, don't. It's an honest—" and he hesitated.

"Mistake? No, I meant that I hit his kid with a rock and everything. That's bound to make him slightly miffed."

"Well, don't worry," Pop said. "I'll be with you."

I had never been to Big Farley's house. The front yard resembled a free-form junk art sculpture—footballs, baseballs, bats, bikes, and dolls were strewn out over the spotty grass. A lone white birch tree stood over the front steps, leaning in toward the house where its branches had rubbed a raw spot in the paint near the roof. The house itself was clay-brown and tiny, tinier than ours. Its shingles were warped and hung cockeyed in places, and there seemed to be a white film over the front picture window.

In the driveway was a police cruiser and a disassembled motorcycle under a canvas tarp. And of course the Ford, Officer Bigger Farley's light brown Ford, which I would have recognized in a heartbeat after last night. Just seeing it again gave me a start.

A German Shepard was tied up to the railing by the side entrance, and as we pulled into the driveway, it reared up on its hind legs, barking and snarling.

The side door opened and out stepped Mr. Officer Bigger Farley, dressed in a stained T-shirt and shorts. He acknowledged Pop with a grim wave and grabbed the dog's chain, viciously yanking it toward the house. The dog actually flipped over, landing on its back, sending a shard of pain through *my* back, but the damn thing never stopped barking. In fact, it went a little nuts, to tell the truth.

We got out of the car.

"Don't mind her," Officer Bigger said. "She likes people."

"For lunch," Pop whispered.

"Come on in," said Officer Bigger. I checked his eyes. They were actually pretty tiny eyes, and pink, like a hamster's, He twitched slightly as he squinted at me.

We sidestepped the growling dog and entered the kitchen. It was dark green and smelled like French fries and sour milk and the first thing my eyes went to was the refrigerator. There, smack dab in the middle of the door, was a heart cut from red poster paper with little sprinkles of that silver dust teachers are always making kids put on their art projects. In the middle of the heart, scrawled in black crayon with the proper misspelling, were the words, "Hapy Mother's Day Mom, Henry Jr. 1955."

Well, that was just fabulous. Big must have been king around the house for God's sake. I mean, his mother had left the damn thing on the refrigerator for *six years*. The heart was surrounded by other, smaller school dabbles, mostly from the other kids, but here was Big's paean to his mom, looming large in the middle of the collage.

"So, you want to talk to Henry," Officer Bigger said.

No, I said to myself, it's *you* I really want to see, up close. Again.

"Thanks for taking the time to let us come over," Pop said.

"I don't know why you want to do this," Officer Bigger said. "Boys are boys and they have fights. It happens all the time. Maybe Henry should be the one apologizing."

"Maybe," Pop said. "So Dub, did you want to say something?"

"Uhm, Mr. B—" I said, "Farley. Henry didn't fall on that

rock." I gulped, searching for a reaction. Officer Bigger had none. "I threw it at him and hit him."

Old Bigger's eyes squinted for a split second, took me in. He shifted his weight.

"I know that, son. I know he couldn't have fallen on a rock and got that kind of a cut. I'm a policeman, you know."

Upholder of the law.

"But I only threw it—" I said in sort of a thin voice.

"Because Henry went at you with a knife," finished Officer Bigger.

"Doug," I said. "Not me, he went after Doug."

"The kid with diabetes?" Officer Bigger said.

"Yes," Pop said. "And, aside from what we came here to do, I think the knife problem has to be addressed." Pop pulled himself to his full height.

Officer Bigger's eyes twinkled slightly. "Oh, I've addressed it all right. I have done that, yessir, don't you worry. But I didn't know he went after the kid with diabetes."

Apparently, in Officer Bigger's world, almost knifing someone with diabetes is a whole lot worse than almost knifing someone whose pancreas is operating a hundred percent.

"I just wanted to register that we are fully aware of the knife," Pop said, "and to make sure that you are aware of it."

"It was my knife," Officer Bigger said. "I ought to be aware of it. Anyway, as it turned out, my kid pulled a knife and your kid pulled a rock. I'd call it even."

"Except for who pulled what first," Pop said evenly.

Mr. Farley cleared his throat and leaned casually against the fridge, his elbow touching the Big Farley heart. "Well, now. Maybe," he said, "just maybe Henry was provoked."

"How do you mean?" Pop said.

"Well, it's no secret that there's been trouble in your neighborhood," Officer Bigger said, cool as a winter's day. "We've all been patrolling over there. Look what happened last night."

Sure, let's look.

"What's that got to do with the boys' fight?" Pop said, warily.

"Well, your kids were at the library with that Negro girl. Who knows, maybe they were carrying a chip on their shoulders. You know how kids are when they get with their friends. They think they're protecting them, when there was no danger in the first place."

"They very well may have been protecting the Dubois girl," Pop said. "But tell me, how is that provoking your son Henry?"

"Well," Officer Bigger said, "I'm not saying they were, and I'm not saying they weren't. But with the way they feel about that Negro girl, and with your column in the paper the other day, who knows? Maybe they felt she was about to be threatened, and maybe they wanted to protect her, and maybe they got a little anxious. You understand what I'm saying, don't you Mr. Teed?" Officer Bigger Farley had a twinkle in his eye, that I'm-so-mean-I-can-bite-a-bulldog-and-get-away-with-it look.

"What you're saying is," Pop said, with a slight edge, "that your son was carrying a knife yesterday just in case he became involved in an altercation with some overprotective, zealous friends of Ricky Dubois? You're saying your son was armed just in case he had to protect himself?"

Officer Bigger dropped his arms to his side. "Look, Mr. Teed," he said, "you called me so's you and your boy could come over here and apologize. I didn't call you, this was your idea. I was prepared to leave it as boys will be boys and forget the whole thing. If you want to apologize, do it. Then get the hell out."

"Fine," Pop said. "I think that's a fine idea."

"Where's Henry?" I said.

"Henry, get out here," Officer Bigger growled.

"I didn't do nothing," a pathetic sort of voice called out from the bowels of the house.

"Now!"

I heard a groan, and in a moment Big Farley shuffled into the kitchen. When he saw me and Pop, his eyes widened, and he dropped his hand to his side in a defensive position.

Big Farley was a big as ever, but he seemed stooped, almost cowed. And, next to his father, he was as big as a circus midget. A bandage over the rock cut was wrapped around his skull, and he looked like that Revolutionary War soldier marching with the fife. One eye was blackened, and a puffed, swollen cheek completed the picture of a guy whom the gods were about to give up on.

Mrs. Farley suddenly appeared from another room—I hadn't heard her footsteps—and stopped at the doorway. She was in house slippers and a light, half-sleeved smock, her hair back in that bun, like always. Her eyes, blinking like mad, darted to Pop and me, then to her son, then quickly to her husband and back to her son. I looked down at her left arm, and a dark purple bruise oozed from beneath the sleeve hem. She caught my eye, and instantly lifted her arms and crossed them, covering it.

"There's nothing here, Margaret," Officer Bigger Farley said. "You can go." It wasn't a request, it was a command, delivered low and whispery from the back of his throat. Instantly, she turned and left as quietly as she'd come in.

Big watched her exit, kept his eyes on the spot she'd just left for a moment, then turned back to us. "What do you want?" he said, his voice thick.

"Jesus, Big," I blurted out, "what happened to your face?"

He glanced furtively at his father, then averted his eyes. He looked at me as if I were a messenger from hell.

"What do you want?" he repeated, this time to me.

"Well, I just came to say," I said, "that I'm sorry."

"I didn't do nothing," he said. He was confused. I felt genuinely sorry at that moment for Big. He was a big, mean ox for whom life used to be a series of wanton and unpunished violent acts. Now his life was out of his control, not that he ever controlled it very well to begin with.

"No, *I'm* the one who's sorry," I said. "For throwing the rock."

"Oh," he said. That was it, just "Oh."

I let it hang there for a moment, sensing that the gracious thing for Big to have said would have been something like, "Think nothing of it, I was about to kill your friend anyway." But, no such luck. He just stood awkwardly, aware that if he opened his mouth he would probably implicate himself in some deeper crime and bring down the wrath of Officer Bigger Farley once again.

I said, again, "So, I'm sorry for that."

Big stood with his mouth slightly open, and I could see coagulated blood on the inside of his lip.

"Okay," he said.

Of course, the gracious thing for Officer Bigger to have said at that point would have been, "Why don't you say you're sorry, too, Henry?"

But instead he said, "Well, that's that."

"Then that's that," Pop said. "Dub, let's go."

"One more thing," I said. Suddenly I felt wildly strong, or wildly reckless, I'm never sure which. But I had to see a reaction. I also had this notion that blowing a little smoke wouldn't hurt. I turned to Officer Farley and said, "About last night."

His eyes widened, but he kept his cool, cleared his throat, just slightly. "Yeah?"

"I'm sorry I said it was you. I just told the other policemen what I thought I saw. But now, I know I was mistaken."

His eyebrows furrowed, and he lightly brushed his hand along the tattoo, a tattoo of a screaming eagle, on his forearm. This lopsided sneer, sort of an Elvis-with-gas smile, crept across his face. "Just doin' my job," he said, as if he'd just rescued some old lady's cat from a tree.

"Okay," Pop said. "I think we're done." We turned and Pop opened the kitchen door. The goddamn dog started to go ape, and Officer Bigger stepped by us to grab its chain. We walked by him, and as we did, I stole a look at his eyes.

You know how sometimes you want to say something so badly to someone that you look at them and think it so hard, so loud, that you're sure they must have heard it? That's what I did to Officer Bigger on our way out the door. I thought a thought so loud I almost closed my eyes to concentrate. I thought: "Your move, you bastard."

Only, I don't think he heard. He glanced at me from the corner of his eye as he yanked on the dog's chain, but gave no sign of recognition. Pop and he didn't exchange a word, or even shake hands. We piled into our car and were gone, just like that.

Pop and I didn't talk much on the way home. He did ask me if I felt better about having apologized to Big Farley, and congratulated me on going one step further and apologizing to Officer Bigger. I lied and said I felt cleaner inside about the whole damn thing, and even asked him if I did well enough for God's sake, and he told me to stop being sarcastic and he was proud of me and all the rest of it, and then he said a curious thing.

Pop said, "I don't like the way Officer Farley called Ricky 'that Negro girl.'"

CHAPTER 10

As Pop and I pulled up to our street, we saw Grandpa Constantine's big yellow Cadillac parked in our driveway.

Any other time, it would have been a bad sign; today, it was worse. The irony was that I could remember Grandpa's car in our driveway maybe twice in the last ten years, and one of those times was when Grandma had died.

Pop reacted in an apropos sort of way: "Damn."

In the house, Doreen and Susan sat at the kitchen table looking pretty glum, and Grandpa paced the floor, a cup of coffee in his hands. He met our entrance with a hard gaze.

"Things are not going good," he said. Only he said it like this: "Tinksa not goongood."

"Fine thanks, and how are you?" Pop said.

"Niggers got this place turned upside down, got the boy upside down too," Grandpa said.

"Dub," I said, by way of introduction.

Doreen sighed. Susan, almost imperceptibly, rolled her eyes.

"It's not *Negroes* who've got this neighborhood turned upside down," Pop said, sounding tired and resigned, "it's other people. The Duboises are not blowing out their own doors with shotguns."

"Lookit dis," Grandpa said. He walked to the kitchen table and held up the newspaper. A small headline, near the bottom of the page, said, "Shotgun Used in Suspected Racial Attack."

"I saw it," Pop said. "I think it's good, don't you? I called a friend at the night desk, told him to get the story from the police."

I hadn't seen it. Doug had delivered my papers that morning, and I'd spent the better part of the day in bed.

"Reporters," Grandpa growled. "And that column of yours. What the hell you trying to do? These people got guns now. It's not safe here."

"I agree," Pop said. "It's a shame."

"That all you can say?" Grandpa said. "What about your family, your wife and kids. What about their safety?"

"I'd say they've all been brave," Pop said. "I'm proud of them."

"Proud?" Grandpa said with disdain. "Proud gonna get them shot. Them nig—."

"I'll ask you not to use that word in my house," Pop said.

"They don't belong here," Grandpa said, sounding uncannily like Doreen had the day before. He squinted at Pop. "Because they niggers."

"That's it," Pop said as he turned a harsh glance toward Grandpa Constantine. "You kids leave the room."

"Pop," Susan said.

"Susan!" Doreen said.

"Pop!" I said.

"Out," Pop said.

Of course, we all know that when an adult asks kids to leave, it's the same as saying, "Why don't you go to another room and spend the next twenty minutes with your ears glued to the door."

So that's what we did.

Their conversation was more or less the same for a while, although Grandpa did manage to refrain from using the word again, at least during the parts we could hear. They shouted back and forth, with Doreen throwing in an occasional "Mr. Avenging Crusader" and things like that, and finally they got around to accusing each other of not having our best interests in mind. That made Pop angry, and he said, "This is the best place for them at a time like this," to which Doreen said, "Well, that's good for you but not for me!"

And it was about then that I knew Doreen would go home again with her father. It was a common practice with her, as if you hadn't seen that by now. But this time it was worse. The signs were all there. She was like an atomic bomb, sizzling.

Only this time she was determined not to go alone. "Susan!" she said. "Walter! Come in here."

"You're coming to Grandpa's with me for a few days," she said.

"Damn right," Grandpa said.

"Why?" Susan said.

"Because it's not safe, that's why," Doreen said. "I turn my back and you and your brother get into some fight over this, this girl, then someone shoots at their house, and your brother, who has been missing all night, is practically in her arms in the back yard watching the whole thing happen. Then they accuse a policeman! And that woman, that *Dubois* woman! That's why."

"Dub and I have taken care of the fight thing, Doreen," Pop said. "Dub apologized."

"What? *Dub* apologized? Who *started* the whole thing?" Then she realized that she was moving herself into a position of having to defend me. "No," she said, "I don't want to hear it. The children are coming with me, and that's that."

"Damn right," Grandpa repeated.

"Stay out of this," Pop said.

Doreen's jaw dropped for the second time in twenty-four hours. It stayed that way.

Grandpa slammed his hand down on the table. His eyes practically left his face and his skin turned close to black as his accent got thicker with rage. "Who da hell you tink you are?" he hissed.

A strange calm seemed to overtake Pop. "If you really want to know," he said, "I'm everything you hate. I am your daughter's husband."

Grandpa shook and spit flew out of the corners of his mouth. I had this fleeting thought that this must be what it looks like when someone is about to have a massive stroke.

"In my young days I coulda chewed you up and spit you out," he growled.

"In your young days," Pop said, "you would've ordered someone else to chew me up and spit me out."

"Ungghh," Doreen groaned.

Grandpa walked over to Pop and drew his chest up against Pop's, invading his personal space something terrible. I actually feared for Pop at that moment.

"You son a—," Grandpa said, and hesitated. Pop's eyes winced as Grandpa breathed heavily. "I'm gonna let that slide outa respect for my grandchildren," Grandpa said. "I'll be out in the car. Dis ain't over." And he stalked out.

Pop looked at Doreen, whose mouth was slack. "Doreen," he said. "The kids stay."

"Oh, really," she grunted. She then began to giggle, at first just a little trickle of a giggle, then it got louder. It was a scary thing to watch.

"Well," she said between heaves, "well, well, well. What does it matter anyway? I'm only their mother, I guess."

"No," Pop said, "we're a family. We should stick this out together."

"Family? Oh, that's a lovely thought, Walter. A family. I loved the way you just treated my father. Just like family." Doreen shook with laughter.

"But, you see," she continued, "I have no say here anyway. My children are out running around town in a gang, fighting, *taking care of it later* behind my back. My husband spends his nights guarding a house full of strangers and makes himself a target for this person with a shotgun—"

The next thing I said, I wished I hadn't said it almost as soon as I said it. I guess I blurted it out. But, my God, who was thinking these days?

"And," I said, "there are the phone calls, too."

Pop shot me a glance that could've dropped Floyd Patterson at twenty paces.

"Of course, those too," Doreen said. And then she laughed again, a hollow, vacant chuckle.

"I'm sure we'll find out who's been doing those things," Pop said, "all those things. But the point is, we should try and stick this out here, in the neighborhood, as a family. We shouldn't run."

Doreen stood up, slowly. It sort of hurt to see her stand like that, as if she was an old woman, her bones brittle and creaky. Like Mrs. Oliphant. She looked defeated, in a final and irreversible way.

"I'll be at Papa's," she said. "Have the kids call me every day."

Susan reached out for Doreen's arm. "Mom," she said, "stay." She started to sob a bit. "Please?"

"Honey, it's been written on the wall since that family moved in here," Doreen said. "This is not for me, and I am so very tired."

"Doreen," Pop said, "please, stay with us." He raised his eyebrows at me.

"Doreen," I said, "I'm sorry about the fight and running away and staying out all night." And I was, I really was at that moment. Doreen looked like hell, finger on the phone or no finger on the phone. And I sort of felt like hell, too.

She looked at me as though she'd met me for the first time in our lives. "I do believe you mean that, Walter," she said. "I'll be upstairs packing."

Pop went up with her, and within ten minutes or so they came down with her bag and they both had wet eyes and I wished life could have been better for all of us just then. But it wasn't. Doreen kissed us on the cheek, the ripe smell of wine thick around her. She said the usual things, things like be good and mind your father and call me every day and I'll be back soon and all that. But even though she'd done this before, gone off to stay with her father, this time it was different. It seemed sadder, and permanent. It was as if the divide had just now widened beyond our ability to cross it, as if she was burdened with so much sadness that it would keep her away forever. The whole thing was awful and contrary and Susan broke down crying in the middle of it and finally had to run up to her room.

Pop escorted Doreen out to the car, and she got in next to her father who scowled at Pop the whole time. As they drove off, I felt as if we'd all come to a turning point in this whole Ricky thing, and that something was about to happen. Maybe it was that I had the Mr. Officer Bigger Farley information in the palm of my hand and I felt as if I could control it, him, and everything by simply having the knowledge. Or maybe it was that I was so tired of it all that I believed it was about to be over, that something would happen to cause the whole thing to just end. Who knows what I thought. Like Doreen, I was so very tired.

My punishment for having brained Big Farley was only one-third completed after I'd apologized to Big and left him standing dumbfounded in the kitchen next to a paper heart that said "Hapy Mother's Day Mom, Henry Jr. 1955."

The next thing I had to do—and I don't mind saying this—I had to write an incredibly stupid letter to the Chief of Police, apologizing for having sent the police out that night looking for me. I mean, in the first place, I always had the impression that it was their *job* to drive around looking for kids who are lost or missing or whatever. And since it was a police officer's son who had started the whole bloody thing, I couldn't see why I had to be the one to take the blame again for having put them to task by looking for me. After all, I had prevented Big from committing murder, something that would have at the very least embarrassed the hell out of the department. I even began to fantasize that they should even *thank* me, perhaps give me a medal or something for stopping Big in his tracks.

That reasoning got me nowhere with Pop. Where it got

me was straight to my desk with a pen and some paper, with the instructions, "Make it sound like you mean it."

So I wrote—did I say this before?—a deeply stupid letter to the chief, which said in part that I was sorry I had wasted the taxpayers' time and money and had upset everyone at the station by making them interrupt their coffee breaks to run around at night with spotlights and flashlights and all that. Well, I didn't really say the thing about the coffee breaks, but I wanted to, I can tell you that.

I also said that I had no intention of ever running away again, and had learned my lesson thank you very much and how could I have been so thoughtless blah, blah, blah, and then I clicked into overdrive.

At the end of the letter, I went into this passionate bit about how I now realized that the police were top-notch professionals and a credit to the town, and had acted heroically in trying to find me and were an inspiration to us all. So much of an inspiration that, on top of being indescribably grateful, I was now considering a future career in law enforcement, I was so goddamned inspired. I even said that I'd be honored if I could serve with Officer Henry Farley someday.

Hell, I figured, a little irony might help make me feel better.

After I finished the letter, I passed it by Pop for inspection. As he read it, his eyebrows rose and his first comment was, "Laying it on a little thick, aren't we?"

"You said to make it sound like I meant it."

"That's right, but I didn't say to make it sound like you were campaigning for sainthood. Anyway, it'll do. What's this about wanting to become a police officer and serve with Mr. Farley?"

"Anything's possible."

Pop told me what the third part of my triumvirate punishment would be. After apologizing to Big Farley and writing the letter to the Chief of Police, I still had a price to pay, mostly, I suspect, because Pop wanted to demonstrate to Doreen that we were sincere about my atonement and everything.

"No circus," Pop said. "You're grounded."

"Pardon?" I felt my heart skip a beat.

"No circus," he said, "until the last day. You can go that one day so you can see the Big Top show."

"Pop, you don't know what you're saying."

"I do," he said, "I do."

"Pop," I whispered. I was hoarse. "Really, you don't know what you're saying."

But it was final. He made it clear. I would go to the circus only once, on its final day in town. With the circus due to arrive in a couple of days, Big Farley had, in effect, ruined my entire year.

I drifted through the next couple of days like the haze over Hartford. I just didn't feel like moving. Doug was appropriately astounded by my punishment, and even felt a little guilty. After all, I was grounded because I had saved his life. In fact, at one point Doug even said, "Then I won't go to the circus either."

"Don't be a nut," I said, "it's not your fault."

"No, it is, sort of," he said. "I mean, Big was trying to kill me when you tried to kill him."

"Actually, now that you mention it," I said, feeling sorry for myself, "you did sort of bring it on yourself. Big was probably out to kill you because you waved that rubber around in his face last week at the Nike Site. Jerk."

"Wait a minute, wanker-face," Doug said, "I was saving *your* hide."

"Scum-breath."

"Pus-for-brains."

"Well," I said, "there's nothing we can do about it now."

Doug pondered for a moment. "Anyway, I mean it," he said. "I won't go to the circus either, until you go the last night."

"Get out of town," I said. "That's stupid. I'm the one who's grounded, you're not. So what if you have all the fun. I'll just stay home and watch my life crumble into minuscule, insignificant atoms of boredom as you and everyone else *in the entire world* just laughs it up and has a grand old time at the circus. Only, remember to think about me when you're riding the Slalom of Death. Just think, 'Good old Dub, he saved my life and now he's at home watching "You Bet Your Life" for about the zillionth time'."

"Hey," Doug said, "I said I'd stay home."

"I'm just kidding." And I was, sort of. "Jerk."

Susan was equally aghast at the whole thing, but was more pragmatic.

"Well," she said, "No sense in both of us having a bad time."

"What ever happened to loyalty?" I said. "You're my sister, for God's sake. Even Doug said that he'd stay home with me."

"You don't believe for a minute that he'd really do that, do you?"

"No. But it was a nice gesture, anyway."

"Okay," she said, "then because I have this enormous amount of empathy I'll stay home with you, too, just like Doug won't."

"Thank you," I said. "Jerk."

When Ricky came by, later that same day, it was more difficult to tell her. Don't ask me why, it just was.

She came sauntering up the street wearing a light green dress, her tawny hair braided in threes, bobbing behind, just like it did the first time we saw her. God, it was good to see her. Doug and I were sitting on his front stoop, reading comics.

"Hello, there, boys," she said, in a chirpy sort of way.

"Hey, Ricky Slick," Doug said.

"Ricky Slick?" I said.

"It's a nickname," Doug said.

"You have a nickname for Ricky?" I said.

"Sure, what's wrong with that?"

"You've got nicknames for each other? When did all this start?"

Doug's eye twinkled. He clearly relished the moment. "Recently," he said.

"Actually, just now," Ricky said, "except that my father has always called me that." Doug looked crestfallen.

"So, what's your nickname for Doug?" I said.

"I don't have one," Ricky said. "Should I think of one?"

"How about 'Spike' or 'Killer' or something like that?" Doug said.

"I can think of a whole lot of words that rhyme with Doug," I said, "like 'Bug' or 'Slug.' Or 'Lug.' The list goes on."

"I don't think I would call someone 'Killer'," Ricky said.

"I vote for Doug Slug," I said, and shot him this maybe-it's-joke-maybe-it's-not glance.

"Anyway," Ricky said, and scuffed the ground. "Daddy just put his foot down."

"What do you mean?" I said.

"Daddy is determined," she said, "to send us back to Louisiana."

I thought about her hugging me the other night, and how I had been thinking about that hug almost constantly since then.

"I really don't know what to expect," she said. "I've spent summers there, with Grandma. But I've never lived there."

It sure was a great hug.

"But you're not going forever," Doug said.

"No," she said, "just until they catch…him."

"When are you going?" I said, clearing my throat.

"After the circus," she said. "After it leaves town. Daddy says we have to stay away until it gets better up here or until he gives up on the police ever catching these people. That's what he said, at any rate."

"You'll miss school," I said.

"I haven't even thought about it," she said.

The three of us hung in silence for a moment.

"Circus sets up tomorrow," Doug said, trying, valiantly, to save the situation. "You excited?"

"Ever," Ricky said. "I've been looking forward to it, despite all that's been going on."

"Dub can't go," Doug said.

"Really?" Ricky said. She was surprised. "Why?"

"It's a long story," I said, "but it has to do with me crowning Big and then running away. It's incredible, it really is."

Ricky squinted her eyes and cocked her head. "Dub," she said, "I just want to say, you know, about what my mother said to your mother the other night—"

"You heard that, too?" I said.

"Yes," she said. "I'm sorry."

"Jesus," I said.

Ricky stood silently, as if that was like telling her old and tired news or something.

Doug's mother appeared at the front door. "Doug," she said. "It's your father on the phone."

Doug's face went dark, and he looked at Ricky, then at me. "Okay," he said, quietly.

"Why, hello, Rebecca," Doug's mother said. "How are things at home?"

"Fine, ma'am," Ricky said, "thank you for asking."

"Well, you tell your mother again that if she needs anything, needs my help, she knows where to find me."

"Much obliged," Ricky said.

"Doug, it's long distance," Mrs. Hammer said.

Doug left, muttering, "I'll be right back."

I turned to Ricky. "So, you really have to go?"

She looked at me in a strange way, and her face seemed, at that moment, fragile as a bougainvillea blossom. "That's what Daddy says. Of course, I don't want to go."

She sat down in Doug's place.

"You know, Dub," she said, "it was really nice that night. Before Officer Farley came by." She shot me a sweet, soft smile. My face turned hot, but I just nodded, I guess.

"So," she said, "no one believes us. That it was Officer Farley, I mean. Even my daddy thinks we must have seen ghosts."

"Mine, too," I said. "Looks like Susan and Doug believe us, though. At least, they say they do. But they don't talk much about it, like they want to believe us but they really don't, you know? Besides, there's nothing they can do about it, anyway."

"Somebody's got to believe us, eventually," she said, firmly. "It would clear everything up, and we could get our lives back to normal."

"I know that. But if we tell on him again, if we keep bringing up the story, he'll come straight for us. He's got the perfect alibi for that night *because* he's a cop. He thinks he's safe. Especially now that I told him I must have made a mistake."

"What?" Ricky said.

I described my forced trip over to the Farley den to apologize to Big for the rock incident, and how I faced Officer Farley.

"Dub," Ricky said slowly, as if talking to a child. "Why would you tell him that? That almost gives him…permission. To do it again."

"He's going to do something anyway. I just wanted to throw him off, to see his reaction, and you know what? It felt good."

"Well, fine for you," she said, miffed. "I'm glad you feel better."

"I'm sorry Ricky," and I was, sort of. But at the same time, a thought occurred to me. It was a whisper, the hint of a idea. "If we had proof, real proof we could show someone, we could nail him."

"You already said it, Dub. He's a policeman, he can lie his way out of anything. He's mad, you know that."

"I know," I said.

"And you apologized to Big Farley," Ricky said, turning back to my visit. "I find that odd."

"You and about a hundred other people. Even, I'm sure, Big Farley, if he has any inkling at all what I was doing there. But in a way, Pop was right, it *was* the right thing to do. I did feel more like a man. Don't ask."

"All these heroics," Ricky said. Her bottom lip quivered and she shuddered slightly, then got hold of herself. "He's trying to kill us, you know," she said.

"No, he's not," I said, half-convinced. "He's just trying to scare you off."

"He's a mean, awful man," Ricky said.

Then, I don't know if it was the emotion built up over the last several weeks, or if it was simply Ricky sitting there in the morning sun with her hair braided in threes, but I blurted out, I mean I really had no control over it, "I don't want you to go, Rebecca."

I mean, I called her *Rebecca* for God's sake. But it sounded so pretty, and so right, that I blurted it out again. "Rebecca," I said.

Ricky's bottom lip quivered again. "Dub," she said, "I—"

"Hey, Ricky!" a voice boomed. It was Susan, coming out from our house.

Ricky turned quickly away from Susan and wiped her eyes. Then she turned back. "Hi," she said, back to being chirpy. Our lives were getting awfully schizophrenic lately.

Susan walked over to our lemonade table. "Dub, Mom is on the phone," she said. "She wants to say hi."

"What is this, wayward-parents-on-the-phone-day? Can't you say I'm out? In Siam or somewhere?"

"Just go in and say hi," Susan said, "it won't kill you. She's trying to be extra responsible and caring and everything."

So, I went into the house and left Susan and Ricky at the lemonade stand. Ricky gave me kind of a curious look as I walked away, a look that made me wonder if blurting out "Rebecca" was the right thing to do. Of course, when it comes to genuine blurting, there's not a whole hell of a lot a person can do about it anyway.

I picked up the phone.

"Hi, Doreen," I said.

"Walter, honey, how are you?" Doreen's voice seemed distant and tinny, almost empty, as if she was a robot or something.

"Not bad, Doreen. How are you?"

"Well," she said, "lonely, I suppose. But I'll be back in a few days. Won't that be nice?"

"Sure," I said. Which was sort of a lie—what I mean is, I didn't really know what would've been nice.

"Everything's okay at home?" she said.

"Yes," I said. "Pop's at work, and Susan and I are hanging around. Everything's great, really."

"Are you sad about not going to the circus?" she said.

"Yes," I said.

"Well, I'll tell you what," she said, getting awfully chirpy herself all of a sudden, "I'll come home soon and we can all go, as a family. How's that? We'll get good seats and sit in the front row at the Big Top show, and we'll have a lovely time. It'll be fun, don't you think?"

I had to admire her for her fortitude, and for trying to make something out of a situation that was beyond her control. Then I began to feel sort of, I don't know, blurry.

"It'll be great, Doreen," I said.

"Well, good," she said, "I'll call tomorrow at about the same time, okay?"

"Okay, Doreen," I said.

"Bye, honey," she said, and the phone clicked. I didn't hang up my end.

You know how sometimes you want someone to say

something like "I love you" for no particular reason other than an "I love you" would sound pretty damn good at the moment? Well, you just want them to say it, no matter who it is, even if it's someone who'd have been the last person you wanted to say that a few days ago, or even a few seconds ago. Sometimes you just want to hear it, for God's sake, from anyone.

I guess I did at that moment, because after Doreen hung up the phone and there was a dead silence, I felt a weight well up inside me, a heavy, ugly weight inside my chest. I needed to get rid of it, because I started to have a hard time breathing. I started to gasp, and I stared at the phone in my hand.

And I thought, *Rebecca.*

Then, I guess it was sort of like blurting again, I slammed the receiver down on the phone, and it felt so good I picked it up and slammed it down again. Then I slammed it again, and again, and again, I don't know how many times—it's not the sort of thing a guy counts, after all—and all I remembered was the phone ringing as I slammed it, hard, again and again like an annoying insect. Finally, when I came out of it, which was more or less like opening your eyes at dusk, I was in the hall with a bunch of phone parts all over the place and the weight in my chest was heavy like a sack of sand. My right hand was skinned along the knuckles, and—this was my punishment I guess—the pain in my back kicked in like an old sore deprived of its scab. I stood silently for a few minutes, breathing like an emphysema patient, until I got some control back.

"Christ," I said, and I left the whole mess right there, for God knows what reason.

When I got back outside, Doug had rejoined Susan and Ricky. They all turned to me.

"What happened to your hand?" Susan said. "Are you okay?"

"I dropped the phone," I said. "How's your dad?"

"Peachy," Doug said, and he looked away.

"Anyway," Susan said, "back to C.D. Now, I'm going for 'Carlo,' and what, how about 'Dubois?'" Only she pronounced it "Dubwah." Ricky, I swear, blushed.

What they were talking about was what the 'C.D.' part of the C.D. Lorenzo Traveling Family Circus and Carnival name stood for. This was a guessing game they'd played for years, ever since we first went to the circus. Susan, in particular, had been extra interested in this for some time now.

Lorenzo was the sort of guy who would drive the girls crazy whenever he walked into the ring, or whenever they saw him strolling around the circus grounds or wherever—he apparently had this mystical charisma and smoldering sexuality, like a rock-and-roller. Personally, I think his appeal was related to the fact that he was the owner of the circus and seemed to have this great supernatural life, touched by the gods with riches, fame, and great animals.

It didn't hurt that C.D. Lorenzo was good-looking in a steamy sort of way. He was tall and dark, and had a thin, black mustache that he twirled at the right moments, adding to the mystique that caused girls like Susan to conjecture that his name was possibly 'Carmen Dibrezzio' or whatever. He was youngish, about thirty-five or so, and used a badly faked and indistinct European accent whenever he made announcements in the ring, or whenever he was in public.

"So, what is this Mr. C.D. Lorenzo like?" Ricky said.

"Cow Dung," Doug said, and laughed.

I guess I don't need to tell you that C.D. did not enjoy the same popularity with the boys as among the girls.

"We'll talk about it later," Susan said, and winked at Ricky. "They wouldn't understand."

At that, I sort of went into overdrive. Again.

"Understand?" I blurted. "Susan, did you know C.D. Lorenzo probably has all his ringmaster suits made in Perth Amboy? Do you understand *that*?"

"Perth Amboy?" Doug said.

"Yes," I said. "Perth Amboy! Or somewhere like that. *That's* what C.D. Lorenzo is all about."

"So?" Susan said. "What does this have to do with C.D. Lorenzo's name?"

"Him," I said, "the man himself, is what I'm talking about. He's not some European count, the guy's probably from New Jersey, for God's sake."

"So what if he's from New Jersey?" Susan said.

"That's it! See, you've got this whole thing wrong. Here you girls are throwing this hero worship at this guy who buys his suits in *Passaic* for God's sake, but whose fake accent makes him sound like he just stepped off the boat from *Paris* with his arms stuffed with bread loaves and whose name is probably Chuck Dumpy or something like that, and all I'm trying to say is—"

"The world isn't always what it seems," Ricky said. "That's what you're trying to say?"

"Precisely," I said, and then, like a moron, I said it again. "Precisely."

"Clear enough to me," Doug said. "You're losing it again, aren't you?"

"No! All I mean is what the world needs is less faking, less *lying*. Don't you see it?" I teetered forward just a little, enough so that Doug leaned toward me. My bloody hand began to ache, and my back was as tight as a pinball spring.

Susan stepped forward and grabbed my arm. "Dub," she said. "Knock it off."

Susan's eyes were dark, and I could see fear and anger in them. Her temper had flared, but she was more confused than anything.

"Okay," I said.

Now, you're not going to believe this, but, in an instant, after I said "okay," I was okay. Sort of. I mean, I calmed down, in a slightly agitated way. They all stared at me with small fears on their faces.

"I had a point," I said.

"The point's taken," Ricky said, and she, in particular, squinted hard at me. "You're very tired."

Well, who can comment on behavior like that? Certainly not me. God knows what was happening to me, and to Ricky and the rest of us. Things were just getting more bizarre and at a faster rate than ever, and my body, including my back and hand and weighted chest, was wracked and I was tired enough to not even think about it. All in all, it was an annoying way to be.

What I remembered next was a small conversation between Ricky and Susan where they decided to get together later, and Susan said, "Okay, I'll call you."

"I had better call you," Ricky said. "We changed our number again, and Daddy said not to give it to anyone. Not that he suspects anyone in particular, but he said it's better not to give it out. That way we can eliminate certain people."

"Our phone's out of order anyway," I said, dazed.

Susan sighed. "Let me check."

She disappeared into the house, leaving Doug and Ricky and me out in front of Doug's house.

"Are you okay, Dub?" Ricky said.

"Copacetic," I said. "Top flight."

Susan came out of the house, and her face was ashen. "Where did you drop the phone from?" she said. "The Mercury capsule?"

"It bounced a couple of times."

"Well," she said, "The extension works anyway. Ricky can still call."

"When did your father change the number?" I said.

"Yesterday," Ricky said.

"Who's got it?" I said.

"No one," Ricky said. "No one at all. Not even family back in Louisiana. Just Daddy, Mom, my grandmother, and me. And of course," she hesitated, "the police."

Things broke up after that, and I never did get to finish my conversation with Ricky, at least not that day.

Later there was a little bit of hell to pay for the way I beat up the phone. Pop came home from work and took one look at it and asked me if I'd been having a rough day. He asked me if I was aware what the cost of a new phone was, and I said no, but I guess since I was the one who'd dropped it, I guessed I'd be finding out soon enough. Pop told me to cut the charade, Dub, you didn't drop the phone, did you? I mumbled something about maybe I didn't quite drop it, you know, like an average, everyday, simple drop, but maybe I helped it along or something. That's when Pop told me that I had to call the phone company tomorrow to order a new phone—same model, same color—and I might as well start counting my newspaper route money because a good chunk of it was going to pay for the thing, and did I have anything more to say about it?

I told Pop that no, I guessed I'd said enough about it, and he replied, yes, I suspect you have. But when he said that he had this sadness covering his face, and I thought: All this dread, everywhere. It's like a disease. But he didn't tug at his ears.

I slept like a dead man that night, possibly the deepest sleep I'd ever had. I had dreams that were deep and dark and intricate, but if you were to ask me today what they were, I couldn't tell you. They were the kind of dreams that make you even more tired while you're asleep.

Nevertheless, I still managed to get up early the next day to do my paper route. I found Pop, as usual lately, seated in his car in front of the Dubois's place as the sun came up over East Hartford. He was asleep and looked peaceful, as did the house, and I didn't wake him up.

Later that morning, a Saturday, Pop came back from his guard duty and reported that all was well and no incidents had occurred during the night. Actually, nothing had happened at the Dubois's place since the night Officer Bigger Farley had blasted the front door, which was, if I remember correctly, only the previous Tuesday. I was reminded of the packed agenda of the week, starting with Pop's column appearing on Monday, and culminating in the fight, then my flight, the shotgun, my apology to Big Farley, and, of course, the great bits about hugging Ricky in between.

"Did the police come by?" I asked Pop.

"As usual," he said. "Actually, I'm impressed by their concern, especially since the shotgun night."

"Was Officer Farley with them?"

"Dub," he said, "Let's not go though this again. Anyway, I don't know. The police came by during Herb's shift. He told me about it."

Then Pop took off for the newspaper, leaving us with instructions to either call Doreen or wait for her phone call. As soon as he pulled out of the driveway, Susan said we'd better call Doreen first and get that out of the way because we had big plans for the day.

"The circus is in today," she said. "We're going down to watch them set up."

"Great," I said. "I'm not supposed to do that."

"Why not?" Susan said. "Pop said you weren't supposed to go to the circus, but he didn't say anything about not going to watch them set up."

Entirely true.

We called Doreen, and that went fine except for the part when Grandpa Constantine answered the phone and didn't recognize me. I had to explain to him that I wasn't some phone salesman peddling Hawaiian vacations or whatever, and that I was only calling to speak to our mother, to which he replied, "I don't know, some kid," as he handed the phone over to Doreen.

Doreen was pretty cheery, and it sounded like she'd gotten some rest and was having a good time relaxing at her father's place. She asked after Pop and Doug and reiterated that she would be back before the last Big Top Show so that we could all go as a family and be nuclear and everything, and then, out of the blue, as if she'd read my mind in a belated sort of way, she said, "You know I love you, Walter."

I blurted out something about loving her too, and got flustered and quickly handed the phone over to Susan, who had this pithy sort of conversation with Doreen about swimming and tennis and all that. Then, Doreen must have told Susan that she loved her, because suddenly there was Susan getting slightly flustered and blurting out, "I love you, too," to Doreen.

When she hung up, Susan tried not to look at me.

My stomach, which was in knots by then for any number of reasons, flipped a few times, and I said, "I wish she would get better."

"Me, too," Susan said.

I called the phone company and made an ass of myself trying to order a new telephone. They couldn't believe I wasn't some kid making a crank call—I could almost hear them roll their eyes through the phone. I started to get steamed—I actually thought I was going to lose it again and start blathering about C.D. Lorenzo's New Jersey-made suits—until Susan grabbed the phone from me and said, "Yes, thank you, now when can we have this phone installed? Here, let me check my schedule. Yes, Monday at three would be fine, thank you very much." She hung up.

"If you ever want to convince someone you know what you're talking about," she said, "just check your schedule. Adults are always checking their schedules."

The day's plan, which Susan had apparently worked out with Doug and Ricky the day before (me being a psychological outlaw for pretty much that whole day) was that we would ride our bikes down to the vacant lot behind Woolworth's, where the circus would arrive in a couple of hours to set up for the first night's activities.

It always amazed me that C.D. Lorenzo and his troupe could pull in like that, in apparent disarray, and in five or six hours have the whole damn circus set up and ready to go for the evening.

But they always managed to do it, and do it efficiently. I liked watching them offload the animals from the trucks. Some animals, like the Bengal tigers, the lions, and some of the bears were offloaded in their cages. Others, like the horses and chimps, stepped off the truck in chains and were led to cages or to an open corral area.

Whenever Simba came off his truck, which was a pretty damn big truck that had the words "SIMBA, PRIDE OF THE AFRICAN JUNGLE" emblazoned on the sides, he always stepped off like the president steps off of his airplane. He would stop at the top of his ramp, squint slightly in the sun, and flap his giant ears as if waving to a crowd. And, in fact, he usually had a crowd waiting for him.

Once, several years before, a trainer had seen me at the edge of the crowd as Simba stepped down the ramp. He called over, out of the blue, and asked if I wanted to touch the elephant. I stepped over, and Simba held out his trunk as if on cue for me to touch. The trainer said go ahead, touch him. I reached out and scratched the trunk, as if I were scratching a dog's back. It was rough like sandpaper, dusty, and warm, and Simba's moist breath smelled like hay. I looked up and saw him looking down at me in a curious sort of way, as if following the lines of his trunk.

This time I sat on my bike next to Doug while we listened to Susan explain all the workings of the circus to Ricky. Ricky took it all in like a trouper, and didn't seem in the least bit bored. The circus people worked quickly, lifting and hoisting tents and great spans of steel and track as they assembled the booths and rides that would later become a small city on the fair grounds. They sweated a lot and were profane as hell, and there was great excitement in the whole thing. The crowd was large, about fifty people, most of them kids on bikes. I scanned the faces and noted that Big Farley wasn't anywhere to be seen, nor were any of his gang.

"Wonder where Big is," I whispered to Doug.

Doug surveyed the crowd. "Nursing his wounds," he said.

At one point C.D. Lorenzo walked by us, shouting in that accent—you wanted to puke hearing it—"No, no, no, ovah heah, ovah heah wid zee canopy!" I thought Susan was going to die the way she choked on her words as he passed by. Then, as if the whole thing was a bad scene in a worse movie, C.D. did the unimaginable. He turned to Susan and Ricky, and winked. Just that, he winked, and passed by. I thought they'd both pee their pants, I really did.

"Oh, C.D.," Doug whispered in a lilting voice, "so nice of you to stop by and say 'allo!"

"Shut up, Doug," Susan said.

I picked up on it. "Shall we zee you at zee show lateah, Misteah C.D.?" I said.

Susan whipped around to me. "I guess *you* won't have to worry about that," she hissed.

"Guess not," I said.

"Now, come on," Ricky said, softly. "He's just another guy. Are you boys jealous?"

If you ever want to get a guy really jealous, the best thing do is tell him is that he's jealous, because then he'll deny it so adamantly that there is no doubt in his mind that he's jealous.

"I'm not jealous!" we both said.

Suddenly a door swung open at the back of Simba's trailer. The crowd strained and a few kids hushed each other, and Simba emerged from his cavern, led by his trainer. His trunk came out first, and he appeared to be sniffing the air. I imagined he was checking by smell to see if this was a place he'd been to before. Apparently, when he was satisfied that it was, he stepped gingerly, as gingerly as an elephant can step, to the edge of the platform. He stopped and did his little ear-wave, thanking the crowd for showing up. One of the kids in the crowd started to clap, a totally inappropriate gesture, and he was slapped down by a friend. It was a time for awe, not clapping. I tried to focus on Simba's eyes, but he was far enough away so that all I could imagine was him scanning the crowd for someone he knew. I thought briefly about raising my hand and shouting, "Simba! Over here! I'm here."

But, of course, I didn't.

The trainer then led him down the platform and off around the side of the truck. They headed in a slow-motion jaunt toward the elephant area, where Simba would be kept, staked to the ground by a long chain and metal pin sunk four feet into the dirt. I know that because I once watched Simba's trainers preparing the area, and it took two men twenty minutes to pound that stake in. It seemed a particularly bad way to live, speaking for Simba, but my hunch is it was better than living in a cage. But not much better.

After Simba was led away, the highlight of the whole thing was over as far as I was concerned. I said something about taking off before Pop got home from work, and Doug agreed that it would be a good thing to do. Susan said she wanted to stick around for a while and Ricky decided to stay with her—both, I imagined, to get another look at C.D. Lorenzo, the pride of New Jersey. That sort of hurt, but there were other things on my mind, other things that had to get done and done soon before Mr. Dubois sent his family to Louisiana.

I had to figure out some way that I could get Ricky aside and talk to her about Officer Bigger Farley and his shotgun, and what we ought to do about it. I didn't have her phone number, and I couldn't see myself just riding down there again out of the blue. I was sort of a suspicious character these days as far as Mrs. Dubois was concerned. She had never quite gotten over the fact that I had been out in their back yard with Ricky that night Officer Bigger blasted her front door in.

Nevertheless, it was urgent I talk to Ricky soon. We had to try and figure a way to keep her in town. We had the knowledge, we had the bad guy, and we had to find a way to stop it without putting Ricky's life even more in danger than it already was.

I had to know how she wanted to handle it, because I sure wasn't handling it very well.

CHAPTER 11

Doug held off going to the circus for three days, commiserating with me and my deeply unjust punishment. When he finally broke down, to his credit he came to me first to tell me about it.

"I have to go to the circus," he said.

"Hey, don't tell me about it," I said. "A guy's got to do what a guy's got to do."

"I just wanted you to know."

"It's fine."

"I mean, I tried," he said. "But the Cyclops Man, you know, and the Alligator Boy."

"I said it was okay."

"And the cotton candy and Toss-the-Softball, I just—"

"Doug, it's fine."

"I saved all this money."

"Doug."

"And the Tilt-a-Whirl."

"Doug!"

"Hey, you don't have to get snippy about it."

Also to his credit, Doug came back every day and described to me what he'd seen and done, yet managed to keep the excitement down to a minimum. He even tried to act bored about the whole thing once in a while.

"The Cyclops Man's third eye is fake," he said one day.

"Oh?"

"Just a big fat mole there, smack in the middle of his forehead. And he puts make-up on it to make it look like an eye."

"Imagine that," I said.

"What a gyp. Wasted a quarter."

"What about the dog in the cannon?" I said. His face went blank.

"You know, remember when you and Lance talked about how they got the dog into the cannon by tossing a cat into it?"

"Oh, that," he said. "Yeah, well, they must be saving it for the last night. You'll be there, you'll see."

"I'll be there," I said.

"Lorenzo is still walking around like he owns the place."

"He does own the place."

"True enough," Doug said.

Later that week two letters to the editor appeared in the newspaper, commenting on Pop's column of the week before. It was a surprise to us all, and Pop read them both and was mighty pleased that someone had taken the time to write something about his column, even though the first one wasn't exactly laudatory.

In the first letter, a Mr. Duquette of Hartford wrote that he thought the whole issue wasn't about racism and intolerance and all that, but about values and how a neighborhood had a right to preserve its values, both property and family, because a neighborhood is somehow the God-ordained root of all things good and right in America. His point was that if Negroes had a right to move into our neighborhood, then people in the neighborhood had a right, as guaranteed, he reminded Pop, by the Constitution, to protest. Mr. Duquette went on to say that while he didn't think that burning a cross in someone's yard was all that smart, he could understand why someone would be driven to it. He ended by saying that Pop should mind his own business.

"But I am minding my own business," Pop said, and had kind of a hoot over the whole letter.

The next letter was written by a Dr. Mark Weeks of Manchester. It said, in whole, "Three cheers for Walter Teed!"

Later during the morning the letters appeared, Doreen called from her father's place and had a long conversation with Pop. I gather it went something along the lines of her telling him that she didn't want to say I told you so, but see what happens when you go public with your fantasies and so on and so forth. But the call didn't seem to affect Pop much at all. He just puttered around the house for a while before he went to work, muttering—I swear I heard this—"Three cheers, well I'll be."

Susan and Ricky continued to get along pretty gloriously, and I really didn't get all that bent out of shape when they went off to the circus every day for fun and games. It seemed right for them to do it. Susan did sympathize with me about having to stay home and all, and was worried that I'd been acting so weird lately, but she also kept talking about how wonderful it was to finally hang around with another girl and talk about, well, whatever they talk about, so I couldn't begrudge her that. She told me that, initially, Mrs. Dubois was reluctant to let Ricky out of the house to go to the circus because of the threats and danger, but finally relented in the face of Ricky's constant haranguing. Ricky could be pretty damn focused when the time came for it.

As well, helping Ricky's circus cause was Mr. Dubois's insistence that the family act as normal as they could, rather than let the vandals get their way. Of course, old Mrs. Oliphant had been ready to go back to Louisiana ever since the cross-burning—I'll bet she'd been half-packed for weeks—and she objected strongly to her granddaughter putting herself squarely in danger, especially in the midst of a godless, profane spectacle such as a circus. Myself, I suspected Ricky wasn't in any danger at the circus, because we assumed that it would be unlikely for Officer Bigger Farley to start blasting away in broad daylight in the middle of a fairground. I also suspect that Mr. Dubois, for other reasons, felt Ricky was in no danger either. There were likely to be hundreds of Negroes at the circus, and I'm sure that he felt the probability of a racial melee breaking out was small.

And, I did run into Big Farley.

I had taken to riding down to the library once a day, mainly because there wasn't a whole lot else to do with everyone gone to the circus and to work all day long. And I thought I was on an Ernest Hemingway kick. All I had known about Hemingway was that he was a famous novelist who looked like a polar bear and had shot himself in the head recently, just before the Fourth of July. Pop said that Hemingway had not only been a famous novelist, but a good novelist as well, and he'd suggested I take out a book called *The Old Man and the Sea* to get acquainted with his writing.

I dropped off my James Baldwin novel, of which I hate to admit I'd read about three pages. I tried, I really gave it that old shot, and I think Baldwin is a real whip of a writer, but in the end every sentence of that book was a struggle for me, given Ricky's situation I mean. I'm going to read it soon, though. I know that now.

So I picked up *The Old Man and the Sea* and read it in a day. I began to think Hemingway was on to something about fate and frustration and bad luck, and I liked the fishing parts, but the whole thing made me feel sort of melancholy because Hemingway had shot himself. I couldn't figure why someone who had such a gift for writing would want to do something so damn contrary. I mean, it was a shame, and I said as much to the library lady when I returned the book.

"Did you know that Hemingway shot himself?" I said as I brought *For Whom the Bell Tolls* up to the desk.

"Yes, I did," she said. "*For Whom the Bell Tolls*, Walter?"

"I mean," I said, "right in the head, just recently."

"Yes, it was very tragic. Will someone be reading this to you?"

"It must have been a heck of a way to go, staring down a shotgun barrel with your toe on the trigger."

"I'm sure," she said. "But life isn't very nice sometimes."

"I wonder what he was thinking when he did it? Was he thinking he couldn't write anymore? You know, he gets up one morning and says, hey, it's all over, I've got nothing left to say to anyone, ever again. Then, wham, his brains are wallpaper. Go figure."

"Walter, please. You seem pre-occupied with this."

"Of course, he had to have been a sad person. That book about the fisherman, that was as low as things get. Nothing went right for the old guy. He works so hard and he's so *noble*, and then the sharks come and eat his fish. I wonder if Hemingway's own books depressed him, you know, even made him do it?"

"Walter, *For Whom the Bell Tolls* is not precisely uplifting either. Do you know what this book is about?"

"No, I don't, that's why I'm taking it out," I said, probably too loudly, because at that moment one of the other librarians shushed me.

"Don't you see?" I whispered. "He wasn't only tragic, he's dead."

"Walter, I think you should try a Mark Twain book," she said. "I think that fight with Henry Farley has disturbed you quite a bit."

"Maybe," I said, "I guess."

"Have you seen Henry around lately?" she said, sure that was my problem.

"No," I said, "But I'd be ecstatic to see Henry Farley around, I really would."

"Really," she said. "For whatever reason?"

"Because he wrote a Happy Mother's Day card to his mom once."

The librarian squinted her eyes. "Walter, take your book, go home, and have a long nap."

She quickly punched up the card and handed me the book. "Two weeks," she said. "Good luck."

So I left and rode over to Mr. Hwan's shop, and later got my wish about Big Farley.

Mr. Hwan was alone in his shop, looking as tired as ever. Actually, he sort of sighed when I came in the store. Not that I blame him for sighing or anything. Things had not necessarily gone well for him every time I'd been in there lately.

I poked around the comic books and considered striking up a conversation with him. But, as it turned out, I needn't have worried about it.

"So, where are friends?" Mr. Hwan said, out of the blue.

Startled, I said, "They're at the circus."

"And you? Every day you in my shop. No circus?"

"No circus," I said.

"Why?"

One of the great things about people who didn't grow up speaking English is that they pull no punches. I mean, another person might have said, "Oh, that's too bad. Any particular reason why you're not going to enjoy the one thing you look forward to all summer and for most of the year?" But with Mr. Hwan, that would have been tantamount to reciting President Kennedy's Inaugural speech.

"I'm being punished," I said.

"For hitting Henry Farley with rock?"

"You heard about that?" I said. I don't know why I was surprised. Mr. Hwan's family lived all over town, and they would have paid very close attention to the Big Farley gang and their movements.

"Yes, for hitting Henry," I said.

"He was going to stab friend, who? Douglas, true?"

"I guess," I said.

"Bad boy," Mr. Hwan said. "Bad blood."

I hoped he'd elaborate. He didn't.

Then, for whatever reason, I said, "His father is a policeman, you know."

Mr. Hwan looked at me as if I'd just informed him that most people are born with opposable thumbs. "I know," he said.

I waited again, hoping that Mr. Hwan would continue. He didn't. But since we were having this semi-animated conversation, I pushed on.

"Say," I said, "didn't the gang spray-paint your place once?"

"Oh, that, sure, sure, sure." Mr. Hwan seemed to actually relish the memory. "That boy, Ralph, he spray 'Slants Go Home'."

"Really?"

"Ralph is stupid boy," he said. "Or Henry stupid, whoever make him write it. Because when he spray it, I was *already* home. Watching Jack Benny." He chuckled.

I remembered Doug's tall story about Ralph. "Mr. Hwan, mind if I ask you a question?"

"Okay, okay." He'd begun to laugh. Apparently, the stupidity of the spray-paint job was just too much to bear.

"How did your cousin Wing catch Ralph?"

"How? How you mean how?" He was full-guffawing now. The laughter caught, and I started to chuckle.

"I mean, didn't Wing have a gun or something?" I said.

"Gun?" Mr. Hwan broke down, holding his sides. "No gun! No gun here. Very funny, gun!"

"Then, how did he do it?" Tears began to gather at the corners of my eyes.

"He just walk up behind Ralph and grab him. Gun? Very funny, gun!"

"And then?" We were both laughing like idiots.

"And then Wing call police and Officer Farley and another policeman take away Ralph. Simple." Mr. Hwan's mood sobered. "No gun," he said, and wiped his eyes.

"Just that?" I said and wiped my eyes, too.

"Yes," Mr. Hwan said. "Officers and Ralph just go away. With spray-paint."

"Officer Farley didn't say anything to Wing?"

Mr. Hwan was silent for a moment, as if weighing his response. "No," he said. "Wing say that Officer Farley and other police stand by car for a while, talking." He cleared his throat. "Making joke. Laughing."

"Laughing?" I tried hard to imagine Officer Farley laughing. "About what?"

"Who knows? People laugh." But his look told me that he knew exactly what people laugh about when they're around people like him.

"Didn't Wing fill out a report?" I said.

Mr. Hwan sighed again, then looked toward the front of his shop. "Nothing," he said. "Ralph just go home to his fatha."

"Then Officer Farley didn't make an official—"

Mr. Hwan clapped his hands together and said, "You like something or we talk all day?"

End of conversation. "Comic books, I guess," I said.

I went over to the rack and pulled out a couple of Green Lantern and Sergeant Rock comics, and put them on the counter. Mr. Hwan was busy loading cigarettes into slots behind his cash register.

I put my money on the counter. Mr. Hwan sighed again and pushed the coins back to me. "No pay today," he said.

I didn't know what to say.

"You fatha very brave to write in newspaper," he said. "You stay away from Henry Farley. Big trouble."

"Well, thanks, Mr. Hwan," I said.

"And stay away from fatha." He turned quickly.

I walked out of the store, dazed and wondering how much Mr. Hwan knew about Officer Farley, or the other cop for that matter. Thinking about it now, I guess that Officer Bigger wasn't really all that hard to figure out, particularly for people like Mr. Hwan and his cousin Wing, or people like Ricky. No official reports, not for slants.

I said thanks and got on my bike and took off. As I rounded the corner of Main and Silver Lane, there was Big himself, straddling his bike on the sidewalk, smoking a cigarette. One of his gang was with him.

I couldn't avoid them, and, in fact, almost ran straight into them. It would have been a classic accident, and if I'd been looking the other way the three of us would have ended up in a heap all over the sidewalk. I slammed on my brakes and we stared each other down for a moment.

"Hey," I said.

Big looked much like he had the week before, sort of puffy in the face. The bandage on his head had been reduced to a small cotton gauze held on with tape. He flicked the butt away.

"Hey," he said.

We sat on our bikes, trying to figure out what to do. Big, incredibly, seemed embarrassed.

The gang ferret stared quizzically at Big for a moment, then shrugged his shoulders and said, "Hey."

"Hey," I repeated.

The three of us sat and looked everywhere but at each other. I had this urge to whistle, but that really would have been too much.

"Well, I guess I'll be going," I said.

"Where to?" Big said.

I was dumbfounded. I searched his face for anger or a trace of vengeance, and I saw nothing.

"Home, I guess," I said. "You?"

"Just hanging around."

I took a chance. "Not going to the circus?"

He breathed deeply. "Grounded," he said.

"Me too," I said.

"I know," he said.

Since we were having this congenial conversation and all, I figured, what the hell, we're in broad daylight on a busy street corner. What could go wrong?

"Big," I said. "You never burned that cross on Ricky's lawn, did you."

He calmly took out another cigarette and lit it. "Heard about it," he said.

"Or spray-painted their car," I said.

"Nope," he said.

"Or threw that brick through their window."

"Listen, what do I give a shit about niggers? I got my own problems."

"Mr. Hwan's store?"

"That was Ralph's idea. What is this, a lie-detector test?" I dropped it. We were silent for a moment.

"Look," I said. "I wasn't trying to kill you."

"Aww, screw it," he said, looking down. He flicked the cigarette away. "I gotta go."

He pulled up on his bike and started to pedal away, the other boy behind him. "See you," he said over his shoulder.

I was amazed. I had never heard Big's voice in a normal conversational tone. I mean, it's not like we were ever going to be chummy or anything, or start slobbering over the good old days, but this was a big change in Big.

I was sure he'd told the truth, that he'd had nothing to do with the vandalism at Ricky's home. Yet I wondered what he knew about his father's involvement. I rode away with a vague idea in mind, the same germ of an idea that I'd had when talking to Ricky the other day. It was a strange plan, but powerful, and the more I thought about it, the more it made sense.

When I got home, I settled down to what I thought would be a long afternoon of reading *For Whom the Bell Tolls* and Sergeant Rock. They seemed related, somehow. But, fairly quickly I was reading Sergeant Rock and Green Lantern, and *For Whom the Bell Tolls* had taken a place on my shelf for what would become a two-week stay, ending my Hemingway phase.

As I went in to the kitchen to make myself a peanut butter and mustard sandwich, the phone rang. It was Doreen.

"Hi, honey," she said. "What's doing?" Her voice was bouncy.

"Making myself a sandwich," I said.

"Peanut butter and mustard?"

"As a matter of fact, yes."

"That's nice."

"How are you?" I said.

"Fine, just fine," she chirped. "I'm resting, that's all."

"Grandpa?" I said.

"He's fine as well," she said. "A little tired, he's getting old. Is Susan home?"

"No," I said, "she's probably at the circus."

"With Ricky?"

"I expect so," I said, warily.

"Well," she said, "I'll give you a call tomorrow. I'm looking forward to coming home Saturday. The circus should be fun."

"Sure will," I said.

"You be good, and have your father call me later tonight, okay?"

"Okay."

"I love you, Walter."

"Me, too, Doreen." And then I guess I flashed back to my talk with Big, and, "Doreen," I said. "Doreen?" But her end was dead.

I still had to ask. "You didn't make those phone calls, did you?"

About five minutes later, as I ate my sandwich, the phone rang again. This time it was Ricky.

"Why aren't you at the circus?" I said.

"How many times can you go to a circus?" she said.

"You wouldn't believe," I said.

"I know, I know, that seems to be the case. I thought I might find you at home, and I wanted to see you, alone. Don't you think we should talk about Officer Farley?"

"Sure. Where are Susan and Doug?"

"Still at the circus," she said.

"Come on over," I said. "No one's home." The moment I said that, my heart sort of jumped around.

"I'll be right there."

After she hung up, I panicked. This is the way my mind worked: Brush your teeth! That's it, brush those crummy teeth! And comb your hair. Pick up the comics and wipe the crumbs off the counter, and pick up those stinking socks! And I ran around in a frenzy, wiping this and brushing that, for what seemed like only an instant.

Because the doorbell rang, and I realized how very close our homes were to each other. I spit on my hands and ran them through my hair, and opened the door.

Ricky stood in the doorway. She smelled of baby powder.

"Hi, Dub," she said.

"Hi." I think I stared at her for a moment.

"Is that mustard in your hair?" she said.

"Uh," I said, "maybe." I ran my hand through my hair again and came up with a small wad of gooey mustard.

"Jesus wept," I said.

"Can I come in?" she said.

"Sure."

As she walked in, I excused myself to the bathroom to run a face cloth over my head to get the mustard out. The cloth was cool and refreshing, so I wet it down and wiped my face again. I'd begun to sweat like an ice bag on a summer day.

"So, what do you think we should do?" she said as I came into the living room. Ricky had plunked herself down on my mother's favorite chair.

"Well, here's how it stands," I said. "I wish we could convince Pop and your father that Officer Farley is the bad guy. But that won't work, at least right now. And telling the cops again won't do a thing. Remember, some other cops might be involved, or at least turning a blind eye." I told her Mr. Hwan's story about Officer Farley and the other laughing cop, and how they never filed a report on Ralph.

"My God," she said. "But we can't think that. Let's just think it was Officer Farley, alone."

"But what if it's true? I mean, weren't the cops

conveniently someplace else the night he shot out your door?"

"It could be a coincidence," she said. "They were out looking for you, Dub, so he knew the house was unguarded. And two men laughing, that doesn't mean anything at all."

But Ricky was upset by the thought. Her lip sort of quivered.

"Okay," I said, and I tried to sound convincing, "let's just say it was Officer Farley. Alone."

"Maybe we *could* get evidence or something," she suggested. "I mean, like you said the other day."

"Exactly."

"Like those tire tracks the police took photos of," she said, "or the shotgun shells they collected. If we could show that they're Officer Farley's, the police would have a case."

"Of course, he *is* the police," I said. "He'd know how to turn that around, make it look like it didn't belong to his car or to his gun."

She hesitated. "I just don't know what else to do. And if we stay quiet about it, he'll just come back again."

"I know," I said. It was maddening, it really was. For a moment I thought I might reach out and touch her, but found myself wanting the cover of night and a half-moon for that.

"What is it about people?" Ricky said. "What's going on in their minds?"

"My guess is, in Officer Bigger Farley's case, we'll never know."

"What have we ever done to him? What is he? And now the phone calls have started again."

My mind raced. "But, no one has the number," I said.

"Dub, don't you see?" she said. She shifted in her seat, and a waft of baby powder flew away from her. "Only my family has it, and they haven't given it to anyone, not even to you or Susan or your father.

"And," she continued, "we haven't even given it to my father's people at the college. But the police have it."

Well, of course. That sealed it. I guess I'd known ever since we'd found out about Officer Bigger Farley. I guess I'd always known that my mother, however screwed up she thought our lives were, would never have done something as horrible as that. But, as these things tend to go, I'd messed that up, too. I'd not only suspected Doreen had made the calls, I'd talked to Pop about it as well. It was a huge mess. All of a sudden, an almost violent wave of guilt grabbed me from top to bottom, and I shuddered. That's the thing about guilt. When it happens, it really hits you, like a tidal wave or something.

"Are you okay, Dub?" Ricky said.

"Yes," I said, "Yes, I'm okay. Really."

"It's got to be him," Ricky said. "It's Officer Farley who's been making the calls. He's been the one behind all of it. Everything."

"He's a mental case," I said.

"Which makes him more dangerous," she said, "more than we thought."

Just then, it came to me, clear as a fall day. My idea, the same plan that had hit me when I'd met Big Farley on the street, would be Ricky's best hope. The thought came quickly, and almost left as quickly because Ricky shifted again in her chair and, I don't know, it wasn't really a sexy sort of shift or anything, but it threw me for a loop.

"Look," I said. "Ricky, what if we *can* actually get that evidence you mentioned, evidence even a crooked cop couldn't change. Say, catch him in the act. That'll solve it, and, since we're now sure he's the one behind all the rest of it, it'll solve everything."

"Catch him in the act of what? Making a phone call?"

"No, we catch him at your house, doing something. Vandalizing the place. Like we said, he'll probably come back. If we can catch him then we'll have real evidence."

"Dub, he had a shotgun the last time. Remember? I should think we are a bit beyond laying traps. Officer Farley could kill someone."

"He could," I said. "But how else are we going to get him? Like you said, we can't catch him making a phone call." Man, I was happy it wasn't Doreen. So what, I thought, my mother is a racist bigot and a depressed person, but at least she didn't make the goddamn phone calls.

"How, then," she said, "do we catch him?"

Just at that moment, Ricky threw back her head and her braids flipped over her shoulders. To me, it had the same effect as if she'd reached over and grabbed me hard around the neck and dragged me down to the floor in some kind of wild wrestling match. She was like a horse tossing her mane.

"Okay," I said, and fought to throw off the image. "First of all, we still can't tell our fathers about this, because their first reaction would be to go to the police, which won't work, we know that. But let's just say you suggest to your father, since this Saturday night is the last night the circus is in town, that maybe you should all go as a family."

"It's already planned," Ricky said. "Daddy wanted to do something special. Because then we leave for Louisiana."

"Don't think about that," I said. "Don't worry. See, I'll be allowed to go on Saturday, too. In fact, my whole family will be going, on account of I won't be grounded anymore. Next you get your father to call the police to ask them to step up the patrols that night because no one will be home or parked out in front and so on. It's a reasonable suggestion, he'll probably think of it himself. Now, if that doesn't bring out Officer Bigger, nothing will."

Ricky looked at me as if I'd suggested she torch the house herself. "Why," she said, "would we want to bring out Officer Bigger?"

"Because," I said. "I've got a plan."

She blinked. "Okay, so we're all at the circus. Officer Farley knows we're all there. How do we catch him?"

"Well, first we'll have to tell Susan and Doug," I said. "And get them in on the plan."

"Which is?" Ricky said. When this girl focused, she focused.

"Then we have to get someone to be at the house while we're all at the circus. Someone to spring the trap on Officer Farley."

"And the trap is?" she said.

"It's a trap where we not only catch him in the act, but we get some evidence as well. A picture. A photograph."

"A photograph," she repeated.

"I've been thinking. I've got a camera, one of those instants. You take the picture and you pull the film out from the bottom of the camera, and it's developed, right there. It's got flash bulbs."

"So, you're proposing that as Officer Farley steps up to the house with his shotgun, he'll stop to pose for a photograph?" Ricky rolled her eyes.

"Of course not," I said, "but something like that. Now, here's the other part. Doug has a siren, one of those fake police sirens, only it's pretty loud. It operates on batteries. His mother gave it to him for his birthday last year. It's loud, and in the dead of night, it'll be really loud."

Ricky sighed. "Go ahead."

"Right," I said, enjoying it, "say Officer Farley pulls up and steps out of his car with some gasoline and a cross, whatever. Now, our guy hides in the dark at the corner of the house until Officer Bigger does something incriminating, like pulling out a can of paint—"

"Or a shotgun," Ricky said. "Let's not forget the shotgun."

"Right," I said, "or a shotgun. Now, as soon as Officer Bigger is in the act, our guy steps out of the shadows, snaps the picture—"

"Which Officer Bigger sees instantly because of the flash," Ricky said.

"Right, instantly," I said. "But he can't react because he's blinded by the flash. Then our guy jumps back into the shadows, hits the siren and heaves it into the bushes, and runs like hell into the woods at the back of your house."

"With Officer Farley running after him," Ricky said, "with a shotgun. Let's not forget the shotgun."

"Right, the shotgun," I said. "But Officer Bigger won't have time to chase our guy. He's startled, he's dumbfounded, and there's a whole lot of racket going on. His eyes are blinded by the flash, and all he can hear is the siren. This incredibly loud siren. He's not going to run after our guy, because he's parked his car, maybe even left it running, somewhere near the front of the house. He's not going to rummage around in the bushes for the siren while the thing is waking up the whole neighborhood. He's going to jump into his car and disappear the hell out of there! Like he did last time. He's a chicken, at heart."

"Or simply shoot," Ricky said.

"He might shoot," I said, "but he's startled by the flash, and far enough away from the corner of the house so that he'd have to run to get a good shot. Too much time. Our guy would be long gone, into the dark and the woods. Remember, the siren is still screaming."

Ricky heaved a huge sigh my way. "Dub," she said, "this is insane."

"No, it's not. If it goes well, we've got a photograph of Officer Bigger *at the scene*. He can't talk his way out of that!"

"What if," Ricky said, "Officer Farley lies again, says that he was just there to check up on the place, just like he did last time?"

"That's where our guy has to be smart. He can't just snap the picture as Officer Bigger gets out of the car. He has to wait until Officer Bigger begins to *do* something. And he's too clever to use the same story twice, especially when he knows there's someone out there with a photograph of him doing something nasty. No, he'll run, and he'll be scared."

She shook her head. "Fine," she said. "Let's just say, for

the sake of argument, that this insane plan might just work. Who is going to be this 'our guy'? There *is* danger involved—let's not forget the shotgun. And all of us will be at the circus. Who is going to snap the picture?"

"I know just the person," I said. "It has to be someone who's fearless. Someone who wouldn't care if there was a shotgun involved. Someone who would do it because of the cloak and dagger aspects."

"Who's that?" she said.

"And he'd have to be able to use a camera," I said, "and run fast. And he'd have to have a stake in this. He'd have to have his own reason to catch Officer Farley in the act."

"So, who is that?" she repeated.

"If my thinking is right, that person would be Big Farley."

I surprised myself. I hadn't completely worked it out until that moment, but it was instantly clear to me that Big was the best choice. Ricky wasn't convinced. Her eyes went wide and she exhaled as if the last breath had left her body. She slowly leaned back in the chair.

"It makes sense, doesn't it?" I said.

She twisted a braid with her finger. Finally, she said, "Not even a bit." Her voice was even, controlled.

"It makes good sense to me," I said.

"Oh, it does?" she said. "Have you forgotten that those two are *related?*"

"I know that, but—"

"I mean, what if they're in this together? Who's to say that Big hasn't accompanied his father on some of his nighttime excursions? Who can say that?"

"He hasn't," I said. "I know."

"How?"

"I just know," I said.

She shook her head. "Okay, let's say you do know. What makes you think Big will want to turn his father in? Do you think Big is actually going to snap Officer Farley in the act and then turn the photo over to us? It's his *father* Dub."

"He doesn't have to turn his father in," I said. "That's the beauty of the plan. He'll do it to *save* his father from being turned in. And he doesn't have to give the photo to us. That would be crazy, because Officer Farley will suspect you and me right off of having it. No, I have other plans for the photo."

Ricky shuddered. "Yes, it is crazy. This has gone too far, Dub. You've got to see a doctor."

"I don't need a doctor," I said, "we've just got to stop Officer Bigger. We've already turned him in and that didn't work, so we've got to find a way to stop him. I mean, what's more crazy, him doing all this, or us trying to catch him? Who's the real maniac, me or him?"

"But, asking his own son to catch him," Ricky said. "It's going too far. Have you forgotten that just last week Big Farley tried to kill Doug, and that he hates and despises you because you almost killed him with a rock? And that he hates and despises me because I am a Negro? You know, I'm not sure I can take any more of this conversation." Her eyes began to well up.

"I'm not sure what he hates," I said. "I know he hates a lot of things. Maybe not us."

Ricky sniffed.

I began to explain to Ricky how I'd run, literally, into Big Farley and one of the boys, and how we'd had this strange, abbreviated conversation. As I told her the story, I moved closer to her and sat on the arm of her chair, and put my hand on her shoulder. She calmed down a bit. She was warm, and light sweat clung to her blouse. When I finished the story, she remained silent. The house was silent, as if the whole world had shut down for a moment, and all that existed was my hand on Ricky's shoulder.

"I'll handle Big," I said. "I just know that if I talk to him about it, he'll do it. This will work."

Ricky turned and took my hand off her shoulder and into hers. She squeezed my hand. My breathing quickened, and I squeezed her hand back.

I leaned over and brought my face to hers. Ricky's face was warm, and she breathed, "What are you looking at?"

"You smell like grapes," I whispered.

She reached into her mouth and pulled out a wad of grape gum she had wedged in her cheek. She placed it on the side table and turned her face to me. "You can kiss me," she whispered.

"What?"

"I think you ought to kiss me."

"Oh. Sure."

Ricky closed her eyes.

I closed my eyes, too, and for a moment my nose brushed hers. My lips, which were the only dry parts left on my body, brushed her chin. I moved up to her lips and found them to be soft, dry, and slightly open.

And I kissed Ricky Dubois, full and strong, as the warmth of her mouth mingled with the summer afternoon. It was a long kiss. I got used to it.

Suddenly, the kitchen door burst open and the sound of laughter bounced into the house—Doug and Susan.

I opened my eyes and jumped back, knocking over a plastic vase that had been sitting on the coffee table. Ricky shoved herself back into her chair and popped the wad of gum back into her mouth. I jumped onto the couch, grabbed a pillow, and threw it over my lap as Susan and Doug rounded the corner into the living room.

"Hey," Doug said. "You're both here. What's up?"

"Hey," I said, too loudly, "not much." I held the pillow tight.

"How was the circus?" Ricky said. Her voice cracked and she made a show of munching that grape gum as if it were the last piece of gum on earth.

"Great," Susan said. Her eyes darted to the two of us, then she flopped down on a chair, her head tilted. Doug dropped to the floor. "What are you guys doing?" he said.

"Talking," I said. "Just talking."

"Yeah? About what?" Doug said. "Ricky, you got another piece of gum?"

"Oh, sorry," Ricky said. "Last one. Want half?"

"How long you been chewing it?" Doug said.

"About twenty minutes."

"I'll pass. Juice is gone by now."

"We looked for you at the circus," Susan said to Ricky. "What happened?"

"Oh, the usual," Ricky said, her voice wavering. "Chores around the house, that sort of thing. Then I began to think about how we've been going to the circus every day, and Dub was here alone, so I thought I'd pay him a visit."

I could feel their eyes drill into my temple. "So we had peanut butter and mustard sandwiches," I said, "and then got to talking."

"Ugg," Susan said. "Ricky, you actually ate one of those?"

Ricky looked around the room, then threw her arms up in the air and smiled. "Well, a guest takes what a guest is offered," she said.

"You mean you didn't like the sandwich?" I said.

Ricky stared me down. "Perhaps I don't remember," she said, slowly.

"Anyway," Doug said, "That's it for the circus today. I'm taking a breather. Had nine hot dogs so far, and a couple of Orange Slushes. I almost lost them on the last Tilt-a-Whirl."

"Doug," Ricky said. "You're not supposed to be drinking Orange Slushes."

Doug smiled in the luxury of Ricky's concern. I swear to God he almost winked at me. We all fell silent for a moment, a heavy tension in the air.

"So," Susan said, slowly, "what were you two talking about?"

I sat up on the couch and put the pillow aside. "What do you say, Ricky?" I said.

Ricky gave me a quizzical look, then sighed and nodded.

"I knew it!" Susan said. "I knew this was going to happen sooner or later. Damn you, Dub!"

"What?" I said.

"What's going on?" Doug said.

"Damn you, Dub!" Susan said again. "I just knew it."

"Bigger Farley!" I said. "We were talking about Officer Bigger Farley."

Susan stopped ranting. "What do you mean?"

"About catching him," I said.

"What's going on?" Doug repeated.

"You first," Ricky said, and gestured to me.

So it happened that Ricky Dubois and I, for the next half-hour, gave them the full story of our, well, my, incredible plan to trick Mr. Officer Bigger Farley into an act of vandalism, and of my even more incredible plan to catch him in the act by using his son, Big Farley, who knew nothing about the plan as of yet. Of course, as I told the last part Ricky still sort of shook her head.

Susan and Doug remained silent, looking down at the floor, fiddling with rug strands.

Finally, Susan said, "There's something you're not telling us."

"What do you mean?" I said.

She glanced at Ricky, then looked long and hard at me, then went back to Ricky again. "Nothing," she said in this exasperated voice. "Anyway, you're saying that instead of going to the police you'll catch Officer Farley yourselves, using his own son to do it?"

"Yes," I said.

"Dub, you've gone mental."

"Wait a minute," Doug said. "I like the plan. Except for the Big Farley part. He won't do it. He hates us."

"Well," I said, "maybe. But I'll bet he hates the thought of his father in prison even more. See, it doesn't mean that Officer Farley will be arrested. It just means that the vandalism will stop. That's where the photo comes in. And that's why Big will do it, to *save* his own family." I also thought Big Farley would do it for other, darker reasons, but I thought it best to keep them to myself for the moment.

They all looked at me as if I'd just suggested that Buddy Holly was alive and well in Duluth.

"So how," Doug said, "do you convince Big Farley that his father did it all? How do you prove it to him? No one else believes you. Except us, I mean."

"Big is a lot of things," I said, "but he isn't stupid. I think he knows something already."

"So what if he does?" Doug said. "That doesn't mean he's going to help you."

"I'll talk to Big," I said. "He'll do it."

"What are you, best buddies now?" Susan said.

"Look, it's just a feeling I have," I said. "You've got to trust me on this. For the first time in his life, Big Farley is going to do the right thing. Big will do it."

"But," Doug said, "I could do it. I could take the photo. Besides, it's my siren." Actually, he was right. It was the sort of thing Doug Hammer would take to like a bird to a plate glass window. But, I feared, with the same results. He was clearly hurt by having been left out.

"I'm sure you could, Doug," Ricky said. "Any of us could. And I don't yet understand it completely myself. But I do know Officer Farley has a shotgun, and that the plan is dangerous. Better that Big Farley does it," and she shot me a glance. "At least a father won't shoot his own son."

"Well," Susan said, "I think the whole thing is nuts, that's capital N-U-T-S."

"You've got to trust me," I said. At that moment, I felt, for the first time in weeks, that I could run ten miles. I glanced at Ricky. "I know it'll work."

"That's L-O-O-N-Y," Susan spelled.

"Wait a second," Doug said, beginning to get excited. "I've been thinking just now. There are some fine points to this little plan. The first thing is, we all go the Big Top show because Officer Bigger will be expecting it, right? I mean, you said that Ricky's dad would call the police to tell them to step up the patrols, which will—"

"Cue Officer Bigger," I said, "to get him to the house during the show, because he'll think no one will be there."

"Right," Doug said. "Then, by the time we all get back from the show, we'll know if something has happened at the house. If the siren is on that means the plan worked and Big has the photo. If all is quiet, it means that Officer Bigger never showed up. Either way, we'll know."

"Except," Susan said, "say he doesn't come while we're at the Big Top show. What if he comes later on?"

"He won't," I said, "because he knows that Pop and Ricky's father will be back guarding the house, like they do all night, every night. Except during the time they're at the Big Top Show."

"But," Ricky said, "what if Officer Farley shows up and Dub's plan *doesn't* work? Say if Big doesn't show? What if Officer Farley does something really bad?"

"The plan will work," I said. "But if it doesn't, and if Bigger does something horrible, then all hell will have broken loose."

"Or what if Officer Bigger never shows up at all?" Ricky said.

"He will," I said.

We all sat, lost in thought.

"If Dub's plan does work," Ricky said, "how do I explain the siren to my father?"

"He'll think it was another prank," I said. "He'll turn it off, he'll be angry, and then he'll sit in the car in front of the house again—for the last time. Doug, your name's not on the siren, is it?"

"No," Doug said, and his eyes were bright with enthusiasm. "I'm liking it Dubby, liking it a lot. Is this going to be great or what? I'm in."

Susan looked straight at Ricky and me. "On one condition. No more secrets, okay? No more secrets."

I swallowed hard.

"What about it, Ricky," Doug said. "Are you in?"

Ricky nodded her head, slowly at first.

"I'm in," she said.

CHAPTER 12

I had two days to contact Big Farley to convince him to stand guard at Ricky's house on Saturday night—to catch a criminal who would turn out to be his very own father.

The thing is, maybe Big had the morals of a seagull, but I knew he'd do it. All the signs pointed to it. First, I was convinced that, deep down inside, Big had a twisted sense of justice that would allow him to possess the knowledge that his father had done the deeds—and that this sense of justice would allow him to use that knowledge in his own productive way. Second, no matter how bad Officer Bigger Farley treated Big and his family, no matter how often he beat them and bullied them, I knew that Big would not want to see his father go to jail. No kid would, even if his father was Adolph Hitler.

In other words, I knew Big would be more than happy to have something on his father—and to save him from jail at the same time. It's not that I thought it would be easy to talk to him about Officer Bigger's pleasant little nighttime excursions, but, and here's the important thing, I also sensed that Big might already have an idea, an inkling, about what his father had been up to. I'd felt it since that time we'd talked after bumping into each other on the sidewalk. He'd been subdued, almost reflective. As if he had something to say but couldn't find the words. At the very least I figured if I talked first and fast enough, he would listen. After that, it was all up to fate.

I had a couple of other things to think about in the next few days. First, Doreen would be coming home on Saturday, and that was bound to reopen an old kettle of fish I would've just as soon kept closed for a while. Her unpredictability couldn't help but get in the way during what would most likely be a delicate time in our lives.

I suppose I was glad Doreen was all rested and everything, at least it seemed she was from her phone calls, and I was happy that she'd be home again—Pop had been a little out of sorts for the past week or so, and both Susan and I felt that something was missing in the house, sort of like if the refrigerator had up and walked out for a few days. Not that I'm comparing my mother to a refrigerator, although you could play around with the obvious metaphors, such as the cold and frosty but nourishing aspects of both and all that, but that would be stretching it. What I'm saying is, Doreen wasn't there, and we all felt it.

I also had to contend with the fallout from Susan over what she though Ricky and I had been doing in the living room that day. Not that she avoided us, but I felt a slight edge, a tiny irritability from her. At least once in a while.

For instance, one day Doug and Susan went off to the circus again, by themselves, without asking Ricky. Of course, asking me was out of the question because I was grounded, but you'd have thought they might have asked Ricky. Later that day I found Susan up in her room, reading a book. When I asked her how the circus was, she'd said fine, how's Ricky? She didn't say it in a particularly nasty way or anything, it's just the fact she said it that made her feelings obvious. I told her I hadn't seen Ricky during the day, which was true, and that I was sorry for whatever it was she was mad about, and she said not to worry and then looked at me and shook her head from side to side in a slow way, as if she were sort of nauseated.

Doug seemed to be at ease about the whole business. He took everything in stride, and generated a lot of enthusiasm for the plan. He even went out and bought new batteries for his siren, so that it would have maximum strength on the night it was needed most. He did, however, conspicuously avoid talking about Ricky.

Which was a good thing, because I had no clear understanding what really happened between us—other than the fact that I'd kissed her, and she kissed me back, and we both enjoyed it and that I think we did it pretty well, actually, given the circumstances. I had thoughts about what would have happened if Doug and Susan hadn't walked in on us, and I thought about that often. I even began to fantasize about the future, about what we would have said to each other if we were older and wiser and knew what to say in situations like that. And I began to understand, although I had known it all along without admitting it, that I lived and breathed Ricky Dubois.

That realization suddenly made the whole thing, our plan to catch Officer Bigger, crystal clear and more urgent. I had never forgotten that Ricky and her mother and grandmother were due to leave for Louisiana after the final Big Top show.

I had to contact Big Farley, and soon.

I couldn't call him on the phone. He would have seen that as suspicious. And then there was the possibility that I'd get Officer Bigger on the phone instead.

"Oh, Officer Farley," I'd say, "I didn't expect to get you."

"I live here," he'd say in a brusque sort of way.

"Well, I'd like to talk to Henry, if you don't mind."

"What about?"

"Oh, I don't know. Just about setting a trap to catch you in the act of violating the public trust, you miserable bigot."

And I couldn't just ride my bike over there either. Suppose I just ran into Officer Bigger right there on the front porch with that demented dog barking like it had just swallowed a hot coal? No, I'd have to think of a way to nonchalantly run into Big and get him alone without arousing suspicion, then tell him the whole story and hope that he doesn't take my head off when I casually mention that it's his father we're after. Tall order, little time.

As it turned out, I got my wish, in an indirect way, when I rode down to Zikker's Pond on Friday morning to try and think the whole thing through.

I rode the little path toward the rock, but before the pond

became visible, I heard the voices of several boys in some sort of raucous play. They shouted and laughed, and I had a gut feeling I'd heard those voices before. As I rounded the corner to the pond, I knew I had heard those voices before. It was Big and a few of his thugs. They had two baseball bats—a bad sign—and were hitting what appeared to be rocks into the pond. After each hit, they'd yell and stamp their feet and generally whoop it up.

I knew this might be my only chance to talk to Big, and desperation pushed me on. I stopped by the rock. They fell silent and the bats went down to their sides. Big, who was smoking a cigarette, stared at me blankly.

"What do you want?" he said. The cigarette hung from the corner of his mouth in a bad attempt at sophistication. I saw nothing in his eyes.

The rest of the boys looked angry and apprehensive. They obviously saw this as an opportunity to repair the debacle of the Great Library Battle. A couple of them looked at Big. A couple looked down at the bats.

Without thinking, I plunged into it. "I've got to talk to you," I said.

"About what?" Big said, abruptly.

"About something."

"So, talk," Big said.

"Alone," I said.

"Alone?" one of the boys said. "Alone! Who do you think you are?" He started to laugh. I recognized him as the one who had kicked me in the back during our savage fight.

Big took this in, then he squinted at me. He turned to his gang member and said, "Shut the fuck up."

"Huh?" the boy said.

Big turned back to me. "What do you mean alone?"

"It's pretty important," I said.

Big considered this for a moment. One of the boys started to say something, but Big held out his hand, like a cop stopping traffic. The boy shut up.

"Okay, Teed," he said. "let's hear what you got to say." He turned to the boys. "Scram, all a you."

"What?" another boy asked.

"I said scram, as in leave, as in depart," Big said, with heavy sarcasm. "As in vamoose. As in right now."

I had to hand it to Big. Where this ironic bent came from, I still have no idea, to this day.

The boys, confused, walked dejectedly to their bikes. "Wait for me at Jackson's," Big said. It was a pool hall.

"Yeah, yeah, sure," said the back-kicker. He turned to the others, "Let's get out of here so's some people can talk." A few of them laughed nervously, but not loudly. Big still had cache as far as rank terror was concerned, that was clear. They got on their bikes and rode slowly away.

"Yeah, fuck you very much," Big said after them.

I walked over to Big, and looked into the bucket from which they'd taken their rocks. But inside the bucket, there were no rocks. There were five or six frogs, hopping limply against the side in a vain attempt to escape.

Big looked at me and then at the frogs. He let out an ugly chuckle and picked up a bat. "Wanna try?" he said. "It's called Frog Home Runs."

"You're hitting frogs?"

"Yeah," he said.

"With bats?"

"No, with my dick," he said, and chuckled again.

"But, that kills them."

"Bright, Teed," he said. "You're a genius. You'd die too if you were a frog got hit by a bat. So, do it." His eyes twinkled.

I actually debated for a second whether to pick up a frog and give it a light but manly tap into the dark green water of Zikker's Pond. I debated this as a method of gaining Big's confidence, but I couldn't bring myself to even think about it longer than it took for the bile to rise into my throat. Puking would've ruined everything, so I swallowed hard.

"Well," I said, "it's not something I do every day."

"I know," he said. "And I can see in your face that you don't want to do it now. Because you're a pussy."

This was a bad turn in the conversation.

"But that's okay," he said. "'Cause me, I ain't no pussy."

To prove his point, Big reached down into the bucket and pulled out one of the hapless frogs. He bent over and grabbed a bat, then tossed the flailing frog into the air and nailed it with a dull, sickening plop. The frog, which was dead as it left the bat, twirled limply and arced for about forty feet, then plopped into the water.

Big shoved the bat into the water and pulled it out, wiping it with his shirt. He turned to me. "Got it?"

"I got it, Big," I said, reeling and lightheaded.

"Now, what's this thing you got to talk about?"

"Well," I said, deciding that if I hesitated I would chicken out and slither off, defeated, "it's about Ricky Dubois."

"The nigger?" he said.

"Well, yeah," I said. No use being heroic. "It's about what's been happening at her house."

Big reached in his pocket and pulled out another cigarette. He lit it and took a slow drag, like Robert Mitchum in the movies. "I told you I got nothing to do with that."

"I know," I said. "That's why I want to talk to you. We want to catch the guy who's been doing it."

His eyes flashed. "What do you mean?"

"I mean, we want to catch the guy who's been smashing windows and pumping bullets into their front door."

"Cops' job to do that," he said.

"Do what?" I said.

"Catch the guy," Big said, "what did you think I meant?"

"Well, that's the problem," I said.

Big didn't say a word. He took a drag from his cigarette. His brow furrowed. He was thinking hard.

"We have to be the ones to catch the guy," I said, "not the cops."

"Why?"

"Because," I said, "well, because, it's just better that way." I noted that Big still had the frog bat in his free hand.

"Teed," he said, "I don't get you."

All of a sudden, just like that, I felt incredibly sorry for Big Farley. It choked me up for a second, honest to God.

"Listen, Big," I said, "what if I told you that the guy is well-known, maybe even someone you know, like maybe even a public person, say even someone who's—"

Big cut me off. "What the hell are you saying?"

"I mean, Big," I continued, "let's say that the guy is for instance a cop, and probably a good cop for that matter, but let's say that he's, you know, he's done something wrong, that he's maybe made some mistakes, and let's say that you know—"

"You're babbling," Big said. "You always like this?"

"Well, I don't know," I said feverishly. "Jesus, it's not easy talking about this, you know, because the guy—"

"Is my father?" Big said.

I snapped back as if I'd been hit by the bat, and Big flicked his cigarette into the water. I thought to myself, incredibly under the circumstances, that floating cigarette butts would be bad for the frogs.

"Yeah," I said.

"So?" Big was as calm as could be, as if we were talking about the Yankees or something.

"You knew," I said.

He took a deep breath. "Teed, let me put it to you simple. The other day at my house you told my old man that you made a mistake about that, and that you were sorry. So leave him alone, okay? He didn't do nothing. After that, it's none of my goddamn business. How's that?"

"But it's my business," I said without thinking. "She's my friend. If it doesn't stop, they're leaving town."

"Like I said before, what do I care about niggers? Let them leave."

"We're going to stop him, one way or the other."

"It wasn't him," Big said, harshly.

"So why did you say it was your father?"

"I didn't say it," Big said. "I didn't say that. You were jabbering about cops and people I know, and I know you told the other cops it was him that night, so I put two and two together and I just figured you were getting around to my father. Again. What, you still trying to get back at me?"

I decided to take my chance. "Well, it is him. I know it's him."

Big's eyes flashed again. "Yeah? How do you know that?"

"I saw him," I said, "that night. I saw him do it, Big. So did Ricky."

"Oh, yeah? Prove it."

"Do I have to? You know something, don't you? You've been suspecting it, too."

Big regarded me as a person might regard an ant. "Look, Teed, tell me one good reason why I shouldn't smash your face in right here, right now, with this bat?" He shook it.

I closed my eyes. "Because you would have already done that if I was lying. And because, one way or the other, sooner or later, he's going to get caught. But if we catch him, we just make him stop. If someone else catches him, he's a goner, he goes to jail. Then what have you got Big? You've got a father in prison."

I opened my eyes. Big had put the bat down.

"I'm sorry," I said. "But it's the truth."

Big blinked, his eyes knitted in anger. But he kept quiet.

"Look," I said, "I'm not trying to hurt anyone, I just want it to stop. I know you don't want your father to go to jail. Nobody believes it's your father except me and Ricky. Not my father, not Ricky's father, not the other cops, I think. No one. But you know it, too. I promise to keep it that way."

"If no one believes you, then what the hell difference does it make," Big said, but his voice had gone slightly hoarse.

"Because sooner or later he'll go too far," I said. "And even he won't be able to get out of it."

"But when the niggers leave, it all stops," he said. "So who cares?"

"There will be another family, and another one after that. Black people will be moving in all over the place. But you'll be in control, you can save him. From himself."

"What?" he said. He wiped his nose with his shirt-sleeve.

"Look," I said, "first you tell me you know it's your father, so we all go into this with a clear mind and we all know what we're up against."

"Fuck you. Next?"

"And you promise to help us stop him."

Big let out a deep breath. "What? You're nuts," he said. "Fucking nuts."

"I know, and that's why it's you I'm asking. Only you can save him. Like I said, we don't call in the cops or hurt him or anything. We just make him stop. Beyond that I can't say until you give me your word."

"I'm going to repeat myself, Teed," he said. "I should break your ass right here and now."

"But you won't," I said. "Because I'm going to repeat myself, too. You know it's the truth."

Big stood silently and wrestled with his conscience. I could almost hear the wheels turning up there. It was a mighty struggle, and I knew it involved elements of Big's rotten family life and his father's cruelty, as well as the contradictory and appalling possibility that his father might go to jail. He couldn't have been in a worse situation, and I did not envy him that. Yet there existed here a lesser of two evils, and I trusted Big would see it soon enough. But first we had to overcome the hurdle. He had to admit his father's guilt.

Big suddenly looked exhausted. "I got to sit down," he said. He started to walk toward my rock.

"On that rock?" I said.

"Yeah, that rock," he said.

"What do you know about that rock?"

"I know it's a fucking rock," he snapped. "And I want to go sit on it."

"Yes, but," I said, "is it, I mean, special or something, that you have to sit on that rock?"

"Teed," he said, "I have never understood you. I think you're fucking loony-tunes, I really do. I always have. But I don't want to talk about the goddamn rock, okay?"

"Fine," I said, and we walked over to the rock.

Big lit another cigarette, and I realized that he'd been buying time to think about how he was going to approach this.

He blew smoke through his nose, then wiped it again with his sleeve. He was beginning—I swear this is true and if I didn't see it with my own eyes I'd never have believed it—but he was beginning to tremble. He took a long drag and blew smoke as he said, "Why do you think it matters to me, Teed? I mean, what if I was to tell you, and this isn't true, but what if I was to tell you that I don't give a shit about my old man. I mean, what if I couldn't care less. Maybe I'm better off he's locked up. I still got my mom, the rest of us. So what if he goes to jail, piece of shit. What if I told you that, huh?"

"You just did. Besides, whether or not you care, he's still your father. Look, Big, it's not up to me to make your family life perfect. Maybe my family isn't perfect either. But he's your father, and how's it going to look if your father is in jail? For a long time. How are you going to feel?" I pulled out the stops. "Especially knowing you could have prevented it."

Big hung his head and looked at the ground, and worked that cigarette for all it was worth. Smoke billowed around his face, as if his head was on fire. The wheels were turning again, fast and hard.

"Teed," he said, finally, "you should be a priest, you know? You're good at making people feel shitty."

"Thanks. I guess."

He let some smoke drift out of his nose. "So you say it's my father. I don't. But you say I can save his ass from jail. Well, I don't give a shit about him going to jail. But, other people would. I guess." I remembered the "Hapy Mother's Day" heart on his refrigerator, and I thought about how that kind of thing could make a guy cry.

"Look, alright?" he said. "You give me your word that none of this never gets beyond you and me. Otherwise, I'll say it's not true and then I'll kill you."

"Sounds reasonable," I said.

"I mean that," he said, and he shifted. "Okay? So this is between you and me, right?"

"It is."

"Okay," he said softly, and his shoulders dropped. "Okay. I'm only going to tell you this once. I'm not saying that my old man did anything, because I don't know. Honest. But he don't like niggers, it's as plain as that. For a long time, even before they moved into your neighborhood, half the time all's I hear from my old man is niggers this and niggers that. He comes home from work, he's steamed about something and he starts yakking about spooks. I don't personally give a shit about them, but I never heard him this bad until them people moved in. He watches TV and them stories about the buses down south, and he's complaining about everybody and how the world is going to hell. Then your niggers moved in and he's always talking about how this woman is married to this white guy, and how that's about the worst thing that could ever happen that a white person marries someone who ain't white.

"Anyway," he continued, "I never seen him get so worked up about it. And my mom tries to calm him down every once in awhile, you know, talk to him, and he just yells at her and–" Big hesitated, "everything. Anyway, he was more or less always pissed off. But I never seen it like this, not until them people moved in down your street."

I shook my head in agreement. Best to say nothing, I thought.

"You understand that's not real proof, right? I mean, lots of people hate niggers. Right?"

"Sure, Big."

"Well, anyway," he said. "Then later—I don't know about the other stuff, the cross and the brick and what have you—but then there was that day you and me had the fight." He stopped and ground out his cigarette. Up until now, Big had been positively effusive, and I realized this was the first time I'd ever heard him say more than three sentences in a row. His story poured out.

"So," he said, "that night he's really pissed off at me for having his knife, the one I used in the fight. Well, I didn't actually ever use it, you know? I just had it there, in case, just in case. I never stabbed no one."

I realized this was Big's way of almost apologizing for going at Doug Hammer with the knife. "I know you never stabbed anyone," I said. I figured this was all water under the bridge, at least for now. Under the circumstances, I mean.

"So that night he takes me home and really wails into me, I swear to Christ. I mean it, he was crazy mad. I never even went to the doctor's for, you know, that bump on my head. My mom wanted to take me but he wouldn't let her, so she just slapped some stuff on it and then a bandage, and then we left it alone. But my father was sure as hell mad at me."

At this point Big's voice started to waver a bit.

"So," he said. "So then I went to sleep that night and later there he is, in the dark, at the edge of my bed. Shaking my arm, because I was asleep, you know? And I wake up and he's standing in the dark and he goes, just like this, he says, 'Henry, you awake? Listen, don't you ever go fighting them nigger lovers again, got that?' He goes, 'Niggers'll be leaving soon. I got that under control.' Then he leaves, and that was that."

I just nodded my head.

Big dropped his head and his back began to heave. He buried his face in his hands and then, incredibly, balled his fists and began to smack the side of his face, hard, first one side, then the other.

"Big," I yelled.

"Leave me alone!" He smacked his face a few times more, in a rhythmic pattern, really hard, and then slowed down. He calmed a bit, and the heaving stopped.

He looked up, and his eyes and face were red from the smacks. But there were no tears. Big had beat his tears away. He cleared his throat. "So, anyway," he said, and inhaled deeply, "that's all I know. Then you and your old man came around later that day, and I never said anything to anyone."

"Big," I said, slowly, "are you okay?"

"Of course, goddamnit," he said. "Now, that's not proof of anything, right? Because beyond that I'm not saying shit. But I been thinking about it, and that's all I'm going to say about anything."

I knew this sort-of-admission was as far as Big Farley would go.

"And all this stays between you and me," he said. "Right? Or else, Teed, I swear I'll kill you."

"Okay," I said. Big looked down to the ground and kicked a stone into the water.

"Do you want to save him?" I said.

He looked up.

"Otherwise," I said, "they're going to catch him someday." I played my last card. "Think about your mother, Big."

His eyelids flickered.

"I've got a plan," I said.

He thought for a moment. "And we don't turn him in. I mean, no police." It wasn't a question.

"I think I have a way we can avoid that," I said. "I gave you my word."

"You know, Teed, I'm still fucking amazed you would even ask me this."

"Well," I said, "I'm asking you because you're the one who will eventually end up with the evidence, and I figure that type of thing should be kept in your family. That's why."

Big was intrigued. "What evidence?" he said.

"Are you with me?"

Big exhaled through his nose. "I don't know."

"It's the best way," I said. "You're the only one who can save him."

Big rubbed his temple, and exhaled hard. "I don't even know what you're talking about, and it already sounds crazy."

"I know. So, are you with me?"

Big squinted his eyes and looked directly at me. "What's this plan?"

And that's how it happened that I enlisted Big Farley in our plan to thwart his own father's rage against the Dubois family. I explained the plan to him, fully trusting, at that point, that he would not turn around and deliver the plan to his father. I had no way of knowing that to be a fact, of course, but it was a chance I had to take. That, and I knew, I just knew, he wouldn't.

I told Big about the plan to provide his father with an opportunity to come to the house while everyone, night guards included, were at the final Big Top show watching clowns and elephants and The Flying Zalubras. I included details about the camera and the siren, and what we would eventually do with the photo if his father actually took the bait. Only I didn't say "took the bait" because we were in a delicate situation here and I didn't want to make Officer Bigger come out sounding like a flopping carp or something.

We agreed that Big would tell his folks that he was going down to the Big Top Saturday night, but would instead sneak off to the Dubois home and camp by the side of the house until either his father came by, or the Duboises returned home, at which point the fathers would start their night watch.

We would leave the camera and siren in a bag behind a bush on the left side of the house for him to find. Big said he could figure the camera and the siren out, but his only concern was that the police might come by on their stepped-up patrol and discover him hiding there. And they would instantly accuse him of all the mayhem and vandalism.

"Part of the game, Big," I said. "You've got to be clever."

"Right," he said, now slightly, weirdly enthusiastic. "Clever."

We agreed to link up on Sunday at two in the afternoon, the day after the final Big Top show, to find out what had happened. Meaning whether or not he got a photo. We agreed to meet right there, at the rock at Zikker's.

"And we don't turn him in," Big said, repeating my promise like a mantra.

"We don't have to," I said. "That'll be up to him."

When we parted it was with some anxiety and a sense of danger, but I knew we both felt we had taken the best step to correct something that had been bothering us, in different degrees and for different reasons, for a long time. I had faith that Big was sincere, and when we stood up to go, I offered my hand. Big, whose hands were, by the way, grimy with frog entrails, took it, shook it, and left without a word.

The countdown to the big night ticked away. Pop and Mr. Dubois continued their night shifts, and I met Pop there on Saturday morning as I delivered the paper.

Doreen came home later that morning, dropped off by her father, who stayed in the car and didn't say a word when Pop went out to grab the luggage. But, that bit of unpleasantness over, Doreen and Pop got all affectionate and happy and their mood seemed to catch. I began to look at Doreen with different eyes. Well, slightly different eyes. I mean, now that I absolutely knew she wasn't the one who'd made the phone calls, it made a whole lot of difference, no matter how she still felt about Ricky and her family. Actually,

I might as well admit this: I was happy to see her, and she seemed happy to see me.

We talked and laughed and made plans to go to the circus, although Doreen didn't ask about Ricky or her family.

The rest of Saturday morning was hectic. Doug and I rode down to the drugstore to buy some fresh film and flashbulbs for my camera. Susan went over to Ricky's and later reported that Ricky's father had called the police to tell them there wouldn't be any neighbors on night shift at their house because all the families would be out at the circus, and would they mind stepping up their patrol just a bit and all that. The police had agreed to see what they could do, and I knew at that instant that Officer Bigger Farley was somewhere, somehow, digesting the information. Susan said there had been a slight snag when Mrs. Oliphant had insisted on staying home while the others went to the circus. But, again, Mrs. Dubois wouldn't have it. She'd told her mother that she wasn't going to allow someone to throw bricks through the windows with an old woman in the house, and she insisted her mother come along, if not for the entertainment, at least for safety's sake.

Another notable thing had happened while Susan was at the Dubois place. Mr. and Mrs. Dubois went out to pick up a car, a used car. Ricky explained that a couple of days earlier, her father had gone down to a dealership and picked out a car he would use around East Hartford. The reason for the new car was that Mrs. Dubois, her mother, and Ricky would be driving the Chevy down to Louisiana.

That part of the equation had become real.

Late in the afternoon, after Doug and I had loaded the camera with film and found the siren, we put them in a paper bag and went down to Ricky's place. Our intent was to find a way to drop it off behind the bush at the side of the house, where Big Farley would find it later.

The hours had moved quickly and the plan had fallen into place so far, yet I was nervous as we pulled up to Ricky's place. I mean, we had quite a few people involved now, including Big, who after all had once tried to stab someone, as well as Ricky, Doug, and Susan. And I was responsible to see that this whole thing came off. There seemed to be plenty to be nervous about, not the least of which was Officer Bigger Farley's shotgun.

As we pulled up we found Mrs. Oliphant in the front yard, bent low, watering a low honeysuckle bush. I remembered my earlier fantasy of saving her from Big and his gang using that very hose to force-feed water into Big's gullet. It seemed like a long time ago.

"Hi, Mrs. Oliphant," I said, as she turned slowly to watch us roll up the driveway. I couldn't help notice how old she looked.

She shrugged her shoulders and nodded.

"Is Ricky in?" I said.

"'Spect she is," she said in a creaky voice, bending back over the flowers. To me, it sounded as if she hadn't used her voice for a while, as if she hadn't spoken to anyone in weeks.

"Can we just go in?"

"Sure can," she said. "What's in the bag?"

"Oh, this?" I said, swallowing. "It's—"

"A camera," Doug said. "Ricky wanted to take pictures at the circus tonight. She wanted to borrow Dub's camera."

"Yeah," I said.

"Ricky has a camera," Mrs. Oliphant said.

"This one's an instant," Doug said.

"She has an instant," Mrs. Oliphant said. "Bought it for her myself."

"Oh, well," I said, "maybe she wants two cameras? Lot of action tonight, you know."

"And hers is on the blink," Doug said, grasping. "It's broken, so she needs another one."

Mrs. Oliphant straightened up and considered us with heavy eyes. She wiped her brow. "Devil out tonight," she said.

“Ma’am?” I said.

“Ricky’s inside, no need to knock.”

She went back to her flowers.

We dropped off the camera and siren, and Ricky assured us that she’d be able to place the bag behind the bush before her family left for the circus. Everything else was in place, and we wished her and each other luck, and agreed to meet first thing in the morning to find out what, if anything, had happened. Then we left. We knew the chances were good that we wouldn’t see each other at the show, since there’d be hundreds of people from all over, from Hartford and as far away as New Haven for this, the final Big Top show of the C.D. Lorenzo Traveling Family Circus and Carnival.

Before we left, I gave Ricky a quizzical look, sort of a call-me-later look, at least that’s what I tried to do. I’m not sure she got the message. If she did, she never acted on it. Not that I blame her, but I just wanted to talk to her one more time before everything kicked in. I had this thought it would have been sort of like the soldier who has this final, emotion-packed conversation with his betrothed before he goes off to war. I’m not even sure what I would have said, but it didn’t matter, really. It just would’ve been nice.

Dinner that night started out sort of spooky. As we were about to dig in, Doreen asked that we all join hands for a moment. “Pardon?” Pop said.

“Let’s just say grace,” she said, but her voice was soft, and she raised her eyebrows. “For me, okay?”

I couldn’t remember the last time we’d said grace at the dinner table. It could have been years ago, it could have been never. I mean, we’re Catholic and all that, but somehow grace never figured in the daily routine. But we all cleared our throats, almost in unison, and Susan and I shot each other these what-the-hell kind of looks, and held hands, me with Pop and Doreen, and Susan on the opposite side of the table doing the same.

“Who would like to offer the blessing?” Doreen said.

"Mom, it's your idea," Susan said, and Pop cleared his throat another time.

"Pop's the writer," I said. "He'd be good at it."

"Let's not make a federal case out of this," Doreen said evenly. "For once can we have a loving family moment without the bickering?"

"Sure, I'll do it," Pop said. I had this dread that he'd bring up the black Jesus Christ business again, but, as it turned out, he kept it simple. He bowed his head and said, "Bless this table and family. May the Lord keep us all together and safe, and the world safe for every single person in it, for all time."

"Amen," Doreen said, and squeezed my hand, softly. It was the hand-squeezing equivalent of a smile, and it felt nice. After that it got pretty cheery, not that I expected it to be full of jokes and family fun and everything. But it sure turned out that way, much to my surprise. Doreen seemed to have become a different person. I didn't see the sullen pauses, the sloppy wine talk, the anger, or the flying broccoli that usually comes to our table. Actually, it seemed as if she'd never even done those things, had never hated Ricky Dubois, never goaded Pop for his beliefs and actions. If I held my breath and closed my eyes, it was almost as if she'd always been a happy woman and I'd never ever seen that hard, amber glint in her brown eyes.

Doreen laughed and told stories about her week with Grandpa. She told one pretty raucous story about how Grandpa had taken her down to Goodwin Park to feed the ducks, just like he used to when she was a child. They'd brought along some bread crumbs and things in a bag, and when they'd arrived at the duck pond they'd discovered literally hundreds of ducks in and around the water, ten times as many, she said, as there were when she was a little girl. And the ducks weren't as timid as they used to be. These ducks were aggressive, snapping at each other and Grandpa for the food and honking like the world's biggest traffic jam.

They generally made a mess of things. It got so bad that the ducks started to go after the bag of breadcrumbs, nipping at Grandpa's fingers as he pulled out a handful to feed them. Pretty soon, they started to engulf him, as if they'd never been fed in their lives. Then one duck flew straight into his face and Grandpa shouted, "That's it, you stinking birds!" and stuffed the bag of breadcrumbs down the front of his trousers.

Which was, as it turned out, a bad move.

In an instant, Doreen said, those ducks started to flap and scream as if they'd been dealt a challenge. They jumped up to snap at Grandpa's crotch, which made him all the more flustered and angry as he tried to fend them off. Pretty soon there were about a dozen ducks nipping at his trousers. It must have been quite a scene, as he slapped ducks away from his crotch and screamed, "Sons of bitches!" and she said she almost fell down laughing before she waded into the mess and hauled him out and dragged him away from the ducks, back to the car.

I thought it was pretty funny too, and I near split my sides as she told the story. Susan and Pop were both delirious, thumping their forks on the table and wiping tears from their eyes. It was a pretty racy story coming from Doreen, and I had to admit I admired her for it. I mean, she'd actually made fun of her father and even repeated the "sons of bitches" part, which, I realized, she might never have done two weeks earlier. It was good seeing her laugh like that as she tried to finish the story.

"Then," she screamed, "we get back to the car and you know what he says? He says, 'Good thing I had that bag down there for protection, them ducks would've made me a girl!'"

And she hooted and Pop hooted and it was a pretty damn funny ending to the story and we all felt that warmth people feel when they're laughing, and then Susan managed to blurt out, in the middle of it all, "I don't get it."

Doreen said, "Don't you see, honey? If he hadn't put the bag there in the first place—" and we all laughed again.

"I got that," Susan said, "I mean, why were the ducks so hungry?"

"They probably weren't all that hungry," Pop said, wiping his eyes. "They just got caught up in a frenzy. Or maybe they knew what it would take to rile Grandpa, and did it for fun. In other words, they acted like me."

Even Doreen laughed at that.

Anyway, not one of us mentioned Ricky or her family during dinner, not that I'd expected it—that would have been too perfect. But, nothing awful was said about them either, so I'd have to give the dinner an even rating for tolerance. It was, I guessed at the time, a start.

After dinner, we cleaned up, jumped in the car, and made a beeline for the circus. Doreen even gave Susan and me each a five-dollar bill and said to have a good time with it.

The Big Top shows were at six and eight-thirty that night, and we had planned, as had Doug and Ricky, to go to the later show. We had about two hours to kill, and we let Susan lead us around because she had been to the circus almost every day that week, and had just about every ride, every game, and every food booth mapped out.

The arcade part of the circus was just like a county fair. The rides were, of course, insane, and Doreen and Pop understandably demurred when we invited them to join us on the Tilt-a-Whirl, or the Loop-a-Loop Roller Coaster. Pop did join us for some bumper car action, and Doreen and Susan went on the Fun House ride. We all got lost in the House of Mirrors and had a great time running around screaming like we were at the Alamo, watching our bodies and heads and necks grow long or squat in the trick mirrors.

As we walked around the grounds, I became aware of the ride operators and throw-the-darts guys and others at the game booths, perhaps for the first time. Maybe it was because they were about the strangest looking group of people this side of a reflection in a frying pan. In fact, they were a pretty hideous bunch if you want to know the God's honest truth. Most were in tattered T-shirts and greasy trousers, with hair that looked as if it had been spiked with transmission oil. Their teeth grew in several shades of tan, or were missing altogether, and the result was that they all looked as if they were aliens from another planet in search of a good dental plan. I swear that one or two of them were drunk the way they shouted and carried on with people walking by their booths. And their hands looked as if they'd been dipped in grape juice a long, long time ago. That I noticed. I mean it, their hands were the worst. And to a person, they looked bored.

Ditto with the ladies who ran the hot dog and cotton candy booths. They were puffy, bulky women whose hairdos had seen better years, and who talked with cigarettes hanging from their stubby teeth. Their booths smelled of sweat, cooking fat, and fruity perfume. The whole crowd, men and women both, struck me for the first time as sad but happy they'd found each other. They seemed to regard us in the same manner.

I detected a lot of New Jersey accents, which meant they were all from the land of C.D. Lorenzo, which explained a lot, at least in my mind. Also for the first time, I thought that their lives, moving around the country in truck caravans and so on, might not have been as romantic as it seemed.

The barker in front of the freak show tent, which we bypassed—but not without me sneaking a look through the canvas at a man standing in a loincloth who'd stuck what appeared to be metal skewers through his cheeks, the Human Pincushion was my guess—was a young guy. He couldn't have been more than twenty or so, and was dressed nattily in a vest and straw hat. He kept up a patter that was loud and boisterous, and promised direct contact with the Eighth Wonder of the World, the Two-Headed Goat.

"How about you sir?" he said to Pop as I was dragged

from my peephole at the tent. "Just two thin quarters for a glimpse at the most amazing people and animals on the face of the earth!"

"I don't think so," Pop said.

"How about the boy! He's interested! Get him an education he'll never get in school!"

"I don't doubt that," Pop said as he dragged me away.

"Another missed opportunity, ladies and gentlemen!" the barker shouted to the crowd. "Don't you miss it, too! Come see the Human Fly! The—" and his voice faded off in the general cacophony of the bells and whistles of the C.D. Lorenzo Circus.

We didn't bump into Doug or Ricky, nor their families, as we'd expected. In fact, I didn't see anyone I knew.

At about eight, I looked at my watch and realized that Big Farley was probably in place at the Dubois home.

By the time we bought our tickets and made our way into the Big Top with our stuffed Yogi Bears and other animals, the tent was filling rapidly. Still, we managed to get good seats. They weren't ringside, but were just behind the front row, where we would have a perfect view of the action. They were the best seats we ever had, in fact. The tent hummed with the energy of the large crowd, and the smell of hay and animals was strong. It was a pleasant smell, one that I'd always liked, and it certainly didn't foreshadow the strangeness that later followed.

I checked my watch again. It was almost eight-thirty, and dark outside. Big was surely in place. Turning back now was impossible.

Soon enough, amid the din of the tent, the lights flickered, then dimmed, then went completely out. The crowd squealed, and I could hardly hear C.D. Lorenzo's voice over the speaker system: "Welcome ladies and shentlemen to zee greatest Big Top spectacle in zee univeahrse." At that, the crowd went berserk.

A spotlight popped on at center ring, and C.D. Lorenzo

stood in his red and gold uniform, waving and blowing kisses to the crowd as if he'd just stepped off his throne to greet his inanely adoring subjects. Shrieks, about a jillion of them—I am not kidding—erupted and filled the tent. Susan was part of that whole spectacle, and, if the truth be known, Doreen got in a few high-pitched squeals as well. It wasn't easy to watch grown people in these embarrassing states, all because of a greasy fake guy who had an inexplicable hold on their lives for the moment. Whatever the hold was—perhaps our lives were so dull that someone like him, someone so obviously self-absorbed, could grab our interest for a week just because he owned a bunch of imprisoned animals and employed midgets to toss buckets of feathers—it spoke volumes about our small town. Hey, it spoke volumes about me.

The show began.

It turned out to be the most memorable show in the history of the C.D. Lorenzo Traveling Family Circus and Carnival.

It started off with a bang, literally, as C.D. gestured to the corner of the ring—well, it wasn't a "corner" exactly, because the thing was a ring, after all—and a roving spotlight settled on the huge cannon that would blast several times that night. The Human Cannonball, dressed in a crash helmet and suit that looked like the one Commander Shepard had just worn into space, stood by the cannon and waved to the crowd. He would not only be shot from his cannon several times during the show, but would, at one point, crawl into a wooden crate with dynamite and blow the whole thing to smithereens—and emerge unscathed. He would ride a motorcycle through rings of fire, and later up a ramp to take a flying leap over a line of kneeling horses.

But for now, his charge, so to speak, was to inaugurate the Big Top Show with a big cannon blast. As for my discussion with Doug and Lance about the flying dogs and exploding cats, I looked around to confirm what I knew was true—but had niggling doubts about anyway—and to my relief saw no cats or dogs anywhere. I filed that away for later discussion with Doug.

Sometime between the Flying Zalubras high-wire act, which featured one of the lady Zalubras hanging by her teeth on a small ring suspended from a unicycle, and the tiger act, I checked my watch: nine-twenty. The show would go on until past ten.

The show was fairly standard as far as the acts went. C.D. Lorenzo was of course annoying, but managed to keep the show going at a nice clip, and when it finally came time for Simba, The Pride of the African Jungle, to come out the crowd had been whipped into a frenzy.

Actually, Simba didn't really have his own act. He was more an embellishment to other people's acts. He stood on his hind legs, and then on his front legs, while a sagging woman in sequins and fake Indian headdress who called herself Princess Kikimamoona, a name she probably found on a sign by a small lake somewhere in upstate New Jersey, knelt under his body to prove that Simba was so well-trained she wouldn't think twice about letting his precariously balanced tonnage loom over her. Simba even curled his long trunk around her and raised her high in the air, a move that was definitely a crowd pleaser. That part seemed to make Princess Kikimamoona happy as well. In a perverse sort of way, if you want to know the truth. She faked a swoon and, I swear it, smiled at C.D. Lorenzo.

The other part of Princess Kikimamoona's act involved a chimpanzee, an old circus stalwart that had been around ever since I could remember. The reason I remembered him was simple. He had a gimp leg. He was a chimp with a limp. I know all chimpanzees sort of teeter and totter when they walk, but this chimp had a limp, there was no doubt about it. The bad leg was shriveled and shorter than the other, and the chimp almost dragged it along as he moved from place to place. It didn't seem to hinder him, though, and he was on and off Simba like a rocket, doing handstands, flips, and generally chattering up a storm.

Simba went through his paces like an old pro, but his age had begun to show. He didn't seem to move as quickly as necessary when Lorenzo snapped the whip, and he even stopped once and sort of looked around, as if confused, before he walked up to Princess Kikimamoona and placed his huge, padded foot gently on her stomach.

I checked my watch at about ten. It was time for me to wonder what had happened at Ricky's place.

The final act in the Big Top show was the grand procession, where the bears, horses, tigers, Simba, and other animals joined the clowns, jugglers, Flying Zalubras, animal trainers, Human Cannonball, Princess Kikimamoona, and all the rest for a final two or three loops around the ring. It was always a bang-up way to end the show, and I cannot recall a time when the cheering crowd did not turn into a foot-stomping, clapping, screaming monster as the animals and circus people circled the ring, waving, blowing kisses, and generally looking like gods descended from Mount Olympia.

Then it happened.

Now, circus animals are trained, I know, but apparently some are slow learners in the area of bladder retention. Or maybe they aren't slow learners but want to make a sort of statement, to say something the rest of us can understand, because I know they can communicate when they set their minds to it—I'm positive of that. Don't ask. It's a thing you take on faith. I mean, they could be reciting the Gettysburg Address in their own grunts and whinnies language and we wouldn't know a damn thing about it unless they wanted us to, much the same way we wouldn't know if Mr. Hwan says, "American boy or ingrown toenail, which is worse? Boy, by far," under his breath every time we walk into his store, which actually might be the case.

As the procession rounded my side of the ring, the chimp and Princess Kikimamoona swayed back and forth on

Simba's back like Indian maharajas while the calliope piped this bouncy theme music through the Big Top tent, drowned by the squeals of East Hartford, Connecticut.

And Simba stopped to pee.

Which may be understating it. What I can tell you right here and now is that it wasn't your normal stream that dribbled from between his legs. It was a gush, a roar that raised wood chips and warm mud from the sawdusted floor of the circus ring, splattering the front rows of spectators, where I sat with my family. Princess Kikimamoona's eyes went wide, then quickly turned to peeved slits. She looked down and adjusted her straps and sequins, all the while making a face as if the family dog had walked into the sitting room and started humping her leg. The procession, including the horses, clowns, tigers, the Flying Zalubras, animal trainers, and C.D. Lorenzo himself, leading Simba in front, came to an abrupt halt, bumping into each other like the Marx Brothers flying around a corner.

Simba stood his ground, as I suppose anyone would, and let loose a regular Niagara Falls. At first I was amazed, stunned actually, but within moments I realized what he was doing. I jumped up and whooped, screamed in honor of Simba, in honor of all elephants, for a reason I can only now attribute to stupid exhilaration. The chimp whooped, too, and took the opportunity for a bit of tumbling and somersaulting atop Simba, all the while grabbing his crotch and flapping his lips, screeching in an odd, satisfied grin. That was when Princess Kikimamoona turned to him with a distinct horror, as if it had suddenly occurred to her that she was in the company of a demented chimpanzee on top of a urinating elephant.

Within seconds though, it wasn't just me whooping. The crowd began to point, then laugh, then shriek. And it was in honor of more than Simba's attitude. As he stood there and his stream continued to ricochet into the stands, as he let his body relax and become *involved* in it, what we really whooped about was his truly spectacular shlong.

Now, penis may be the proper word to use, anatomically speaking, but to tell the truth, as far as Simba was concerned, penis just didn't cut it. It sounds diminutive, almost puny. Most of the words I know, like dink, dick, dong, and dork; or pecker, pizzle, putz, and peter; or even wiener, willy, wanker, or whatever—I guess I don't need to go through the whole alphabet here—none of those words cut it either. If there is a specific word for an elephant's penis, my bet is that it's one huge word.

The crowd roared for the winning size of Simba's whatever, which would very quickly become part of local town lore. It, all forty unfolding pounds of it, swaggered and slapped against his inner thighs, wandering back and forth like a guided missile following its target. It was gray and black and shiny and—I swear I couldn't lie about something like this, no guy could with a straight face—had sort of a hook at the end of it.

Susan, who had covered her eyes while peeking through her fingers, said, "Is that, I mean...is it?"

"Jesus God, yes," I shouted. "What do you think it is, a kickstand?" I grabbed her camera—she wasn't using it anyway—and snapped off a few shots. The errant rocket had now taken on a life of its own, and the screaming front rows dove for cover, ducking like actors in a civil defense film.

As the crowd went berserk, C.D. Lorenzo cussed as he dodged the muddy splash, and for some reason started to whack at Simba's legs with his tiny whip. As if it mattered. Because when Simba was finished and not a moment before, a shiver snaked along his back and sides, which had the effect of knocking off the last drops, and he snorted once, a signal, apparently, to resume the march.

For me it was an image I would never forget, a taste of the other-worldly. I think at that moment I knew I would someday see an elephant, a free elephant in the wilds of

Africa, stomping poachers into pancakes, trumpeting victory to hordes of wide-eyed natives, and thundering triumphantly into a panoramic sunset, guided by his shiny seeker missile.

It was, as well, a yardstick, or two, against which I could forever measure the quality of righteous and embarrassing situations, as in, "That's nothing. An elephant once pissed on my mother."

Of course, the crowd was beyond berserk, partly because Simba had chosen this very public moment to do this very personal thing, which, as I've said, did not strike me as wholly unintended at the time or later. Especially later. It seems to me now that the crowd cheered him on, much like they'd cheer on a marathon runner who'd come from behind to win a race, much like they cheered Jimmy Stewart in "Mr. Smith Goes to Washington."

Lorenzo went from raging anger to grudging bewilderment in record time, because he realized that somehow, in some way, an elephant urinating in the ring was good for business. He got Simba back into the procession and did a couple of extra loops around the Big Top Ring while the audience hooted and stomped like wild people at the bottom of the ninth inning of a bases-loaded, two-outs, two-strikes, three-balls, tied baseball game. The procession looped around until the crowd let up a bit, and finally C.D. Lorenzo led the animals and circus people out of the Big Top and into the night air of their last day in East Hartford, Connecticut.

People were already standing as the lights went on and C.D. Lorenzo's voice could be heard booming over the loud-speaker system: "Zank you ladies and shentlemen, we hope you enshoyed zee show. We weel return nex yeeah for an even biggeah and betteah extravaganza, and we hope you will shoin us once again. Until zen, Ciao!" The crowd cheered and clapped some more. Then, the speaker clicked as if someone had tried to shut the mike off, and I heard, faintly, "Morons."

Pop heard it too—his head whipped around—and I figure a couple of others must have heard it. But the crowd was in the noisy process of exiting the tent, and I don't think more than a handful of them would have believed me if I told them that C.D. Lorenzo held them and everything except their money in contempt.

Ciao, indeed.

Outside the tent, Susan said, nervously, "Great show, wasn't it?"

"I need a shower immediately," Doreen said.

Pop walked slowly, as if he were contemplating something. Suddenly, he snickered to himself. "Not surprised," he said.

"I was," I said, thinking his reference was to Simba's stupendous anatomy.

"Not that," Pop said, "although, I've got to say I've never seen anything like it."

"Enough of this talk," Doreen said. "And neither, thank God, have I."

"Thanks," Pop said.

"Get me to a shower," Doreen said.

"Did you hear what Lorenzo said?" I said.

"When? What did he say?" asked Susan, ever anxious to gather new information about her hero.

Pop stopped walking and regarded Susan. He put his arm around her shoulder. "Nothing," he said. "I didn't hear anything."

"What did he say, Dub?" she asked.

I caught Pop's glance and said, "Well, he said 'ciao.' Which is Italian. I thought Lorenzo was supposed to French or something, with that accent."

"The accent," Susan said, "is fake, as we both know, and his last name is Lorenzo, which is Italian, okay? And why shouldn't someone say 'ciao' if they want to say 'ciao?'"

On the ride home we talked about the circus, and Pop

and I exchanged glances whenever Simba's name came up. His last act, I could tell by Doreen's attitude, was never going to be a proper topic for discussion, so we pretty much let it go. At least for the time being. Still, in the long run the 1961 C.D. Lorenzo Circus would become legendary for that, as would Simba.

As we pulled into our neighborhood, I had an idea.

"Pop," I said. "are you going to take a shift at the Dubois's tonight?"

"Later," he said. "I'm taking three to six."

"Why don't we swing by," I said, "and see what's up?"

"Your mother wants a shower," he said. He said it as much to change the subject as anything else.

"And it's late, Walter," Doreen said, calmly.

"Can't we just, you know, drive by?" I said.

"Walter, no," Doreen said.

"Please?" asked Susan, who had picked up on the whole thing.

"Well, I suppose just driving by wouldn't hurt," Pop said. "The kids are just concerned. What do you say, Doreen?"

Doreen sighed.

So we swung by the Dubois house on our way home. The lights were on in the place, and I could see shadows moving through the sitting room, as if the family had just come home and were settling in. Which they were, assuming they had returned from the circus just ahead of us. Nothing about the house seemed out of place, and no one was running around as they would have been had there been a smoldering cross on their front lawn or a door caved in by a shotgun blast. Everything was hunky-dory.

I leaned out the window just a bit and listened hard, but the sound of a siren was as absent as the rest of the mayhem I had expected. I felt a surge of despair as I realized that Officer Bigger Farley might not have taken the bait after all. He might never have come to the house.

I wondered how long Big had waited there before he took off, probably cursing me for making him camp out by the house all night.

I turned to Susan and shrugged. She shrugged as well.

We drove home and Doreen and Dad puttered around downstairs while we got ready for bed. I cornered Susan in the bathroom as she brushed her teeth.

"What do you think?" I whispered.

"We'll find out tomorrow, from Ricky."

I suddenly had a horrendous thought. What if Officer Bigger had actually come, and what if he had taken a shot at Big, not knowing who he was? And what if Officer Bigger had winged him, and Big was right now, at this very moment, bleeding to death in the woods behind Ricky's house?

I said as much to Susan.

"Enough with the melodrama," she hissed. "Another shotgun blast would have had the whole neighborhood out on the street again. There would've been police all over. Now, go to bed."

I had another thought. "Wonder what got into Simba?"

Susan looked at me as if I'd told her I'd just eaten a plate of toenails. "You're disgusting. Just go to bed, you pervert."

"Okay, okay," I said. "I didn't mean anything by it."

And so I went to bed. The alarm clock by my bed ticked loudly as I lay there, eye-dry awake, waiting for morning, when we'd finally find out if the horror in Ricky's life was to end.

CHAPTER 13

I woke up feeling heavy, and went out for my paper route. I found everything pretty much as I expected it would be. Pop was outside the Dubois's place, asleep, looking content. Which is probably why this time I decided to wake him. I walked up slowly to his window, which was closed, and lightly tapped it with my knuckle. Pop opened his eyes and turned his head slowly, warily. "Oh," he said from behind his window.

He rolled it down. "What's up, Dub?"

"Want the paper?"

"Yeah, well, give me the sports and—wait, what time is it?" He checked his watch. "I'll tell you what," he said, "give me the whole paper and I'll take it home. It's about time I knocked off anyhow."

"How did it go last night?" I said.

"Fine," he said. "The police were by more than usual. Herb had called them and asked them to step up their patrols since we were all at the circus. But other than that, just another normal night. Except—"

"What?" I said.

"Except that, I don't know, something seemed odd tonight, sort of out of kilter."

"Oh," I said. I tried to be nonchalant. "Like what?"

"I don't know," he said. "It's just a feeling I have. But nothing happened, anyway."

"That's weird, Pop," I said. He cocked his head and regarded me, but decided to let it pass, whatever it was.

I continued along my route for about twenty minutes before I realized I hadn't even looked at the paper myself. Maybe it'd have some news, any news, about an incident at Ricky's place. I stopped and unwrapped one, and there, under the fold at the right-hand corner of the front page, was the headline: "Circus Elephant's Death Baffles Authorities."

I gripped the paper and wobbled as I straddled my bike, and my first thought was, "Of course."

The report was sketchy, but it appeared that sometime after midnight Simba had gone on a rampage. He'd apparently pulled his stake and chain from the ground and attacked his trainer, one Mario Bordonaro. The trainer recalled that when he approached the loose elephant, Simba was "pawing at his chest with his tusks and calling out, like he had some powerful itch in there." Bordonaro went on to say that the elephant had picked him up and tossed him "like a kid's teddy bear" and that the next thing he remembered was a gun going off.

Then, according to witnesses, who I guess were circus people, the elephant charged a circus trailer that turned out to be the living quarters of circus owner and ringmaster C.D. Lorenzo. Somehow Lorenzo had found a hunting rifle and tried to shoot Simba. The shot apparently missed the elephant, who then stepped up to Lorenzo's trailer and tipped it over before collapsing dead. After police and firemen were called, they assisted in rescuing another circus performer, one Alice Raye, who goes by the stage name Princess Kikimamoona, from the tipped trailer. She was unharmed, the elephant trainer was treated and released from Hartford Hospital, and the cause of the elephant's death remained a mystery.

Of course. I folded the paper and finished my route, slowly.

After breakfast, Susan and I went next door to get Doug. He was just finishing a big old doughnut, and, wiping his face with his hand, left the house and jumped on his bike.

"Read the paper?" he said, glumly, as we rode down the street.

I nodded.

"Pretty unfair, if you ask me," he said.

"Yup," I said.

"There's Ricky," Susan said. And there she was, in dungarees and a pink top, sitting on her front steps. When we reached her, she held up her hand and placed a finger to her lips. She looked tired, like she'd had about the same kind of night I'd had.

"Hey," we said.

"Keep it low," Ricky said. "They're still having breakfast inside." She searched our eyes for a moment. "So, I suspect you'll all want to know what happened."

We nodded.

"As far as I can tell," she said, "well, I just don't know."

"What do you mean?" I said. "You don't know what happened? Or you don't know if anything happened?"

"What I mean," she said slowly, "is that nothing seems to have happened."

"What?" I said.

"Let her talk, Dub," Susan said.

"Well," Ricky said, but not before she gave me an eloquent, exasperated glance, "when we got home from the circus, everything at the house seemed fine, nothing wrong. No siren was on, nothing. Then, when everyone was getting ready to go to bed, I slipped outside, just to poke around a bit."

"And?" Susan said.

"Nothing. I checked where I'd dropped off the camera and siren by the bush, where Big Farley was supposed to find them, there they were, just like I left them."

My heart scuttled. "Just like you left them?"

"Just like I left them."

"Then Big never showed up," Doug said, "the coward."

"Who knows?" Susan hissed. "Maybe Big did go, and maybe it was his father who never went to the house. Ricky said that nothing else had been touched."

"Damn," I said. So, there it was. The plan had failed. My

only comfort was that maybe it had failed because the enemy hadn't turned up, and not because the good guys, so to speak, hadn't done their share.

"Nothing happened?" I said. "No fires, no bricks, nothing?"

"Nothing," Ricky said, "thank God."

"Then," Susan said, "it's time to insist that Pop and your father listen to you about Officer Bigger."

"I'm leaving tomorrow, you know," Ricky said. "My father said so."

"Tomorrow?" Doug said, incredulous.

"Tomorrow."

"Listen," I said, "let's just play this out till the end. Let me meet Big this afternoon, like we planned, and let me ask him what happened over at Ricky's. It couldn't hurt. If nothing happened, if it's true Officer Bigger never showed up, then we go to plan B. "

"Which is?" Susan said.

I was shaken. It had come down to this. No one believed us about Officer Bigger, and just when we needed him most to act like the pathetic creep he was, he might have let us down.

"We'll think of something," I said.

"What if Big never shows up at your meeting?" Doug said.

"He will," I said. "It's our last chance." I knew Big would show. It was inevitable, as if it had to happen. It was as though we had some sort of pact that made it necessary for us to believe in each other.

We all stood there, thinking about tomorrow.

"Okay," Susan said. "We'll see what Big Farley has to say. Nothing we can do about it now."

"Look," Ricky said. "I have to get ready for church. So, this afternoon, then?"

"Sure," I said. "After I meet up with Big."

"Dub," she said as she stood up. "I just want to say that I'm sorry about Simba."

"It's okay," I said.

"I mean, I know he was kind of special to you. And I'm just sorry, that's all." She opened the door to her house and took one step in, then turned back. "Maybe it was just his time to be somewhere else."

I thought about that later, and many, many more times later on, and I only have this to say about it: I wish to hell she'd never said a goddamn thing, especially that. I mean it.

Doug and Susan and I jumped on our bikes, and we left.

I told Susan I'd see her and Ricky back at Doug's later, and got ready for my meeting with Big Farley. I felt awful about it, fully expecting him to report that nothing had occurred during the night, and that he'd simply left Ricky's house when it became apparent that his father hadn't taken the bait. I had no reason to believe otherwise.

Nevertheless, just in case things turned out better than expected, I put a pen, two sheets of white paper, a plain envelope, and a stamp in my pocket, and set off for Zikker's Pond as fast as my bike would carry me.

I was mildly surprised to find Big already there, alone at my rock, pacing back and forth, smoking a cigarette. Beneath him, a pile of crushed cigarettes swam in the muck and water of the pond.

His face was screwed tight and he paced like a caged tiger. As I got off my bike he walked evenly up to me and without a blink punched me in the chest. I fell backward, breathless, into the mud.

"That's for fucking up," he said.

"Hi, Big," I choked. "Good to see you, too. Jesus, what was that for?"

"The siren, you idiot! The goddamn siren didn't work."

I stood up and pushed some mud off my hands and

elbows. I walked up to Big and punched him, hard, in the chest. He went reeling against the rock.

"That's so we start off even," I said. Then it hit me. "Did you say the siren! What about the siren?"

"Help me up, first," Big said.

I extended my hand and Big grabbed it, then yanked as hard as he could. I went sprawling face-first in the mud.

"*Now*, we're even," Big said, "Okay, goddamnit?"

"Okay," I said from the ground. "Truce?"

I got up slowly and scraped more mud from my clothes and face. He shrugged and put his hands in his pockets, looked down.

"Anyway," I said, "what happened?"

Big regarded me with resignation, and he shook his head. "He came to the house," he said. He sat heavily and stared at the ground.

"What happened? We found the camera and siren right there, where we left them."

"You probably thought I didn't show up, didn't you?"

"No," I said, lying slightly. "I wasn't sure what had happened."

"I bet Hammer thought I didn't show up."

"Well, we couldn't figure it out, is all."

"Who gives a shit, really," Big said, and he sighed. "I was there all right."

I nodded, and Big acknowledged it.

"You know, I wasn't a hundred percent sure about what you told me, you know, about what he was doing. Until last night."

I didn't want to push Big into talking about it more than he had to at the moment—even though I was crawling out of my skin to know. This couldn't be easy for him.

"Anyway," he said. "I did go. Figured I'd, you know, help my mom out, see what this was all about. Anyway, I get there and find the bag with the camera and siren, and everything looks like it's going about right. I'm crouching in the bushes, just hanging out—I couldn't even smoke a cigarette for Christ's sake, you know? In case someone sees the glow. I'm just waiting. Then a cop car pulls up and they flash a spotlight around the house, just checking. They even flashed the bush I was hiding behind and it scared the snot out of me, I'm telling you. But I didn't run. They didn't see me anyway. I laid low after that, and just waited some more."

"Wow," I said.

Big just nodded. "So then at about, hell, I don't know what time it was, I only know that the neighborhood was real quiet and there were hardly any cars around. Everyone must have been at the circus or something. Anyway, I see this car come around the corner, real slow. I know the car right away, I can tell it from a mile away."

Big paused and ran his dirty fingers through his hair. He was cautious.

"So he drives by the house, extra slow. Then he turns around up the street and slows down again. In the meantime, I'm sitting behind that bush and I can't move an inch. I got the camera and siren in my hand, and I just wait."

Then I asked another one of the stupidest question I've ever asked another guy in my life, but, for some reason, I had to know. "How were you feeling about it?" I said.

Big looked at me as if I'd asked him what it was like to stick a burning twig in his eye. "Shitty, what do you expect?" he said.

He continued. "Then he stops, backs up, and parks in front of the house, on the opposite side of the street. I'm ready, ready as sin, but he doesn't get out of the car. He just sits there, looking."

"Was he in uniform?"

"No, he was off-duty. It was his car, not a cop car."

"Jeez, so he just sat there?"

"No," Big said, surprised. "Just for a while, like maybe a minute or two. Meanwhile, I'm sitting there and I need to piss and the whole thing looks like it's going nowhere. You know, I was beginning to think he was just there checking on the house, like the rest of the cops. That the whole thing was a bust. That you were wrong. But finally, he steps out of the car."

"Great!" I said, which was the second stupidest thing I said to Big that day. I caught myself, but badly. "I mean, well, that's good."

"Sure," Big said, and spit. "It was fucking great. Anyway, he steps out of the car and looks around. And he's got a bottle in his hand, like a whiskey bottle or something. Only the bottle has something hanging out of it. I don't know, it looked like a rag. He's holding the bottle low, by his side, and then he walks, real quick, but kind of loose, you know? Right over toward the bush I was sitting behind, like he knew I was there for Christ's sake."

"That sounds like the spot me and Ricky were when we saw him."

"Yeah? Well maybe he was looking for you guys, whatever. I mean, he comes straight for me and I'm thinking I'm dead for sure. Then he stops and we got maybe ten feet between us, at the side of the house. And then, Jesus, I hear this rhyme, this kid's rhyme. He's humming this rhyme."

"What rhyme?" I said.

"You know, that one that goes, 'Eenee, meenee, meinee, moe,' like that."

I had no response, except horror.

"Go on," I said.

"And then I smell the gas. The bottle smells like gas."

"Holy Moly," I said.

"But I couldn't even breathe, for God's sake, or he'd hear me. I mean, he could have just about reached out and grabbed me, right there. Then, he pulls his lighter from his pocket, and I know right then and there that he's going to light the bottle and throw it at the house."

"Did he?" I said.

"Hold on. See, he's humming that song, and he's taking

his time. I know this is the moment, so I got my finger on the button of the siren and my other hand on the camera button. Then I flick the siren, thinking I'm going to snap the picture and book outa there like nobody's business."

"And?" I said, almost breathless myself.

"And nothing, that's what. The goddamn siren doesn't work. It's dead. And the next time I see Hammer I'm going to break his legs because I think he set me up. He knew the thing didn't work."

"It wasn't his fault," I said. "We put new batteries in it just a couple of days ago."

"Yeah, but did you ever test it to see that it worked? Did you hear it? Maybe it never worked in the first place. Maybe the damn thing is busted. Or maybe Hammer busted it, on purpose."

"Well, I don't know," I said, thinking, hey, anything is possible. I hated to think that, I really did. But I couldn't discount it.

"But you're alive, you're here," I said. "And the house didn't burn. What happened?"

Big made a show of pulling out a cigarette and lighting it. He punctuated the rest of his story by jabbing and gesturing with the cigarette, giving the distinct impression he needed to do something with his hands.

"Anyway," he continued, "Even though I'm rattled, I still got the camera in my other hand. I stand up just a little, so I'm still sort of half-way behind the bush. He's flicking away at this lighter, kind of having a hard time with it, you know? So, anyway I pull the camera around the bush and aim it in his direction, but I don't even know what I'm shooting at because I woulda had to stand up all the way to aim it good. So I just reach my arm around the bush. And I hit the button."

"Holy Cripes," I said. "You got a picture?"

"Sure," Big said. "Got it right here in my pocket." He patted his hip pocket. "You and Hammer didn't even check the film in the camera did you? None too bright, Dubby."

"Well, let's see it!"

"Hang on," Big said. "At least let me finish the story."

"Yeah, sure, go ahead."

"Well," he continued, "so the flash goes off and I hear him shout something, something like, 'What the hell?' or something like that. But by that time I'm running my ass off toward the back of the house, with the camera in my hand and the picture coming out the bottom. Tell the truth, I think I was running before I even snapped the picture. I don't know."

"Did he come after you?"

"I never looked back. I'm just booking it out through the woods, and I hear him say something like 'Who's that?' and then 'Shit!' but by that time I'm way into the woods. After a couple of seconds, I hear a car start up and squeal out of here, so I just sit down and let my heart slow down. It was him. He was gone, just like that."

"So, let's see the picture!" I said.

"Hold on," Big said, jabbing the smoke. "Jesus Christ. There's more."

"Go on," I said. I was about to have an apoplectic fit.

"So I wait a few minutes until I calm down, like about twenty minutes. Just to make sure he's gone. Then I sneak back to the house slowly, real slow, you know? Who knows what's going to happen next?

"Well, nothing happened. The car is gone, and he must've took the bottle of gas with him too. Nothing is different. So I take the picture and put it in my pocket, then I put the camera back in the bag with that lousy siren—that way I unload the camera and nobody can put me together with any picture. And I take off. I get home before him, I don't know where the hell he went, but I crawl into bed and the next day here I am. Just like that."

I was silent, awestruck. But I couldn't hold it any longer. "The picture, Big! The photo!"

"Yeah, that," he said, and reached behind to pull out a

photo from his pocket. Big Farley, with trembling hands, handed me the picture.

The photo was blurred, as if the person who'd taken it had been moving as he snapped it. Which, as Big had said, was exactly the case. But it was clear enough. The figure in the photo stood diagonally, as if the camera had been tilted at exposure. It showed Officer Bigger Farley from the waist to his eyes, standing sideways with a blurry Molotov cocktail in one hand and what appeared to be a sparking lighter in the other. On his forearm was the tattoo of a screaming eagle. Behind him was the outline of the Sullivan place across the street, dark and slightly blurred, but at least it placed Officer Bigger at the Dubois house. Officer Bigger's eyes were half-closed, but there was no doubt that they were his eyes. And face. The top of Officer Farley's head was cut off, but the image, the essence of the photo was unmistakable. It was a man about to do damage with fire.

I held the photo out to Big. "I'm sorry," I said.

Big took the photo, stared at it, and put it back in his hip pocket. Then he pulled it out again, and stared at it some more. "Yeah," he said, and turned his head. It was as if the presence of the photo confirmed his father's crime, once and for all, and the act of looking at it made it more real than it was. All of a sudden Big stood up and walked to the edge of the water.

Big Farley choked, for the second time in days, smacking himself with his fists, choking to stifle the tears, choking on snot and salt, choking on the bad taste in his mouth. He lit another cigarette and spat out the smoke, as if it offended him. He paced, sat down, and paced again. He walked over to the water, picked up some stones and savagely threw them into the water. He kicked mud piles. He never cried, never said a word. I never said a word.

Finally, exhausted and bloodshot, Big sat down on our rock. He nodded.

I nodded.

"I guess it could be worse," he said, trembling.

I knew what he meant. "We'll never know," I said. "But now we can make things right."

"No cops, right? No one but you and me?"

"And your father," I said.

"And I get to keep the picture," he said. "I don't want Hammer, or your sister, or even the nig—the girl to see it."

"It's yours to keep. If he goes after them again, you'll know what to do with it."

He contemplated that. "Let's just finish this."

"Let's," I said.

And we moved to the second phase of our plan. Which was: We would write an anonymous letter to Mr. Officer Bigger Farley, right then and there, on the paper I'd brought, describing our little piece of evidence. We would stuff the letter into the envelope, and deliver it posthaste, anonymously again, into Officer Farley's hands. Whereupon he would read it and all hostilities toward the Dubois household would cease and desist. End of plan, end of story.

Big had agreed to the general plan in principle, but now wanted to know details. First, what exactly would we say in the letter? Second, how would we deliver it? Third, since his father knew that Ricky and I had seen him at the house during the night of the shotgun, what would prevent him from believing that we were the ones who also took the photograph? And what would prevent him from coming after us to get it? Big had thought this through fairly quickly, and admirably, I'd say. I knew his questions stemmed not only from a desire to make it work, but from a desire to protect his father from committing more crimes.

"Good points, one and all," I said. "Okay, first, you and I will write the letter together, so we agree on everything. Second, we deliver the letter by U.S. mail. I've got the stamps right here. Third, yes he knows we saw him that other night, but if we do a good job with the letter he won't come after anyone. If he does, I have my own alibi. I was at the circus, with hundreds of people. And who has the photo? You. And I'd never tell him that."

Big nodded again. "Let's do this fast."

So we wrote the letter. First we had to go to the edge of the pond to wash the mud from our hands, which we let drip-dry because our clothes were also full of mud. I pulled out the paper.

"You write," Big said. "He might recognize my writing."

"I'm left handed. I'll write with my right hand," I said, balancing the paper on my knees. "That way no one will recognize it."

"No," Big said, "then it'll only look like you wrote it with your right hand. Hold the pen in your fist, like you were holding a—" He stopped himself.

"A what?" I said.

"A knife," he said.

We haggled back and forth over wording and so on, even over spelling—Big felt we should spell key words wrong to lead his father off the trail, while I maintained that spelling words incorrectly would point directly at a bunch of kids, not that Big was all that much of a speller in the first place. I pointed out that we wanted Officer Farley to believe it was possible that an adult took the photo, and an adult wrote the letter. Anyway, we finally settled on accuracy. I also warned Big that we had to be a little tough in the letter, even threatening, just to show we meant business, something he agreed on after a while, but only after a while. To tell the truth, the whole miserable business was awfully delicate and strange, but we finally came out with this:

Dear Officer Farley,

We know what you have been doing, and we think you should not do it anymore. We want you to stop. You remember that flash you saw on Saturday night while you were holding the bottle filled with gasoline? It was a camera. So now we have a picture of you trying to light that bottle to throw at the house. It is a very good picture. It is very clear. It would solve the case of who has been bothering that family. You would definitely be found guilty. Jail is not a nice thing, and think of your kids.

We could turn in the picture today if we wanted to, but we have decided to give you a second chance because we are thinking of your kids. We just want you to stop the things you have been doing, even the phone calls, and to never, never bother that family again. If you do, we will send a letter and copy of the picture to the newspaper, and to the chief of police where you work . Then we will send a copy to the FBI.

In order for us not to turn over the picture, we want you to write a letter immediately to Mr. Dubois saying you are sorry, and what you did was wrong, and you will never do it again, to anyone. You have to write exactly that. If it makes you feel better, you can say that you must have gone temporarily mental or something. Don't worry, you don't have to sign your real name, just sign it "A Changed Man." That's so we know for sure you wrote the letter. Write it and mail the letter the same day you get this. If they don't get the letter RIGHT AWAY with those exact words, then we think you will be really sorry. Okay?

Don't bother to go hunting for the picture because it is not in the hands of who you think. It is in the hands of someone you would never expect. If Mr. Dubois doesn't get his letter, or if anything bad ever happens again, that person will turn the picture over in a heartbeat.

Justice has spoken.

Sincerely,

Concerned Citizens of East Hartford

PS: We have a carbon copy of this letter.

The part about thinking of your kids was Big's idea, and he was proud of it. The bit about the FBI was also Big's idea, because he said that's how police forces work, that the FBI is more powerful than town police forces. The last bit about justice has spoken and concerned citizens and all that was my idea. Of course, we lied about having copies of the photo and letter, but we weren't dealing with the Pope here for God's sake.

Big questioned the bit about the phone calls, and I had to explain to him what had been happening with the calls and that the police were just about the only ones who had the phone number. Just covering bases, is how I explained it. Big finally agreed to it, but not without some protest. He's never seen his father do anything like that, he said, so why accuse him? I explained that we had to convince his father that we knew the score, completely, and then I finally admitted that we were maybe ninety-nine percent sure that Officer Farley had made the crank calls. Big explained that he had flunked percentages in school, but what the hell, he supposed it was okay.

The parts about Officer Bigger going temporarily mental and signing it "A Changed Man" were my idea. The thing is, it's not that I wanted to punish Officer Bigger, although that would have been sweet. The main problem was time. I wanted him to get our letter and send his off as soon as possible. Ricky was due to leave the next day, and in order for her father to cancel that trip, it had to be clear to him that the danger in the neighborhood was over. How we hoped to accomplish that in such a limited time, short of turning in Officer Farley right then and there, was the root of the problem. And turning in Officer Bigger was not an option. Big had my word on that.

But if we could persuade Mr. Dubois to postpone the trip for a couple of days, then the letter from Officer Bigger would arrive, and everything would be solved. That's how we figured it, and that's how we left it.

When all was said and done, it was a pretty damn good letter, and we were happy with it.

Before we folded it, Big took the only clean part left on his shirt and wiped the paper. He said he thought he'd heard that paper was a good source of fingerprints. He folded the letter with his hand inside his shirt, then wiped the envelope clean after he stuffed it. I began to respect Big a whole lot more than I'd ever thought possible.

We addressed the envelope to "Officer Henry Farley, East Hartford Police," along with the street address which Big knew by heart. We added "Warning, Very Personal," both for effect and because we both thought we'd once seen something like it on "Dragnet." Finally, I stood up and tossed the pen deep into Zikker's Pond. All evidence of our involvement seemed to be in order.

I licked the stamp and fixed it, then put the letter in my pocket and stood up.

"I'll find a mailbox," I said. "He should have it by Tuesday. And Mr. Dubois should have the apology by Wednesday. Then we get back to normal."

Big stood up as well. "Sure," he said, and shuffled a bit.

"Well," I said, "that's that."

"Sure is," Big said. "Cigarette?"

"Don't smoke," I said.

"Yeah, that's right."

"Well, what do you think?"

"I think we did good," he said.

"Me too."

"Yeah."

"Well," I said. "I guess that's the end of that."

"Yep," Big said.

"I guess we should lay low," I said, "until this thing blows over."

"Yeah," Big said. "Shit's going to hit that old fan."

"Sure is," I said.

"Well," Big said. "I guess that's that."

"Yeah," I said. "We did good. You. You did great, really."

"I suppose," Big said. "So." And he cleared his throat.

Incredibly, he held out his hand.

It was the second time I'd ever touched Big Farley, except in matters of violence and mayhem. I took his hand, which was strong and rough, and pretty grimy at that, but I didn't mind. So was my hand. We shook.

"See you later," I said, and turned to my bike.

"Okay," he said. "Hey, Teed."

I turned back to Big Farley. "Yeah?"

"Is that rock yours?"

"Which rock?"

"You know, the one we been sitting on."

I hesitated, then blurted out. "Yeah, it's my rock."

"Well, I never told anyone this, but it's mine, too."

I nodded at him. "I thought so," I said. And Big Farley mounted his bike and rode away.

A half-hour later I mailed the extortion letter to Officer Bigger Farley, remembering to carefully wipe my fingerprints from the envelope before I dropped it into the box.

CHAPTER 14

Susan and Ricky and Doug and I got together at Doug's place after dinner to discuss my meeting with Big Farley.

I made a long story short for them, and related Big's adventure at the house, including a detailed description of the photo, and our ultimatum letter to Officer Bigger. I did this in about two minutes. They were, as I'd expected, dumbfounded.

"So it worked," Doug said.

"Great!" Susan said.

"Big actually showed up," Doug said. "Imagine that."

"Thank God he did," Ricky said.

"But wait," Doug said, "I'm sure that the siren worked. It should have worked, I mean we put new batteries in it."

"Well," I said, "it didn't, but it all worked out for the good. Turns out he didn't need a siren anyway."

"But I don't want him to think I tried to sabotage him," Doug said. "I might think he's a no-good lying scum-bag who tried to murder me, but I wouldn't do that to a person."

"I know," I said. "We'll see how it all turns out, don't worry."

"Did Big actually help you write the letter?" Doug said, amazed.

"Yes," I said. "I can't explain it. It's like it was his mission or something."

"Or maybe he's just showing a new part of himself," Susan said.

"Listen, let's not forget that this is a guy who came after me with a knife," Doug said. "But still, I can't figure him out. I don't know if I'd trust him all the way yet."

"Sometimes there are no other choices," Susan said.

"Anyway, I mailed the letter," I said.

Ricky drummed the picnic table with her fingers. Finally, exasperated, she said, "I'm leaving tomorrow."

"Look," I said. "I've got a thought. What if we can get your father to postpone the departure? Say, two or three days? By then the response should have come from Officer Bigger, and everything will be settled."

"Not likely," Ricky said. "It's all set. We're driving down, Mama and Grandma and me. They're almost packed and everything. The worst of it is, Grandma is itching to go. She has been like that since Officer Bigger burned the cross on the lawn way back when. It's all she talks about. She walks around the house mumbling about this devil town and this Satan city and that sort of thing. I can't see Mama agreeing to delay the trip."

"Well, let's say we talk to them," I said.

"And what do we say?" Susan said. "That everything will be okay because now you have proof that Officer Farley did all this? What if they ask for the photo?"

"We can't mention Officer Farley again," I said. "I gave Big my word. And he has the photo anyway, that's the way we had to work it out. But we have to try talking to them. And we have to try now."

"So what are you going to say?" Doug said.

I started to walk toward my bike. "I don't know," I said. "Ricky, is your father home?"

"He is," she said, "but, Dub, what are you going to tell him?"

"We'll just blurt something out, for God's sake. I don't have a clue. But we have to do it now."

"You're going to give Big Farley away," Doug said.

I was on my bike. "Are you coming?" I said.

They shrugged their shoulders yes, figuring, I suppose, that I was going to be weird again and they might as well be there to see it rather than hear about it later. They were right.

Several minutes later we stood in front of Mr. Dubois on his lawn while he shook his head slowly, his brows knitted.

"That, Dub," he was saying, "is one of the darndest things I've ever heard in my entire life."

"Well," I said, "I'll agree with you on that. It's hard for me to believe it myself. But that's what I've heard, and that's why I'm here, just to relay this small piece of information. Which just might help you make some decisions."

"Okay," he said, "let me see if I got this straight. You say that one of your friends has a friend who has a friend who has a friend and so on, and that person knows something about what's been happening to my family?"

"Yessir," I said. "He's not saying who said what, only that he heard this through the grapevine."

"Okay, and you say this friend has heard that the people who've been vandalizing my home have decided to stop?" he said.

"Yessir," I said. "Only it wasn't people, it was a person, I guess. Just one guy."

"This isn't about Officer Farley again, is it?"

"No, no. I mean, we must have been wrong about that."

"Okay, so this friend," Mr. Dubois continued, "says that this person has decided to stop because...why?"

"Well," I said, "according to Bob—"

"I thought you said your friend's name was Oliver."

"Oliver. Yes, well, it is, as a matter of fact. I mean, his middle name is Oliver. You know, it's not like anyone is going to give a kid a first name like Oliver or anything. Sometimes we call him by his initials, you know, B.O., just for fun. My guess is that his parents had this strange sense of humor and—"

"Dub," Mr. Dubois said, "just go on with the story."

"Okay. Anyway, Bob heard from his friend's friend and so on that this guy, the one who has been making the calls and shooting shotguns and so forth, has, well, found the Lord."

"Found the Lord. That's what I thought I heard you say."

"Yessir. He's found the Lord."

"A religious conversion."

"I expect so."

"And he's decided not to bother us anymore."

"That's what the word is."

"He's sorry for his sins."

"Well, he ought to be," I said.

"Do you think he'd be sorry enough to come and talk to me about it? Or to turn himself in to the police?"

"To tell the truth, sir, I highly doubt that."

"Do you know his name?"

"No, none of us does. Neither does Bob."

"So you think the vandalism is going to stop."

"I'd be willing to bet on it."

"Have you told your father this?"

"No, sir."

"The police?"

"No, sir," I said.

"Then, the only people who know about this are the four of you and your friend Bob Oliver."

"And the bad guy himself, I guess."

Mr. Dubois exhaled heavily. "Dub," he said, "this wouldn't happen to have anything to do with the fact that Ricky is due to leave tomorrow, would it?"

"Tomorrow?" I said. "Is it tomorrow? That soon! Ricky, you didn't even tell us."

Ricky rolled her eyes.

"Of course not," Mr. Dubois said. "Now listen, son, and I think all of you should listen carefully. I admire your attempt and respect your feelings of friendship here. You've all been a great help to us. But the truth is, the man who has violated my home is dangerous, very dangerous, and this is not something to play around with. People's lives are in jeopardy. I have no choice but to remove Ricky and my family from the danger. Do you all understand?"

They nodded.

"Well, sort of," I said.

"Not sort of," Mr. Dubois said. "That's the way it is. No arguments. Ricky, do you understand?"

"Yes, Daddy," she said.

"Good. Look, it's not like Ricky has to go away forever. It's possible, right now anyway, that she'll come back just as soon as the police resolve this. Then we'll all get on with our lives. What do you say?" His eyes darted around, as if he had something more to say but couldn't say it.

"Well, sir," I said. "With all due respect, maybe if you just waited a day or two things might just begin to resolve themselves."

"Dub, you've called me 'sir' about eight times in the last three minutes and to be frank, it sounds like you've got something up your sleeve. What is this 'day or two' business, if you don't mind me asking?"

For a split second, I thought I might spill out the Big and Officer Bigger stories and swear Mr. Dubois to secrecy. But I had this image of Big crouching behind the bush waiting for his *father* for God's sake, and another of his tiny mother blinking like a frightened mouse, and I knew I couldn't say it.

"Well, I don't know," I said. "Wishful thinking, I guess."

Mr. Dubois nodded, then sucked on his gums. "Listen, why don't you kids come by in the morning and say good-bye to Ricky. We can have juice and scones or something, sort of like a little going-away party. Bring your father."

We nodded assent.

"Anyway," Mr. Dubois said, "I've got to get back in the house and help with the packing. I'll see you in the morning." He turned and walked back into his green house.

"You tried," Ricky said.

"Found the Lord?" Doug whispered, and he stifled a chortle.

Ricky stifled another one. "Sorry for his sins?"

"You're a mental case!" Doug said, and he burst out laughing. It was infectious, and soon I was laughing and

Ricky was laughing and, in a minute, the four of us were pushing each other, wrestling and laughing and hurting because we were tired and because the plan had almost worked and because we still had hope that it would work.

And because we really liked each other.

And, minutes later, as we left her, I thought that Ricky's glistening face and disheveled hair would have made a pretty damn fine photograph itself.

"It'll be fine," Susan said. "Your father will get the letter in a couple of days, and then call you up and tell you to come on home."

"Yeah, don't worry," Doug said. "You'll be back up here before you know it."

"I'm not worried," Ricky said. "Really."

That night, I stayed up late and wrote a short note to Ricky.

As I delivered my papers the next morning and came upon Pop's car parked in front of the Dubois place, I understood the long road we'd traveled. It was insane, this business. Officer Bigger Farley was truly dangerous, and I'd let him walk through our fingers on a whim of loyalty to an old enemy, his son. That, in itself, was crazy. Was it any crazier to know that a murderous man in uniform was loose to practice his violence again? The threat of the photo couldn't stop a guy like him forever. For a while, probably, but not likely forever. But then, what is there in this world that isn't slightly crazy, when you get right down to it.

According to Pop, the night-vigils would stop a couple of days after Ricky and her mother and grandmother left for Louisiana. Mr. Dubois was the one who said they should stop. He'd said he could handle any further trouble himself.

So, on that Monday morning we all went down to the house, all of us except Doreen, to say good-bye to Ricky and her mother and grandmother. Mrs. Hammer went along with Doug.

It was a long scene, an awkward scene. The worst of it

was that I never got a chance to talk to Ricky alone. As usual, I don't know what I would have said to her anyway, and I don't know what she would have said to me. If we'd been alone, maybe we would have finished that kiss we'd started so long ago. Maybe we would have finished the hug that had been interrupted by Officer Bigger Farley's shotgun that night. Maybe we would have finished a simple conversation. As it turned out, we never had the chance.

When all was said and done, Mrs. Dubois and Ricky hugged everyone in sight and Mrs. Oliphant shook hands while they said their good-byes. Susan started to cry, and so did Ricky, and they hugged for a long time, a nice long time. Doug threw his arms around her and gave her more or less a bear hug, so tight that Ricky grunted. Doug started to snuffle. When Ricky came to me, her cheeks were wet and she smelled like roses, and we squeezed each other with the world around us gone dark. As we did, Ricky leaned into my ear and whispered, "Don't worry, I'll come back soon."

I started, I don't know, to cry a bit, and I reached into my pocket, amid the general confusion of everyone else's good-byes, and slipped her the note I'd written the night before. I knew she wouldn't open it there, that would've been too embarrassing for both of us. I knew she'd wait until they were well down the road to tear its flaps apart and pull out the paper to read my message. Which said—I swear this is true even though I know you won't believe it—it said, "You'll come back soon, don't worry. Love, Dub." I swear to God Almighty.

They piled into the car with much hand waving and horn-honking, and then pulled out into the street and moved down the road, and were gone, just like that. The last sight I had of Ricky Dubois was a shadow in the back seat of the '57 Chevy, waving through the rear window.

Pop asked Mr. Dubois, who was drying his eyes, if there was anything he could do for him. Mr. Dubois thanked him but, no, he had to go to work. So Pop invited him over for dinner that night, a move he hadn't cleared with Doreen, which made me roll my eyes but then I thought, what the hell.

Who cares.

We went home and things settled down quickly. Doreen turned all peaches and cream, using this bouncy new step around the house, smiles for everyone. To completely attribute it to Ricky's departure would make Doreen seem silly and immature, but the fact is, I'm sorry to say, the shoe fit. She even leveled this sort of "I-told-you-so" attitude at Pop every now and then, which was doubly irritating. She enjoyed it just a bit too much.

Meanwhile, the rest of us, including Pop, walked around wide-eyed, like we'd just been told we had the plague or something. I was on edge about everything, but mostly about the letter from Officer Bigger. I knew Mr. Dubois would get it soon. I mean, I hoped it would come soon. I couldn't relax, I couldn't hang out with Susan in the willow tree, I couldn't go riding with Doug for more than ten minutes before I had to stop and go home. And wait for the word, somehow.

When the phone rang late that afternoon, I jumped for it, and Susan raced down the stairs and stood behind me. It was Mr. Dubois.

"Dub," he said, "would you tell your father and mother I won't be able to make it to dinner tonight, but thanks anyway. I've just got too much to do."

"Sure, Mr. Dubois." I took a chance. "Any news?"

"Well, they just left this morning Dub. They're not even half way there yet. They'll call as soon as they get to New Orleans, don't worry."

"Okay. But any other news?"

He hesitated for a moment. "No, no news. What do you mean?"

"Nothing, really. Just asking, that's all."

"Okay, well let your parents know I appreciate the offer, but I can't make it."

We signed off, and Susan searched my eyes. "Nothing," I said. "Yet."

The next day, the day after Ricky pulled out of town, Doreen asked me to take a ride down to Patrick's Farm stand over on Silver Lane to pick up some tomatoes.

"Squeeze them, Walter, but not too hard. They should be deep red and juicy, but not split, and they—"

"Doreen?" I said.

"Yes, Walter?"

"They're tomatoes, for God's sake."

She regarded me for a moment, but, and this the measure of our post-Ricky Dubois times, she let it go. "Well, you just use your judgment," she said in this sunny Doris Day voice.

The day was perfect for late summer, with a hint of cool in the morning air and not a cloud in the sky. I pedaled fast, my eyes on the road, thinking about all that had happened, when a dark shape, a car, slowed down along side me. It was a police car.

It was Officer Bigger Farley's police car.

My nose went dry and my breath stuck in my throat as he passed me, his right turn signal on, and pulled in front. He held his hand out the window, signaling me to stop, then beckoned with his finger. I got off and walked my bike to his window. He was alone, and stared straight ahead at the windshield.

"Morning, Dub," he said in a low, silky voice. He didn't look at me, and his hands stayed on the wheel.

"Morning, sir," I croaked.

He exhaled heavily, but stared straight ahead and said, "That bike of yours registered?"

"Registered?"

"Yeah," he said. "Registered."

"Yessir. The plate's on the back fender here," and I pointed, but his eyes remained front and center.

"Good," he said, slowly. "Good." He turned to me. His tiny eyes were pink and glazed, almost wet, as if he hadn't been sleeping too well. He'd shaved, but missed a few spots, and a vacant grin lay frozen across his face. "So how ya doin'?"

"Fine, sir."

"You know, I been thinking. Maybe you and me should have a talk." The words slithered from his lips.

My voice came out like I'd had laryngitis for about twelve years, and my whole body, even my eyelids for God's sake, trembled. "About what, sir?"

"Oh, about, say, photography? You like photography?"

I glanced up and down the road. A steady stream of cars flowed by, filled with, I hoped, alert and curious people noting the lone cop talking to the kid who appeared to be about to faint. I only hoped they'd note the time for the inquest later. After they found my body.

"Yessir, I like photography."

"Yeah? Me, too. I sure do."

He just waited, so I said, as if we were having this chummy conversation, "Well, I've got to get down to—"

"So, take any good pictures lately?"

"Uhm, sure, a few maybe. One or two, here and there."

"Yeah? Isn't that something," he said. "That's something. Got any you want to show me?"

Jesus oh God. I tried to think fast, but all I could come up with was the truth. Sometimes when you're searching for brilliance you get blind, dumb luck instead, and sometimes you have to trust it.

"Took a few at the circus the other night," I blurted out. "Saturday it was. You know, the night the elephant died. I was there with my family. Saw the whole Big Top show."

He frowned, but in a flash the frozen smile was back in place. "The circus. Right. Your whole family?"

"Sure, it was great. Susan and I took some neat shots of the guy in the cannon."

He turned back to the windshield. "I bet you did," he said, now drumming the wheel with his fingers.

"Matter of fact," I said, now resorting to some judicious lying, "I saw Doug Hammer and his mom there, too, and our other neighbors, you know, that family, a couple of rows behind us. Everyone was there. All night long. We got some terrific snaps."

"Sure, sure you did," he said, staring, drumming.

"You know what? I do believe I saw your son Henry, as well. The whole town must have been there. Great show."

"Yeah, yeah, he was there," he said, distracted. Now gripping the wheel.

I warmed up to it. "Say, Officer Farley, if you swing by my house later on, I can show you our photos of the circus. Want to do that? You can bring some of your photos and I can show you some of mine. We could even trade if you want!"

He didn't respond, just breathed hard it seemed, while passing cars slowed down to see what was going on.

Then, of course, I stepped over the line. It's this bad habit I have. "Did you get a chance to take some pictures at the circus?"

His head snapped to me, eyes focused and black, and he grunted, "What?"

"I mean, you must have been there, right? With Henry and all?"

His nostrils flared but he gathered himself, commendably I thought. Under the circumstances. He blinked a few times, searching my face. "Yeah, that's right," he said. "I was there with Henry. All night. Had a fun time."

"So stop by with your pictures, maybe we could trade. Get any of the elephant and the chimp?"

He cleared his throat, and turned back to the windshield. Drumming his fingers again, his chest rising and falling. Suddenly, he slammed the wheel with his fist and slammed it again, and turned to me, his face twisted and dark. "Where is it, Teed," he snarled, like his son in one of his worst rages. "*Who's got it*?"

I licked my lips, just to make sure they were there, and glanced down at his gun, holstered at his side. As if on cue, his right hand moved to the pistol, brushing its handle with his fingertips. Incredibly, he tried that grin again. "Worried about something?" he sneered. "Sure, why not? I stop a kid for a routine check, but for some reason he panics, dives for my gun. Could be he still has it out for me, who knows? We struggle, maybe it goes off. Poor, crazy kid. You think they wouldn't believe me? *Again*? Now *who's got it*?"

So I did panic. I stepped back out of reach and turned, about to jump on my bike. "Then shoot me," I shouted over my shoulder. "But you'll shoot me in the back. Who's going to believe that?" I squeezed my eyes shut, but all I heard was the sound of passing cars and Officer Farley's engine, idling.

"Turn around," he hissed.

"No."

"I said turn around!"

"I don't know what you're looking for," I said. "But whatever it is, it's in your hands." I squeezed my eyes tighter. It took a moment—it could have been a minute, it could have been an hour—before he growled, whispered almost, "You got this wrong, you *and* your father."

I heard him put the car in Drive. It lurched forward, a squeal from the tires, and was gone.

Not so much as a wave.

I walked my bike to the curb and sat down, trying my best to remember how to breathe.

Sometimes you take your victories in stride, and sometimes they rattle you to the core. After my conversation with Officer Bigger Farley, I was jumpy as a dog at the vet's. Pop was concerned about my agitated state enough to ask me if I wanted to talk about it. He cornered me in the garage the next day, while I was oiling my bike.

"Ricky's leaving really makes a difference, doesn't it?" he said.

I was surprised, and squeezed an extra large dollop of oil from the can.

"Hmm?" he said. "It's pretty obvious, even to me."

"What?"

"Well," he said, "I mean it's pretty obvious that you are very fond of Ricky. And my hunch is, she's very fond of you as well."

"You think so?"

"Take it from me. I know so."

I looked down and noticed that I'd just pumped about half a pint of oil onto the bike chain. Pop disregarded it.

"Do you want to talk about it?" he said.

"It's not just that Ricky left," I said, "it's the whole thing."

"What whole thing?"

"Everything."

"Maybe if you told me what everything is, we could talk about it."

"You know," I said. "Just everything. All these fights, Doreen, the phone calls." Then I just had to slip it in. "And Officer Farley. Then Simba has a heart attack or something and is shot at for it. Ricky has to leave, and she was Susan's best friend, too. It's been a miserable time. That's all."

"That's understating it," Pop said. "Look, I still feel bad about the whole Officer Farley business. In a way, I wish it was him, at least we could have done something. And I do get the impression he can be bad business. But—"

"Don't, Pop" I said. "It's okay."

He nodded.

"You know," I said. "Doreen didn't make those phone calls."

"I know that," he said.

I was startled. "How?"

"Because we're married. I know her very well, and, really, so do you."

"I guess," I said.

"Don't worry," Pop said. "I suppose the question would be when did you decide for sure it wasn't your mother? That would be the question, but I'm not going to ask it."

"Why?" I said.

"Because," Pop said, "I think you know something that you haven't told me, and I think it's a secret that I'll let you keep, by yourself, for yourself. I'm not sure what it is, but one thing I do know. What is between a person and his conscience is never a simple thing. Do you get that?"

You don't know the half of it, I thought. I cleared my throat. "I got it, Pop."

"Look I've been worried about you. You've been about half-stretched for a long time now. Way back when you smashed the telephone, something was obviously wrong and I wish we'd talked more then. But now I think we need to seriously think about having some long talks, you and me. It's not an easy life, Dub. In fact life can get downright ugly, often, and in my opinion the only way to get through it successfully is to talk to the people who love you, and the people you love. And I love you very much."

I nodded, and said, "I know."

"I've got to go down to the newspaper later," he said. "If you want to talk about it, why don't we take a ride after dinner and get an ice cream cone or something. Just you and me, the guys."

"Sure, Pop," I said. "That would be great."

He walked over and put his hand on my shoulder, and squeezed gently. "You may be needing a new bike soon," he said. "You're getting a little big for this one. We'll talk about it." Then he was gone.

Later that day, as I sat in the den watching TV, Doreen came into the room.

"Your father just called, Walter," she chirped. "He said not to forget about your ride tonight. He said maybe Susan wants to come, too. Where is Susan, by the way?"

"She's up in the willow tree," I said. Susan had been spending a lot of time up there since Ricky left town. "She's reading a book."

"That girl," Doreen said, "is going to fall down and break her neck someday."

When Pop came home later that day, I swear this is true, he walked through the *door* tugging his ear. He had a brief, whispered conversation with Doreen, then turned to me and said, "Let's forget dinner. Why don't we go out for a ride right now and get that ice cream."

"Sure," I said.

"Where's Susan?"

"I'll get her," I said. I went down to the basement, where Susan was communing with Elvis via a stack of forty-fives she'd relentlessly played since she'd come down from the tree. She lay on her back on the floor, with her head in her hands. Her eyes were closed.

"Pop wants to go for a ride," I said. "He's nervous. Something's up."

Susan opened her eyes and sat up. She reached over and turned down the hi-fi. "What?"

"Pop wants to go for a ride, just the three of us. Something's wrong."

"What's wrong?"

"You got me. Maybe Mr. Dubois finally got the letter from Officer Farley, and maybe the letter said to go to hell I'm coming after you anyway. God knows. It's all nuts."

"Well, let's go," she said. "We'll find out."

We got into the car with Pop, with Doreen at the front door waving as we pulled out. We were only going for a ride for God's sake, but there she was at the front door waving as if we were on our way to Dahomey.

Meanwhile, Pop's eyes darted this way and that, and he fidgeted with the rearview mirror like a crazy man, as if he was trying to win some award for rearview mirror positioning. He looked into the back seat, where Susan and I sat.

"Well," he said, and his voice cracked. "Nice day, isn't it?"

Which is the worst thing a guy can say to a person, it really is.

"I'm thinking it just got worse," I said.

"Too bad about that elephant, eh?" he said.

"Yeah," Susan said, and frowned.

"I mean," Pop said, "well, I haven't the slightest idea what I mean."

We drove for a while, the three of us silent. Pop bounced around in the front sit a bit and tugged at his ear here and there. He tried to whistle something, but blew air mostly.

Finally he took a long breath and exhaled loudly, drummed his fingers on the steering wheel. "Listen," he said. "I have some bad news."

Susan and I exchanged glances, and leaned toward the front seat..

"Well, there is some good news," he said. "But, Christ, what's the difference?"

"What good news?" Susan said.

"You know I love you kids," Pop said, and he glanced at us in the rearview mirror.

"That's the good news?" Susan said.

"What did we do?" I said.

"Nothing," he said. "Nothing at all. You've been the best, all that a father could ask for." He took a deep breath. At that point, we passed the lot behind Woolworth's, the circus grounds. The grass and dirt were scrubby and oily, and paper and discarded cotton candy cylinders blew along the ground.

"Pop," Susan said, exasperated.

"Sorry, honey." He pulled the car into a the parking lot at Woolworth's, and drove to the far end. No other cars were near us. Pop cut the engine and turned to face us. It was only then that I saw how lined his face was.

He took a deep breath. "Ricky won't be coming back," he said.

Susan's eyes went wide. "What?"

"What do you mean?" I said. "Never?"

"Afraid so," he said. "I'm sorry. I talked to Mr. Dubois today on the phone. He has an offer to teach down at Tulane, back in New Orleans, and he's decided to take it. He feels it's all been too much up here, too much trauma for his family. Too dangerous, and I can't say I disagree with him. He has to do what he feels is right."

"Never?" Susan said. "She's never coming back?"

"Yes, honey."

Susan's mouth was open, her brow dark. "That's," she said. "That's just, that's really… just absurd."

I was numb. I couldn't think of a thing to say, or do, so Susan did it for me. She started to sob. Pop got out of the car and came around to the back seat. He crawled over me and sat between us, and he put his arms around Susan and me, and I started to sputter when it hit me.

"What else?" I said.

"What do you mean?" Pop said.

"You said you had some good news," I said. Susan raised her face from her wet fists.

"Oh, that," he said, as if it was an old memory. "I guess it could have been good news. It turned out to be no news. It was a letter."

"What letter?"

"Mr. Dubois got it in the mail. It was from a person who said he'd been the one who'd been vandalizing the house, and that he was sorry he'd been doing it. The letter said that he'd seen how wrong he was and how bad it was, that he said he was stopping it as of now. It was signed 'A Changed Man.' Awfully strange. But I certainly hope so."

"So that means they're coming back?" Susan sniffed.

"Sorry, Susan. I asked the same question. He said he weighed it very hard, but his decision is final. The teaching job down there is good one, it's his alma mater, and that's where they're from, their home. He can't see them coming back here to bad memories."

For some obscene reason, I laughed.

"What is it, Dub?" Pop said.

"It's just a bad joke. That's all."

"Dub, we can't think about it that way."

"No, Pop," I said. Then, to myself, "Justice has spoken."

I closed my eyes.

Just then Susan sighed deeply, and opened the car door. She bolted out and stomped across the parking lot, kicking at trash on the blacktop.

"Susan!" Pop said.

He got out to follow her, then leaned back into the car. "Dub, don't take it hard. At least the man apologized, if we can believe the letter. And all of this, I mean everything, could have been avoided if the guy had never started up in the first place. It's horrible, but it's a victory. It is. Somehow."

Pop followed Susan, and I was left alone in the back seat of the car, eyes closed, with nothing to do.

CHAPTER 15

This would be a great place to talk about how Ricky eventually came back and we all lived happily ever after in our terrific little town, but that's not what happened so I'll drop that fantasy right here and now. This isn't some fairy tale where the knight slays the dragon and saves the princess. The best I can say is that in real life the dragons don't appear to be much different from the rest of us, and I guess it's only pure, stupid luck when the good guys win. And maybe there were, as Pop said, some victories. Take Big Farley, for instance. Every once in a while we pass in the halls at school, we nod, he jams his hands in his pockets and walks on. My guess is that it's his way of saying he's sorry about the whole goddamn thing. And I believe him. But here's what surprises me—I'm even happy for him, in a way. I mean, I helped the guy, and I'm actually glad for that. His home life might have been rotten before Ricky came to town, and it probably wouldn't win any American Family awards now, but at the very least Big Farley knows, deep inside, that no matter what his father does to him or to anyone else, he has a small cushion, a good-luck charm, that he can call on if the going gets tough.

And it's not as if my life is one huge, heaping bag of regret. In fact, I have this notion that some day all of this, even that queasy feeling I have that no one is really in charge, will somehow make sense. Or at the very least, I'll learn to live with it. Who knows, maybe I'll see the face of Jesus on a walnut and get divine inspiration, or maybe one day I'll be bouncing my grandkids on my knee and I'll look into their faces and, wham, hello Mr. Finally-Gets-It. Things like that are always happening to people, when they least expect it. I'll be waiting.